THE

Italians

RICO, ANTONIO & GIOVANNI

THE
Italians
COLLECTION

August 2015

September 2015

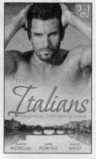

October 2015

November 2015

December 2015

January 2016

THE
Italians

RICO, ANTONIO & GIOVANNI

KATE HARDY
KATHERINE GARBERA
SUSANNE JAMES

Published in Great Britain 2015
by Mills & Boon, an imprint of Harlequin (UK) Limited,
Eton House, 18-24 Paradise Road, Richmond, Surrey, TW9 1SR

THE ITALIANS: RICO, ANTONIO & GIOVANNI
© 2015 Harlequin Books S.A.

The Hidden Heart of Rico Rossi © 2012 Kate Hardy
The Moretti Seduction © 2009 Katherine Garbera
The Boselli Bride © 2009 Susanne James

ISBN: 978-0-263-91573-0

026-1215

Harlequin (UK) Limited's policy is to use papers that are natural, renewable and recyclable products and made from wood grown in sustainable forests.The logging and manufacturing processes conform to the legal environmental regulations of the country of origin.

Printed and bound in Spain
by CPI, Barcelona

THE HIDDEN HEART OF RICO ROSSI

KATE HARDY

I dedicate my fiftieth romance to Gerard—
who always believed in me—with all my love

Kate Hardy lives in Norwich, in the east of
England, with her husband, two young children,
one bouncy spaniel and too many books to
count! When she's not busy writing romance or
researching local history, she helps out at her
children's schools. She also loves cooking—spot
the recipes sneaked into her books! (They're also
on her website, along with extracts and stories
behind the books.) Writing for Mills & Boon has
been a dream come true for Kate—something she
wanted to do ever since she was twelve. She says
it's the best of both worlds, because she gets to
learn lots of new things when she's researching
the background to a book: add a touch of passion,
drama and danger, a new gorgeous hero every
time, and it's the perfect job!

Kate's always delighted to hear from readers, so
do drop in to her website at www.katehardy.com.

CHAPTER ONE

'UM, *MI SCUSI?*' Ella dredged up the little Italian she'd learned from the phrasebook as she stood at the hotel's reception desk. 'I think I have a sightseeing tour booked this morning?'

'*Sì,* Signora Chandler. With me.'

Ella's jaw almost dropped as she turned around to see who'd spoken. This couldn't be her tour guide, surely? The man looked more like a model for a perfume ad. He was tall, with slightly dishevelled dark hair held back from his eyes by a pair of sunglasses, dark eyes with unfairly long lashes, and the most sinful mouth she'd ever seen.

He spoke perfect English, with the slightest, sexiest hint of an accent. And she was going to have to keep her libido on an extremely tight leash. No doubt the man was used to English tourists who were too full of hormones melting at his feet and he knew how to deal with them kindly; all the same, Ella didn't want to make a fool of herself. She'd already done that quite enough, this past year.

'I, um, *buongiorno.*' She held out her hand.

When he took it, it felt as if her temperature had just gone up five degrees.

This was crazy. How could she possibly react like this to a complete stranger—a man she'd only just met and knew nothing about, other than that he was an employee of the hotel where she was staying?

Not that he was wearing a uniform like the other staff. Instead, he wore a crisp white shirt, the neck unbuttoned far enough to show that there was a light sprinkling of hair on his chest and the sleeves rolled up to just below his elbows, teamed with stone-coloured chinos and boat shoes that would be comfortable for a long day's walking tour of the city. Casual, and yet utterly, utterly stylish, as only the Italians could be.

Ella's best friend Julia would immediately dub him 'sex on legs'. And she'd be right on the money. He was *gorgeous*.

'Are you ready, Signora Chandler?' he asked politely.

No, not in a million years. 'Of course,' she fibbed, forcing herself to sound as professional as she would to one of her clients.

'I'm Rico,' he said.

Why did her tongue feel as if someone had glued it to the roof of her mouth? 'Uh—Ella,' she responded, hating the fact that she sounded so pathetic and gauche.

'Ella.' Her name sounded like a caress, the way he said it.

Help. She really needed to remind herself that she was twenty-eight, not seventeen. And she knew only too well that charm like his was all surface and no substance. Been there, done that and worn the T-shirt to shreds.

'Shall we go?'

'Sure.' She gave him her best attempt at a sensible smile.

'So this is your first time in Rome, and you want a tour of the major sights, *sì?*'

'Ancient Rome, the Spanish Steps and the Trevi Fountain,' she confirmed.

'*Bene.* Then we'll start with the Colosseum. Apart from

the fact that it's the nearest site to the hotel, the queues are relatively short at this time of day.'

She followed him out of the hotel and resisted the urge to pinch herself. She, Ella Chandler, was actually in Rome—The Eternal City. The place she'd wanted to visit for years, though they'd never been able to afford a holiday when she was small; by the time she was earning enough to pay her way, her friends had talked her into going somewhere else with them. This time, she was pleasing herself. Visiting the place that had captured her imagination as a child, far more than tales of princesses and castles.

'I've always wanted to come to Rome, ever since I saw a picture of the Colosseum in a book as a little girl,' she said to Rico. 'I mean, I know it's not one of the official Seven Wonders of the World, but to me it was.'

'It's the largest surviving ancient Roman building,' he said. 'It's not quite as well preserved as somewhere else I'll take you to see today, but it's still pretty spectacular.'

He told her about the history of the place as they walked down the street, and Ella found herself relaxing with him. Then, as they reached the bottom of the street, she stopped dead and just stared.

'Wow. I can't believe we were just walking down a modern street with cool shops and houses—and here it is. Right in the middle of things.' The ruin was huge and just...*awesome*. There was no other word for it. Up close, the Colosseum was exactly what she'd always thought it would be like, really living up to her dream.

'That's one of the things about Rome,' he said with a shrug. 'A building might look modern, but beneath it there's likely to be the foundations of something like this.'

Clearly he was used to it; didn't they say that familiarity bred contempt? He didn't seem anywhere near as impressed by it as Ella was. But she was entranced by the sheer majesty of the ruin; and she was glad that Rico was sensitive enough to let her absorb the atmosphere rather than breaking it up with chatter.

She was gorgeous, Rico thought as he looked at Ella. Very much an English rose with that pale skin, golden-brown hair tied back at the nape of her neck, and blue-grey eyes. An old quote floated into Rico's head: *non Angli, sed angeli.* Not English, but angels.

Ella Chandler was as beautiful as any Botticelli angel. Particularly as she didn't seem to be the slightest bit aware of how lovely she was. And she had a natural beauty—not like half the guests in his hotels, who were manicured and spray-tanned and coiffured to within an inch of their lives.

Why was she on her own in Rome? He knew that she was booked into the honeymoon suite, but he also knew that she'd signed in as Ms Chandler rather than Mrs. So had this trip to Rome originally been planned as a honeymoon? Maybe her fiancé had let her down at the last minute, and she'd decided not to waste the booking and had come to Rome on her own. Or was there some other reason?

Rico reminded himself that it was nothing to do with him. He was her tour guide today simply as part of his on-going review of the Rossi hotel chain, checking that they were meeting their customers' needs with every single service they offered. Right now, that meant taking Ella Chandler through the fast-track queue to a place she'd wanted to visit for years and years and years, and making her dreams come alive.

'I never expected to see gladiators and emperors everywhere,' she said, smiling as she saw the characters wandering round.

'It's fun and adds to the atmosphere,' he agreed. 'But

I'd say just enjoy the view, unless you want to pay through the nose for having your photograph taken with them.'

'Oh. So they're not official—not part of the Colosseum itself?' She looked disappointed, and then slightly wary.

'They're freelance. And sometimes they can be a bit pushy. But they won't be pushy with you, because you're with me.' He smiled. 'And I'm happy to take as many photographs for you as you wish. It's all part of the tour service.'

'Thank you.'

Once they were through the entrance and he'd paid for the tickets, Rico took Ella through into the building, showing her where the different classes of people would have sat to enjoy the shows. He took photographs of her with the iconic arches of the Colosseum behind her and a view over the arena and the basement; even though she was wearing sunglasses in the bright Roman sunlight, he could tell that her smile reached her eyes. And her pleasure in the place was infectious. He'd grown used to thinking of it as just one of the buildings near his hotel. But seeing Ella's reaction made him look at the building again. And he could see what she saw: a truly spectacular place, more than just the iconic symbol of the city. This was the epicentre, where emperors had held processions and entertained the entire city. Where ordinary people had seen lions and bears and elephants, creatures they would never see in their daily lives.

On the second floor, he took her through to the temporary exhibition. 'Apart from the written sources we have, the graffiti gives us a pretty good idea of the kind of spectacles people saw here.' He showed her a leaping wolf scratched into the stone, and a gladiator fighting with a net. Ella pushed her sunglasses up to rest on the top of her head so she could take a closer look, and the expression of sheer wonder in her eyes fascinated him. How long had it been since something had enthralled him like that?

Too many years to count...

At thirty, Rico was jaded way beyond his years—and he knew it.

Not that he was going to beat himself up about it. He didn't have time. He had an empire to run.

When they left the Colosseum, Rico took Ella past Constantine's triumphal arch. 'This is my favourite view of the building,' he said, stopping to give her time to turn round and admire it.

'It's spectacular. Everything I thought it would be,' she said softly. 'Thank you so much.'

'Hey, it's my job,' he said. Mainly to remind himself that she was a client, and that made her off limits. And even if she wasn't off limits, she wasn't his type. He always dated tall, slender, sophisticated women who knew the rules and didn't make any emotional demands on him. In return, he gave them the lifestyle they wanted. Temporarily. Nobody had ever tempted him to make it permanent.

He forced his thoughts back to the job in hand. 'Let me show you through the Forum next.'

'Is this the place where Marc Antony did the speech— well, according to Shakespeare?' she asked.

He laughed. 'Yes. Normally you can hear half the tour guides declaiming it.' He pointed to some columns in the distance. 'The spot where he gave the funeral oration is at the New Rostrum—over there by the Temple of Saturn.'

'Is that what you do, as a tour guide? Declaim the speech?'

She had dimples, he noticed. The cutest, cutest dimples.

And it took Rico a real effort to concentrate on her question instead of reaching over to touch her cheek, to find out if her skin was as soft as it looked. What on earth was

wrong with him? He never got distracted like this. *Ever.*
'I can do. Unless you'd rather do it?'

'I know it's a bit touristy, but would you mind if I did?'

'Sure. Do you have a video setting on your camera?
I could film it for the people back home, if you like.'

'That's so nice of you.'

No, he most definitely wasn't *nice.* His last girlfriend
had said he was a machine, totally focused on his work—
because he'd refused to change his rules for her. But he
supposed that Rico the tour guide would be nice, at least
on the surface. 'It's what I'm here for. To make Rome feel
like home for you.'

Ella showed him how the camera worked and her fingers accidentally brushed against his. Awareness flooded
through his whole body and he almost gasped. He couldn't
remember the last time he'd reacted this strongly towards
someone; and it was as much as he could do to concentrate on taking the film while she declaimed the speech.

'You have a very clear voice, and you spoke it well,'
he said when she'd finished and he handed the camera
back to her.

'Thank you.'

She blushed. Very prettily. He couldn't help wondering
what she'd look like, all flushed and drowsy with pleasure.
Pleasure that he'd just made her feel.

Enough. He really shouldn't be thinking about Ella
Chandler in sexual terms. She was a client, for pity's sake.
So what if she was the first woman to intrigue him like this
in more than three years, since he'd taken over as CEO of
Rossi Hotels? He knew how fleeting sexual attraction was.
And he didn't have time to let her distract him.

As they walked back up towards the Via Nova, Ella
looked enchanted by the wisteria that grew along the wires,

the leaves making a kind of canopy and the pale purple blooms hanging down.

'Hand me your camera and smile,' he directed, and took several shots of her with the wisteria framing her.

There was a secluded corner of his roof garden just like this. And he suddenly had the strongest vision of kissing her there under the night sky, her palm cupping his cheek and his hands tangled in her hair, her mouth opening underneath his to let him deepen the kiss...

Help. He needed to get back to a neutral topic. Fast. Something that didn't make him think about sex. This was so inappropriate, it was untrue. Plus it unsettled him that she could have this sort of effect on him. He'd never found it hard to concentrate on work before.

'What do you do at home?' he asked.

'My job, you mean?' She shrugged. 'I'm an accountant.'

'And you enjoy it?'

'It's a safe job.'

He noticed she hadn't said that she enjoyed it. Odd. Why had she gone for a safe job, rather than one that would make her happy?

As an accountant, she probably spent most of her time at her desk. She didn't look the type to hit the gym or go running every morning. He'd already taken her on a longish walk, climbing up stairs and across uneven ground; and, since she wanted to see several other landmarks as well, they still had a fair bit of ground to cover. Exhausting his customers wasn't a good business idea. He'd better schedule in a rest break.

'Time to flop, I think,' he said. 'Let's go and have some lunch.'

He took her to a tiny *osteria* where he knew the food was good, and found them a table in a little courtyard with vines growing across like a canopy to protect diners from the midday sun.

'This is fabulous,' Ella said. 'I can't believe Rome's so green.'

'What were you expecting?'

'I don't know.' She shrugged. 'Something like London, I guess. With a pile of ruins at the edge of the city, not in the centre of things. But this is amazing. It's special. The fountains and the architecture and the ruins and the greenery—it's like seeing all of history mixed together at the same time, yet nothing's out of place.'

That hadn't really occurred to him before, but he realised that she was right. Rome *was* an amazing place. How had he let his home city become just wallpaper?

'And I loved that wisteria in the Forum.'

He knew she'd love the lilacs in the Borghese Park, too. Though it was too far to go there today, and anyway he was showing her just the highlights of the city that she'd asked to see.

A crazy idea bloomed in his head. The more he tried to ignore it, the more insistent it became. Maybe he could spin out this tour guide thing for a little longer. Ella didn't have any trips booked for tomorrow, and he knew she was staying in Rome for three nights. He hadn't taken a day off in months and he had nothing desperately urgent lined up for the rest of the week, so it wouldn't take his PA long to reschedule his diary.

'It didn't say anything in the brochure about lunch being included,' Ella said, looking slightly concerned. 'I take it this is an extra? I'll pay for both of us.'

That was the accountant in her speaking, he guessed. She'd clearly worked out that tour guides didn't exactly earn enormous salaries, and it was kind of her to offer to pay for his lunch. Unexpected, too; he was used to being the provider, and her offer threw him slightly.

And then there was the fact that Rico wasn't usually a tour guide. His income was more than adequate for his lifestyle. The offer had been kind, but no way would he let her pay for lunch. It went too much against the grain. He gave her his sweetest smile to forestall any arguments. 'Absolutely not. It's all part of the tour.' It was a complete fabrication, but maybe it was something he should take into consideration for the future.

The problem was, he hardly ever carried cash. If he took out his credit card, his cover would be blown—because what would a humble tour guide be doing with a platinum credit card? And he was really enjoying being just an ordinary man, instead of having people bowing and scraping to him or demanding things from him. Ella was reacting to him just for himself, instead of what he stood for, and that was so refreshing. He wasn't ready to give that up. Not just yet.

He made a mental note to have a quiet word with the waiter and ensure that he paid at the bar, where she wouldn't be able to see his credit card.

'If you're sure, then thank you very much. Do you recommend anything?' she asked.

'It depends what kind of thing you like.'

Oh, and that had come out so wrong. It sounded sleazy. Like a come-on. His voice practically oozed sex.

Though he had to admit, he wanted things to go further with Ella Chandler. A lot further.

Luckily she didn't seem to notice that she'd put him into such a spin.

'Is there something traditionally Roman on the menu that I could try?' she asked.

He scanned the menu swiftly. '*Cacio e pepe*—it's a

kind of thick spaghetti with a pecorino cheese and black pepper sauce.'

She smiled. 'That sounds lovely. I'd like to try that.'

'I'll join you.' He ordered them a salad as well, and paused. 'Would you like some wine? Red or white?'

'Dry white would be lovely.' She bit her lip. 'I'm afraid I'm not very sophisticated. One glass is enough for me at lunchtime.'

'That's fine by me. And it's nothing to do with sophistication—more to do with common sense. Alcohol's dehydrating, and it's warm today even for Rome,' he said, wanting to put her at her ease and enjoying the grateful smile she gave him.

He ordered two glasses of pinot grigio and a jug of water. When the waiter brought their drinks, he also brought a basket of good Roman bread, flavoured with rosemary. Ella reached for the bread at the same time as Rico did, and her fingers brushed very lightly against his; it made him feel as though he'd been galvanised.

He never reacted to anyone like this. Ever.

But there was something about Ella Chandler, and he really had to make an effort to stop himself twining his fingers through hers, bringing her hand up to his mouth and tasting her skin, brushing each knuckle with his lips.

Especially as she looked completely unaffected by their brief contact. No way was he going to make a fool of himself.

'Wow. This is fabulous,' she said when she'd eaten her first bite of bread.

God, her mouth was beautiful. A perfect rosebud. Again, he had to hold himself back from leaning forward and touching his mouth to hers, brushing his lips against hers until they parted.

And it wasn't just sexual attraction. There was more to

it than that. Spending time with someone who enjoyed such simple pleasures… It had been way too long since he'd done that, Rico thought. His last few girlfriends had been more interested in the lifestyle he could give them. Tickets to exclusive events, the finest champagne, designer jewellery. Ella seemed very different. He wasn't sure whether she fascinated him or unnerved him most. He didn't have a clue what made her tick—or why she was affecting him like this. This wasn't supposed to be happening.

'So have you done this job for very long?' she asked.

'A while,' he said. It depended on what you defined as 'this job'. He'd been running the hotel chain for three years now, but he'd worked in the business during the school holidays ever since he was fourteen, doing every single job in the company—right from cleaning the rooms through to making strategic decisions. Even now he did a stint in every role in the business during the year, to make sure he kept abreast of the issues his staff faced and could see where things could be improved for the customers.

'Do you have family here?' she asked.

'Some.' Again, it depended on how you defined family. His parents lived in Rome, but he wouldn't class either of them as family. Not after his upbringing.

He could see her slight frown at his evasiveness, and added, 'My grandparents live here.' They'd rescued him from the mess of his parents' marriage and kept him safe. They were the only ones in his life who hadn't wanted him for what he could give them. Or maybe even that wasn't strictly true; after all, his grandfather had groomed him to take over the business, knowing that it would be a total disaster in the hands of his only child, Rico's father. In Rico's hands, the business was safe. To the point where he was planning to expand it outside Italy.

Rico managed to keep the conversation light for the rest

of lunch—and he was pleased to notice that Ella ate with enjoyment, rather than picking at her food and being boring about calorie and carb intake.

And then it was time for the next ace up his sleeve. He'd taken her on the route where she would see the back of the Pantheon first, a squat building with moss creeping over the patched brickwork; he could see from her face that she thought the building a little dingy and dowdy, and was expecting to be disappointed.

Until they came into the square and she saw the front, the huge triangle with its inscription commemorating Agrippa and the enormous columns supporting the porch.

'Oh, my God—that's just what I expected a real Roman temple to look like! And those doors are just *huge,*' she said, wide-eyed.

'Allegedly they're the originals, though they've been restored so much that there isn't actually much original material left.'

Inside, Ella looked overawed as she stared up at the dome and the enormous opening in the centre that was the building's only source of light. 'This is stunning. I can't believe this building is nearly two thousand years old, and they built that huge dome without any of the equipment that construction companies take for granted nowadays. I mean, just *how* did they do it?'

That expression of wonder was back on her face. Although Rico had been to the monument countless times, enough to be almost immune to its beauty, seeing it with her was like seeing it with new eyes; he, too, caught the wonder, as if it were the first time he'd ever seen it. And how amazing it was. It made him want to hold her, feel a physical connection between them as well as a mental one.

Though he could see the disappointment on Ella's face when they reached the Spanish Steps and she stared up the white marble steps to the balustrade and the obelisk, framed by the white church at the top.

'Give it a couple of weeks for all the azaleas to come out and it'll look a bit prettier,' he said.

She wrinkled her nose. 'Sorry. I guess I expected the Spanish Steps to be a bit more...well...' Her voice tailed off and she gave an apologetic grimace.

Special, he guessed. 'They're just steps,' he said gently. 'Where tourists sit to take a rest. Though the square at the top by the Trinità is pretty at weekends; it's full of artists sketching.'

She looked up, as if imagining it.

'Come on. You'll love the Trevi. That definitely lives up to its reputation.'

They could hear the water gushing before they even got into the square, and when they managed to skirt the crowds he could see from the look on her face that the fountain was everything she'd expected. 'Wow. It's huge,' she said. 'I can't believe how white it is, and how clear and blue the water is. And look at the way it's carved.' Her eyes glittered with delight. 'The horses—their manes look as if they're real, not stone, and they're billowing in the breeze, and the water sounds like the thundering of their hooves.'

Rico normally thought of the Trevi Fountain simply as a tourist trap; but right then he could see what she saw. And he was surprised by how stunning it was.

The steps leading down to the fountain were thronged with tourists; Rico managed to shepherd Ella to the front, where she could sit on the edge of the fountain and he could take a photograph of her throwing a coin over her shoulder as a promise to herself that she'd come back to Rome.

'Is it supposed to be three coins?' she asked.

He smiled. 'No. If you're thinking of the film, that's referring to three different people throwing a coin in.'

'I thought I read somewhere...' She flapped a dismissive hand. 'Never mind.'

He knew exactly what she meant—he'd read it, too. Throw in one coin to return to Rome, two for a new romance, and three for a marriage. Was that what she was looking for? he wondered. Marriage or romance?

Though it was none of his business. And he definitely wasn't looking for either marriage or romance. No way was he repeating his parents' mistakes. He kept his relationships short and sweet, ending them before they stopped being fun.

'The fountain was built at the end of Agrippa's Acqua Vergine. It's meant to have the sweetest water in Rome—though I wouldn't try drinking it,' he added hastily, 'and people are definitely discouraged from trying to paddle in it.'

'*La Dolce Vita,* right?' She smiled. 'My best friend's an English teacher and a film buff. She told me about it.'

He could just imagine Ella standing under the fountain the way Anita Ekberg had, letting the water pour down on her. Making her T-shirt cling to her body like a second skin. And then he'd have the pleasure of peeling it off later...

Right now, he thought wryly, he could do with some cold water himself. Ella Chandler was making him seriously heated.

Officially, this was the end of what she'd asked to see. He knew he ought to ask her if she wanted him to escort her back to the hotel or put her in a taxi; but he found himself reluctant to let her go. Weirder still, he found himself actually giving into the impulse to keep her with him a little longer. What the hell had happened to his self-control?

'Time for a rest,' he said, and found them a quiet table

at one of the little *caffès* in the nearby streets. When she'd chosen what she wanted from the menu, he ordered her a glass of *spremuta,* freshly squeezed ruby orange juice, and an espresso for himself. He gulped it down in one mouthful, then gave a rueful smile as he caught her raised eyebrows. 'Sorry. It's one of my bad habits.'

There was a tiny glitter of teasing in her eyes when she said, 'Dare I ask what the others are?'

'No.' But the coffee hadn't restored his common sense. The words came out of his mouth before he could stop them. 'Do you have plans for tonight?'

'Why?' She sounded wary.

'I wondered if you might have dinner with me. If you weren't doing anything else?'

She blinked. 'Dinner?'

'Something simple. Traditionally Roman.' Or maybe he could cook for her. He knew the perfect place to set a table. Even the swishest restaurant in Rome didn't have a view as good as where he had in mind.

Dinner.
A date.
Part of Ella was surprised and pleased that such a gorgeous man was asking her out; yet part of her wanted to run as far away as she could. She might be over Michael now, but it didn't mean she wanted to repeat the experience. To get involved with someone, even briefly. To make herself vulnerable.

And yet this was Rome. The Eternal City. How lovely it would be to share her first proper evening in Rome with someone. And Rico was only asking her out to dinner, after all. It wasn't as if there were any future in this.

Would it really be so wrong to say yes, or to enjoy the

attention? A bit of harmless flirtation might give her back some of her confidence in herself after Michael's betrayal.

Though thinking about Michael meant that she needed to ask Rico something. It was going to be embarrassing, but no way was she going to do to someone else what Michael's lover had done to her. 'I'm assuming you don't have a wife or a girlfriend?'

'No. I'm single.'

'Me, too.' Just so it was clear. And she intended to stay that way. She wasn't giving anyone else the chance to let her down, the way all the men in her life so far had let her down. Her father, her fiancé…

She was tempted to make an excuse, however flimsy. Tell him she was tired. That way, she wouldn't risk getting closer to him.

Yet there was something about Rico that drew her. She enjoyed his company. And these three nights in Rome were meant to be fun. Given that neither of them had any ties, then maybe she should take the risk. Say yes.

'OK,' she said finally. 'It'd be nice to have dinner with you.'

'Are you vegetarian, or is there anything you don't like to eat?'

'No. And I don't have any food allergies, either.'

'Good. Then I'll meet you at the hotel,' he said. 'I'll call for you at eight.'

CHAPTER TWO

BACK at the hotel, Rico saw Ella into Reception, and then went through the back into his office. His PA was tidying her desk, clearly just about to leave for the evening. 'Lina, I know it's late and I've given you absolutely no notice, but can you clear my diary for the next three days?' he asked.

'Of course. Is something wrong? Your grandfather's ill?' she asked, looking concerned.

'No, he's fine.'

'Your father?'

No, and Rico certainly wouldn't drop everything to rush to his father's bedside. He was well aware that Lina knew it, too; she'd worked for the Rossi chain for longer than he had, long enough to know exactly why Rico had no time for his parents and never would. 'I'm just taking some time off.'

She blinked. 'Are *you* ill?'

'Very funny.' He glowered at her briefly. 'I'm not that driven.'

'Actually, you are, Rico.' She patted his arm to soften her words. 'Look, nobody's going to be around at this time of the afternoon, so there's no point in making any calls now. I'll deal with it first thing tomorrow and move all your meetings.'

'Thank you. I'll have my mobile with me if you need to get in touch. Text or voicemail, that is,' he added.

'I'm not going to call you. It'll do you good to have a break.' She paused. 'So are you going anywhere special?'

'Maybe.'

She gave him a wry smile. 'I should know better than to ask *you* a personal question.'

He grimaced. 'Sorry. I don't mean to be rude.'

'But everything personal is off limits. I know.' She rolled her eyes. 'Tell me again why I put up with you?'

'Must be my charm,' he teased back. Then he grew serious again. 'Thank you, Lina. I do appreciate you.'

'I know you do, *tesoro*. It's why I put up with all your impossible demands.' But she was smiling. 'Go and have some fun.'

'I will.' His step already felt lighter. Which was crazy. There wasn't any future in this; Ella Chandler was a tourist, only here for a couple of days. But maybe, just maybe, Lina was right. Having a little fun in his life would do him good.

Rico left his office and headed for the butcher's. It had been a long time since he'd last gone shopping, and it felt odd to be so domesticated. He came home via the greengrocer's, the baker's and the deli; then rolled up his sleeves and began preparing dinner, humming to himself as he worked.

What did you wear for dinner in Rome? Ella wondered. She'd expected to find a little *trattoria* somewhere and just watch the crowds as she ate, or maybe study the more detailed guidebook to Rome she'd brought with her. She'd packed a pretty, floaty summer dress at the last minute; hopefully that would be smart enough, especially if she put her hair up. She knew it wouldn't be smart enough if Rico took her somewhere seriously posh; then again, he knew the city better than most, so he was more likely to take her to a small, out-of-the-way place with amazing food and where it didn't really matter what you wore.

At precisely eight o'clock, there was a knock on her door.

She opened it, and he smiled at her. 'Ella, *bellezza*. You look lovely.'

He was wearing a different white shirt, this time teamed with faded jeans; he looked utterly gorgeous and her heart skipped a beat.

Reminding herself that this was just dinner, she asked brightly, 'So where are we going?'

'I thought I'd cook for you.'

She blinked. 'You cook?'

He shrugged. 'It's not that difficult.'

True. Though Michael had never cooked. He'd always left it to her. And she'd been fool enough to let him get away with it.

'You have a very expressive face,' Rico said. 'It looks to me as if you've been dating the wrong kind of man.'

He could say that again. 'Perhaps,' she said. This definitely wasn't the time or the place to moan about her ex. 'But I'm over him.' And she was following the old saying to the letter: the best revenge was living well. Thanks to her lottery win, she was going to follow every single dream she'd ever had. Ones that Michael most definitely wouldn't have shared.

Rico took her to the end of a corridor, then tapped numbers into a small, discreet keypad to open the door. She followed him up the stairs and they ended up in the most enchanting roof garden she'd ever seen. There were tiny fairy lights twined through the greenery, and one corner was draped in wisteria.

'Oh, this is beautiful,' she said in delight.

He looked pleased. 'I'm glad you like it.'

There was a table laid for two in the centre of the garden, with a candle on the table and wine chilling in an ice bucket. And she had the clearest view of the Colosseum, with the three lowest tiers lit from the inside and the moon rising above it. 'This is just amazing. Is this your place?'

Yes. But, if he told her that, then she'd know he'd been economical with the truth about being a tour guide. And he liked the fact that she was responding to him as a man, not as the head of the hotel chain; he still wasn't quite ready to give that up. 'It's borrowed,' he said. Which was an equivocation: he was borrowing it from himself.

She looked slightly worried. 'Are you sure the owner doesn't mind?'

'The owner definitely doesn't mind,' he reassured her. 'Please, take a seat. May I pour you some wine?'

'Thank you.'

He held her chair out for her, then poured them both a glass of wine. 'I'll just go and get our antipasti.'

He brought out a platter of *bruschetta* to share.

'Wow, this is fabulous,' she said after the first taste.

'Thank you.' He inclined his head, playing it cool, but inside he was pleased. Particularly as she ate without fussing about carbs or calories; the last three women he'd dated had toyed with their food, and it had irritated him hugely. He loathed pretence.

And the fact that right now he was pretending to be something he wasn't… He pushed that aside. It was only a tiny white lie. And it meant he could be himself with her, instead of the man everyone expected him to be.

She complimented him on the pasta Alfredo he served

for the next course, and on the spring lamb served with rosemary potatoes and garlicky spinach.

'It's very simple Roman food,' he said with a smile.

'And you've taken the time to make it. To spoil me. I appreciate that,' she said.

'I have a confession to make,' he said when he brought dessert through. 'Puddings aren't my strong point. I bought the panna cotta from the local deli.'

'But you've taken the time to present it nicely,' she pointed out.

He raised an eyebrow. 'You're not a hotel inspector in disguise, are you?'

She laughed. 'No. I'm just a boring accountant.'

'You're not boring at all,' he corrected. 'I'm enjoying your company.' He smiled back at her. 'And I know you weren't fishing for a compliment, before you say it.'

'I'm enjoying your company, too,' she said shyly.

'Good. Come and look out over Rome. This place has great views.' He took her hand, drew her to her feet, walked with her to the edge of the terrace.

She leaned both hands on the balustrade to look out over the city; the churches and buildings were all lit up so brightly that every detail was visible. Rico couldn't resist standing behind her and resting his arms on the balustrade on either side of hers, while he pointed out what all the buildings were.

This close, he could smell her perfume; it reminded him of spring violets. And, with her hair up, her nape was bare and way, way too tempting. The spaghetti straps of her dress were no barrier to his lips at all…

With an uncontrollable impulse, he dipped his head so he could kiss the curve of her neck; she shivered and leaned back against him. Her skin was so soft against his mouth, so sweet—and it wasn't enough. He spun her round to face him and brushed his mouth against hers. He could feel her lips parting, inviting him to deepen the kiss; he loved the way she responded to him, her shyness melting beneath his mouth.

He could feel her breasts pressing against him and he slid one hand between their bodies so he could caress her. Through the thin material of her dress and the lace of her bra, her nipple was hardening; he rubbed his thumb against it, and she gave a little gasp of pleasure.

Good. So it was the same for her. This crazy, unexpected surge of desire.

And right now he really needed to see her. To touch her. Skin to skin.

His hand went to the top of the zip at the back of her dress. 'Ella. May I?' he whispered, drawing her back away from the edge so that the greenery gave them privacy again.

She nodded, and he slid the zip down to her waist. He hooked a finger into one spaghetti strap and slid it down, then the other, coaxing the material down to her waist. Her bra was strapless, lacy and very, very pretty; but it was in the way. He needed to see her right now. He unsnapped her bra, let it drop to the floor, then cupped her breasts in both hands. 'You're beautiful,' he said softly. *'Bellezza.'*

She blushed. 'I, um…'

Yeah. He knew. This wasn't the time for words. He kissed her again, hot and urgent; when she tipped her head back, he kissed his way down her throat, then took one nipple into his mouth and sucked. Her hands slid into his hair, urging him on.

Rico's senses were spinning. He was so aware of the softness of her skin, the sweetness of her perfume. When he finally straightened up and looked at her again, desire lanced through him. She looked gorgeously dishevelled, naked to the waist and with wisps of hair escaping from their confines. He wanted to take her hair down properly, see it spread across his pillows.

But the fact he wasn't touching her had clearly broken the connection between them, because she bit her lip. 'Rico. We can't do this.'

Second thoughts? Well, he'd never forced anyone and he wasn't going to start now. 'OK,' he said softly, and touched the backs of his fingers to her cheek briefly to reassure her before he started to restore order to her clothes.

'I mean, not *here*.' She blushed.

His fingers stilled. 'Not here?'

Her blush deepened. 'It's your friend's apartment.'

No, it damned well wasn't, and his bed was only metres away. All he had to do was pick her up and carry her there.

But he'd started the evening letting her think that the place belonged to someone else. Telling her the truth now would make things way too complicated. He was just going to have to roll with the story he'd created. And how he wished now that he'd told her the truth, right from the start.

She cupped his face with one hand. 'But I do have a suite downstairs,' she whispered. 'We could go there.' She paused and swallowed hard. 'If you want to.'

If he wanted to? How could she possibly doubt that he wanted to? Wasn't it obvious how attracted he was to her?

He kissed her. 'Yes, I do. Though only if you're sure.'

'I'm sure.' Her voice was still shy, but definite. 'But shouldn't we, um, clear up here, before…?' She gestured to the table.

So very English. It made him smile. 'It's fine. I'll deal with it later,' he reassured her, and finished restoring order to her clothes before taking her hand. 'Let's go,' he said softly.

They left the terrace and he led her down the corridor

to her room in silence. Her fingers tightened round his;
and he knew she was nervous because when they reached
her door, she dropped her card key.

He retrieved it for her, opened the door and ushered her
inside. He switched on the table lamps so that soft light
spilled into the room, turned off the overhead light and
pulled the curtains.

When he turned to face her, she was biting her lip,
looking nervous.

He took her hand, drew it up to his mouth and touched
his lips briefly against her skin. 'Ella, if you've changed
your mind, I understand.'

'I'm...' She looked away. 'I don't want to disappoint
you.'

'It's fine to say no. I'd never force a woman.'

'I didn't mean that.' She still wasn't looking at him.
'I'm...um...maybe not very good at this sort of thing.'

Her meaning sank in. She thought she'd disappoint him
because she was no good at making love? The way she'd
responded to him had told him that she wasn't hugely experienced, that she was maybe a little shy. And he had
the strongest feeling that someone had damaged her confidence. Who or why, he had no idea—but he could do
something to fix this. To show her that it wasn't true. To
prove to her that she was a beautiful, desirable woman.

'Ella *bellezza*,' he said softly, 'the first time between us
isn't going to be perfect. But that's not a problem. It means
we have time to explore each other. Time for me to learn
what takes your breath away, and for you to learn what
makes my pulse spike.'

This time, she looked at him. 'So it's not a problem?'

He gave her a reassuring smile. 'No pressure, no worries. This is just you and me. And, if you change your
mind, all you have to do is tell me to stop.'

'I…' She blew out a breath. 'Sorry. I'm being really wet, here.'

'No. It sounds to me as if someone made you feel bad to make himself feel better. So I'd say it was his problem, not yours.' He sat down on the bed, scooping her onto his lap. She was definitely struggling with doubts, but not doubts about him. Doubts that another man had put into her head.

The only way he could think of to reassure her was to kiss her. Softly. Gently. Coaxing her to respond to him. Stoking up the heat between them, touch by touch.

He slid one spaghetti strap down over her shoulder and kissed her bare skin. She closed her eyes and tipped her head back; he took the hint and kissed a line across her throat, lingering at the point where a pulse was beating hard, then nibbling the curve of her neck.

She gave a murmur of pleasure, arching against him, and made no protest when he unzipped her dress again. He slid the other thin strap down, and let the floaty material fall to her waist.

'Yes,' she whispered as his fingers found the snap of her bra and undid it.

Colour bloomed in her cheeks as he cupped her breasts, teasing her nipples with the pad of his thumbs.

'You like that?' he asked, already knowing the answer but wanting to hear her say it.

'I like it.' Her voice had deepened.

'Good.' He guided her back to her feet, then dropped to his knees in front of her, gently easing her dress down until she stood before him in nothing but a pair of lacy knickers and high-heeled shoes.

'Nice view,' he said softly. 'You're beautiful, Ella *bellezza*.'

She didn't look as if she quite believed him. Well, there was something he could do about that.

'I'm going to enjoy this,' he said. 'Your skin's so soft. And you smell gorgeous.' He traced a circle round her navel with the tip of his tongue. 'You taste good, too.'

He slid one hand between her thighs, cupping her sex through the lace of her knickers. She shivered.

'I want to see you,' he said softly. He wanted to see her abandoned to pleasure, lost to his touch. 'I want to touch you, Ella. Taste you.'

She shivered again. 'Yes.'

It took him half a second to stand up, scoop her up in his arms and settle her against the pillows. He'd meant to loosen her hair, but he couldn't wait for that. All he could think about was making her totally lost to pleasure.

He kissed her, this time more demanding; this time her response was more confident. More abandoned. Just how he wanted her.

It was a moment's work to strip the last tiny bit of lace from her skin. And then he kissed his way down over her abdomen, taking his time until she wriggled beneath him, arching her body and sliding her fingers into his hair to let him know she wanted this just as much as he did.

He could taste just how aroused she was with the first long, slow stroke of his tongue along her sex. Sweet and salt, and most definitely responsive. She whimpered as he teased her clitoris with the tip of his tongue, swirling round and then sucking hard, varying the pace and pressure until finally he felt her go rigid beneath him, and heard her cry out his name as her climax hit her.

Rico shifted up the bed and held her close. 'OK?'

'Very OK. Thank you.' She dragged in a breath. 'Oh, my God. I'm completely naked, and you're still fully clothed.'

'Because I got a bit greedy,' he said with a grin. 'You can always do something about it, if you want to.'

She unbuttoned his shirt; almost shyly, she skated her fingers along his pecs. 'You feel good.'

As she undid the button of his jeans and slid the zip down Rico felt his control begin to shred. Right now he really, really wanted to be inside her. But he needed to take this at her pace, to make sure she was comfortable with him.

And she took her time undressing him, stroking every centimetre of skin she uncovered, moving her fingertips in tiny circles against his skin and arousing him until he was on the verge of losing control. By the time she'd got him naked, he could barely speak, except to croak the words, 'Condom. My wallet. In my jeans.'

She fished his wallet out of his jeans and handed it to him. He retrieved the little foil packet, but his hands were shaking too much to deal with it. She smiled and took it from him, then unwrapped it and slowly, slowly rolled it onto him. Rico was almost whimpering with the need to bury himself inside her; he sat up, pulling her towards him so that she was straddling his lap, and then sighed with pleasure as she eased herself down onto him.

Oh, my God, Ella thought as she straddled him. This was meant to be just a fling. A one-off. But, seeing the pleasure blooming in his face, feeling the softness of his skin against hers and the hardness of his muscles... The sheer intensity of their connection shocked her.

It wasn't supposed to be like this. It was meant to be carefree and fun and mutual pleasure. No emotions. And certainly not this strange feeling that this was meant to be—because she didn't want to get involved again. Didn't want to feel. Didn't want to risk her heart being shattered again.

She pulled herself together. Just.

'Is that good for you?' she asked huskily.

'*Sì*. Yes.' He stroked her face. 'Thanks to you, I can barely think straight in my own language, let alone in English.'

Pleased, she leaned forward to kiss him.

He slid his hands into her hair so he could angle his mouth more closely to hers, kiss her harder. Working purely by touch, he found the pins that bound her hair, removed them and dropped them off the edge of the bed, then sighed with pleasure as her hair fell over her shoulders. '*Bellezza*. I like your hair down. You have glorious hair.' He stole another kiss.

She rocked over him, taking it torturously slow; Rico's control snapped and he wrapped his arms round her so he could push deeper, harder. And finally he felt her body tightening round him, pushing him into his own climax.

Wow. He certainly hadn't expected it to be that intense between them. Not this first time. He couldn't even remember the last time someone had made him feel like this, the last time when sex had felt this special.

Not willing to give up the connection between them just yet, he held her close. But eventually he had to move to deal with the condom. 'Wait for me,' he whispered.

When he came back into the bedroom, she'd slid under the covers. Clearly she'd gone shy on him.

'OK?' he asked softly.

She nodded, but he could see the awkwardness in her face.

He sat down on the edge of the bed. 'Ella. This doesn't mean I'm going to make demands on you. Or that I'm going to just walk away and ignore you, either. It's up to you where you want this to go next.'

She swallowed hard. 'I'm only here for two more nights after this.'

So there was a defined limit. Just how he liked his relationships. They could have some fun and then just walk away. 'Maybe we can see a little more of each other while you're here in Rome.'

'When you're not working, you mean?'

He smiled. 'Actually, I happen to be off duty for the next couple of days.'

She gave him a sceptical look. 'In the middle of tourist season?'

'There isn't a tourist season in Rome any more,' he said. 'Visitors come all year round. So I can take time off whenever I want to.' He paused. 'If you'd like me to show you a bit more of the city, then I'm at your disposal.'

She thought about it, and smiled. 'Thank you. I'd like that.'

'Good.' He leaned over to kiss her, keeping the contact light and non-demanding. 'So, it's a date. Shall I call for you after breakfast? Say, half-past eight?'

'Half-past eight. That'd be good,' she said.

'Bene.' He pulled his clothes on. 'Then I'll see you tomorrow.'

'Hang on. I'll come with you and help clean up.'

He smiled. 'No, it's fine. It won't take me long. And you look warm and sweet and comfortable. Stay where you are.' He kissed her again, this time lingering until his pulse spiked and she looked flushed and incredibly sexy. 'Sweet dreams, *bellezza.*'

Ella curled back under the duvet as Rico left the room. This was the last thing she'd expected to find in Rome. Romance. A fling. And the way Rico had made her feel…

Funny, she couldn't hear Michael's voice in her head

any more. The justifications, the sharp comments about how he'd had to look elsewhere for his pleasure because she didn't have a clue how to please a man. Now she knew it really wasn't true; she'd most definitely pleased Rico tonight. To the point where he'd actually admitted that he couldn't think straight.

So maybe Rico was right and Michael had dumped his own shortcomings on her. It hadn't all been her fault.

And tomorrow—tomorrow was suddenly full of promise.

CHAPTER THREE

AT TWENTY-FIVE minutes past eight, the next morning, Ella was ready to go. As she'd expected, Rico knocked on her door at eight-thirty exactly. He was wearing pale chinos and another crisp white shirt; clearly he wore the same kind of clothes off duty as he did when he was working.

He glanced at her feet and gave an approving nod. 'Good. Flat shoes. They're comfortable to walk in?' he checked.

'Very,' she confirmed.

'Good. Let's go, *bellezza.*'

Ella locked the door behind her and Rico ushered her out of the hotel. She tried not to be disappointed that he hadn't taken her hand. Then again, they needed to be discreet; this was the hotel where he worked, and having a fling with a guest probably wasn't something that the management would approve of.

Did he have flings like this with many guests? She pushed the thought aside. Even if he did, it didn't matter. She wasn't looking for for ever. These few days in Rome were just for her, and she was going to enjoy them. No guilt, no complications—just fun. A few moments out of her real life.

'So where are we going?' she asked.

'To find beautiful views,' he said. 'And something a

little unusual. And, this afternoon, I think we can do something fun.'

She smiled. 'Sounds good to me.'

As they walked down the street towards the Colosseum, Rico's hand brushed against hers. The light contact sent a tingle all the way through her. Another brush, then another, and finally he was holding her hand, his fingers curling round hers. It made her feel like a teenager, which she knew was utterly crazy; and yet she couldn't help smiling. Today was perfect. A cloudless blue sky, the jumble of ancient and modern buildings that was Rome, and an incredibly charming, gorgeous man to keep her company as she strolled through the streets.

A man who'd given her so much pleasure last night. A man who'd made her see stars. And who might just do that again tonight…

They wandered through the streets together, until they came to a stone wall and she looked over it and saw the river. 'Wow. I had no idea the Tiber would be so green.'

'It's fast-moving, too.' He pointed out a line of ducks that were struggling to swim against the current, then finally gave up and went with the flow.

She rested her arms on the stone wall and peered into the distance. 'Is that the Vatican?'

'That's the dome of St Peter's you can see, yes—but, if you want to go there, I'd suggest going very early tomorrow morning,' he said. 'The queues at this time of day will be horrendous.'

'Well, you can hardly go to Rome and not visit the Vatican,' she said, taking a snapshot of the dome framed by the branches of the trees overhanging the wall.

He smiled. 'OK. I'll book us a tour for tomorrow.'

She blinked. 'But you're a tour guide. You'd actually

take a tour with someone else? Or is that like market research for you?'

'We need a licensed Vatican tour guide and I don't have a Vatican pass,' he explained. 'But right now I have lunch in mind.'

They walked hand in hand along the Tiber. Rico stopped by one of the bridges. 'I know I'm not officially a tour guide today, but I'd be failing in my duty if I didn't tell you that this is the oldest bridge in Rome, built nearly two thousand years ago.'

'You mean it's an original Roman bridge?' And yet it looked as firm and strong as if it had been built with the newest technology. 'Wow. It's amazing to think we're walking in the footsteps of people who lived all that time ago.'

'The more things change, the more they stay the same,' he said softly.

Trastevere, on the other side of the river, was incredibly pretty; the houses were painted in a soft wash of terracotta or saffron, vines grew on balconies and terraces, and large pots of shiny-leaved green shrubs graced the doorways. And Ella thoroughly enjoyed their leisurely lunch in the square outside the church of Santa Maria. Sharing a glass of wine with him, seeing the desire glittering in his eyes— brighter than the golden mosaics outside the church that glittered in the sunlight.

Once Rico discovered that she enjoyed looking round the ancient churches, he smiled. 'That's excellent, because I was planning to take you to see something a bit unusual in another church, just across the river.'

'Unusual' hardly did it justice, Ella thought as she looked at the huge stone disc on a plinth in the portico of the church of Santa Maria in Cosmedin. It contained the carved face of a wild man; his mouth was open beneath his moustache, and wild hair and a beard surrounded his face. There was a crack in the stone going right to the edge from his left eye, and another crack running down from his mouth. Ancient and very, very imposing.

'It reminds me a bit of one of the Green Men you'd see in an English church,' she said. 'What is it?'

'The *Bocca della Verità*—the Mouth of Truth,' he translated. 'In medieval times, if you were accused of lying, you put your hand through the hole in the mouth. If you could take your hand back unscathed, you were telling the truth.'

'And if you were lying?'

He shrugged. 'Then the Mouth would eat your hand.'

'Seriously? You mean someone stood behind the stone and actually cut off their hand?' Very rough justice. Though she knew a couple of people who would've fallen seriously foul of the Mouth. Her father. How many lies had he told? To her mother, to his wife, to however many women who had made the same mistake as Ella's mother and fallen in love with a charming, handsome and utterly faithless man.

And her ex. How many times had Michael told her he was studying at the university library, when he'd really been doing something else—or, rather, some*one* else—entirely? Another charming, handsome and utterly faithless man.

Or maybe the fault had been hers. For not learning from her mother's mistakes. For trusting Michael in the first place. Whatever; lying was the one thing Ella really couldn't and wouldn't tolerate. And she'd never let herself get involved with another charming, handsome and utterly faithless man again.

She pushed the thought away. 'Wow. That's really bloodthirsty.'

'I don't think anyone actually chopped off anyone's hand. The fear of what would happen was enough to make people tell the truth,' Rico said. 'The stone's actually a Roman drain cover, and the face is thought to be that of the god Oceanus.'

'It's certainly imposing.' And there was a queue of tourists posing for photographs, holding one hand through the Mouth of Truth.

'It's touristy, yes,' he said, following her gaze, 'but it's a little less common than people doing the "Friends, Romans, countrymen" speech.' He touched her cheek briefly with the backs of his fingers, as if to let her know that he hadn't been criticising her—merely stating a fact. 'Shall I take your picture?'

'Yes, please.' She joined the queue to have her photograph taken with the Mouth, and paid her donation.

'Would you like me to take your picture?' she asked when he'd taken the shot.

'No need. I live here,' he said with a smile.

For a moment, she thought he looked a bit shifty. But that was ridiculous. What possible reason would Rico have to lie to her? No. That was sheer paranoia, brought on by thinking about the men who'd let her down so badly in the past.

He took her for a quick peek at the Circus Maximus, the ancient chariot-racing stadium; then they caught the Metro to the Piazza del Popolo and climbed up the steps to the Borghese Park.

'I can't believe it's so *quiet* here,' she said as they wandered along the path. 'All you can hear is birdsong—no noise from the traffic, no sirens blaring from the police cars or the ambulances.'

'I come here whenever I need some peace,' he said. 'We could walk round, or we could take a *riscio.*'

'What's a *riscio*?'

He gestured to people passing them. 'A pedal cart for four with a sunshade on top. They do two-seaters, as well.'

'A side-by-side tandem, you mean?'

'Something like that.' He smiled. 'We can see a bit more of the park, this way. And it's fun.'

She wasn't so sure about that five minutes later, when they were heading towards a roundabout and, however she turned the wheel of the *riscio,* she couldn't get the pedal cart to change direction. The notice in the middle of the car warned about needing to brake downhill, and the risk of the cart toppling over. Where was the brake? Panic flooded through her.

'The steering's only connected on my side, *bellezza,*' he told her, reaching out to squeeze her hand. 'Turning your wheel won't make any difference.'

Ella was practically hyperventilating. How could he be so calm? 'There's a road train over there and we're going the wrong way round the roundabout!'

'We drive on the right in Italy, so we go round the roundabout the opposite way to how you drive in England,' he reminded her. 'It's fine. We'll give way to the road train. There's nothing to worry about. Just sit back and enjoy it.'

'Enjoy…?' she asked wryly, beginning to wish they'd just walked.

'Ella, trust me.'

Ha. He'd unconsciously zeroed in on the one thing she wasn't sure she'd ever be able to do again. Trust someone.

'I won't let you get hurt,' he said, gently touching her cheek with the backs of his fingers. 'I promise. And I never break my promises.'

She didn't know him well enough to know whether he was spinning her a line. But she'd go with it, for now.

Once they were round the roundabout and she got used

to the way the cart moved, she found that she actually *was* enjoying it. Just as Rico had promised, they could see more of the park this way; and they could stop wherever they liked to take a closer look at a fountain or a sculpture.

By the time their hour was up, Ella was relaxed and had even agreed to swap places with Rico and steer the *riscio* herself.

'Not so bad, was it?' he asked, sliding his arm round her shoulders.

'No, it was fun, once I'd got used to it,' she admitted, putting her arm round his waist.

They walked back past a bunch of teenagers on rollerblades negotiating a line of tiny, tiny cones. Ella was amazed at how they skated in and out without knocking any of them over, their feet crossing each other, and yet they didn't trip or fall.

The fascination must have shown on her face, because Rico said, 'Dare you.'

'Me? But I...' She hadn't been on roller skates for years, let alone rollerblades.

'Dare you,' he repeated.

Well, these few days were all meant to be about having fun. 'You're on.' It was hard enough to skate in a straight line at first, and she knew there was no way she'd be able to negotiate that double slalom of cones. But then the man in charge of the cones took pity on her and gave her a wider-spaced course.

'Wow, I actually did it!' she said at the other end.

'You were magnificent,' Rico said, kissing her.

'And now it's your turn.'

'Mine?' He looked surprised.

'You challenged me. Now prove that *you* can do it.'

The expression in his eyes grew heated. 'What are the stakes?'

She shrugged. 'You tell me.'

He leaned forward and whispered in her ear, 'If I do it without knocking over a cone, you let me do whatever I want to you tonight. If I fail, I'm completely in your hands.'

She shivered with pleasure. 'That sounds good to me.'

He licked his lower lip. 'Right now, I'm not really sure whether it would be more fun to win or to lose.'

'Do it properly,' she told him. 'I don't like lying and game-playing.'

'OK, Ella *bellezza*.' He kissed her swiftly, then put on the rollerblades.

She wasn't surprised that he managed to skate the same course that she did with relative ease. The man in charge of the cones winked at her and set up a more demanding course with a double slalom.

Rico spread his hands, grinned—and then showed off thoroughly. He was as graceful as a ballet dancer as he moved through the slalom course, his body all clean, flowing lines; Ella was aware of how many other women in the gathering crowd were giving him admiring looks.

He almost knocked over the very last cone, which teetered but stayed where it was. He skated round to Ella, then swept into a deep bow before taking her hand, turning it over and kissing the throbbing pulse in her wrist. Desire skittered through her.

'You've done that before, haven't you?' she asked, not wanting him to see how much of an effect he had on her.

'Now and then. Though I'm a bit out of practice.' He took off his skates and handed them back. 'Come on. Let's go and chill out.'

They ended up by the lake, watching the fountain in the middle.

'I can't believe how blue the water is. It's so pretty here,' Ella said. 'What are the trees?'

'Lilacs.'

'They're not like English lilacs. They don't smell the same, either. But they're lovely. This is really special.'

This was where Rico always came to chill out, because it was one of the few places in Rome where you could enjoy nothing but the sound of birdsong; but the park had become almost background scenery to him over the years. The delight in Ella's face as she looked around made him see the place anew. She was right. It *was* special.

They lay in the dappled shade under the lilacs, holding hands and looking up at the sky. He leaned over and stole a kiss. 'So how come you're in Rome on your own?'

She shrugged. 'It was just the way it worked out. Now was the only time I could go, and my best friend's a teacher—she can't take time off in term time.'

'And you have no family who could go with you?'

For a moment, she looked sad. 'No.'

'And your ex?' That was still bugging him. The man who'd made her doubt herself so much. 'Is that why you were booked in the honeymoon suite? And he let you down?'

'No. I planned the trip after we split up.' Her mouth tightened. 'And he's staying *permanently* ex, no matter how many flowers or grovelling letters he sends me.'

Flowers and grovelling letters? 'Maybe he realised he'd made a mistake, breaking up with you,' Rico said.

'Actually, he didn't dump me. I was the one who walked out,' she told him, lifting her chin. 'As for making a mistake…that's a charitable conclusion.'

'One you obviously don't share.'

She gave a huff of mirthless laughter. 'He probably heard on the grapevine that I won the lottery. Not millions and millions, but a decent amount—enough to give me six months' sabbatical from my job.'

Hmm. So was this the reason why she said that money didn't matter? Rico propped himself up on one elbow so he could look at her properly. 'And you're using the money to travel?'

'A little bit. Actually, I only booked the honeymoon suite because it overlooks the Colosseum. I know it's pathetic, but…'

He pressed a finger to her lips. 'No, it's not pathetic at all. If you wanted a room with a specific view, it doesn't matter what the room's called. Only the view counts.' He smiled at her. 'So where else are you planning to visit?'

'Just Rome, for now. It's the one place I've always wanted to see.'

'Is there anywhere else on your travel wish list?'

She shrugged. 'Vienna, but I don't have time right now. When I get back to London, I'm going to be up to my eyes.'

'Back in the job you described to me as "safe"?' He stroked her face. 'Maybe this money's a chance for you to change your life, find a different job—something you really love doing.'

'That's exactly what I'm going to do,' she said. 'This six months' sabbatical—I'm setting up my own business. If I can make a go of it, then I'll resign properly and concentrate on my business. If I fail, then I still have a safe job to go back to.'

She hadn't let her win go to her head. And she was planning to change her career the sensible way, with a back-up plan. As an entrepreneur himself, Rico knew that meant there was a much better chance of her business succeeding. 'So what's your new business going to be?'

'You won't laugh?'

Why on earth would she think he'd laugh at her? He frowned. 'Of course not.'

She took a deep breath. 'I make cakes.'

'Like cupcakes?'

'Yes, but mostly I make celebration cakes—birthday cakes, wedding cakes, that sort of thing. I've done it for years for friends and colleagues.'

He could see in her expression that it was what she loved doing. Which begged another question. 'You didn't think about making that your job when you left school?'

'I did, but accountancy was safe.' She grimaced. 'We struggled a bit with money when I was growing up. So I wanted to have a safe job, one where I knew I wouldn't have to struggle for money all the time—I even trained on the job rather than doing a degree first, so I didn't have a mountain of debt when I finished studying.'

He'd never been short of money, but he could understand where she was coming from. 'But what you really wanted to do was to decorate cakes.'

She nodded. 'I've done some part-time courses. I did a week's intensive course on sugarcraft, the year before last—how to do embroidery and lace-cut work and stencilling.'

He smiled. 'Embroidery? That sounds more like fashion than baking to me.'

'No, it's a special sort of icing.' She sat up and took out her mobile phone. 'Like this one—I made this last month for a friend.' She handed the phone to him.

He studied the photograph of the wedding cake with its delicate lace. 'You made that?'

She nodded shyly.

'Wow. Forgive me for being rude—I'm sure you're very good at your day job—but you're absolutely wasted there with a talent like this.'

She blushed. 'Thank you.'

'So you're going to work from home?'

'Sort of. I've rented a professional kitchen with a small

flat above it. I moved in a couple of weeks before I came to Rome.'

'So when you get back you'll be setting up your kitchen?'

'And making sure I meet all the hygiene standards—I've got a meeting booked in for when I get back. I've done the food safety courses and I've got up-to-date certificates, so it shouldn't be a problem.'

Rico was intrigued. The way she lit up when she spoke about her cakes… 'Do you have photographs of your other cakes?'

'There's a gallery on my website—except I don't have Internet access on my phone when I'm out of England.'

'I do.' He took his phone out of his pocket and flicked into the Internet before handing the phone to her. 'Show me.'

She brought up the page for him, and he looked through it. Her website was nice and clear; it had contact details and an enquiry form as well as giving potential customers an idea of prices, and the gallery of celebration cakes took his breath away.

'These are amazing, Ella. So when did you start making cakes?'

'When I was a teenager. Like I said, money was a bit tight when I was young—I couldn't always afford to buy my friends a birthday present, but I could make them a special birthday cake, something nobody else would give them. My mum was a great cook, and she taught me how to do icing. And I worked in a bakery on Saturday mornings when I was at school; I learned more about different sorts of icing there.'

It sounded as if she'd had it hard, growing up. But he had a feeling that Ella had also had something that money couldn't buy; the look on her face when she talked about her mother told Rico that Ella had been loved for who she was. Something he'd never really experienced. People only wanted him for what he could give them. His mother, for the hold it gave her over his father. His father, for the access to funds for his lifestyle. His grandparents, so he'd be the heir to the business.

What would it be like to be loved just for yourself?

He pushed the thoughts away. 'What does your mum think about your business?'

Ella's eyes grew suspiciously shiny and she blinked. 'I think she would've said I was doing it the right way—following my dream, but having a back-up plan in case it didn't quite work out.' She swallowed hard. 'Mum would've loved Rome. I just wish I'd had this lottery win a year ago.'

'Your mother...she passed away?' he asked as gently as he could.

'Just over a year ago. She had breast cancer. Otherwise she would've come with me and I could have spoiled her—the way she should've been spoiled.'

Given that money had been a struggle when Ella was growing up, and she hadn't mentioned her father at all, Rico guessed that the man had been either feckless or absent. But he wasn't going to push Ella on that, in case she expected him to trade confidences. He didn't want to talk about absent or feckless fathers: his had been both.

But he could appreciate that Ella missed her mother badly: a woman she'd loved dearly and who'd loved her all the way back. 'Ah, *bellezza*.' He put his arms round her and held her close. 'I'm sorry you didn't get to share Rome with your mum. But I'm selfish enough to be glad that I could share it with you.'

'Yeah.' She took a deep breath. 'Sorry. I'm not going to go all maudlin on you. I'm trying to remember Mum with smiles, not tears. That's how she was. The more rubbish life threw at her, the more she found to smile about.'

A million miles from his own mother—the more gifts life gave her, the more she found to grouse about, Rico thought. He stroked Ella's hair. 'I bet your friends loved their cakes.' He would've been thrilled about someone giving him a present like that—something that had taken thought and time and effort, not just a pile of money thrown at it.

'They did. Do, I should say.' She smiled. 'One of my friends designed that website for me on the understanding that I keep her in cupcakes for a month when I get back from Rome, and I make her a Christmas cake that even her mother-in-law can't criticise.'

'Yeah. Families can be too critical.'

She raised an eyebrow. 'That sounds like experience talking.'

'Not everyone has a wonderful family.'

'You're not close to yours?'

That was the understatement of the century. 'No.' And he didn't want to talk about it. 'But that's fine. I'm happy in my job.'

'So what's your big dream?' she asked 'To write the ultimate tour guide?'

'Not exactly.' He didn't actually have a dream. He'd been going through the motions for the last year, just concentrating on making the business be the best it could be and getting it ready for expansion. London, next; then Paris.

'OK. Something crazier, then. To be a rock star?' she suggested. 'Or to design the best Italian sports car in the world?'

He laughed. 'No. I'm fine with where I am now.' Though even as he said the words, he knew they weren't strictly true. There was something missing in his life. Except he had no idea what it was.

And thinking about that made him uncomfortable. He was fine with his world just the way it was. He was in charge of the family business. In charge of his own destiny. What else did he need?

Time to change the subject, he thought. 'Hey. We've been lazing about here for so long, we're going to be able to catch Rome at sunset. Better get your camera out.'

Ella was absolutely enchanted by the sunset. Rico took her back by the Trevi Fountain so she could see it lit up at night, and took more pictures for her.

'Rome's just amazing.' She sighed happily. 'You're so lucky living here.'

'I know.' He slid his arm round her shoulders, enjoying the contact and just strolling through the streets with her. He couldn't remember the last time he'd felt this relaxed. 'Have dinner with me?' he asked. 'I know a little place not far from here where the food's excellent.'

'On condition we go halves.'

He still couldn't quite get his head round that. His last few girlfriends had expected him to pay for absolutely everything—not that he begrudged the money at all, but he'd grown a bit tired of being taken for granted. 'We'll go halves,' he agreed. 'On condition you let me buy you dessert somewhere else.'

She smiled. 'It's a deal.'

They shared a simple meal of bruschetta and a bowl of pasta; although Ella ordered a salad, she didn't pick at it and ignore the rest of her meal. She enjoyed everything. And she was like nobody he'd ever met. Again, he wasn't sure whether that scared him or fascinated him most.

Afterwards, Rico took her to the best *gelateria* in Rome.

'Wow. How do you expect me to choose from all these flavours?' she asked. 'They all look so gorgeous.'

Eventually she picked ginger and cinnamon, and they walked back through the streets, holding hands and eating *gelati*. She sighed with pleasure as they reached the Colosseum. 'I love this building. It's everything I thought it would be.'

'Yeah.' He couldn't resist kissing her. And when he saw her back to her room, he couldn't resist kissing her some more. Kissing turned to touching, and touching ended with him making love to her in the shower.

Afterwards, he tucked her into bed.

'Thank you for today,' she said softly. 'It's been really special.'

She was right. It *had* been special. Which set all his alarm bells ringing; this was meant to be just fun. She was vulnerable; she'd been hurt badly by her ex and had lost her closest family. And he could only be her Mr Right Now. What did he know of families, of love and protection? For both their sakes, he needed to rein back a bit.

It was just as well that tomorrow would be their last full day together. He was dangerously close to actually wanting to get involved with her. Which would be a seriously bad idea.

'My pleasure, *bellezza,*' he said lightly. 'See you in the morning. Sweet dreams.'

CHAPTER FOUR

THE following morning, Rico took Ella to the Vatican on the Metro. As they walked through the museum, Ella was amazed to learn that they were actually walking on original Roman mosaic floors, ones which might once have lain in an emperor's villa; and then on marble floors that had once graced the Colosseum itself. The tapestries and sculptures were beautiful too, but what really stunned her was the Sistine Chapel.

'I didn't think it would be this huge,' she said to Rico. One corner had been left dark, so you could see how much work had gone into the restoration of the chapel and cleaning the paintwork. Ella just stood and gazed at the paintings, loving the depth to the blue sky. And the famous view of God reaching out to Adam with his finger, something she'd seen on postcards and in magazines, was much more awe-inspiring in real life.

'That was really incredible,' she said to Rico as they left the chapel to go to St Peter's. 'I honestly wasn't expecting it to be that special. Thank you so much for bringing me here.'

Outside, there were the two Swiss guards with their saffron-and-purple striped uniforms, and the guide pointed out the building that contained the Pope's apartment and the window where he gave the blessing every Sunday.

The church itself was gorgeous, and Ella lingered by Michelangelo's *Pietà*. 'It's amazing to think that he was only twenty-four when he carved it. Four years younger than I am now.'

'Doing what he loved. Making the most of his gift,' Rico said. 'Which is what you're about to do, too.'

'I hope so. Though sometimes I wake up and wonder just how crazy I am, setting up a new business in the middle of a recession.'

'You already have a customer base, and word of mouth will bring you more. And when you have transferable skills that you can use to keep your cash flow ticking over, if you really need to. No, you're not crazy at all,' Rico said. 'You're doing the right thing. And when you're old, you can look back without regrets or wondering what would've happened if you'd given your dreams a chance.'

'I guess so.'

They wandered back outside into the sunshine, and Rico showed Ella the disappearing columns.

'That's clever.'

'And you're thinking about how you can use that on a cake, aren't you?' he asked, smiling.

'Something like that,' she admitted. She looked at the obelisk in the centre of the square. 'I take it that that's another of the Egyptian obelisks that seem to be everywhere?'

'Yup. Caligula brought it to Rome, and it was moved here from Nero's circus by the order of Pope Sixtus V,' Rico told her. 'Apparently, it took four months to move it across Rome, and the men who moved it had to do it in silence, on pain of death.'

'Wow. That's a bit harsh. I assume that's another medieval thing, like the Mouth of Truth biting off the hands of liars?'

'Roman history's not *totally* gory,' Rico said, laughing.

'Gladiators, Nero, Caligula… I rest my case.' She spread her hands, laughing back.

They walked back into the city, stopping every so often to look at the gorgeous cakes in the windows of the *pasticcieri*. There were lilacs and orange trees everywhere, and Ella loved every second of it.

As they crossed the Tiber Ella asked, 'Can I take you to dinner tonight?'

She wanted to take him to dinner? That was a first. Normally, Rico did the asking. And normally, Rico did the paying. The only time someone else offered to treat him, there was usually an ulterior motive—an obvious one at that. Not being able to see a motive made him feel out of his depth, to the point where he was lost for words.

'Sorry. Of course you're probably busy. I assumed too much,' she said when he was silent.

'No, I'm not busy. And, yes, I'd like to have dinner with you.'

'And it's my bill,' Ella said firmly.

That was what he didn't get. He couldn't help asking, 'Why?'

'You cooked for me, that first night. Obviously I can't return the favour because I don't have access to a kitchen here, so the best I can offer is buying you a meal in a restaurant.' She smiled. 'I would say let's go to the swishest restaurant in Rome, but I'd guess you have to make a reservation months in advance, and anyway I don't really have anything suitable to wear.'

'Plus it would be incredibly expensive. Michelin stars and what have you don't come cheap,' he warned.

She shrugged. 'The money doesn't matter. Remember, I won all that money, and I'm under budget here anyway. I can afford it.'

Rico hid a smile. Ella might be planning a new career as a baker, but she still talked like an accountant.

'And anyway, it'd be a treat for me as well,' she added, as if trying to persuade him.

'I'll see what I can do,' he said. 'I have a few connections.'

She smiled. 'Thank you.'

'Let's have a coffee and I'll make some phone calls.'

He gulped his lukewarm espresso down, as usual, and made a few calls. Luckily Ella's Italian was nowhere near good enough to follow what he was saying. There was one particular restaurant he had in mind; the food was stunning, and there was always a huge waiting list to get a table. But it also happened to be owned by a very good friend of his, and if there was a chance he could call in a favour...

He was in luck. The *maître d'* also agreed to let him settle most of the bill beforehand and give Ella a much smaller bill at the end of the night, to Rico's relief. No way was he letting her pay for a meal *that* costly, lottery win or no lottery win. And sorting this out beforehand meant that he was still in control. No surprises.

'The good news is, I have a reservation for us at eight tonight,' he said when he'd finished the call. 'The bad news... Do you have a little black dress with you?'

She grimaced. 'No.'

'It might be an idea to buy one.' Normally, he'd just go to the Via Condotti with his current girlfriend and let her loose in the designer shops with his credit card. But he had a feeling that Ella would refuse to let him buy her a dress and shoes. And if he explained that he could afford it— and could more than afford to take her out to one of the fanciest restaurants in Rome every night of the week—he had a feeling that she'd react badly. She'd told him at the park that she didn't like lying or game-playing. Though he wasn't playing games—merely taking the chance to be seen for who he was, for once, rather than for what he stood for. And surely one little white lie wasn't that bad?

'Can you recommend any shops?' she asked.

'It depends what you want. The big designers have shops on the Via Condotti.'

She wrinkled her nose. 'Sorry, I'm not really a designer person. How about something…well, not cheap and cheerful, but not ridiculous designer prices, either?'

He loved the fact that she was so no-nonsense. And he'd just bet that she shopped efficiently, rather than dragging round every shop and then going back to the first one at the end of a long, miserable day. 'Sure. Let's go.'

Rico discovered that he'd underestimated her on the efficiency front. 'Colour me impressed,' he said. 'I've never met a woman who could choose a dress *and* shoes all within the space of twenty minutes.'

Ella frowned. 'That's incredibly sexist.'

'No. It's based on painful experience,' he said with a grimace.

'You've been dating the wrong kind of woman,' she teased.

Now he'd met Ella, he was beginning to think that himself. Which was ridiculous. He didn't want a relationship; he'd seen first-hand just how messy things could get, and he never wanted to be in that position himself. But there was something about Ella Chandler. Something he couldn't put his finger on. Something that drew him and scared him at the same time.

They bought cold drinks at a *caffè* and sat watching the world go by for a while, relaxing in the sun.

'Our table's booked for eight,' Rico said. 'So I'll have a taxi ready for us at seven-thirty and I'll pick you up at your room.'

'That'd be great. Thanks.'

He saw her back to the hotel, then sat on his terrace for a while, thinking about Ella. It would've been nice to share the fading afternoon with her here, but the explanations would be way too complicated.

He showered, shaved and changed into a suit, then went to meet Ella. When she opened the door to him, he whistled in appreciation. She'd chosen a very classic black dress and plain high-heeled court shoes: simple, but very effective. 'You look lovely.'

'Thank you.' She blushed prettily. 'You look nice, too.'

'*Mille grazie.*' He bowed his head in acknowledgement of the compliment. 'Shall we go?'

At the restaurant, he had a rapid conversation with the *maître d'* in Italian to make sure that what he'd arranged that afternoon still stood; and then they were shown to their table. Just what he'd asked for; it was right by the plate-glass windows with a view over the city.

Watching her pay the bill didn't sit well with him, but he could see that she wanted to do something nice for him, so he smiled. 'Thank you. That was a real treat.'

'My pleasure. I'm glad I shared it with you. And the food was fabulous.'

Rico itched to take her to his rooftop garden again and dance with her in the starlight, but he contented himself with taking a taxi back to the hotel and making love to her in the big, wide bed of the honeymoon suite until they were both satiated and drowsy.

'So tomorrow, you go home,' he said, lying with her curled in his arms.

'My flight's at four in the afternoon.'

'Which means you need to check in by two, so you need to leave here at, say, one,' he mused aloud. 'You can leave your luggage here—the staff can put it in secure storage until you're ready to collect it—and I'll drive you there myself.'

'Are you sure?'

'Very sure.' He kissed her. 'And maybe tomorrow I can show you a bit of underground Rome.'

'The catacombs, you mean?'

'They're a bit of a way out of the city. No, it's a church just round the corner from the Colosseum. There's a Roman house in the basement, and you can actually hear the river running past as you walk through the rooms.' He smiled. 'And then I guess you'd like a last look at the Colosseum before we go to the airport and grab something to eat.'

'That all sounds great.'

'And I'd better let you get some sleep. *Buona notte, bellezza.* Sleep well.'

He lay awake that night, thinking about Ella. On paper, he knew it was completely crazy; they lived in different countries and she was just about to start a business venture that would take up all her time and then some. But she'd made him feel like nobody else had made him feel, and he wanted to get to know her more. To explore where all this was coming from. To find out why she was affecting him this way.

He just had to find the right words to tell her who he really was, and that he'd been a little economical with the truth. Hopefully she'd understand that he hadn't been trying to hurt her or cheat her; he'd just wanted her to see him for himself, not as Rico the hard-headed businessman or Rico the boyfriend with deep pockets. Then maybe, just maybe, they could find the time to explore where this was taking them.

* * *

After breakfast, Ella finished packing and headed down to the hotel reception area to organise leaving her luggage in their secure storage area. Rico was already there, though he was busy talking to some of the other hotel staff. They were speaking rapid Italian, so she didn't have a clue what they were saying; but something struck her as odd. The hotel receptionist seemed very deferential when she was talking to him. Given that Rico was a tour guide, surely his status would be the same as that of the receptionist? They were colleagues, not boss and employee.

And then she heard the receptionist say, '*Sì,* Signor Rossi.'

That was definitely deferential. Why wasn't the receptionist calling him by his first name?

'May I help you, *signorina?*' the other receptionist asked.

'I—um, yes. *Grazie.* I'd like to check out.'

'Of course.' The receptionist sorted out the bill and gave Ella an extra receipt for the city tax.

'May I ask…who's that man over there?' Ella gestured over to Rico, who was still earnestly in conversation with the other receptionist.

'Signor Rossi. He's very easy on the eye, no?' The receptionist smiled.

Yes. Rico was very easy on the eye. But this was the second person to use his formal name rather than his first name. Rossi. Something rang a bell there, and she couldn't remember why. 'Who is he?' she asked.

'The CEO of Rossi Hotels. We have three sister hotels in Rome,' the receptionist explained, 'though Signor Rossi is based here.'

Rico owned the hotel.

So he wasn't a tour guide at all. He'd lied to her. Ella felt sick. How rubbish was her judgement? Even for a casual fling that wasn't supposed to matter, she'd managed to find herself someone who lied. So much for the promise she'd made her mother at her deathbed. *Promise me you won't make the same mistakes I did, Ella.* Ella had promised. And what had she done? She'd planned to marry a cheat and a liar. OK, so she'd found out the truth in time to stop her making it worse and actually marrying Michael, but here she was in Rome, making the same mistake all over again; having a fling with a handsome, charming and faithless man—someone who'd lied to her right from the start.

What an idiot she'd been. Stupid, naïve and oh, so gullible. She'd thought she'd connected with him—that she knew him. But she hadn't known him at all.

Well, she'd had more than enough lies in her life. And lying was the one thing she couldn't forgive or forget: her own, very personal, hot button. If Rico could lie over something as unimportant as his job, what else would he lie about? Had he lied about being single, too? Was that why he'd never suggested spending the night with her—because he'd gone home to his partner?

The idea made her feel sick. And she really, really wanted to go home. Right now.

'Would you be able to order me a taxi, please?' she asked the receptionist. 'To the airport?'

'Of course, *signorina*. What time would you like it?'

'Now, please.'

'*Sì,* of course. Would you like to wait in the lounge, round the corner? I'll come and find you as soon as your taxi arrives.'

'*Grazie.*' With one last look at Rico—the man who'd made her feel like a million dollars, yet had lied to her consistently—Ella went into the lounge.

Please let the taxi be quick.

* * *

It was the first time Rico had ever regretted living at the flagship hotel in the Rossi chain. Normally he didn't mind dropping everything to sort out a problem with a difficult guest. But why did it have to be now?

Stupidly, he hadn't taken a note of Ella's mobile phone number, so he couldn't call her to tell her he was going to be a little late. 'Mr Banks is waiting for me in his room, yes? I need you to stall him for three minutes, Gaby, while I make a phone call,' he said.

'Will do,' Gabriella said, looking relieved. 'Thank you, Signor Rossi.'

'Prego,' he said politely, trying not to show his irritation.

He rang Ella's room; there was no answer. So either she was still having breakfast in the hotel's restaurant or she was in the shower, he guessed.

'Gaby, can I ask you to get a message to Signora Chandler for me? She's in the honeymoon suite. Tell her I've been delayed, and I'll be with her as soon as I can. If she'd like coffee, whatever, then it's on the house, OK?'

'Of course, Signor Rossi,' the receptionist said.

Rico took a deep breath and summoned a smile. From what Gabriella had told him, Mr Banks sounded like the kind of guest who'd complain if he couldn't find something to complain about. But, all the same, he was a guest and deserved courtesy and attention. Hopefully Rico would be able to sort out all the misunderstandings—and then Ella would be waiting for him.

Ella sat in the back of the taxi, barely paying any attention to her surroundings as the driver took her through the outskirts of Rome and onto the motorway towards the airport.

Why had he lied to her? That was what she didn't understand. Why had he pretended to be somebody else? Was he so rich, spoiled and bored that he got his kicks from making a fool out of people?

What an idiot she'd been, letting herself fall for every word he'd said. Accepting everything at face value. She really ought to have known better. The man she'd spent three days with—the man she'd let into her bed and started to let into her heart—just didn't exist. Rico the tour guide was a complete fabrication. Rico the CEO was a complete stranger; she knew nothing of his true self.

As for that coin she'd thrown into the Trevi Fountain—well, she had no intention of ever coming back to Rome.

Finally, Rico left Mr Banks smiling and satisfied. The man had to be the most difficult guest he'd ever encountered—the room was too small, the towels were the wrong size and hadn't been laundered, the pillows were too flat, the bed was too hard, the air-conditioning didn't suit him, and as for the city tax that tourists had to pay on top of an already extortionate hotel bill...

Rico had listened, empathised and made suggestions. And he'd upgraded the man's room, even though he suspected that Mr Banks was the kind of customer who booked the cheapest room in every hotel he stayed at and then complained until he was upgraded to the best suite. He'd gently explained that anyone staying in Rome had to pay the city tax, and Mr Banks' travel agent should have told him when he booked that several other cities in Italy, including Venice and Florence, levied the same tax on visitors. And he'd also very politely pointed out the notice in the bathroom asking guests to help the hotel be more environment-friendly by leaving the towels that needed laundering in the bathtub and putting the ones they didn't mind re-using on the towel rack. If Mr Banks wanted all his towels laundered every day, that was fine.

He took a deep breath. At least now he could see Ella.

Except she wasn't waiting for him in the lounge next door to the hotel reception, as he'd expected. Maybe she'd missed the message and was waiting for him in her room, he thought, and rang her room. Again, there was no answer.

He frowned and went over to the reception desk. 'Gaby, did you manage to get hold of Signora Chandler?'

'Ah, Signor Rossi. I'm afraid not. She'd already checked out and left.'

What? He couldn't believe what he was hearing. Why had Ella gone without a single word to him?

'Maria booked a taxi for her.' Gabriella gestured to the other receptionist.

'A taxi?'

'To the airport.'

'Right.' He could see that Maria was busy with a guest. 'Can you ask her to come to my office for a quick word when she's free?'

'Of course, Signor Rossi.'

'Thank you,' he said, keeping a lid on the hurt and anger that threatened to bubble over, and headed for his office.

'Rico? I thought you were taking three days off?' Lina said when he walked through the door.

'I changed my mind.' Warning her silently not to ask, he closed his office door behind him.

Ten minutes later, there was a rap on the door. 'Signor Rossi? Gaby said you wanted a word.' Maria looked worried.

'Come and sit down,' he said, forcing himself to give her a reassuring smile. It wasn't her fault that Ella had left without even saying goodbye. 'I believe you booked a taxi for Signora Chandler?'

'Yes.'

'Did she leave a message for me?'

'No.' Maria frowned. 'Is something wrong?'

Yes. But how could he explain it without making himself look a fool? 'She's a friend of the family,' he fibbed. 'I was going to give her a lift to the airport this morning, but then...'

Maria rolled her eyes. 'Signor Banks.'

He should've reminded her that they should always be ultra-polite about a guest, however difficult, but he understood exactly what she meant. 'Gaby was going to give Signora Chandler the message that I'd been delayed, but she'd already left before Gaby could find her.'

'But Signora Chandler pointed you out in the lobby and asked me who you were. I told her.' Maria frowned. 'If you were giving her a lift to the airport, why didn't she know who you were?'

Oh, great. Now he was tangled in a real web of lies. His own fault, for not being honest in the first place. All he could do was bluff it out. 'Nonna knows her grandparents. We don't really know each other.' That last bit at least was true. He'd thought he knew Ella—but how wrong he'd been. 'I guess she saw I was busy and thought I might not be able to get her to the airport in time.' He smiled at Maria. 'I just wondered if she'd left me a message. But no matter. Thanks for clearing that up for me.'

'*Prego.*' Maria smiled back and left his office.

Rico leaned back in his chair. Maria had told Ella who he really was—and Ella had obviously realised that he'd lied to her. But it had been a white lie. He hadn't done it to hurt her, and she'd completely overreacted to the situation.

Perhaps it was just as well that she'd gone and they'd never have to see each other again. He could go back to his normal life. No more strange feelings that something was missing. What he'd shared with her had been good sex and nothing more. A holiday fling. He'd obviously spent too long in the sun—and that crazy idea of trying to make things work between London and Rome was just that. A crazy idea. Ella Chandler was nothing special. He didn't need her, he didn't want her, and he was perfectly happy with his life as it was.

CHAPTER FIVE

FOR the next three weeks, Ella was busy—more than busy. She spent her time working her way through all the local cafés and sandwich businesses to see if they wanted to stock her cupcakes, talking to managers at function rooms and taking samples of her cakes to see if they'd put her on their recommended supplier lists for celebration cake bakers, planning the launch party for Ella's Cakes, and making sure that all the invitations were sent out on time.

When she crawled into bed at night, she should've slept like the dead. Except she couldn't get Rico out of her head. Which made her even crosser with herself. Why was she thinking about a man who'd lied to her? Especially as she couldn't see a single reason for him to need to lie.

Yet still she dreamed of him. Every single night. And it was driving her crazy.

Rico couldn't get Ella out of his head. He kept telling himself that it was because she was the one who'd ended it and that usually he was the one who called it quits; it was just hurt pride making him feel that way. She wasn't anything special. He was being an idiot.

And yet he found himself brooding. He didn't even sit on his rooftop terrace any more, watching the sun go down and the lights of Rome bloom in the darkness—because all he could see was Ella and the delight on her face as she looked out over Rome.

He really needed to snap out of it. Focus. It wasn't as if he had nothing better to do. He had all the details through of The Fountain, a boutique hotel in Bloomsbury; the initial figures stacked up, so all he needed to do was go and see it for himself, see if his gut feel told him it was the right place for Rossi Hotels to expand in London.

London.

Where Ella was.

Maybe he should look her up while he was there. Then he could prove to himself once and for all that what they'd had was nothing out of the ordinary—and he could finally get her out of his head.

Julia plucked a leaflet from Ella's hand and replaced it with a glass of wine.

Ella shook her head. 'I don't need this, Ju—'

'Yes, you do. Just one sip,' Julia said. 'It'll help you relax.'

'I'm fine,' Ella protested.

'I've known you since we were ten. I know when you're panicking,' Julia said dryly. 'And you really don't need to, you know. Everyone's going to turn up and it's going to be a raging success.'

'That, or the local ducks are going to be having the biggest party in the world tomorrow morning,' Ella said gloomily.

Julia just laughed. 'The ducks don't stand a chance. Once people taste your cakes, they'll be thinking up excuses to have cakes made for them.'

Ella put the wine down untouched and hugged her friend. 'Thank you. I really appreciate your support. You know, you're the sister I never had.'

'You, too.' Julia returned the hug.

To her horror, Ella felt tears sting her eyes, and blinked hard. 'Oh, God. I've gone all wet. I'm not going to be able to do this.'

Julia patted her arm. 'Of course you are. Think about it. You've been working like crazy, totally overdoing things, so it's not surprising you're tired and feeling a bit emotional. Today's a big deal for you. Your dream's finally coming true. Take a swig of that wine and then a deep breath, and you'll be fine. And remember that you make the best cakes in the whole wide world.'

This time, Ella did as her best friend said.

'OK?' Julia asked gently.

'OK.' Ella squared her shoulders. 'Let me go through my list. Wine, soft drinks and glasses, tick. Coffee and tea, tick. Cakes, tick. Business cards on every table, tick. Display book on every table, tick. Extra supplies for filling up plates in the kitchen at the back, tick.'

'Smile, tick,' Julia added.

Ella forced herself to smile. 'Yes.'

The function room was full; people were chatting and talking and clearly having a great time. Rico noticed that there was a woman refilling the plates with beautiful cupcakes in different colours. Clearly Ella's launch party was a success and the cakes were going like—well, hot cakes.

It took him a matter of seconds to locate her. She was at the far side of the room, talking to someone and writing on a pad—or was she sketching? She looked animated, almost glowing with pleasure. A kick of desire went through him. He could remember how to make her glow even more than that…

Oh, for pity's sake. It was just sex. He hadn't slept with anyone since Ella had left Rome; he'd been too busy to date, and this was just a physical reaction to abstinence, he told himself. There was absolutely no reason why his heart should be thumping like this. And he absolutely wasn't going to give into the temptation to march over to her, sweep her off her feet and kiss her until they were both dizzy. Apart from anything else, it looked as if she was talking to a potential customer. He wasn't going to barge in and spoil the deal for her. It wouldn't be fair.

Maybe some coffee would clear his head and bring his common sense back. He went over to the tables where hot and cold drinks were being served, accepted a mug of coffee from the woman serving, and smiled appreciatively at her when she encouraged him to help himself to some cake.

He took one of the smaller cakes and the taste exploded in his mouth. Wow. He'd never eaten chocolate cake this good, before. He tried another. The ivory and deep pink two-tone icing turned out to be raspberry, the tartness of the fruit cutting through the sweetness of the icing. And the peach-coloured one was a glorious riot of passion fruit icing on a coconut base.

He was pretty sure Ella had been a very competent accountant, but she'd been totally wasted in the financial world. Being able to cook like this was a gift, and setting up this business was definitely the right thing for her to do. He ought to back off and leave her be. Except something nagged at him to stay.

Something dragged Ella's attention from her client. She glanced up briefly to see what was drawing her, and nearly choked when she saw Rico.

No, it couldn't be him. It had to be someone who looked a bit like him. He was hundreds of miles away, in Rome. And why would he come to her launch party, anyway? She hadn't invited him. And if she'd really meant anything to him—if the time they'd spent together in Rome had been more than just Rico acting a role to amuse himself—then he would've got in touch with her before now. The hotel had all her details from her booking. His silence proved what she'd learned so shockingly on that last day: that it had all been some kind of spoiled playboy's game. He wasn't interested in her. He'd made that clear. He'd lied to her when there hadn't been any need to lie.

But then he caught her eye. Raised his mug. Blew her a kiss.

And every circuit in her brain felt as if it had just fried.

This wasn't fair. Just when she really needed to concentrate, all she could think of was the way that gorgeous mouth had enjoyed every centimetre of her skin, brought her such glorious pleasure. He was breathtaking to look at, and he made her feel like no one else ever had. Which made him incredibly dangerous to her peace of mind.

She hated the fact that she couldn't tear her gaze away from him. That she still wanted him every bit as much as she'd wanted him in Rome.

She dropped her pen. Although she knew it made her look clumsy, at least it made her look away from Rico. 'I'm sorry. I'm not usually this scatty,' she said apologetically to her client. She forced herself to ignore Rico and concentrate on what she did best, planning and making cakes to delight people. Finally she had all the details of the commission, took a deposit and gave her new client a receipt. She was just putting everything in her briefcase when Rico walked over.

'Ella *bellezza*,' he said softly, his voice low and husky; in response all her hormones sat up and begged.

'What are you doing here?' she asked, trying desperately to sound cooler than she felt.

'I think we have unfinished business.'

'No, we don't.'

'You walked out on me in Rome without a word.'

Her eyes narrowed. 'You lied your face off. What did you expect, congratulations and a helium balloon?'

'I think,' he said, 'we need to talk.'

She knew what he meant by that. She'd been there before with Michael. No doubt Rico, too, thought he could exercise a bit of charm and talk her round to his point of view. Wrong. She wasn't repeating her mistakes. 'I have nothing to say to you.'

'Is everything OK?' A tall, statuesque woman appeared beside Ella and gave her a concerned look.

'It's fine,' Rico said, smiling. 'Ella's cakes are amazing. And I was about to ask her to make me a special cake.'

She was looking daggers at him, and the other woman clearly picked up the atmosphere. 'Perhaps I can help you. Ella's been on the go all day.'

'You're Ella's business partner?' he asked.

'Yes,' the woman said.

'No,' Ella said at the same time, and sighed. 'It's OK, Ju. I'll deal with this.'

'Signal me if you need me, Ella,' Julia said, and gave Rico a hard look, as if warning him to go easy on Ella or he'd have her to deal with.

'Your guard dog?' Rico asked.

'My best friend,' she corrected. 'Though, yes, she does look out for me.' She lifted her chin. 'What do you want, Rico?'

'To commission a cake.'

She narrowed her eyes at him. 'I don't have time for playing games.'

'I'm not playing games. I have a business opportunity in London. If I decide to add the hotel to my chain, then

I'll need to have some kind of opening ceremony, and that in turn means I'll need a cake for the party.'

'So that's an "if". Not a definite.' She shook her head in disgust. 'Where do you stop with the lies?'

'I haven't lied to you.'

She folded her arms. 'You told me you were a tour guide.'

'Which I was. For that day. I'm hands-on in my business. I do a stint in every job, every few months, so I can see the issues my staff face and where things can be improved for both customers and staff. The day I met you, I was a tour guide.'

'Why didn't you tell me who you really were?'

'Because.' He sighed. 'Ella, this isn't the place to discuss it.'

'You're telling me.'

'Can I take you to dinner, when you've finished here?'

'Why?'

'So you can continue with your launch party and do what you do best. And then we'll talk.'

'I…'

'We have unfinished business,' he said softly, 'and you know it, Ella *bellezza*.'

She scoffed. 'I don't think so.'

There was only one way to prove it to her. He stooped very slightly and brushed his mouth against hers in the lightest, sweetest, softest kiss. His mouth tingled where it touched hers.

She shivered, and he noticed that her pupils had dilated hugely.

'And that was barely a kiss. If I kissed you properly, Ella, neither of us would give a damn that we're surrounded by strangers. We'd both go up in flames. *That's* what I mean by unfinished.'

She swallowed hard. 'I'm working,' she whispered.

'Which is why I suggested dinner. Afterwards.'

She closed her eyes, looking defeated, and for a moment Rico really didn't like himself for the way he'd pressured her. But he hadn't done anything wrong—had he? 'Just dinner, Ella. When we've talked things through.'

She opened her eyes again. 'OK.'

'Good—and, by the way, your cakes are superb.' He couldn't resist just one taunt. 'I particularly like the passion fruit one.' He put the emphasis on *passion,* and Ella blushed to the roots of her hair.

He winked at her, and disappeared back into the crowd.

Flustered, Ella grabbed the mug of coffee she'd abandoned half an hour earlier and took a gulp of the lukewarm liquid.

'Who was that?' Julia asked, returning to her side.

'It's complicated—a long story.'

'Tell me after.'

'I'm, um, having dinner with Rico afterwards.'

'Rico. Hmm.' Julia raised an eyebrow. 'And although his English is perfect, there's a definite accent there. Would I be right in saying you met him in Rome?'

Ella felt her skin heat. 'Yes.'

'You had a fling with him?'

'Um, yes.'

Julia looked hurt. 'You never said a word to me.'

'It's complicated,' Ella said again.

'You don't have to see him if you don't want to.' Then Julia's eyes narrowed. 'Hang on. I know you've been working like crazy to get things up and running, but I remember the last time you threw yourself into work like this.'

'He didn't do a Michael on me, if that's what you're asking.'

'But he knows about your lottery win?'

Ella nodded. 'That isn't an issue.' She could guess what her best friend thought: Rico was a con-man after her money. 'Actually, the money would be small change to him. He could buy me out ten times over and still have a fortune left.'

'So if he's not after your money, what does he want?'

'Right now, I don't have a clue.' That wasn't strictly true. That kiss had told her a great deal. And it had also made her libido sit up and beg.

Why had he walked back into her life, offering her temptation? Yes, physically it was good between them. Better than it had ever been for her with anyone else. But Rico had already proved to her that she couldn't trust him. She had no idea who the real Rico was. She wasn't stupid enough to put herself back in a vulnerable position; so she'd have dinner with him—and she'd tell him to stay out of her life.

She managed to keep her focus on business for the rest of the evening, though it was a real effort; even when she couldn't see Rico, she was so aware of his presence.

Finally, the last person left the party, and she started to clear up. She could hear noises from the kitchen at the back of the function room, but Julia was in the front with her, collecting plates and mugs. So who was in the back?

She nearly dropped the crockery she was carrying when she walked into the kitchen and saw Rico with his sleeves rolled up and his hands in sudsy water. 'What are you doing?'

He rolled his eyes. 'Ask the obvious, Ella *bellezza*.'

'But…'

'The quicker you're done here, the quicker I get to spend time with you. So it makes sense for me to help you clear up.'

'I guess so.'

He frowned. 'You look exhausted.'

'She's been working crazy hours since she got back from Rome,' Julia told him.

'In that case, I won't drag you out to dinner tonight, Ella,' Rico said.

She had a reprieve?

Then he added, 'I assume you have the makings of an omelette and salad in your fridge, so I'll cook for you instead. Or order takeaway, if you'd rather.'

'I...' She was too tired to think straight. Right at that moment she didn't have a clue what to say.

He sighed. 'You really are exhausted.' He dried his hands, then took the crockery from her. 'Sit down.'

'I've still got things to clear up out there.'

'I'll do it. Don't argue.'

Before she had time to collect her thoughts, he'd made a mug of coffee for Julia and herself, finished clearing up in the function room, and was back to dealing with the huge pile of washing up.

'So how do you know each other?' Julia asked.

'We met in Rome,' Rico said.

'And you've come all this way to see Ella?' She sounded disbelieving.

'I'm in London on business,' he said. 'And I saw the details of the launch party on Ella's website. So I thought I'd drop in and say hello.'

'Hmm.'

Ella could tell her best friend was still suspicious of Rico, though the fact that he was helping to clear up without being asked had redeemed him a bit in Julia's eyes.

'Is there anything else that needs doing?' he asked when he'd finished drying the crockery and Julia had put it away.

'No.'

'Good.' He rinsed out the sink. 'Can I give you a lift home, Julia?'

'No, I'm fine—I'm only two stops away on the Tube.'

Ella blinked at him. 'You drove here?'

'No, I don't have a car in London. I called a taxi.' Rico flicked open his phone and speed-dialled a number. 'Address?' he asked.

'Here?'

'No. *Your* address.'

Of course. She was too tired to think straight. And that kiss earlier hadn't helped. She couldn't stop thinking about it, about the way he made her feel. Bad, bad idea. She mumbled her address at him.

'The taxi will be here in a quarter of an hour,' he said.

It gave them enough time to lock up.

'I think,' he said softly when they were inside her flat, 'you're too tired to talk tonight.'

'I am.'

'You look all in.' He rummaged in her fridge.

She frowned. 'What are you doing?'

'Making you something to eat.'

'I'm not hungry.'

'Tough. You need to eat to keep your strength up. Especially if you're working crazy hours.'

He made her an omelette, then sat opposite her with his arms folded until she ate it. The food was surprisingly good, but then she already knew he could cook. One thing he *hadn't* lied about.

'Aren't you having anything?' she asked.

'I'll eat later.' He flapped a dismissive hand. 'I don't usually eat until late anyway.'

He washed up her empty plate and cleared up in the kitchen. 'I'll call you tomorrow. We can do lunch, or dinner—whatever fits in your schedule.'

'What about yours?'

'I can be flexible.' He touched her cheek gently with the backs of his fingers, a sweet and cherishing gesture. 'Goodnight, Ella *bellezza*. I'll speak to you tomorrow. Sleep well.'

She was pretty sure she wouldn't. He'd just turned her upside down all over again.

And yet she was out like a light the second her head hit the pillow. The next thing she knew, her alarm was beeping crazily.

She showered and washed her hair, and was halfway through drinking a mug of coffee when the phone rang. She grabbed it without looking at the display. 'Ella Chandler.'

'*Buongiorno,* Ella *bellezza.*'

That sexy, melted-chocolate voice undid all the good that the caffeine had done in sharpening her brain again. And she hated the way her libido betrayed her like this, turning her into a puddle of hormones. A pushover. 'Good morning.'

'So, are you having lunch with me today or dinner?'

'Do we really have anything to say to each other?'

'I think we do.'

She sighed. 'Dinner, then.'

'Good. I'll pick you up at eight.'

Before she could protest, the line went dead.

She replaced the receiver. God only knew what she was getting herself into, agreeing to have dinner with him and talk. And yet there was a frisson of excitement running down her spine, and the world suddenly seemed a brighter, more vibrant place than it had since she'd come back from Rome.

'Just remember that he's a liar,' she told herself. 'OK, so he's gorgeous and I have the hots for him. But he's still a liar, first and foremost.' And she had no intention of getting hurt again. Which meant most definitely not getting involved with Rico. Not now, not ever.

CHAPTER SIX

ELLA managed to keep her mind on her work—just—but by half-past seven she was antsy. Rico hadn't given her any idea about where they were going, so she had no idea what the dress code was. She didn't possess a little black dress; the one she'd bought in Rome had gone straight to a charity shop as soon as she'd washed and ironed it.

In the end, she decided to wear one of the suits she'd worn in her office job. Formal and smart might be the way to go. A suit of armour would be better still, but a work suit would have to do.

He was as prompt as he'd been in Rome, ringing her doorbell at exactly eight o'clock. It was the first time she'd seen him wearing a suit, and he looked absolutely stunning. The dark grey material, teamed with one of his trade-mark crisp white shirts and a silk tie, emphasised his good looks. He was utterly breathtaking—and she *wanted*.

'You look very nice,' he said, disarming her.

'Thank you.' And why was it that, even though she knew what a liar he was, her knees still went weak when he smiled? Cross with herself for being such a pushover, she asked, 'Where are we going?'

'My hotel.'

Somewhere private. Oh, help. She remembered what happened when they were in private hotel rooms together.

'We'll talk in my room. And then we'll order dinner,' he said.

'And I get no say in this?'

He spread his hands. 'I just said we'll talk in my room.'

She narrowed her eyes at him. 'You're being bossy.'

He shrugged. 'We agreed to talk. And it makes sense for it to be the hotel; it's neutral ground, and somewhere we won't be overheard.'

She locked the door behind her and followed him out to the taxi. He didn't start a conversation, and she didn't have a clue what to say without making a fool of herself, so they remained in silence until the taxi pulled up outside a boutique hotel in Bloomsbury.

'Fountain Hotel' was etched into the glass of the doors. Definitely a link with Rome, she thought.

'Is this the hotel you're thinking of buying?' she asked as the taxi drove off.

'Maybe.'

She rolled her eyes. 'I'm hardly going to go and tell the world what your plans are and scupper your business deals, am I?'

'I guess not.'

She sighed. 'Rico, what are you doing here? I mean, with me?'

'We have unfinished business, Ella *bellezza*. And we're going to talk about it now.'

They took the tiny lift up to his room. She could still remember the last time they'd been in a hotel room together, and warmth spread down her spine at the memories. Maybe this wasn't such a good idea and she should've insisted on them talking in a public place. Then again, what they were going to discuss was definitely something best done in private. She didn't want anyone else overhearing what a fool she'd made of herself.

When Rico opened the door and ushered her in, Ella was relieved to discover that he'd booked a suite rather than a room. Without a bed in sight, she might just be able to concentrate.

He offered her a seat on one of the sofas. 'Coffee? Something cold? A glass of wine?'

'I'm fine, thanks.' She stared levelly at him as he sat down on the opposite sofa. 'So, where do we start?'

'We can start with why you walked out on me in Rome.'

'You know why. I found out you'd lied to me. I don't like liars.' She lifted her chin. 'Why did you lie to me about who you were, Rico? You let me believe you were a tour guide.'

'Which I was, for that day.'

'Why couldn't you have told me the truth later that evening, when we went out to dinner?'

A muscle twitched in his cheek. 'Because you would've changed.'

She frowned. 'How?'

'Instead of seeing me for who I am, you would've seen me as the CEO of Rossi Hotels.'

She frowned. 'And what difference does that make?'

'You befriended a tour guide, a man you thought didn't have any money. You responded to me as a man. You liked me for who I was, not for my status.'

She looked at him. 'You once told me you thought I'd been seeing the wrong sort of man. It sounds to me as if you've been seeing the wrong kind of woman.'

He rubbed a hand across his eyes. 'Maybe.'

'And, actually, I'm a bit insulted that you think I could be that shallow. I don't judge people by the balance in their bank account.'

He flushed a dull red. 'I'm sorry. I didn't mean it personally. It's just how people always reacted to me in the past.' He raked a hand through his hair. 'I'm making a mess of this. Ella, what I'm trying to say is that I liked who I was when I was with you. I liked the way you made me feel, and I wasn't ready to give that up.'

'But you thought I was shallow enough to respond differently to you once I found out who you were.' She grimaced. 'I'm not sure if that's worse than what I thought originally.'

'Which was?'

She shrugged. 'That you were a bored, spoiled rich kid, and you were slumming it with me—having a joke at my expense.'

'And now you've insulted me,' he said. 'Rich, yes; spoiled, possibly; but bored and slumming it—no way. I never laughed at you, Ella. Far from it.' He gave her a wry smile. 'The irony of it is that I was going to tell you about my real job, that last day. Neither of us wants to get involved; neither of us has time for a relationship. But we're good together. So I was going to suggest that we found a way to juggle things and carry on our fling a little longer.'

She stared at him, stunned. That was the last thing she'd expected to hear.

'OK, so I was a bit evasive about my background.'

'A *bit?*'

'But you're overreacting. It really wasn't that big a deal.'

'Lying's a big deal to me,' she said. 'If you can lie about something small, what's to stop you lying about something else? How do I even know you're single and you're not just turning on the charm? I can't trust you.'

'I'm single. I wouldn't lie about that. I don't like cheats.' He looked thoughtful. 'Who lied to you so badly, Ella? Your ex?'

'Yes. And I was too stupid to see it.'

'You're not stupid,' he said softly. 'But if he was plausible, offering you what you thought you wanted, then maybe it was easier for you not to ask questions or look for problems.'

'Gullible, then.'

'Don't be so hard on yourself.' He took her hand. 'What happened?'

'I...' Bile rose in her throat at the memory. She didn't want to drag it all up again, have the top of her scars ripped open.

As if he guessed her thoughts, he said gently, 'It's not good to bottle things up. It means you don't get the chance to heal.'

He had a point. And maybe if she explained, told him the truth, it would take some of the pain away. Rico had made her feel beautiful in Rome, wiping out the hurt Michael had left. Maybe telling him the rest would help her put it where it belonged—in the past.

'I spent three years supporting Michael while he studied for his PhD. I thought we loved each other.' How naïve and trusting she'd been. 'And I knew he was working hard, juggling his thesis with his teaching commitments, so I decided to surprise him with lunch at the university. I wanted to make him feel good, give him a break. Except he was busy having...' Her breath caught. 'Let's just say he was having a very *private* tutorial with one of his students. And I walked right into the middle of it.'

'How awful for you.' Rico looked sympathetic. 'I take it you had no idea that he was cheating on you?'

'None at all. I thought he loved me.' She swallowed hard. 'But he was just using me; I was someone to pay the rent and the bills. I don't think she was the first of his students he'd had an affair with. And he said afterwards that it was my fault. That I wasn't woman enough to satisfy him.'

'That was his biggest lie,' Rico said. 'It wasn't your

fault at all. He tried to blame his own inadequacies on you.' He pressed a kiss into her palm and folded her fingers over it, and Ella had to swallow hard to stop a sob breaking through at his gentleness. 'You're woman enough, all right. He was the one with the problem.' His eyes narrowed. 'Now I understand what you mean about grovelling letters once he found out about your lottery win. I'm glad you didn't fall for it and take him back.'

'No, because I already knew I couldn't trust him. But I'm still a gullible idiot. I fell for all the lies you told me. That flat you said you borrowed…'

'I borrowed it from myself,' he said. 'I know that's equivocating, and I apologise for that.'

'And you own that swish restaurant, too?'

'No. But I admit that I'm good friends with the owner. We went to school together. So, yes, I traded on our friendship. He found me a table that night.'

'And charged me lower prices, too?' She narrowed her eyes at him. 'I didn't really think about it at the time, but when my credit card bill came through I realised it seemed a bit low for such a posh restaurant.'

Rico sighed. 'OK. I admit I settled part of the bill in advance. I knew it would be expensive and I didn't want to take advantage of you.'

There at least he wasn't like Michael, who'd really taken advantage of her. All the same, it annoyed Ella that Rico had made a high-handed decision without even discussing it with her. 'Don't you think that's just a tiny bit patronising? I told you I could afford it.'

'I know. But it still felt like taking advantage of you.' He wrinkled his nose. 'I'm sorry. I didn't mean to be ungrateful. I guess I'm used to being the one who pays.'

'So you're a control freak?' she asked. 'Except…' She shook her head. 'No, that's not what you were like. Not that first night. When you made all that effort and cooked dinner for me yourself. And you admitted that you're rubbish at puddings so you bought them from the deli.' She narrowed her eyes at him. 'You were telling the truth then, weren't you?'

'Yes. And I really was a tour guide, that day, Ella. Another time, you might've met me as a waiter. Or the male equivalent of a chambermaid.'

She blinked. 'You really clean hotel rooms?'

'And other jobs. I've worked in the kitchen—I probably have the same kind of food hygiene qualifications you do.'

'But you're the CEO of the chain.' She didn't understand. He was the boss. Why was he taking on other roles?

'That's precisely why I do it. Working a short stint in every role is the best way of seeing what issues my staff face, and it also helps me see what would make life better for my guests and for my staff. And my staff respect me for it, because they know I'm not just issuing orders from some ivory tower—they know I've done the job myself, so I'm talking from experience rather than some half-baked theory. And they also know that because I've done it myself, I appreciate what they do.'

'That figures. And the girl who told me about you seemed to respect you.'

'Good.' He paused. 'You overreacted, Ella. I told you one little white lie.'

'It was still a lie.'

'But it wasn't meant to hurt you. Your ex really messed with your head,' he said. 'Or is there more to it than that?'

'He isn't the only one who lied to me,' she admitted. 'Lying is a definite deal-breaker where I'm concerned.'

'Supposing I promise never to tell you anything but the truth, the whole truth, and nothing but the truth, from this moment on?' he asked.

She grimaced. 'You make it sound as if I'm putting you on trial.'

'Isn't that what you're doing?'

He was the one who'd lied. How come she was the one who felt guilty? She sighed. 'Rome—you and me—that was meant to be just fun. A fling.'

'Absolutely. Three days of enjoying each other's company, and we'd never have to see each other again.'

'But now you're here in London.'

'On business.'

'So why did you look me up?'

'To prove something to myself.'

'What?'

He shrugged. 'Doesn't matter.'

He really didn't like talking about himself, did he? He sidestepped questions, or even stonewalled them. She didn't have a clue what was going on in his head. She frowned. 'Where are you going with this? Rico, I'm just starting up my business. Right now I barely have time to sleep.'

'I didn't,' he said softly, 'have sleeping in mind.'

Pictures bloomed in her head, and heat coiled deep in her belly. 'Oh.' Her voice sounded husky, and she was furious with herself for giving herself away like that. She still had the hots for him. Which was crazy, because in some ways he was more of a stranger to her now than he'd been when she'd met him.

'I don't have time for this, either,' he said. 'I have an empire to finish building.'

'That's the dream you wouldn't tell me about in Rome? To build an empire?' She paused. 'Or a dynasty?'

He scowled. 'Not a dynasty. I don't want a family.'

He sounded a little too emphatic. She remembered he'd

said he wasn't close to his family. 'What's so bad about your family?'

'Let's just leave it that they want different things from me.'

'But surely your mum and dad are proud of you? You don't look much older than I am, and you're already CEO of a chain with four hotels in Rome.'

'Sounds as if you've been doing research on me.'

'No. Your receptionist told me about the other hotels. And you're avoiding the question.'

He shrugged. 'I have no idea whether my parents are proud of me and I don't actually care. I barely speak to them, and it suits all of us that way.' He looked her straight in the eye. 'What about you? I know you lost your mum—but if she'd been here I'd bet she would've been really proud of you last night. But what about your dad, your grandparents? Were they there at the launch?'

'My mum was a single parent, and...' She grimaced. 'I don't have a family to be close to. But I have good friends. That's enough for me.'

'Me, too.' He gave her a wry smile. 'Something else we have in common.'

'We're from different worlds. You're—'

'—a bored, spoiled rich kid, slumming it?' he cut in.

She blew out a breath. 'I apologise for that. But you do come from a wealthy background. I don't. My lottery win would be small change to you, but it's absolutely life-changing for me.'

'You're the one who said money isn't important,' he reminded her.

'It isn't what you have that matters; it's the kind of person you are and how you treat others that's important.'

'That works for me,' he said. 'So. You and me.' He drew her hand up to his mouth. His lips were warm against her palm. She closed her eyes as his mouth moved to her wrist; she knew he would be able to feel just how hard and how fast her pulse was beating.

'Ella *bellezza*.' He stroked her cheek and she opened her eyes again. 'Neither of us has time for this. Neither of us is looking for this. But can you honestly tell me that you want to walk away from this?'

'Honestly?' She thought about it. 'No.' She reached up to trace his lower lip with the tip of her forefinger. He had such a beautiful mouth. A mouth that had given her so much pleasure.

He drew the tip of her finger into his mouth and sucked, hard.

Lust curled through her again. 'Rico.' The word felt as if it were poured through sand.

And then they were kissing each other, hot, hard, open-mouthed. He scooped her onto his lap and slid his hands under her jacket; she could feel the warmth of his palms against her skin through the soft cotton of her shirt. Then he tugged her shirt out of her waistband and they were skin to skin. His fingertips moved in tiny circles against her skin, arousing her further. Slowly, slowly, he moved his hands from her back to her midriff, and then upwards so he could cup her breasts. She ached for his touch.

As if he read her mind, he moved one hand so he could unbutton her shirt, then stripped her jacket and shirt off at the same time.

'Your skin's so soft.' He traced the lacy edge of her bra. 'And I need to see you.'

'Yes.' She wanted this as much as he did. Needed it. He might be a liar, a man she could never trust, but he made her body sing.

He unsnapped her bra with one hand, slid the straps down, then tossed the lacy garment away. She closed her

eyes and tipped her head back as he kissed his way down
her throat—hot, open-mouthed kisses, swirling his tongue
against her skin. Her hands slid back into his hair, urging him on.

He opened his mouth over one nipple and sucked; a bolt
of pure pleasure lanced through her. But it wasn't enough.
She knew he could give her more, and she wanted everything he could offer. Every touch, every caress, every taste.

When he released her, she dipped her head and kissed
him.

He was shaking when he broke the kiss. 'Ella, if we
don't stop now...'

'If we do stop,' she said, 'I think I might implode.'

'Me, too.' His eyes were very dark, and his accent was
more pronounced.

She slid off his lap and got to her feet, expecting him to
lead her through to his bedroom. But, to her shock, when
he stood up, he scooped her into his arms and carried her
through to his bed.

'Caveman tendencies?'

'Absolutely. And that means I want your hair down.
Spread across my pillow. While I'm buried inside you.'

Oh, God, the pictures that put in her head.

That silenced her, and he laughed. 'Careful what you
wish for, Ella *bellezza.*'

His smile gave her the courage to say what she was
thinking. 'Right now I wish,' she said, 'that you weren't
wearing quite so much.'

He set her down on her feet. 'OK, I'm in your hands.
Do what you will.'

Her hands were trembling slightly as she undid the
buttons of his shirt. Then she had to deal with his tie. It
had been years since she'd dated a man who wore a tie—
Michael had always gone for the casual college profes-

sor look—and this one felt like silk. Designer. 'Help?'
she asked.

He dealt with the tie and his top button, and shrugged
his jacket off. 'Better?'

'Rico, that needs hanging up.' His jacket had felt soft
and smooth, and she'd bet it cost a small fortune.

'I don't care. I just need you to take the rest of my
clothes off. Preferably in the next five seconds. And you
can lose your skirt, first.'

She lifted her chin. 'Bossing me about, are you?'

He spread his hands and gave her the sexiest grin she'd
ever seen. 'Just making a suggestion. Which you can
choose to accept...or not.'

'So this thing between us—it's equal.'

'It's equal.' He narrowed his eyes at her. 'So will you
just stop talking and kiss me?'

'A request. Polite. Ish,' she said. 'There's a word missing.'

He looked pained. 'Ella. *Please.*'

'Much better.' She kissed him.

Between them, they managed to get rid of the rest of
their clothes, and he took the pins out of her hair. And
then he lifted her up and laid her on the huge, wide bed.
The mattress was firm, but the pillows were soft and deep.
She drew her hand down his side, moulding her palm to
the shape of his body; in return, he traced the curve of her
hip and her buttocks.

'Your move,' he said, his voice deepening.

She drew one finger down his sternum and smiled.

He copied her.

She slid her hand across his midriff. Rico did the same
to her, then slid his hand up to brush the under curve
of her breasts. Ella closed her eyes. 'Oh, yes. More,' she
whispered.

He slid his hand between her thighs to cup her sex; she wriggled, needing him closer.

At last, he drew one fingertip along her sex, teasing her until she was near to clenching her fists with frustration; her breath escaped as he pushed one finger inside her. She tipped her head back against the pillows as his thumb found her clitoris and teased it.

'You like that?' he whispered.

'Yes.' She dragged in a breath. 'But I want more.'

'Me, too.'

Ella felt the mattress dip and realised he was no longer beside her. She opened her eyes. 'Rico?'

'Condom,' he said, rummaging for his wallet and retrieving a foil packet. He ripped the packet open and rolled the latex over his shaft; the bed dipped again as he knelt between her thighs. And then at last he gently eased into her. He held still, letting her body adjust to the feel of his, then stole a kiss. 'Perfect. Just how I wanted to see you, Ella *bellezza,*' he said huskily. 'Your hair spread over my pillow, and me inside you.'

Then he began to move; he took it slowly at first, stoking her desire to fever point. Then it was as if something snapped his control and he moved faster, harder, building the pressure until finally her climax splintered through her. As her body tightened round his she could feel him tense as he reached his own release.

Finally, he eased out of her, and kissed her tenderly. 'Don't go anywhere,' he whispered as he headed for the en suite.

Alone in his bedroom, Ella felt awkward. They were supposed to be talking, sorting things out between them, and yet they'd ended up in bed. And she felt like a tart.

'What's the matter?' he asked when he came back.

She told him.

He sighed, sat on the end of the bed and took her hand. 'First of all, you're not a tart. I didn't exactly have a lot of control, either. I was with you all the way. So don't beat yourself up about it.'

'I guess.'

He drew her hand to his mouth, pressed a kiss into her palm and curled her fingers round it. 'If anything, I'm the one at fault. I was supposed to be taking you to dinner, not carrying you to my bed.' He was still holding her hand as he asked, 'So where do we go from here?'

CHAPTER SEVEN

'WHERE do we go from here?' Ella blew out a breath. 'I have absolutely no idea.'

'Let's start with what we know. Neither of us wants a relationship. Neither of us has time for one.' He paused. 'But.'

'But?'

'It's good between us. Physically.'

She narrowed her eyes at him. 'What are you suggesting?'

'I'm going to be in London for a while. Maybe we can see something of each other while I'm here.' He paused. 'Kind of friends with benefits.'

'We're not friends. We barely know each other,' she pointed out.

'Acquaintances with benefits, then.'

'You're really compartmentalised, aren't you?'

He shrugged. 'It tends to make life easier.'

'So what you're offering me is sex. Just while you're in London.'

'That sounds tacky.'

'But that's what it boils down to.'

'I guess. We're both busy and neither of us wants to get involved.' Honesty compelled him to add, 'But there's something between us.' Ever since she'd left Rome, he'd told himself that she was nothing special. Seeing her again was supposed to prove that.

Except it hadn't.

Not that he was prepared to admit quite that much to her.

And maybe seeing more of her would make this thing burn itself out. He'd get bored, the way he always did. And it would end before it stopped being fun. Before it started being serious.

'What do you want, Rico?' she asked.

He wasn't sure he could answer that. He knew what he'd always thought he wanted—to be in sole charge of the business. Which he was. And the fact that it wasn't enough for him any more, that expanding into London excited him less than the thought of seeing her, made him antsy. He threw the question back at her. 'What do *you* want?'

'You're not supposed to answer a question with a question.'

'What do you want?' he repeated.

She sighed. 'I don't know. I thought I'd got you out of my system. Tonight was supposed to be closure. And look what happened. I'm naked and in your bed.'

He already knew she felt bad about that. Which made it easier for him to admit, 'It was completely mutual.'

'So do we walk away from each other now?'

His head was telling him to run like hell. His heart was telling him to stick around. 'Do you want to walk away?'

'It would be the sensible thing to do.'

The 'but' was loud and clear. She felt the same way he did. Mixed up and torn between the options. Safe and not safe.

'I'm sorry I wasn't honest with you right from the start,' he said.

'I guess you had your reasons for what you did. I think

they're ridiculous reasons, but I suppose you weren't doing it out of a sense of meanness.'

'No, I wasn't. It's the way people are with me—they see me in terms of what I can do for them. With you, it felt different. I didn't want that to change.' She looked so cute, and he was so, so tempted just to lean forward and steal a kiss. But he held himself back. Just. 'I really ought to go and find your clothes, let you get dressed, and take you down to dinner. But I have a feeling that they're going to be pretty crumpled—just as mine are.'

'I didn't think of that.' She bit her lip. 'Everyone's going to look at us in the restaurant when we walk in and jump to conclusions. Worst of all, they're going to be right.'

'Let's order room service. We can eat in the other room. And it means we can try talking again, without an audience.'

'OK. That sounds good.'

He handed her the menu. 'Have a look through and choose what you want.'

He disappeared into the living room, then came back a few moments later with her clothes neatly stacked in a pile, which he placed on the chair. Shortly afterwards, she heard the shower running. He emerged from the bathroom wearing only a towel wrapped round his hips; she wasn't sure whether it was his near-naked body or his smile that made her heart skip a beat.

'Help yourself to whatever you need in the bathroom,' he said. 'By the way, I had a word with Reception. The hotel laundry service can press your stuff for you while we're having dinner.'

Ella felt the colour bloom in her face. 'Oh, God. So they know what we've—'

'It doesn't matter,' he cut in softly. 'We're not the first people who've got a bit carried away and we won't be the last. Anyway, for all they know, you spilled something over your jacket and skirt and had to sponge your suit down.'

She knew he was trying to make her feel better. But it didn't quite work. 'Mmm,' she said.

'Look, there's a robe behind the bathroom door. You're very welcome to use that until your suit's ready. Have you decided what you'd like from the menu?'

'The salmon, please. And can I be greedy and have the chocolate-dipped strawberries for pudding?'

'Great idea.' Though the suddenly heated expression in his eyes told her that he had ideas about the strawberries. Ideas that involved her.

Ella almost, almost climbed out of bed, removed his towel and dragged him into the shower with her. But sense prevailed—just—and she waited until he'd left the bedroom before heading for the bathroom.

The hotel toiletries were gorgeous, citrus-scented, and the towels were large and super-soft. When she came out of the shower, she noticed that her suit and shirt had gone. So he'd kept his word about the laundry service, then.

Dressed in the soft, fluffy bathrobe, she padded barefoot back out to the living room where Rico was waiting for her.

'Thank you for sorting out the laundry.'

'*Prego,*' he said, giving her a tiny bow.

He was fully dressed in a clean white shirt and chinos.

'You're pretty high maintenance, aren't you?' she asked.

'How do you mean?'

'You always wear a white shirt and it's always pristine. I hate to think what your laundry bill's like.'

'Don't you think I do them myself?'

'No. Because I think you've costed out how much that time's worth to you and you'd rather use that time in a more productive way,' she said.

He raised an eyebrow. 'Is that you talking as an accountant, or are you giving me the reason why you use a laundry service?'

'I do my own laundry, actually. Ironing time is good thinking time. And I'm an ex-accountant for the time being.'

'I'll try to remember that,' he said dryly.

'So you're thinking of buying this hotel?'

'It's a possibility, yes.'

'Why London?'

'Because we already have four hotels in Rome, and to have any more would mean we'd be competing against ourselves.'

'Expanding your empire into another country. *Veni, vidi, vici.* Maybe I should start calling you Julius,' she teased.

He laughed. 'London, Paris, then maybe Vienna or Barcelona. I have plans.'

'So that's your dream. To be a hotel tycoon.'

'Maybe,' he said. 'Actually, I like this hotel. There are a few tweaks I'd want to make, but I can see it fitting in with the rest of the Rossi chain. It's big enough to have every comfort, but it's not so big that it's impersonal. The staff care about the guests, and the facilities are good. And the figures stack up. It doesn't need much work to bring it in line with the rest of my hotels.'

'What if the figures didn't stack up?'

'Then I would've looked at other hotels.' He smiled. 'Like you, I have back-up plans. And, talking of your business, I meant to ask—how was your first day, post-launch?'

'Busy,' she said. 'I have a few orders for celebration cakes to take me into the next six weeks, and some regular cupcake orders from a couple of local cafés that will keep me ticking over in between.'

'If you're experimenting with different frostings, I'd be happy to lend my services as a taste-tester. You make the best chocolate cake I've ever eaten.'

'Thank you for the compliment.' She smiled. 'And I might take you up on that taste-testing thing. Provided you're totally honest with me.'

'I'm not going to lie to you again, Ella.'

'I don't mean that—I mean, being polite. Fudging the issue so you don't hurt my feelings. I need to know if something works or not. If it doesn't, then I can tweak the recipe until it does work.'

'Honest feedback's important. It's what I want from my guests, too,' he said. 'OK. It's a deal.'

Room service arrived, and the waiter served their meal at the table that Ella guessed Rico used as a desk during the day. The food was excellent, and by the end of the meal she'd lost her residual shyness and was totally relaxed in Rico's company. It really didn't matter any more that he was properly dressed and she was only wearing a bathrobe.

All the same, she was glad when her suit and shirt arrived, neatly pressed, along with their coffee.

'Don't change back into your clothes just yet. Come and sit with me,' Rico said, shepherding her over to the sofa.

She curled up next to him, resting her head on his shoulder and enjoying the warmth of his body against hers.

'Tell me about Julia,' he said.

'She's my best friend. I've known her since we were ten.'

'And she's an English teacher and film buff.'

'Yes.' Ella was surprised he'd remembered that; then again, to do what he did, Rico needed a keen eye for detail.

'You seemed very close.'

Mmm, and he'd called Julia her guard dog. 'Ju's like the sister I never had.'

'You don't have a brother, either? Your mum didn't re-marry?'

'I'm an only child. And Mum didn't marry my father in the first place.' Ella pulled away from him. Well, he might as well know what he was getting into if he planned to start seeing more of her. Even if it was supposed to be acquaintances with benefits and no emotional entanglement. 'He was already married to someone else. Mum didn't have a clue that he wasn't single until she fell pregnant with me. Then, when she told him she was expecting me, he told her that she'd have to deal with it.' She lifted her chin. 'In other words, get rid of me. Which she refused to do. So he dumped her.'

'That's appalling.' Rico winced. 'I'm beginning to see why you have a thing about lies.'

'It wasn't just Mum he lied to. It was his wife, too. And I'd bet Mum wasn't the first to fall for him—or the last.' She sighed. 'My grandparents didn't react very well to the news that she was expecting me and the baby's father didn't want to know. She was an only child—a very late baby—and they were more like her grandparents than her parents, with an older generation's views on morality.'

Rico sucked in a breath. 'Please tell me they got over it and supported her.'

'Far from it. They said they were ashamed of her. They, too, wanted her to get rid of me. When she refused, they threw her out,' Ella said grimly. 'But Mum managed to find a flat, and when I was growing up she worked three jobs to make sure she could put food on the table for both of us.'

'Which is why you wanted a safe job when you grew up.'

'Financial security.' She nodded. 'And it was fine. I could do my cakes in my spare time. I've just been incredibly lucky and now I have a chance to do what I really love and make a living from it.' She blinked away the threatening tears. 'I just wish I'd won that money when Mum was still here, so I could've treated her and made some of her dreams come true, too. And I would've bought her a flat, given her the security she always wanted and never really had.'

He frowned. 'Didn't your father have to pay her maintenance?'

'Mum wouldn't have taken it, even if he'd offered. It wasn't about the money, for her. And I'm pretty sure he didn't offer in any case. What I found when I was going through her things last year, after she died...' She grimaced. 'When I was a kid, I used to feel it that I didn't have a dad—I really envied my friends who had two parents to go home to, and who talked about their dads teaching them to swim or ride a bike. I didn't even have an uncle. But now I'm glad he's never been part of my life. I don't think he's the kind of man I'd want to know.'

'What did you find?' Rico asked softly.

'Thirty-six envelopes. Each one contained a photograph of me on my birthday or at Christmas, for every single year since I was born. And every one was marked "return to sender".' Ella tried not to grind her teeth. 'Her letters never asked him for a thing. She was only writing to let him know how I was getting on. She told him about me, and she really tried to build some kind of connection between us—but he threw it back in her face every single time. She even sent the letters to his office rather than to his home, so it wouldn't be like rubbing his wife's face in it. But he just didn't want to know.'

'Thirty-six envelopes. And you're twenty-eight?'

'Yes.'

'So he must've kept some?'

Ella shook her head. 'Mum gave up sending them when

I turned eighteen. So now you know why I don't have a family. I probably have half-siblings somewhere out there—who knows how many other women fell for the same lies that my mum did?—but they've never tried to find me, and I don't need them. I have good friends, and that makes me luckier than a lot of people.'

'Did your grandparents soften once they met you?'

'No. Mum tried to stay in touch with them, but they refused to see us. And it's too late for any reconciliation now—they both passed away, some years back.'

'It was their loss, not yours.' Rico pulled her onto his lap and held her close.

For a moment Ella thought that she saw something in his expression—something that told her he understood how she felt because he'd been badly let down himself—but he masked it so quickly that she couldn't be sure.

Sitting so close with him like this made her feel so warm, so secure. And the question slipped out before she realised what she was going to say. 'So do I get to see you tomorrow?'

'Maybe. What time do you finish?'

'I'm not sure. Late afternoon, I guess.' She thought about it. 'I have two celebration cakes to make and flat-ice, and then I need to do some of the sugar work for them, as well as make the cupcakes for the two local cafés who've agreed to stock my cakes. And there's the business admin stuff. If I keep on top of it, then it won't take long. If I leave it to pile up, it'll be a chore.'

'So the cupcakes have to be ready before the cafés open. Does this mean a really early start?'

She smiled. 'That rather depends on whether you call six a.m. early.'

'I'd better get you home, then. It's not fair to make you

burn the candle at both ends. If you want to get dressed in my bedroom, I'll call a taxi.'

'Thank you.'

The phone rang as she walked back into the living room. Rico answered it. 'That's great. Thank you very much.' He turned to Ella. 'That was Reception. They're very efficient—the taxi's here already.'

'Thank you. I guess I'll see you tomorrow, then.'

'I'll see you home. I would've driven you myself, but I haven't sorted out a car yet.'

Outside her flat, he kissed her lingeringly in her doorway.

'What time do you finish tomorrow?' she asked.

'That depends on how my meetings go.' He wrinkled his nose. 'Plus I have a pile of paperwork to get through and a few phone calls to make to Rome.'

'Call me when you're free,' she said.

'I'll do that.' He kissed her again. 'Goodnight, Ella *bellezza*. Sweet dreams.'

CHAPTER EIGHT

When Ella's alarm clock went off at five-thirty the next morning, she woke with a smile on her face. This was everything she'd wanted: being her own boss, organising her own work and being responsible for everything. And she didn't mind the early starts, because she loved what she was doing.

And she loved the way her schedule was coming together. The way she was able to work at a pace to suit her, to music she enjoyed listening to, and she didn't have to change things to suit other people. Perfect.

She baked the cupcake orders for the two local cafés; while the cakes were cooling, she made the fruit cakes and put them in the oven. Once she'd iced the cupcakes, she dropped off the boxes to her clients, then came back to check on the fruit cakes and start making the sugar roses. The Madeira cake was next; finally, when all the large cakes had cooled, she flat-iced them, ready for decorating.

She'd just washed up and put the icing bowls away when her mobile phone rang.

'Hi. You asked me to call you when I was done,' Rico said.

And how crazy it was that hearing his voice made her heart beat faster. This wasn't good. 'Uh-huh.' If she had any sense left, she'd tell him she was too busy to see him. But her mouth had other ideas. 'Are you coming over now?'

'It's a good time?'

Tell him no, her common sense urged.

'It's fine. See you when you get here.'

'I'm on my way. *Ciao, bellezza.*'

Ella had just about finished tidying her kitchen when he arrived.

'Wow, you made these?' he said, looking at the sugar roses. 'They're incredibly delicate. And very realistic.'

'They're for a wedding cake—though it's one that was booked in weeks ago. Normally people book cakes like this at least six weeks in advance.'

'How fast can you do a celebration cake?'

'If it's just a normal-sized cake and I don't have to do carving or armature or lots of intricate sugar-paste work, I can do one in a day—baking it, flat-icing it and basic decoration.'

'Carving and armature?' Rico asked, looking puzzled.

'Shaped cakes. Some of them need support so they don't collapse—that's the armature bit.' She took her display book from the shelf and flicked through it until she found the page she wanted. 'Like my dinosaur.'

'This is a million miles away from what I do in my job,' Rico said. 'I wouldn't even know where to start, making something like that. And how do you get the colours on the icing?'

'I hand-paint it. It's pretty labour-intensive, but I love doing it. Creating someone's dream out of sugar, butter, eggs and flour.' She smiled at him, 'So what do you want to do this evening?'

'Are we talking acquaintances or benefits?'

To her annoyance, she actually blushed. 'Acquaintances. Rico, I hope you realise I don't sleep around.'

'Neither do I. Don't believe everything you read in the press.'

She stared at him, shocked. 'The press follow you about?'

'In Italy, sometimes. It depends who I'm seeing.'

'I'm a nobody, so you should be safe,' she said dryly.

'That wasn't what I meant. But the press blow things up out of proportion and twist a story to suit themselves. If everything they said about me was true, there'd be so many notches I wouldn't actually have a bedpost left. Dating someone doesn't necessarily mean sleeping with them.' He leaned forward and stole a kiss. 'Let's start again. What do you want to do this evening?'

Her mouth was tingling—and that kiss had been the lightest and sweetest of touches. He tempted her so badly that she could barely resist him. 'Do you want to come upstairs for a mug of coffee while we think about it?'

'Sure.' He followed her up to her flat. 'What sort of thing do you normally do in the evenings?'

'It depends what kind of day I've had.' She switched on the kettle and shook grounds into a cafetière. 'I might go to the cinema or out for a drink with friends; I might just go for a walk by the river; or I might collapse on the sofa in front of the telly.' She gave him a wary look. 'I should perhaps warn you I'm really not into clubbing.'

'Good. Me, neither.' He looked at the photographs pinned with magnets to her fridge. 'That must be your mum.'

'Yes.' She had to swallow hard. Even now, a year later, she still missed her mother badly. Missed her smile, her gentle calmness, her common sense.

'She's very like you,' he commented.

'I hope so.' She definitely hoped she hadn't inherited any of her father's genes. Pushing the thought away, she suggested, 'Maybe we can go for a walk by the river? It's really pretty here in Greenwich.'

'I'd like that. And I'd like to see more of London while I'm here. What's the epitome of London?'

She thought about it. 'I guess it'd be something like the Changing of the Guard outside Buckingham Palace. Mind you, you need to be there early to get a decent spot to see it, so it'll have to be a weekend.'

'We'll leave that for Saturday, then.'

She gave him a regretful smile. 'Sorry, I can't make it. I'm working.'

'You're working six days a week?' Rico looked concerned. 'You're risking burnout if you keep up that kind of pace.'

'Unless I have a really big celebration cake to sort out, it's only half a morning on Saturdays, enough to keep the cafés stocked with cupcakes. They're closed on Sundays, so I can take Sundays off,' she explained.

'Let's do the Changing of the Guard on Sunday, then.'

He hadn't given her any idea about his schedule; she didn't have a clue when he was going back to Rome. 'Are you in London for very long?'

'Possibly.'

Which served her right for asking a closed question. Then again, she had the feeling that Rico could turn the most open question into a closed one.

'We should make a list of places we're going to see.'

She rolled her eyes. 'You're such a control freak, Rico.'

'You work with lists,' he pointed out, gesturing to the lists held to her fridge door by magnets.

'I like being organised.'

'Now who's the control freak?' he teased, and kissed her.

If he kept this up, she'd forget all about making acquaintances and go straight for benefits. 'Busted,' she said, and moved away from him to make the coffee—while she still could. 'With you coming from Rome, I guess we should do a tour of Roman London. We can start with the Roman Wall; plus there's a Roman bath near the Strand, and an amphitheatre under the Guildhall. And guide books are bound to list other stuff I don't know about.'

'So you're going to be my personal tour guide of London?'

'Ironic, considering how I met you.' She coughed. 'Except *I'm* not pretending to be a guide.'

'I wasn't pretending. I was doing the job—and I didn't hear any complaints from you,' he reminded her.

'No. You really made the Colosseum come alive for me. You know a lot about your home city.'

'Because I love Rome,' he said simply. 'It's the only place I ever want to live.'

So this thing between them, she thought, had definite limits. She had no intention of moving to Rome, and he had no intention of moving here. Not permanently. So she'd take the warning as read. This was a fling, until his interest waned. She'd enjoy it while it lasted, but she wouldn't expect anything more from him.

He took a mouthful of the coffee she gave him. 'This is good. Thanks.'

'My pleasure.'

'Let's make that list. Do you have a laptop?'

She fetched it and placed it on the kitchen table between them. He scooped her onto his lap and wrapped his arms round her waist. 'Now we can both see the screen,' he said.

'We could both see it perfectly well from where we were sitting,' she pointed out.

'Yes, but this way is more comfortable.' He kissed the curve of her neck.

He was right; it felt good to be held close to him like this. Not that she was going to tell him. She didn't want him thinking that all he had to do was whistle and she'd sit up and beg.

Between them, and with the help of a few websites, they came up with a mixture of the famous sights and some quirky, out-of-the-way places to visit.

'Enough for now. It's a nice evening. Let's go for that walk by the river,' he said.

The sky was streaked with pink feathery clouds as they wandered hand in hand along the path by the Thames.

'Since I'm being your personal tour guide, I should tell you that that's the Royal Naval College,' she said, pointing out the complex of beautiful white buildings and the twin grey domes with their gold clocks and weather vanes. 'It was designed by Christopher Wren.'

'Like St Paul's. Which we need to add to our list,' he said. 'It's gorgeous.'

They carried on down the Thames Path until they reached a waterfront pub. 'I sometimes stop here for a drink with Ju,' Ella said. 'Apparently Dickens used to drink here. And the food's OK, too, if you fancy something to eat?'

'Sure.' They had a drink on one of the wrought-iron balconies, then headed back inside when their food was ready; the waiter had found them a table overlooking the Thames.

When they came back out, the sky was midnight blue, fading almost to white and then deep orange at the horizon, and the buildings of London were all lit up. 'That's the Millennium Dome over there,' she said, pointing out the white dome with its yellow, blue and red spikes. 'It always reminds me of a birthday cake with candles on it.'

'London's beautiful by night,' Rico said. He leaned down to kiss her. 'And so are you.'

'Thank you.' It wasn't just the words that touched Ella. Rico made her feel beautiful in the way he touched her, the way he listened to her. And he really had seemed interested in her job, not just as if he were being polite.

They walked hand in hand back to her flat.

'Do you want to come in for coffee?' she asked, unlocking the door.

'Not coffee,' he said, and dipped his head to kiss her.

By the time he broke the kiss, Ella was shaking with need. She made no protest when Rico scooped her up, pulled the door closed behind him, and carried her up the stairs to her bed. She wanted this every bit as much as he did, matching him touch for touch and kiss for kiss. And it shocked her how quickly he could make her climax. She'd never, ever experienced that kind of intensity before.

When he came back from the bathroom fully dressed, she blinked in surprise. Wasn't he going to stay?

'Not a good idea,' he said softly, as if her thoughts had been written all over her face.

'Will I see you tomorrow?' she asked, hating herself for sounding needy but wanting to know the answer.

'No. I'm up to my eyes. But I'll call you. And I'll see you on Saturday.'

'Sure.' Acquaintances with benefits. That was what they'd agreed. And she'd be a fool to want more. 'I'll see you later.'

Although Ella was busy on Friday, she was surprised to discover that she missed not seeing Rico, and the highlight of her day was when he called her.

Which was utterly ridiculous. She didn't need a man to make her life complete. Especially one who clearly wasn't going to give anything of himself.

On Saturday, Rico arrived at Ella's kitchen at half-past

eight, just when she was putting cupcakes in a box. 'What's that?' he asked, going over to the plate where a single cupcake sat. Then he laughed, seeing his name piped on top of the icing. 'Now that's cute.'

She rolled her eyes. 'You were supposed to ask if any of those cakes were going begging. And then I was going to tell you that, actually, one of them had your name on it, and present you with that one.'

He wrapped his arms round her waist and kissed her. 'I like your sense of humour, *bellezza*. Are you done, or is there anything I can do to help?'

'I'm just dropping these off at the cafés. You can be my delivery boy and carry the boxes, if you like.'

'Delivery boy, hmm? I assume the payment is in cake. But I should ask before accepting the job what the benefits package is.'

Oh, the ideas that put in her head. 'Cake,' she said firmly. She wrapped catering film over his cupcake and put it in the fridge.

He laughed and stole a kiss. 'OK. Today's "acquaintances", too. I get it. Give me the boxes, *bellezza*.'

Once they'd dropped off the cakes, they caught the Tube to Trafalgar Square. 'I used to come here with my mum to feed the pigeons when I was a little girl,' she said, 'but people are banned from feeding them now.'

'I can see why. Their droppings do a lot of damage to stonework, and they're a health hazard. I don't encourage them at any of my hotels, either,' Rico said. He gazed round the square. 'So this is the famous fountain—the one everyone jumps into on New Year's Eve?'

'Well, not everyone. And I imagine this probably feels a bit plain and small to you, after all the gorgeous ones in Rome, but it's had a makeover recently, so it's lit up by coloured lights at night. And the water goes higher now than I ever remember it being when I was a child,' she said.

'No, it's charming,' he said.

They wandered along to see the bronze Landseer lions guarding Nelson's Column. 'I like these, too. Very stately,' he said with a smile.

'We could go to the National, as we're here,' she said. 'Or, as it's a nice day, maybe we can walk by the river. There are usually street performers on the South Bank at weekends.'

'It's too nice to go indoors,' he agreed.

Over on the South Bank, there were indeed the street performers she'd promised: living statues, jugglers, a contortionist, a man making balloon animals for children, and a string quartet in full evening dress playing Mozart.

There were also a crowd of artists, sketching caricatures and portraits of willing punters. He smiled. 'They're like the ones at the top of the Spanish Steps. Rome isn't so very different from London.' He gazed up at the London Eye. 'That's on our list, yes?'

'Yes. I'm not sure whether to take you there by day or by night.'

'We'll do both.' He gave her a wicked grin. 'Seeing as I'm such a spoiled rich kid.'

She sighed. 'I did apologise for that.'

'I know. I'm angling for a kiss better.'

'Oh, you fraud.'

'Please?' He batted his eyelashes at her. 'Pretty please with sugar on it?'

How could she resist? This was a different side of Rico. A playboy, but not a selfish one. And she really, really liked this side of him. Though at the same time it made her nervous. Was this the real Rico? She couldn't tell; and it worried her how easy it would be to let herself fall for him. How could she fall for him when she wasn't sure she could trust him?

When he saw the children playing in the fountain installation, jumping the boundaries between each 'room' made from the fountain jets when they died down, he tugged at her hand. 'Come on. That looks like fun.'

'I'm not sure if there's a set rotation of the walls or if it's random,' she said.

He watched the walls of water for a while. 'Random. Which is more fun. Your choice which way we jump—now!'

She picked the wrong one, and they both got soaked as the water rose up between the grids. Rico simply laughed and kissed her.

'Typical Roman boy—can't resist the fountains,' she teased.

They lay on the grass in Jubilee Gardens to dry out, enjoying the early summer sunshine. 'Do you like Chinese food?' she asked.

'Yes.'

'Good—we'll eat in Chinatown tonight.'

He smiled. 'I love it when you go all bossy on me.'

She coughed. 'Isn't that a bit pots and kettles?'

'A bit what?'

'Pots and kettles.' She flapped an apologetic hand at him. 'Sorry, your English is so good that I forget you might not know all the idioms. It's a saying, "the pot calling the kettle black"—because they were both covered in soot. Or were, in the days when people cooked over an open fire,' she explained.

'Hypocritical, you mean. As in me calling you bossy when I'm just as bad.'

'Yes.'

He leaned over and kissed her until she was dizzy.

'If we weren't in a public place, I'd show you just how bossy I can be,' he whispered.

He'd actually made her forget where they were. And that people were all round them—people who could see him kissing her so passionately, and the way she responded to him. Colour rushed into her face, and he laughed. 'I love the way you blush. You're so cute, Ella *bellezza*. And you're like nobody else I've ever met.'

'I hope that's meant in a nice way.'

'Yes.' And Rico was surprised by how much he was enjoying Ella's company. He could relax with her, be himself, act on crazy impulses and play in a fountain with her— and she didn't complain that her hair was ruined or sulk about getting splashed. He was enjoying himself more than he had in years.

Yet, at the same time, it made him panic. It would be, oh, so easy to fall for Ella Chandler. To be hers for the taking.

But what if, once he let her that close, he wasn't enough for her? Just as he hadn't been enough for his parents. Just as he wasn't enough for his grandparents.

He'd never really loved anyone. And maybe he never would be able to love someone the way that Ella would want to be loved. Maybe it just wasn't in him.

'Come on, *bellezza*. You're supposed to be showing me round London.' And he needed serious distraction from his thoughts. The best way to distract himself would be to carry Ella to his bed—sex always worked—but he'd promised not to rush her. And he had a nasty feeling that sex was different with Ella because she was something special.

Exactly the opposite of what he'd been trying to prove to himself.

* * *

They continued their tour of London; in the evening, she took him to a restaurant in Chinatown. The incredibly abrupt waiter waved them downstairs, where another waiter sat them on a large table with several complete strangers, then banged down a pot of jasmine tea and two handle-less cups in front of them.

'The service here won't have the finesse you're used to,' she said, 'but I promise the food makes up for it. They do the best crispy duck in London.'

'It's an experience, I'll give you that,' Rico said with a grin.

'And we're going halves on the bill. Equals, remember.'

'Sì, signorina.' He dipped his head and gave her a deferential look. She rolled her eyes and punched his arm, and he just laughed.

After their meal, they wandered back through Leicester Square.

'I don't know if I dare suggest stopping here for an ice cream. Not when Italian ice cream is the best in the world,' Ella said, looking longingly in the window of one of the ice-cream shops.

'If you want an ice cream, *bellezza,* that's fine. Though I'll pass, because I happen to know there's a cupcake with my name on it in your fridge and I want to make sure I can do it justice.'

They caught the DLR back to Greenwich, and she produced the cupcake from the fridge. 'Enjoy.'

He savoured every mouthful. 'I'm seriously thinking about kidnapping you and making you my personal pastry chef.'

'So I'd cook at your whim?'

'No. You can cook whatever and whenever you like. Your pleasure will be mine.'

It was suddenly hard to breathe, because she knew he

wasn't just talking about food. And he had a point. She got a real kick out of pleasing him; and it was entirely mutual.

As if he guessed at her thoughts, he drew her towards him. He kissed her until she forgot what day it was, then brought her to an incredibly intense climax before taking it much more slowly and doing it all over again.

Curled up in bed beside him, her head resting on his shoulder, she asked softly, 'So are you staying tonight?'

Stay.

Rico was shocked by how much he wanted to take her up on that offer.

But this really wasn't a good idea. Sex was one thing, but intimacy was quite another. Dangerous. He still didn't want his heart involved. And she was vulnerable; he was pretty sure that most of her assertions were utter bravado and what she really wanted was a family. Something he'd never be able to give her.

Gently, he disengaged himself from her. 'Sorry. I've skived off all day, so I'll have a pile of emails waiting for me when I get back to the hotel,' he said. He knew he was using his business as an excuse, but he didn't want to hurt her. 'But I'll see you tomorrow.' He smiled to soften his words. 'My personal tour guide promised me the Changing of the Guard.'

'Buckingham Palace is nearer you than me, so I'll meet you at The Fountain,' she said.

'Fine. What time?'

'Is nine o'clock too early?'

'Nine o'clock is fine. I'll see you then.'

Ella hid her disappointment that Rico didn't stay. This was a fling and nothing more. So why did she feel so empty as soon as he was gone…?

* * *

On Sunday, Rico was waiting in the reception area of The Fountain when Ella walked in. '*Buongiorno,* Ella *bellezza,*' he said.

'Good morning. Are you ready to play tourist?'

'Absolutely.' He gave her a wide smile.

They were near enough to walk to the palace from his hotel, and eventually joined the queue of people waiting outside Buckingham Palace. At last, the soldiers in their red tunics and tall bearskin hats marched onto the fore-court outside the palace, and he enjoyed watching the spectacle. Though he had a nasty feeling that, more than that, what he was really enjoying was being with her.

She smiled at him when it was over. 'So there you have it. One very British tradition.'

'Nothing like you'd see in Rome. You might get the odd Roman legion and a bunch of senators in the Circus Maximus on a weekend—usually re-enactment groups—but I've not seen anything like this before.'

'I'm glad I've shown you something new.' She laced her fingers through his as the old guard marched away. 'You showed me the grisly bits of Rome. It's time I returned the favour—we'll go and see the Tower of London.'

'So is this the oldest building in London?' he asked as they walked inside the complex.

'Just about,' she said. 'Though your Colosseum's a thousand years older. William the Conqueror started it with the White Tower, and various kings extended the buildings over the years. I remember my mum taking me here when I was small; I was fascinated by the Beefeaters and their hats. And the ravens.'

'Let's go and see the ravens,' he said.

The ravens stalked across a patch of ground by the Wakefield Tower. 'According to legend, the kingdom and the tower will fall if the ravens fly away, so their wings are clipped to make sure they don't,' Ella told him.

'Poor things. They're trapped.' Which was how he'd felt at university. He'd been groomed to take over Rossi Hotels, so he knew that choosing any other career would mean letting his family down; his father was totally useless, and Rico was the only grandchild. The only one who could continue the business. Without him, hundreds of jobs would be at risk, and that wasn't fair on the staff who'd worked for Rossi Hotels for years.

Yet it wasn't fair on him, either, to have all his choices taken away. Frustration at being hemmed in had nearly sent him off the rails; and then his best friend had pointed out that, actually, the world was at his feet because he could take the business in any direction he liked and he didn't have to follow his grandfather's lead.

Which was precisely why his next hotel was going to be in London rather than in Italy. He was in charge, and he was putting his stamp on the firm. And this deal was going to be a lot bigger than the last one he'd made. He was branching out, in more ways than one—and he already knew his grandfather had reservations about it. Well, tough. Rico didn't have reservations. He was going to make this work. And then maybe his grandfather would be forced to admit that Rico was doing just fine.

'The ravens' wings are almost the same colour as your hair,' she said, ruffling it.

He caught her round the waist, spun her round and kissed her; she was pink and laughing by the time he'd finished.

'Now, now. You're not supposed to distract the tour guide,' she scolded, but she was laughing as she spoke.

'How long is it since you've been here?' he asked.

'I'm not sure. Years. But I loved it as a child. The crown jewels, Henry VIII's armour…'

'What's the significance of the polar bear?' Rico asked, gesturing to the sculpture.

'There used to be a menagerie here. Actually, there's sort of a Roman connection, because the Holy Roman Emperor Frederick II sent Henry III three leopards when Henry married Frederick's sister Eleanor. It really snowballed from there; the King of Norway sent Henry a polar bear.' She smiled. 'My mum told me how the bear was kept on a long leash so he could swim in the Thames and catch fish. And then the King of France sent Henry an elephant. Apparently it came up the Thames by boat. Mum and I made up a song together about elephants in the tower, but I can't remember how it goes now.'

How different from his own childhood. He could barely remember either of his parents taking him out; they certainly hadn't told him endless stories or made up songs with him or spent time with him, the way Ella's mother had with her. Materially, Ella's childhood had been poor, but she'd had more than enough love to make up for it. Given the choice between being spoiled and being loved, that was what he would've wanted too; but he didn't think either of his parents had known how to love anyone except themselves. Definitely not each other; and definitely not him.

And why the hell was it bothering him again now? He was grown up and over it. Plenty of people had had it far worse than he had. And he had a great life. He wanted for nothing. Don't be so pathetic, he told himself.

'Rico? Is something wrong?'

He forced himself to smile. 'Nothing, *bellezza*. So what happened to the menagerie?'

'It became London Zoo, just before Victoria became queen.'

'Is London Zoo on our list?'

'It can be.' She smiled at him. 'Anything you like.'

Her sweet, open smile made him feel as if something were cracking inside him. Like the sun shining to melt away the loneliness of his childhood. Ella made his day brighter just by being there. She made him feel better.

And that scared him as much as it reassured him. Ella was special. He really ought to walk away and let her find someone else—someone who deserved her. Someone who could give her his whole heart.

Yet he wasn't ready to let her go. Not yet. Which made him precisely the selfish, unlovable man that was in his genes. Precisely the wrong man for a woman who'd already been hurt by selfish, unlovable men—her absent father and her cheating fiancé.

And Rico didn't have a clue how he could make everything turn out right for both of them.

CHAPTER NINE

ELLA glanced at the screen and frowned. Rico didn't usually ring her during office hours. Was something wrong? 'Hello, Rico?'

'Ella *bellezza,* do you have your diary handy?'

'Yes. Why?'

'I need to book a meeting with you.'

'You're seeing me tonight,' she said. 'Why do you need to book a meeting with me?'

'Because the meeting's going to be about business and tonight's going to be about...' He laughed. 'Wait and see. Though benefits might be involved later.'

Warmth spread through her. 'What kind of business are we talking about?' she asked.

'A potential commission. A cake for a launch party in a month's time. So where do you want to meet? Your kitchen, or my office?'

She frowned again. 'Your office is in Rome.'

He coughed. 'My *London* office.'

Then the penny dropped. 'You bought the hotel?'

'Yup. We're re-launching The Fountain in four weeks. Is that enough notice for you to make me a cake?'

'Should be. Though we'll need to talk about size.'

He gave a rich chuckle that had her blushing.

'Rico!'

'You said it, not me, *bellezza*. OK. So you want to know how many guests I'm inviting and what kind of design I have in mind.'

'And what kind of flavours.' She paused. 'I can make a meeting any time after ten if it's here, and any time after about ten-thirty if it's at your office.'

'Let's make it four-thirty, today, at yours,' he said. 'And, Ella—this is official, by the way. It's a business deal, not a favour.'

'So you're getting quotes from elsewhere?' Some of the bubbles of pleasure burst.

'It's business,' he repeated. 'Though your prices are obviously market rate, and I already know the quality of your product. Give me the right design, and you get the commission. I'll email you the other details. See you at four-thirty. *Ciao, bellezza.*'

By the time Rico arrived, Ella had three pages full of sketches.

'Are those designs for me to approve?' he asked.

'Suggestions. Though I'll listen to what you have to say, first. They might be the complete opposite of what I've come up with.'

'You're the creative one,' Rico said. 'I'd rather see what you've been thinking about.'

'OK. First of all, I could do you a cake in the shape of the hotel. It'd be a scale model, of course.' She showed him the picture she'd sketched from the hotel's website.

'That's good,' he said.

'Or there's the fountain in the courtyard. I could do you a normal sheet cake, decorate it as a garden, and do you a sugar-paste replica of the fountain as a topper. If I use wires, I can do you droplets of water coming down from the fountain.' She showed him the sketches. 'Obviously this isn't *your* fountain. I'd have to come and take photographs of it so I could make an accurate sugar-paste replica. But it's an example of what I can do.'

'Impressive.'

She warmed to her theme. 'Or, if you'd rather the guests had individual cakes rather than slices, I can make a tower of cupcakes with a six-inch cake for cutting, like I do for wedding cakes. And I could do you a smaller sugar-paste fountain on top of the cutting cake.'

'I definitely want a fountain,' he said. 'Given the hotel's name, I'm planning a chocolate fountain and a champagne fountain, too.'

'So maybe the cupcakes would be best. It'd reflect the shape of the other two fountains.'

He smiled. 'I like how your mind works. Price?'

She handed him a piece of paper without comment.

He scanned it swiftly. '*Bene*. It's a deal.'

'I need to make the cupcakes on the day so they're fresh,' she said, 'and then ice them. I take it you're doing an evening launch?'

'Yes. And it'll be on a Saturday. Given that you've got the café orders to do as well, that's going to be a lot of work for you. Do you need me to send over one of my kitchen staff to help you?'

'You wouldn't offer that to my competitors, would you?' she asked.

'No.' He raised an eyebrow. 'But you're pulling out the stops for me. And it's in my interest to make life easier for you.' He leaned forward to steal a kiss. 'Think of it as... extra benefits.'

The pictures he'd just put in her head made her cheeks colour, and he laughed.

'So do you want to borrow staff?' he asked.

'Someone to do the café deliveries would save me some time,' she admitted.

'I'll sort it.'

'What flavour do you want?'

He smiled. 'Guess.'

She rolled her eyes. 'Chocolate. If you've got a chocolate fountain as well, Rico, don't you think that'll be too much?'

'Is there such a thing as too much chocolate?' he asked.

She laughed. 'Now you sound like a girl.'

'Oh, do I?' He looked thoughtful. 'I might just have to make you take that back.'

He stood up, took her hand and yanked her into his arms. By the time he'd finished kissing her, Ella was completely breathless and dishevelled. 'OK. I admit. You're not girly in the slightest. You're all man,' she said. And how. She lifted her chin. 'But I thought this was supposed to be a business meeting?'

'It was. We've concluded our business. And we need to be elsewhere.'

'Do we?'

He produced two tickets from his pocket and handed them to her. The best seats in the house, at a performance where tickets were like gold dust. 'Wow. Rico, how did you…?'

'Let's just say there are some advantages to being a spoiled rich kid.' He stole a kiss. 'Go get your glad rags on, *bellezza*. Let's go and have some fun.'

Over the next couple of weeks, Rico and Ella fell into a habit of meeting up after work. Sometimes they went out; sometimes Rico turned up with a bag full of ingredients, which he stowed in Ella's fridge while he carried her off to bed, then cooked for her; and at the weekends they worked through their tour-guide list.

Ella couldn't remember ever being so happy. Neither of them had made a commitment to the future, but she was beginning to think that it'd be safe to trust Rico with her heart. Because maybe he was the man she'd thought he was, in Rome. Rico the CEO had a public face; she had the strongest feeling that Rico the tour guide was his private face, one he didn't show to just anybody.

On the Sunday morning, Rico rang Ella at six. 'Rise and shine, *bellezza*.'

'So much for my Sunday morning lie-in,' she grumbled. 'Why are we getting up so early?'

'Because today we're going somewhere not on our list. Oh, and you need your passport.'

'My passport?' Still half asleep, she couldn't get her head round the idea. 'Why?'

'Just bear with me on this—it's something I think you're going to like. I'll collect you in thirty minutes, OK?'

Bemused, she showered and dressed, and was ready when he rang her doorbell. When the taxi dropped them off at the airport, she frowned. 'Where are we going?'

'Through here. For breakfast.' Including superb Italian coffee.

'Where are we going?' she asked again, looking at the departure boards.

'That won't help you, *bellezza*. It's not a scheduled flight.'

She blinked. 'You're telling me you have a private plane?'

'No, it belongs to a friend.'

Her eyes narrowed. 'In the same way that your flat in Rome belonged to a friend?'

'No, it really belongs to a friend. Like the restaurant.' He spread his hands. 'Spoiled rich kid territory. Some of my friends have *great* toys. And we share.' He smiled. 'I'm lending Giuseppe my car for a month, in return.'

She laughed. 'Don't tell me—would this be an Italian sports car?'

'That predictable, am I?'

'Sure are,' she teased. 'Where are we going?'

He shrugged. 'About two and a half hours away.'

'Talk about vague! Rico…'

'Just go with it,' he said, and kissed her. 'It's somewhere I think you'll like. I know it's a bit decadent, nipping over to mainland Europe just for the day, but…wait and see.'

She didn't have a clue where they were going until they arrived at Vienna airport. And then she just gaped. 'I can't believe you're taking me to Vienna for the day.'

'You told me in Rome that you wanted to come here,' he said with a smile. 'I assume that's because of the cafés and the cakes.'

'Absolutely.' She could still barely believe he'd whisked her off here just for the day. 'Rico, this is the nicest thing anyone's ever done for me. Thank you.'

'My pleasure, *bellezza*.' He kissed her lightly.

They caught the train from the airport into the city, then changed to the underground and emerged onto the street near the cathedral, with its green and gold chevrons on the roof. 'Wow, what gorgeous architecture,' she said. 'Vienna's beautiful.' The wide, wide street was flanked with five-storey white and pastel-coloured buildings, and she'd never seen so many windows.

'Come on. There's somewhere we need to be.'

'Where?'

'You'll see when we get there.'

Rico had clearly put a lot of thought and planning into this, and Ella was intrigued rather than annoyed by his vagueness.

He took her to one of the oldest *Konditoreien* in Vienna; she was enthralled by the glass cabinet displaying what looked like fifty different types of cake, as well as displays of confectionery.

'Come on. The café's upstairs.' He led her through to the stairs at the back of the shop.

'Wow, look at that chandelier,' she said as they reached the top of the stairs. 'That's beautiful. And this whole place—it's like being transported back into a much more glamorous age.'

'I'm glad you like it.' And he was relieved that it lived up to the pictures he'd seen on the website. 'Apparently the classic coffee here is a melange,' he said, pronouncing the word *mel-anj,* as if it were French rather than German. 'And I think we should have cake to go with it.'

'How on earth do you choose from a selection as tempting as that?' Ella asked, staring at the display. 'Though I guess, as we're in Vienna, I ought to choose Sachertorte.'

He kissed the spot just behind her ear. 'We're going to Café Sacher for that, a bit later. So you can try something else.'

Eventually she chose the Esterhazytorte. 'I love layered cakes,' she said as they went back to their seats. 'We had an Aussie temp at the accountancy firm, and she introduced me to hummingbird cake.'

'Obviously it's not made from hummingbirds, so what is it really?'

'Kind of like carrot cake, but made with tropical fruit. Banana and pineapple, normally, but I've got a recipe for a version that includes mango and passion fruit.' She looked at him. 'You'd really like it. If you're good, I might make you one.'

He leaned closer. 'Good at what?' he whispered in her ear.

She blushed spectacularly, and he laughed. 'Ah, *bellezza.* You're so easy to tease.'

The waitress came with their coffees, two small glasses of water, and two slices of cake.

'Oh, I really like this—it's kind of a cross between a latte and cappuccino but without the icky cocoa on top,' Ella said when she'd tried the coffee.

'I thought you liked chocolate?'

'Not quite as much as you do, and definitely not on my coffee.' She smiled at him and tried the cake. 'This is lush. Almond sponge and hazelnut cream. Try it.' She fed him from her fork.

'Very nice.' He waited until they'd finished their coffee. 'Ready for the next bit?'

'Next?'

The look on her face when they went through a side door and were met by the head pastry chef with white coats and hats, and she realised he'd arranged a tour of the kitchens for her, was priceless.

The worktops were all marble; one pastry chef was working on flat-icing a line of chocolate cakes, while others were mixing batters, making frosting or laying out the delicate pastry for making apple strudel.

But the standout for Ella was a sheet cake with a beautiful Lipizzaner horse on top, which a pastry chef was delicately painting. 'That's stunning. Look at the sugar-paste work on his ears, and the saddle.'

The pastry chef talked her through various painting techniques. Rico wasn't that interested in the details, but he loved seeing the expression on Ella's face. She was clearly taking it all in, asking questions to clarify points here and there.

Yep, he'd definitely planned the perfect day for her. And it was true what he'd told her: in pleasing her, he was giving himself real pleasure. He'd never felt like that before.

'That was amazing,' she said when they left. 'I can't believe you did that for me. Thank you. That was so special.'

'I'm glad you liked it.' He loved her enthusiasm. And it was definitely catching. 'We're right next door to the Hofburg Palace. Do you fancy playing tourist?'

She nodded, beaming. 'I'd love to.'

They wandered hand in hand through the imperial apartments, listening to the commentary from the audio guide.

'Ankle-length hair. I'm not sure I could cope with that,' Ella said. 'Three hours every morning just to have your hair dressed. It'd drive me crazy!'

But she paused in front of a portrait of Empress Sisi in a white dress. 'Wow. She really was beautiful.'

There was a case by the portrait, displaying reproductions of the diamond stars the empress wore in her hair. 'You'd look lovely with those in your hair,' Rico said.

She shook her head. 'My hair's not really long enough. And you'd need dark hair to set them off properly.' She paused. 'They'd look very nice done in icing.'

He blinked. 'You could make them in icing?'

'Sure. I'd use a glacé icing rather than buttercream. And then I'd do the stars separately, in fondant. If you paint white icing with a mix of silver lustre dust and alcohol, it'll look silver. And then you can use white glimmer sugar for the diamonds.'

'Glimmer sugar?'

'The sparkly sprinkles I use on cakes.'

He laughed. 'I love the way you see everything in terms of cake.'

'Well, hey, Vienna's practically the capital of the cake world,' she teased back. 'And you know the saying. When in Vienna...'

He gave her a speaking look. 'It's "when in Rome".'

She grinned. 'It works for Vienna, too.'

They lingered in the gift-shop, and Rico noticed that she looked closely at a replica of the Sisi star. Interesting. But he also noticed that she didn't buy it.

When they'd left the palace, they wandered through the city centre, window-shopping. Rico still couldn't get the diamond stars out of his head. 'You don't wear much jewellery, do you?' He glanced at her. 'Just a watch. And your ears aren't pierced.'

'I'm too chicken to have my ears pierced, and clip-on earrings just aren't comfortable. I do sometimes wear a necklace, but jewellery just gets in the way when I'm working.'

A necklace. He spotted a replica of the Sisi star, made into a choker, in one of the seriously expensive jewellery shops. Something like the one in the palace gift shop, only using real gemstones rather than being costume jewellery. He could just imagine Ella wearing nothing but the choker, and his temperature spiked.

'Time for Sachertorte, I think,' he said, and took her to the famous café. 'Excuse me for a second?' he said after they'd ordered.

'Sure.'

With any luck, she'd think he'd gone to the loo and there was a queue. Making sure she didn't see him leave the café, he made a swift exit, returned to the jeweller's and bought the star choker. He stowed the box in his pocket, where she wouldn't notice it, and came back to join her, all smiles.

'I was beginning to wonder if you'd got lost,' she said. 'Your coffee must be almost cold by now.'

'Which is how Italians drink their coffee anyway,' he reminded her, and promptly downed his espresso in one.

As they walked back through the streets she insisted on stopping at one of the chocolate shops. 'Ju's almost as much of a chocolate fiend as you are. I'd like to bring something back for her.'

He looked in the window. 'It says here that this used to be one of the imperial court confectioners, so they must be good.'

'Give me two minutes.'

He knew from Rome that she wasn't one for dragging round the shops, and was happy to browse through the displays while she picked what she wanted.

He held her hand all the way home to London. Back at her flat, she handed him a bag from the confectioner's they'd browsed in.

'For me? I thought you were buying chocolate for Julia?'

'I did. But I bought some for you, too. I know you love the stuff.' She shrugged. 'It's not much. Just a token, really. But I wanted to say thank you, and let you know I appreciate how much you spoiled me today.'

'*Bellezza,* you didn't have to give me anything. But thank you.' It touched him that she'd thought of him. And she'd bought him a gift that he really appreciated, the tiny Lilliput chocolates that were a speciality of the confectioner's. None of his exes would've done that; he was more used to being taken for granted.

'Since you've just given me a present—I have one for you, too.' He took the box from his pocket and handed it to her.

Ella stared at the beautifully wrapped box, and her heart skipped a beat for a moment. It was clearly from a jeweller's. But of course it wouldn't be a ring. Neither of them had said how they felt about each other; and anyway the box was too big.

She undid the ribbon and opened the box to see a beautiful silver star, a replica of the ones that the empress had worn in her hair; it was a choker on a black chiffon ribbon. She'd almost bought one of these in the gift shop, and with Rico being so observant he'd clearly noticed. And he'd remembered that she didn't wear bracelets or a watch for work. He'd bought her the perfect piece of jewellery. She had absolutely no idea when he'd managed to buy it, but she was thrilled that he'd bought her something so beautiful.

'Thank you. It's gorgeous.' She kissed him.

And this was definitely a kind of declaration from him. A ring was out of the question as it was too symbolic; but she knew he was telling her that, for him, she was as beautiful as that long-ago empress. And maybe, just maybe, he was telling her that he was ready to start opening up to her. Letting her close. Making this more than just being acquaintances with benefits.

'It's been the perfect day.' She held him closer. 'And I'm not ready for it to end, yet. Will you stay tonight, Rico?'

Stay.

He never stayed the night with anyone. It meant letting someone too close. He'd been tempted several times to break his rule for Ella, but he'd held himself back. Just. Though he, too, wasn't ready for the day to end just yet. And one night wouldn't hurt, would it?

'And your alarm goes off when, exactly?' he asked, feigning a coolness he definitely didn't feel.

She grimaced. 'Half-past five. Sorry.'

He smiled. 'I'm not usually up *quite* that early but, for you… Yes.' He kissed her. 'I'll stay.'

CHAPTER TEN

LATER in the week, on impulse, Ella texted Rico. *Taste-tester required.*

It took a while for him to reply, but he eventually came back with, *Happy to interview. Where and when?*

She smiled. *My kitchen, when you've finished today. Arrive hungry.*

And she knew full well he'd have more than one interpretation for that.

Her phone beeped at six. *On way. **Starving**.*

By the time Rico knocked on the door, the cakes were cooled and iced.

He kissed her hello. 'Something smells gorgeous.'

'I hope you're hungry.'

'Very.' He kissed her again, this time more lingeringly.

'Take a seat.' She set three cupcakes before him, a bowl of lemon sorbet and a glass of iced water.

'What's this for?' he asked, indicating the sorbet.

'Cleansing your palate, so you can distinguish between the flavours properly.'

He took a bite of the first one. 'Mmm. That's gorgeous. And the cake's different.'

'The base is hummingbird cake rather than vanilla,' she told him.

He smiled. 'You said in Vienna that you'd make me a hummingbird cake if I was good.'

'And I will, if you are,' she said, smiling back. 'What about the icing?'

He thought for a moment. 'Orange. Yes, it works.'

'It should do, because that's the traditional cream cheese frosting that goes with the cake. Eat some lemon sorbet, now.'

He looked pained. 'Don't I get to eat the rest of the cake? Especially as it's only a small one?'

'Later. You're taste-testing, first.'

He ate a spoonful of the sorbet, then sipped the water. 'OK. Cake two.' He took a bite. 'I like this one more. That's lime in the topping, isn't it? There's more of a zing than the orange one.'

She made a note. 'OK. Third one?'

After more sorbet and more water, he tried the third. 'No. Too sweet.'

'That's vanilla buttercream. I thought it might be wrong with the cake. But I wanted a taste-tester's opinion.' She smiled at him. 'From someone I happen to know is a real foodie and would be honest with me.'

'It needs a proper zing. My vote's for the second, the lime one.'

'Noted. Now I know what I'm doing.'

He looked at her. 'So that was it? Just three?'

'Well, I didn't want to overwhelm you with flavours.'

He looked disappointed. 'And there was I, thinking I had a whole plateful of cakes to try. Like the ones with the pretty icing you did for your launch.'

'The two-tone ones, you mean?'

'Though I guess they're complicated.'

'On the contrary. They're dead easy.' She smiled at him. 'Give me a few minutes, and you can ice your own.'

'You're kidding.'

'It only takes five minutes to whip up a batch of cup-cakes. But you're going to get messy,' she warned. She looked at him. 'That white shirt has to go.'

'What?'

'That white shirt has to go,' she repeated. 'Especially if we're doing coloured icing. I'm not sure your laundry service would be able to get the colour out.'

'So what does that make me, the Naked Baker?' he asked, laughing.

She laughed back. 'Semi. And you can have an apron, if you want.'

'An apron?' He gave her a disgusted look. 'I don't think so.' He took his shirt off. 'Where do I put this?'

'I'll deal with it.' She hung it up out of the way, and smiled. 'Mmm. Nice pecs, Signor Rossi.'

'You could take your shirt off, too,' he said, looking hopeful.

'Ha, you wish. But we're making cake.'

Five minutes later, she had the ingredients and a set of scales on the worktop in front of him, and had him mix-ing up the batter for the cupcakes and then spooning it into cake cases.

He looked at her and smiled. 'This is actually quite fun. I can see why you enjoy it. So what do we do while the cakes are cooking?' he asked as she put the cakes in the oven.

'Trust you to be thinking two steps ahead. We make the icing.'

'And there was I, thinking we'd have time out.'

'Not unless you want the cakes to burn. Focus, man, *focus.*'

He laughed. 'You're so bossy, Ella.'

'Says you,' she shot back, but she was laughing as well.

She talked him through making the icing, step by step, and took the cakes out of the oven to cool. Then she handed him a paintbrush.

'What's this for?'

'I'm teaching you my secret. Two-tone icing is the easiest thing in the world.'

She dropped a nozzle with a rounded star tip into a disposable icing bag, and took the top off the pot of one of the coloured icing pastes she used.

'That looks like ink,' he said, peering at it.

'You're not far off, but it's edible. What you do now is dip the brush in, and draw a line inside the bag. Don't get it on your hands.'

He frowned. 'I thought you said it was edible?'

'It is, but if you really want to explain to your colleagues why your hands are bright purple tomorrow morning...'

'Got it.'

'Now spread the line with the paintbrush. Any way you like.'

He looked speculatively at the brush, then at her. 'Now, if this was melted chocolate...'

What he was thinking was, oh, so obvious. She laughed. 'This is a professional kitchen, Rico. No painting of body parts. It's against all the hygiene regulations, and you know it.'

'Spoilsport,' he said. 'I'm very tempted to try and change your mind.'

And it wouldn't take much for him to do it. She sucked in a breath and willed herself to stay professional. 'I'm teaching you to do the icing—on your request. So pay attention.'

He gave her an insolent salute. '*Sì, signorina.*'

'Now press the bag together so the colour's spread evenly.'

He did so, then lifted it up and inspected it. 'It doesn't look as if there's any colour in there.'

'There's enough. You'll see in a moment.' She took the brush from him, then spooned the buttercream into the bag.

'I see it now,' he said, as the rich, deep purple spread against the ivory-coloured buttercream.

'And now,' she said, 'you simply pipe out the icing until the colour starts to show on the edges.' She demonstrated. '*Voilà,* two-tone icing. And then all you do is start in the middle of the cake and pipe a spiral, slightly overlapping the icing as you go.' She handed him the bag, then fetched one of the cakes and set it on a plate. 'Go for it.'

He tried. 'Nothing's coming out of the bag.'

'Because you're not holding the bag right—you need to grip it between your forefinger and thumb.'

'I am.'

She came to stand behind him, and moved his hands. 'Try now. Push downwards, keeping your finger and thumb jammed flat together so the icing can't escape through it.'

'Problem,' he said.

'What?'

He turned round to face her. 'You just took a step back. It was much nicer when you had your arms round me.'

'I'm going to get in your way when you're icing the cake.'

'No, you're not.' He gave her a speculative look. 'And, as I said earlier, you could lose your shirt. You, me, and nothing in between.'

Oh, the pictures that put in her head. Skin to skin with Rico. '*Not* in my kitchen.' Though it was a real effort not to follow through on his suggestion; right now she was seriously aroused. If he touched her, she'd be lost. And she had to sit on her own hands to stop herself touching him.

He proceeded to pipe a perfect spiral on the cake.

She blinked. 'Either you've done this before, or you're a natural.'

He looked at her. 'I know that movement.' He moistened his lower lip with the tip of his tongue. 'Only not on a cake.'

She frowned. 'I'm not with you.'

He gave her a wolfish smile. 'Then let me demonstrate, *bellezza*.' He put the icing bag down. Before she realised what he was going to do, he'd hiked her skirt up, his hand was inside her knickers, and his thumb was working in a spiral on her clitoris.

'Oh-h-h.' The word was a moan of pure pleasure.

'You're wet for me, *bellezza*,' he murmured.

'Yes,' she admitted, her voice husky.

'Let me take your shirt off now,' he said softly. 'And I don't give a damn about hygiene regulations. I want you. Right here, right now.' His thumb moved again, sending another wave of pleasure through her.

Part of her really wanted to go with this.

But.

'Rico, the blind's up,' she whispered.

He stopped as her words registered. 'So anyone could see in.'

'Uh-huh. And while you being topless isn't a problem, me being topless—or people working out where your hand is right now...' She bit her lip.

'Close your eyes, *bellezza*.'

She did so, and felt coolness against her skin as he moved away from her. Then she heard the sound of the blind being wound down.

'Problem solved,' he said softly, and jammed his mouth over hers. The next thing she knew, he'd lifted her onto the worktop—still kissing her—and her skirt was right up round her waist. A couple of seconds later, he'd removed her shirt and her bra, and his body was easing into hers.

She forgot completely about hygiene regulations and rules. All she could focus on was the way Rico made her feel, the way he took her closer and closer to the edge, setting up a hard and fast rhythm that had her pulse racing to meet it.

He smeared cool icing across her nipple, making her gasp—and then followed it up by sucking the sugary confection from her skin, making her gasp even more as his teeth grazed her skin.

And then her body slammed into climax and she held onto him for dear life, feeling him shudder against her as he reached his own climax.

What had just happened was unbelievable. And Ella knew that she was going to be thinking about this evening every time she iced cupcakes from now on.

Rico helped her clear up downstairs, then demolished most of the mini hummingbird cakes. 'I'll see you tomorrow, *bellezza,*' he said softly. 'Sweet dreams.'

'You, too.' She kissed him goodbye.

As he went back to the hotel Rico really wished that he'd stayed over tonight. So he could wake up in her arms again, even if it was going to be at an unearthly hour.

Which was crazy. It meant he wanted to get involved with her. Seriously involved. The idea terrified him and drew him in equal measure. What did he know of love? And no way did he want to make himself vulnerable.

Though maybe, just maybe, Ella was the one he could trust with himself.

CHAPTER ELEVEN

'SATURDAY,' Rico said. 'The launch party.'

Ella nodded. 'Everything's on schedule as far as I'm concerned. The topper's almost done—and no, you can't see it until the day. No previews allowed. You just have to trust me with it, OK?'

'Of course I trust you.' He smiled. 'Anyway, I wasn't thinking about that, *bellezza*. I was merely checking that you're coming as my guest.'

She frowned. 'Well, I'll be a bit busy, sorting out the cake.'

'That won't take all night, and I want you there with me.'

She wrinkled her nose. 'Rico, I'd be happier in the background. I don't really fit into your world.'

He flapped his hand dismissively. 'Sure you do.'

'How? You own a chain of glamorous boutique hotels. I make cakes.'

'You make *fabulous* cakes,' he corrected. 'And, excuse me, who is it who always tells me that it's not how much money you have, it's how you treat other people that matters? You're good with people. And I want you with me.'

Put like that, how could she refuse? 'OK. Though I don't have anything suitable to wear to a launch party. And I

really don't have the time right now for clothes-shopping.'
She sighed. 'I guess I'll just have to make the time.'

He drew her close. 'Could you shop online, get stuff
delivered to you and try them on when it suits you? Then
you wouldn't have to drag round the shops.'

'Then I'll have to wait in for the courier,' she grumbled.
'And if they turn up when I'm out on a delivery, it'll be
the next day before they can re-deliver, or I'll have to trek
over to their warehouse to pick it up.'

'Get everything delivered to the hotel, and I'll ask my
PA here to return the things you don't like.' He paused. 'Or
tell me the kind of thing you want and I'll ask her to call the
designers and get them to send in a selection of dresses.'

'My own private fashion show, you mean?' She shook
her head. 'It's very sweet of you to think of that, but you
know what I think about designer clothes. They're over-
priced and they only suit one body type. Which isn't mine.'

'I happen to like your body type, so don't even think
about changing it.' He moulded her curves with his hands.
'Or turning into one of those boring women who count
every single calorie and every single carb.'

That made her smile. 'Hardly, doing what I do for a
living.'

He stroked her face. 'Would you let me buy the dress
for you, *bellezza?*'

She folded her arms. 'Thank you for the offer, but I can
buy my own dress.'

'I know you can, *bellezza.* I'm trying to do something
nice for you, not be a control freak.' He gave her a rueful
smile. 'It's my fault that you have to go clothes-shopping,
so I'm trying to minimise the time impact for you.'

She leaned her forehead against his. 'And I'm being
an ungrateful cow. Sorry. It must be the wrong time of
the month.'

'No, you're just really busy at the moment and I'm making demands on time you don't have. But I do want you at the party with me, Ella *bellezza*.'

'I'll be there. Is your family coming to the launch?' she asked.

'No. My grandparents are too frail to travel.'

Yet again, she noticed, he didn't mention his parents. And she was curious—why was Rico estranged from them? She still hadn't persuaded him to open up to her about his family, even though she'd told him all about her own difficult background.

Before she could ask anything else, he switched the subject back to her clothes. But she noticed. And she wondered.

Rico was busy keeping the Italian side of his business ticking over on the phone and by email while the English side was coming together; the time he could spend with Ella before the launch was severely limited, and it put him out of sorts. With her, he felt grounded. And when he realised that, it put him out of sorts even more. He didn't want to rely on someone else for his happiness, even if that person was as sweet-natured as Ella.

The day of the launch dawned, and the whole hotel was busy preparing for it while minimising the disruption to their guests. Rico barely had time to speak to Ella during the day, apart from kissing her hello, giving her a key to his suite so she could change into her dress for the party, and telling her to see the chef if there was anything she needed from the kitchen.

Though he did see the cake just as she added the finishing touches.

Ella had made him a pyramid of cupcakes swirled with alternate white and dark chocolate ganache; at the top was a white chocolate iced cutting cake with tall curls of chocolate standing round the outside, topped with a sugar-paste fountain, with droplets of water coming down on almost invisible wires.

'Ella *bellezza,* that looks amazing,' he said.

'You really do like it? You're not just being polite?' she asked.

'I'm not being polite,' he reassured her. 'It's perfect.' He kissed her. 'Thank you.'

Once the party started, Rico had interviews to give and journalists and photographers to show round. He noted how many photographs were taken of the cake; Ella would definitely get some good publicity from this. Which she deserved—she'd worked hard to make sure the cake was perfect for tonight.

After the journalists, there were the movers and shakers, people who could use their conference and event facilities, and Rico went into full sales mode.

But best of all was when everyone had gone home. Everyone except Ella, dressed in a very plain black dress and high heels, with the glittering star he'd bought her in Vienna at her throat and her hair pinned in a swish updo. Desire kicked through him. He'd never seen her look more beautiful.

'I never got to dance with you tonight,' he said.

She smiled. 'That's OK.'

'No, it isn't. And I've neglected you all evening.'

'Because you were working and you had a lot of people you needed to talk to.' She stroked his face. 'It really is OK, Rico. I understand.'

He was so used to demands from his previous girl-friends that the lack of them from Ella floored him slightly. 'Everyone loved the cake. The picture might end up in a few colour supplements—and on the Internet,' he said.

'Good. Just make sure there's a picture of it on your hotel website with a link to mine,' she said with a grin.

He grinned back. 'It sounds like you're building an empire, Ella *bellezza*.'

'Maybe. Right now,' she said, 'I'm really, really happy. Life doesn't get any better than this.'

'You know what? I was thinking just the same. But, actually, it does get better.'

She frowned. 'How?'

'I'm kidnapping you.' He scooped her up and strode over to the lift.

She laughed. 'Rico, are you taking me to your suite?'

'Better than that.'

He set her on her feet once they were inside the lift, and made sure her body was in full contact with his all the way down, so she was left in no doubt about his arousal. Once the doors had closed, he kissed her until they were both breathless; the lift doors had opened and closed several times before he realised that they were on the floor he wanted.

'This isn't the way to your suite—or did you move after I got changed?' she asked.

'This is just for tonight.' He opened the door to the honeymoon suite.

Just as he'd planned, there was a bottle of good champagne on ice. He plugged his MP3 player into a dock, and a smoky-voiced jazz artist started singing a love song to the accompaniment of a piano and double-bass. Then he turned the lights down low.

'Dance with me, Ella *bellezza?*' he said.

Oh, wow. Today had been a big deal for him, she knew. The launch of his first hotel in London—his first hotel outside Italy. He'd been busy with the launch party for weeks, talking to journalists and potential clients, making sure he got the right attention for the business.

She'd stayed in the background tonight, knowing that his work needed to come first and not wanting to be in the way. And she'd watched him, proud of the way he didn't let a single question put him off his stride. He knew everything about the hotel and its staff; he hadn't had to ask anyone else to clarify a single thing for him.

And yet, despite everything that had been going on, he'd still planned these quiet moments just for them. She had no idea when he'd found the time to think about it, let alone organise it, but it touched her to the heart.

She smiled. 'I'd love to dance with you, Rico.'

And there, in his arms, dancing with him, it hit her. *She'd fallen for him.*

She couldn't pinpoint the exact moment when, but she loved him. She loved his strength, she loved his sense of humour, and she loved the way he could switch from hard-headed businessman to intensely focused lover. She loved the way he noticed things but didn't make a fuss about them. And the quiet way he dealt with things had taught her that she could trust him. He didn't make promises unless he knew he could keep them. Since Rome, he'd been scrupulously honest with her.

And she was sure that he was finally letting her closer. OK, so he hadn't made any kind of declaration, and she had a feeling that Rico would rather stick pins in his eyes than talk about emotions—but that didn't mean he didn't feel them.

She wasn't going to tell him how she felt about him in words—she didn't want him to back off—but she could tell him with her body.

This time, when he kissed her, there was no holding

back—within seconds the kiss turned deep and demanding and hot.

And actually, no, she wasn't going to hold back the words. She'd just have to say them in a way she knew he'd accept. 'Rico,' she whispered, 'I want you.'

'I want you, too,' he whispered back.

And she had the strongest feeling that they meant the same thing by 'want'.

Rico unzipped her little black dress, slowly eased it down so she could step out of it, then hung it carefully over the back of the sofa. The diamond star at her throat glittered; he still hadn't got round to telling her that it was diamond and white gold, not silver and cubic zircona. And he really hoped she wouldn't consider it a lie when he finally confessed. OK, so he hadn't corrected her assumption that it was costume jewellery; but that was a little bit of misdirection rather than an out-and-out lie, so he could spoil her without her feeling bad about it.

He gently removed the choker and kissed his way along her throat. 'Your skin's so soft.' And her perfume was light and enticing, making him want more.

Her underwear was lacy, the black in sharp contrast to her ivory skin. He hooked his fingers under the straps of her bra and drew them down to bare her shoulders. 'You're lush, Ella *bellezza,*' he said, his voice low. 'Absolutely lush. You make me ache for you.'

In answer, she kissed him hard.

He undid the pins in her hair and let it fall down. *'Bellezza.'* His voice cracked with desire; he picked her up, carried her through to the bedroom, and lay her down on the four-poster bed.

'I think you're a little overdressed, Rico,' she said with a smile.

He considered stripping for her, but he knew that right now he didn't have the patience to have any kind of finesse. Instead, he stripped in ten seconds flat, then finished removing her clothes.

'What happened to seduction?' she asked, laughing.

'I just can't wait any more. I need you now.' He paused only long enough to grab a condom to protect her. And then at last he was where he wanted to be, inside her, her body tightening round him, warm and wet and welcoming. He pushed deeper; she sighed with pleasure and slid her hands into his hair, drawing his head down to hers and then kissing him, demanding and giving all at the same time.

This was what he'd needed all day. His Ella.

Her body tightened round his, tipping him into his own climax. He held her tightly, wanting this moment to last for ever.

Though of course it couldn't. He went to the bathroom, then came back to lie beside her.

'It's Saturday night. Stay with me tonight?' he asked. 'I'll drive you home tomorrow, or if you give me your key I'll drive over first thing in the morning and pick up a change of clothes for you.'

She smiled. 'Yes.'

'I forgot the champagne. I guess I rushed you a bit.' He kissed her. 'Sorry.'

'Nothing to apologise for. I wasn't saying no.'

'I guess. Stay there.' He went to fetch the champagne and glasses.

'That's so decadent, drinking champagne in bed,' she said, accepting a glass from him. 'Mmm, and this is nice stuff.'

'Glad you like it, Ella *bellezza*.'

'And I like this room. A proper four-poster.'

'And there's a whirlpool bath in the bathroom.' He eyed

her speculatively. 'Which I think would go very well with the champagne.'

She rolled her eyes. 'The Roman boy goes in search of yet another fountain.' But she let him lead her into the bathroom. And he thoroughly enjoyed taking a whirlpool bath with her, teasing her and arousing her until she climaxed again under his touch.

Later that night, Rico lay awake. He never asked his girlfriends to stay over. If anything, he made sure they didn't get that close and he kept them away from his private domain. But having Ella beside him—he couldn't even begin to explain to himself how it made him feel. All he knew was that he wanted this. And he wanted more.

And it scared the hell out of him.

She'd been hurt before. What if he let her down? He'd promised her that he wouldn't let her down...and he didn't intend to. But what if he failed? He hadn't been enough for his parents to love him. And he knew that his grandparents had seen him as the heir to the hotel empire rather than for himself. Could he be something more than that, for Ella?

In business, he never doubted his judgement. Emotionally, it was a whole different ballgame. And one where he didn't have a clue what the rules were.

Waking with her in his arms was definitely something Rico wanted to do again. It made the whole morning feel full of sunshine.

'Well, Signor Hotel Tycoon, what are the plans for today?' she asked.

'Whatever you want to do. I'm in your hands.'

She gave him a truly sensual smile. 'Good. I have an idea...'

An idea that blew his mind and put a smile on his face.

And, after he'd driven Ella home to change, Rico enjoyed walking along the river with her again.

'So now The Fountain is relaunched, does this mean you're going back to Rome?' she asked.

'Not yet. I'm spending the next week doing a few hours in every role, so I can work out what the staff training needs are.'

She gave him a speculative look. 'You're going to be a waiter, then?'

'Yes.'

'I'm so tempted to come and pester you and be a difficult client.'

He just laughed. 'You can try. I'm good with difficult clients.'

'Hmm. That sounds like a challenge. When exactly are you on duty?'

'Tuesday morning. Ready for morning coffee at ten o'clock.'

She grinned. 'Oh, this is going to be *such* fun.'

On Tuesday morning, Ella dropped off the orders at the cafés, then headed for Rico's hotel.

'Good morning, madam. May I show you to a table?' Rico asked.

He was dressed the same as the other waiters, in a fitted burgundy jacket, white shirt and black trousers. And he looked utterly delectable. She smiled at him. 'Thank you. May I have a table with a view of the garden?'

'Of course, madam.' He ushered her to a table, held the chair out for her, then brought her a menu.

When he came back to take her order, Ella purred, 'What do you recommend?'

He gave her a sultry look. 'That depends whether

madam is in the mood for light and frothy, or dark and intense.'

She burst out laughing. 'Rico, you're a terrible waiter. I hope you don't say that sort of thing to all your clients.'

He grinned and took a seat opposite her. 'Only to you. What I recommend for you, madam, isn't actually on the menu.'

She went hot at the thought.

'But, if I'm recommending something to you as a customer, then I think you'd like the cappuccino here. And, yes, I'll ask them to hold the cocoa dusting because I know you hate it.'

'Sounds good to me. Anything else?'

He went back into official waiter mode. 'All the cakes are fresh today, madam, if you'd like to make a selection from the counter.'

'Is your counter as good as the one we went to in Vienna?'

He gave her a speaking look. 'The Fountain Hotel isn't a specialist patisserie, madam. But I believe we are looking at a new supplier. The hotel owner has made a recommendation to the head chef.' He glanced at his watch. 'Who might have time for a word with her right now, if madam isn't busy.'

She smiled. 'I only came to test your waiting skills, Rico.'

He grinned. 'I believe in multi-tasking. Seriously. I told John about the hummingbird cakes, and he says he'd like samples.'

'Then I'll make a proper appointment and bring samples with me,' she said.

'Hmm. I might have to work a shift in the kitchen, that day.'

'Behave. And I must tell the head waiter that his staff

leaves a lot to be desired. I ordered a cup of coffee about half an hour ago and my waiter still hasn't brought it.' She tapped her watch.

'It wasn't anywhere near half an hour ago. And *you're* the one who wanted to talk.' He rolled his eyes. 'All right. Hint taken. I'll go and get your coffee, *bellezza.*'

When he came back, he had other customers to attend to; Ella watched him, and he was thoroughly charming, smiling and paying attention to what his guests wanted. The four middle-aged women he served would definitely be repeating their visit, she thought. He'd made all of them smile and feel special.

Though not *quite* as special as the way he made her feel.

Then she took a sip of the coffee.

It was absolutely vile.

She blew out a breath. She knew Rico would want to know the truth, but she'd have to find a nice way of telling him.

He came back over to her table. 'Is everything OK, *bellezza?* You've barely touched your coffee.'

She bit her lip. 'Rico, I'm so sorry. It's just, um, not how I'd normally have a cappuccino.'

'You mean it tastes revolting?' He frowned. 'That's not good. I apologise on behalf of the kitchen, and obviously I need to keep an eye on quality control. Or maybe change the coffee machine they use at the moment. May I?' He tasted it, then looked at her in surprise. 'Ella, it tastes fine to me.'

'Maybe it's me.' She shrugged. 'I'm probably overtired and I've drunk too much coffee lately,' she said.

'Let me get you something else.' He came back with a peppermint tea.

It was really refreshing, and the first sip took away the slight queasiness the coffee had induced. 'That's lovely.

Thank you.' She paused. 'Would you do that for all your customers?'

'Yes. You don't think you're getting special treatment just because you happen to be dating the owner, do you?'

She laughed. 'Well, am I?'

'Well, I wouldn't actually taste anyone else's coffee,' he admitted, 'and I wouldn't be sitting here opposite them, chatting. But I would make sure that anything they weren't happy with was replaced.' He sighed. 'You're a distraction, *bellezza*.'

'Go and do your work, *garçon*,' she teased.

He leaned over to steal a kiss. '*Garçon*, indeed. I'll see you later. And I meant it about ringing John. I want those hummingbird cakes on the menu.'

'Yes, sir.' She gave him a teasing salute. 'Can I pay my bill?'

'No. Because it's on me,' he said. '*Ciao, bellezza.*'

Later that evening, lying on the sofa with Rico, Ella stroked his hair back from his forehead. 'Sorry I put you off, this morning.'

'Actually, I quite liked having you around. Though I did have to explain to the other ladies I was serving that I was actually the owner of the hotel doing a bit of quality control work, and you were my girlfriend—my staff didn't really go around kissing random customers.'

She laughed. 'Were they very disappointed?'

He laughed back. 'Oh, you're such a bad girl.'

'So are you happy with the way things are going at The Fountain?' she asked.

'Yes. I have a good team. Some of the management needs replacing, but I'll handle that myself until I get the right person to do it.'

'So you're staying in London for a bit longer?'

'Yes.' But wild horses wouldn't drag it from him that the real reason he was staying was Ella. He could quite easily send a manager from one of his other hotels to take over in London, but right now he wanted to be in London. With her. And if he had to make up excuses to do it, so be it.

CHAPTER TWELVE

'IT's officially lunchtime, but obviously you're working through your lunch break today,' Rico said.

'No, I'm having a proper break. See?' Ella gestured to her plate and glass.

Rico eyed her sandwich and grimaced. 'That doesn't look very nice, Ella *bellezza*.'

'Actually, it's gorgeous.'

'What is it?'

She smiled. 'Marmite and celery.'

He looked completely baffled. 'Marmite?'

'It's an English thing, a yeast-extract spread,' she explained. 'Very savoury. People either love it or hate it. Try a bite.' She gestured to the plate.

He did as she suggested, and then had to take a gulp of her orange juice to take the taste away. 'Ella, how can you possibly eat that? It's repulsive!'

She shrugged. 'As I said, people either love it or hate it. I'm on the pro side.'

He pulled a face. 'I'll believe you. Otherwise I'd say it'd have to be a food craving.'

She rolled her eyes. 'I'm not pregnant, Rico.' Then she went white.

He felt his eyes narrow. 'What's wrong, *bellezza*?'

She lifted one hand, gesturing to him to wait; she was

clearly running through something in her head. 'Oh.' She bit her lip.

'What?'

'I'm late.' She took a breath. 'Two weeks late.'

Rico went cold. 'Is that normal for you?'

She bit her lip again and shook her head. 'Though it's probably just because I've been working madly. Last time I worked this hard, my periods went all over the place. And we've been careful.'

But the only one hundred per cent guaranteed contraception was abstinence. And he knew she knew it, too. 'Ella, you need to do a test.'

'You're overreacting.'

He stared at her in disbelief. 'Your period's two weeks late, you say that's not normal for you, and you tell me I'm *overreacting?*'

'I don't have any other symptoms of being pregnant.'

'Yes, you do.' Memories slid into his head. 'The other day, you didn't like the coffee and it tasted perfectly normal to me. And you're tired all the time.'

'Because I've been working hard. You're probably right about burnout. And I haven't been feeling sick or anything like that.'

Oh, man, was she in denial. It was all adding up for him. Nastily so. 'Not everyone feels sick. My best friend's wife didn't. You need to do a pregnancy test,' he repeated.

'It's not the kind of thing I have just lying around my bathroom, you know.' She narrowed her eyes at him.

'Fine. I'll go and buy one. Is there a pharmacy near here?'

'I don't need to do a pregnancy test,' she repeated. 'I'm fine.'

He folded his arms. 'Where's the pharmacy?'

'Don't bully me, Rico.'

'I'm not bullying you.' Though he was having a hard time containing his irritation. She was being ridiculously stubborn about something that would take only minutes to sort out. If the test was negative, they could both start breathing again and go back to normal. If it was positive...

He didn't even want to think about that right now. 'OK, if you're not going to tell me, let's do it the quick way.' He grabbed his mobile phone, flicked into the Internet and tapped in her postcode. The website brought up a list of the nearest pharmacies. 'Right. I'll be back in a minute.'

She scowled. 'You're *so* overreacting.'

No, he wasn't, he thought as he banged the door closed behind him.

If she was pregnant... Oh, hell. He'd always sworn he'd never have children, never subject another living being to the kind of childhood he'd had. But how could he possibly walk out on his child? He didn't want to be like his father had been, feckless and absent. Rico wanted his child to grow up feeling secure, knowing that both parents always would be there for him or her. A home and a life with the kind of structure and security he hadn't had until his grandparents had stepped in.

On the other hand, he didn't want to make his parents' mistakes and get married for the baby's sake. And, given how Ella's engagement had ended, he knew she wasn't going to be particularly warm to the idea of marriage, either. Though she'd admitted that she'd missed having a father, growing up.

Would she want to make a go of it with him? Though, if she did, he didn't have a clue where to start. How to be a father. How to be part of a loving family. It was completely outside his terms of reference.

What a *mess*.

Maybe she was right, and he was overreacting. But his gut told him that this was trouble.

He found the pharmacy, bought a pregnancy test kit, and went straight back to Ella. The second he walked through the door, she looked as if she was spoiling for a fight. Which wasn't what he wanted, at all. He just needed to know the truth. To know where they stood.

He handed her the packet. 'I need to know for sure, Ella. One way or the other. Please.'

That last word seemed to take the wind out of her sails, and her shoulders dropped. 'OK. I'll just be a minute.'

Though she seemed to take for ever. Why did women take so damned long to go to the loo? Rico wondered, trying to stem his frustration.

She came out holding the test stick. 'We're meant to keep it flat,' she said.

'OK. How long does it take before we get the result?'

'Two minutes—I read the instructions before I did the test.'

Oh. So that was why she'd been such a long time.

Both of them stared at the stick.

'There's a blue line in that window,' Rico said, pointing to it.

'That's the control window. It shows the test is working.'

She sounded calm, but he noticed she was gripping the stick so hard that her fingers had turned white.

A second blue line started to appear. And then it turned into a plus sign.

Positive.

She stared at him, looking utterly shocked.

Rico could barely breathe. This couldn't be happening. It really couldn't. 'One of the lines is fainter than the other.'

'It doesn't matter—if there's a plus sign, it's positive,' she said. She shook her head, as if trying to clear it.

'Pregnant. I...I can't be. I just can't.' Her face was filled with panic. 'I've just got my business off the ground. It's absolutely the wrong time for me to be pregnant. How am I going to be able to carry on the business, when I'm looking after a baby?'

He felt sick. 'So you want a termination?'

'I need to think about this.' She put her head in her hands. 'A termination would solve all the problems,' she muttered.

True. Though, if his parents had taken that route, he wouldn't be here now. And Ella wouldn't have the same dilemma in front of her. But he hated the thought of a termination. They'd just made a new life together. OK, so it hadn't been planned. But snuffing it out, as if it wasn't important... All his instincts told him that no, it wasn't what he wanted. Not at all.

Though he didn't have the right to put pressure on her. And he needed to know how she felt about this.

'Uh-huh.' He was careful to keep his voice neutral.

She looked up again, her expression tortured. 'I can't get rid of a child just because it's not convenient for me.' She dragged in a breath. 'I wasn't planned, but my mum never gave up on me, and I'm not giving up on this baby, either.' She lifted her chin. 'I promised my mum on her deathbed that I wouldn't make the same mistakes that she'd made. She never made me feel as if I was a mistake.'

Rico flinched. That definitely wasn't true for him. He'd been planned—but only by one of his parents, and not because she'd wanted him for himself. And both his parents had made him feel as if he was a mistake. A nuisance, one they only put up with so they could get the lifestyle they wanted.

'So you want to keep the baby.'

'Yes.' Her eyes were very clear. 'Which doesn't mean I'm expecting anything from you. Financial or otherwise.'

'It's my baby, too.' And, the way he saw it, there was only one way to give their baby stability and love. A traditional Italian family background. And he'd make damned sure he made a better job of it than either of their fathers had done. 'We're getting married.'

'What?' She stared at him in seeming disbelief.

'We're getting married.'

'Because of the baby?'

He rolled his eyes. 'What do you think?'

'What century are you living in?' she asked. 'People don't get married nowadays just because they're having a baby.'

'We're getting married,' he repeated.

'We are *not*.' She put her hands on her hips and glared at him. 'You told me you didn't want a family.'

'That was before you were pregnant. I'm doing the right thing by you.'

She laughed, but there was no mirth in the sound. 'Listen to yourself—do you have any idea how pompous you sound?'

'The baby is having my name.'

She rolled her eyes. 'Obviously I'll name you as the father on the birth certificate. But that's as far as it goes. You don't want a family, Rico. You don't want to get married. And I'm sure as hell not going to trap you like that and make you resent me for it later.'

The way his mother had trapped his father. She had a point. But Rico wasn't his father and Ella wasn't his mother. Surely they didn't have to repeat those mistakes?

The only way she was going to understand was if he told her about his past, the way she'd opened up to him. Trusted her. Asked her to help him change their future.

She took advantage of his silence to state her terms. 'I expect absolutely nothing from you, Rico. It's up to you how much time you want to spend with our child but, make no mistake, our child will be living with me.'

'Our child will be living with *both* of us. And we're getting married,' he repeated.

'My mother brought me up as a single mother. I've turned out perfectly fine. Our baby will be fine, too.'

She might be fine, but he definitely wasn't. 'Ella, I don't want our baby to grow up the way I did. My parents…'

There was no way out. He was going to have to tell her. Every last dragging bit of it. Even though his throat felt clogged with the words. 'My mother got pregnant with me at eighteen. On purpose. So my father would have to marry her.'

She stared at him. 'Are you saying you think I got pregnant on purpose?'

'No, of course I'm not. We're both sensible and our baby's a surprise to both of us. And you're very far from being manipulative and selfish. You're nothing like my mother.' He raked a hand through his hair. 'Ella, I don't find this easy to talk about. At all. And the only reason I'm telling you now is because it's the only way to make you understand.'

'Understand what?' She looked completely baffled.

He blew out a breath. 'I'm going to have to trust you to keep this to yourself.'

Hurt flickered on her face. 'When have I ever given you any reason not to trust me?'

'Never. I know. That came out wrong.' There was a horrible, salty taste in his mouth. 'I'm…it's…' He shook his head in frustration. Why was it so damned hard to say it? 'Hell, I've always been articulate. And yet this…it makes me feel as if my mouth's full of glue and the words can't come out.' He took a deep breath. 'I don't see my parents, Ella. I have nothing to do with them, other than giving them an allowance.'

'You give your parents an allowance?' She looked utterly shocked at the idea.

'We have a deal. They get the money to fund whatever the thrill of the month is, and they stay away from me. It suits us all perfectly.'

'Rico, I…' Her eyes were full of bewilderment. 'Why don't you want your parents anywhere near you?'

'Because they're not nice people, Ella. I'm better off without them. They never wanted me in the first place.' He couldn't look at her. Couldn't bear to see the pity in her eyes. But he owed it to her to tell the truth. 'Living with them was a nightmare. My mother got pregnant deliberately so my father would have to marry her, and she'd have the lifestyle she wanted. But they were both way too young to settle down. And they weren't suited. At all. All they did was yell at each other.'

Even now his skin felt clammy with the memory of it. 'Every day they had a fight, usually over something completely trivial. And I hated living like that. I hated all the shouting and the smashing things and the slamming doors. I went into myself, barely spoke or communicated with anyone. My teachers told my parents that I might need to go to a special school.' He dragged in a breath. 'It wasn't that I had developmental problems. I just couldn't cope with what was going on around me at home, so I closed off from everyone.'

'Oh, Rico.' She put her arms round him and held him close, as if protecting him. 'You don't have to tell me any more.'

'Yes, I do. So you can understand why I want our child to have a secure, stable home. My parents split up several times when I was little. Sometimes my mother took me with her, just to spite my father, but most of the time she forgot about me.' He dragged in a breath. 'They split up for good when I was four, nearly five. And then there was this battle for me. Not because they wanted *me*—they wanted what I represented.'

She said nothing, but she stroked his hair back from his forehead. As if she was trying to soothe him, take the pain away.

Nothing was going to take that pain away.

'For my father, I was his heir.' He smiled grimly. 'Not that Nonno was stupid enough to hand over the reins of the company to him. My father spent nearly as much money as my mother did. Fast cars, which he crashed. Boats he never even used before he sold on, at a loss. He had a real nose for investments—ones that failed, that is. But I was his bargaining chip for the future. As long as he had me, Nonno would always bail him out. Which made me a gold-mine. I wasn't his son—I was the means to an end.'

'What about your mother? I mean—she carried you for nine months. She must've adored you when you were born.'

How could Ella be that naïve, that trusting? Or maybe that was what came from knowing you were loved for yourself. Something Rico had never, ever had. 'No. For her, I was a way to get at my father. Keeping me meant that he didn't have me, and that made her feel she'd won the fight. Not to mention the extra allowance that came with me to support her lifestyle.' He sighed. 'I lived with her for a while after they split up for good. Not that I saw much of her. She slept in late every day because she was out partying every night. I had a series of indifferent nannies who brought their boyfriends round and stuck me in front of the television in the afternoons while they were...'

He coughed. 'Let's just say they were otherwise engaged behind a locked door.'

'That's awful.' Her arms tightened round him.

'And then, when my mother finally got full custody of me because the courts agreed my father was too feckless to look after me, she planned to send me to boarding school, so I'd be out of her way. She told her friends all about it when I was playing quietly in the corner of the room. I have no idea if she knew that I could hear every single word she was saying, and even if she did I don't think she cared.' He looked at Ella. 'I had everything money could buy. Every toy—all I had to do was mention it, and it would be there in every colour and size the manufacturer made. My parents tried to outdo each other in who could give me the biggest presents.'

'But you didn't have someone there for *you*. Your childhood was the total opposite of mine,' she said softly. 'My mum couldn't afford to buy me much for my birthday or Christmas. My clothes were all second-hand. But she was always there for me. She read me stories every night—from library books, because she couldn't afford to buy them. And I always, always, knew how much she loved me. She told me every single day.' She stroked his face. 'I was the lucky one, Rico. That's the kind of upbringing I want for my child. Money doesn't matter. It's how you are with people that matters.'

He knew that was true. And it turned his blood to ice. He had intentions—the very best intentions—but how would he know how to be a parent? He'd had very little to do with children. He was godfather to his best friend's children, but it was a nominal title. He was as bad as his grandparents, giving plenty in the material sense but no emotional support. He'd merely made an educated guess that his goddaughter's favourite colour was pink and his godson liked toy cars. That, or he asked Sofia, their mother, what they wanted for birthdays and Christmas.

'So did you end up at boarding school?'

'No. In the end, my grandparents took my mother to court and got custody of me.'

'So they loved you enough to rescue you.'

'To rescue the heir to the business,' he corrected. 'They sent me to various medical experts to sort me out and eventually I started talking again.' Though Rico had a feeling that that'd had less to do with the doctors and more to do with the fact that his grandparents didn't shout at each other or throw things. That he'd felt *safe* with them.

'And then, once I was reading and writing and starting to catch up with the rest of my class, my grandfather started pushing me to achieve more at school. I started work in the family business when I was fourteen. And he made it clear he expected me to do well in everything. If I wasn't top of the class, he wanted to know why. If I dropped marks in an exam, he expected me to go through it all again and work out where I'd failed and why, so I got it right next time. And if I made a mistake with the accounts or the business projections, he'd drill me in how to read a balance sheet until my head ached.'

'Did he ever say "well done"?' she asked softly.

Rico shrugged. 'He made me CEO three years ago, when he stepped down as head of the business. I guess that's the same thing. He trusts me not to mess it up. I have the final say in what happens.'

'Maybe he isn't good with words. Some people aren't good at saying what they feel.' She stroked his hair. 'What you said about your dad... He was an only child, yes?' At Rico's nod, she continued, 'Maybe your grandparents couldn't have any more children after him, so they spoiled him, poured all their love into him and gave him everything he wanted. The way he turned out, your grandparents knew they'd got it wrong. They didn't want to make those same mistakes with you, and that was why your grandfather was so hard on you when you were growing up. Like being the opposite of the way they'd been with your father, so you'd turn out OK.'

Rico had pretty much come to that conclusion himself. Though he'd rather die than actually ask his grandparents if they loved him. 'I don't want my child to grow up like that. I want to be there for my child—to be the kind of father...' He couldn't say it. He just hoped she'd realise what he meant. The kind of father he wished he'd had.

'But you're asking me to marry you for completely the wrong reason. Surely even in this day and age people get married because they love each other?'

He blew out a breath. 'That's the one thing I was hoping you weren't going to ask of me.' Because he wasn't sure he was capable of doing it. He didn't have a clue what a normal family was like. He didn't know how to love, the way she wanted him to love her. And it scared him to hell that he'd be a failure at it.

He looked absolutely terrified. And suddenly a lot of things were clear to Ella. Rico, who was calm and efficient and terribly good at business, was completely at sea when it came to emotional things. From the way he'd grown up, he didn't know how to give his heart, and he was always going to hold back from her.

Unless she could teach him to love. Give him the security he'd never had as a child. Make him realise that she valued him for himself, not for what he could give her or do for her.

If she married him, their baby would have the security she hadn't always had as a child. Two parents. What she'd always wanted, when she was younger and before she found out what a louse her father had been.

It wasn't about the money. At all. But, if she didn't marry Rico, she knew she'd struggle to cope with the business. She'd have to give it up, just when she'd got it off the ground and was doing well—that, or find a business partner to share the workload and give her time to spend with her baby, because she had no intention of neglecting her baby in favour of her career. But how could she possibly trust her judgement to find the right business partner when she was all over the place, emotionally and hormonally?

'I need to think about this,' she said. 'And right now I want to be on my own.'

For a second, she thought he flinched—as if she'd pushed him away. Given how much she knew he'd been pushed away by people in his past, it made her feel guilty. 'A lot of the time, Michael talked me round to his way of thinking, and I let him,' she said softly. 'I don't want that happening with us. Not with something this important. I just need a little time to work things out in my head—and to be sure I know what I want. And then we can talk about it, work it out between us.'

'Fair enough.' He'd switched back into efficient businessman mode and shut himself off again. She could see it in his eyes, hear it in his voice. 'Even if you decide not to marry me, Ella, you'll have my support. And I know you said it wasn't about the money, but I also know you had it hard growing up, and I'll make sure you don't ever have to worry about finances again—you or the baby. Call me when you're ready to talk.'

And he walked out without another word.

Part of Ella wanted to run after him, to tell him that she loved him and they'd work it out together. But part of her wasn't sure they could. Not if he was going to keep hold-

ing back from her. The way he could switch off like that…
she really didn't understand how he could do that. How he
could compartmentalise things so easily. Or maybe that
was his defence mechanism, and together they could learn
how to break it. Give him the chance to love her and their
baby, make a real family together.

She surveyed the kitchen. She had plenty to do. But
work could wait. Right now, she really needed to be somewhere else. She needed to think about what was happening. What Rico had offered her. If it was enough.

An hour later, she was sitting in the cemetery, putting
flowers in the vase in front of her mother's headstone.

'I wish you were here,' she said. 'You would've been
such a fabulous grandmother. Full of stories and love and
laught—' Her voice cracked halfway through the word.
'Oh, Mum. I don't know what to do. If Rico asked me to
marry him because he loved me, I'd say yes like a shot.
But it isn't why he asked me. It's so his child won't grow
up like he did. He wants to make our baby feel safe, secure, nurtured. But that isn't the same, is it?' She dragged
in a breath. 'I promised you I wouldn't make the same mistakes you did. But here I am, with an unplanned baby.' She
sniffed. 'I know you wouldn't have been like your mum
and told me to get rid of it. Rico doesn't want me to get rid
of the baby, either. I'm not under the same kind of pressure
you were. He's not like my father or Michael. He's not a
cheat. And he'd never be unfaithful to me. I guess that's
one mistake I wouldn't be repeating.'

But? She could almost hear her mother's voice asking
the question.

'But I don't know how he feels about me,' she whispered. 'I don't know if he knows how to love. Nobody's
ever really been there for him or loved him for himself.
And I think he's scared of loving me or the baby.'

She bit her lip. 'I don't want to do this on my own. You did a brilliant job with me, Mum, but I'm not you. I need someone to share this with. Someone to share the baby's first smile, the first tooth, the first word, the first step. Someone to share the tough times, to hold me when I'm panicking and tell me everything will work out just fine because we're a team.' She dragged in a breath. 'I need more support than you had. Ju would help, but it's not fair to burden her; and now I've found what I really want to do with my life, I don't want to go back to being an accountant. I know I'm being greedy, but I want it all. I want this baby, I want my career, and I want...' Her voice cracked again. 'I want Rico. I love him, Mum. He's a good man. Just a little bit lost, I think. And maybe—maybe if I let him close to me and the baby, it'll teach him to let us close to him, too. To make him realise it's safe to love us.' She bit her lip. 'And let me know it's safe to love him, too.'

Ella walked home the long way. Thinking, all the time. Could she marry Rico, knowing that he didn't love her and might never be able to love her? Could she take the risk that he'd change when the baby arrived, that he would at least fall in love with their child?

She didn't think he'd fight her for custody of the baby. Not when he'd been stuck in the middle of a custody battle himself, as a child. But what was the alternative? That he'd simply be a source of financial support? That felt wrong, too.

The more she thought about it, the more she was sure that this was the only chance Rico would ever give anyone to get really close to him. For both their sakes—and their baby's—she had to try.

When she got in, she picked up the phone.

He answered immediately. 'Rico Rossi.'

'It's Ella. I'll marry you. But I want you to know it's not about the money. It's about *sharing*.'

'Uh-huh.'

She really should've gone to see him instead of calling him. She couldn't tell a thing from that cool, neutral voice on the other end of the phone—and she needed to know how he *felt*.

Asking him would be pointless. She knew he'd stonewall her. He'd told her so much already this afternoon; no doubt right now he felt vulnerable, and he'd go into panic mode, shutting off his emotions.

Well, she felt vulnerable, too. And shutting off wasn't on her agenda.

'That means I want you to go to the scans with me. And the first ante-natal appointment.'

'Of course. I said I'd support you, Ella.'

'And,' she said, 'since we're getting married, we might as well move in together now and get used to each other, first.'

'Fine. I'll sort out an apartment here.'

'At the hotel? You're in Belgravia, Rico. Half an hour away from here. That means I'll have to get up at five in the morning to commute back here in time to start baking.'

'You don't have to commute. You can use the hotel kitchen for your work.'

No. But the only way he'd accept her refusal would be if she put it in business terms. 'That's going to make everything much more complicated. How am I going to work out my costings and my accounts, when I don't have the fuel bills to back them up? What if I get an emergency commission and I can't do it because your chefs are already using the ovens to cook for the hotel guests? I can't interrupt your business for mine.'

'I'm sure we can sort something out.'

He really was missing the point. 'I've been here before, Rico. I let someone talk me round and make decisions for me. And it all went wrong. I don't want to let that happen again, especially with a baby to consider. I want to stay *here*.'

'I'm not Michael.'

'I know.'

'And I'm not your father—or mine. I'm not going to let this fail, Ella.'

'It sounds as if you're talking about a business, Rico, not a relationship.'

He sighed. 'Business is my term of reference, Ella. It's what I'm good at.'

What about love? Though she dared not ask that. 'Rico, you do realise that this whole thing scares me as much as it scares you?'

'I'm not scared.'

She coughed. 'You promised me that you'd never lie to me again.'

He sighed. 'I know. And I told you more this afternoon than I've ever told anyone. I'm all out of words. This is the best I can offer right now, Ella.'

What choice did she have? She already knew she was in too deep. That walking away from him now would break her heart. The only thing she could do was to try with him. To teach him how to give the love that nobody had ever given him.

He'd try his best. She knew that—he'd already told her he didn't intend to be the kind of father either of them had had. But was his heart too damaged to let him be who they both wanted him to be?

'So you'll move in with me—see how it goes?'

'Do I have a choice?'

'Sure you do. You can stay in your ivory tower.'

That made him laugh. 'Ella. This isn't going to be easy for either of us. I'm not used to sharing my space. And I'm really not used to living in a broom cupboard.'

'Don't you think you can slum it for a bit, rich boy?'

'I'm definitely not answering that.' To her relief, there was a flicker of amusement in his voice. 'I'll see you later, *bellezza*. And I'll bring my suitcase.'

'Thank you.' She managed to wait until she'd put the phone down before she started crying.

Rico was going to try it her way.

And she hoped to hell they were doing the right thing.

CHAPTER THIRTEEN

TRUE to his word, Rico moved into Ella's flat that evening, and he was the one to commute to work in the mornings. He didn't make a single complaint about how small her flat was or suggest again that they should move back to The Fountain. Ella wasn't sure whether to be more relieved or surprised that he'd capitulated so easily. Did this mean that he was going to give them a real chance?

And it felt odd to be sharing her home again. To wake in the night to find a male body curled round hers. To have his razor jostling on the bathroom shelf with her hand scrub, his toothbrush next to hers in the mug, his suits next to hers in the wardrobe.

If they could make this work, then maybe her world would all come right again.

If they couldn't…

No. That wasn't an option. Somehow, she had to break through his barriers so they could make this work between them. Somehow, she needed to teach him that it was safe to love. And then it would be safe for her to love him, too.

But over the next couple of weeks she noticed that, despite their physical closeness, Rico was putting more emotional barriers up between them. Was she simply being paranoid, or was there a trapped look in his eyes? She didn't have a clue what was going on in his head, but she was pretty sure it had to do with what he'd told her about his childhood. Telling her had clearly made him feel vulnerable, and he was guarding himself again.

Didn't he know by now that he could trust her? That she'd never, ever hurt him? That she wasn't like his mother or the girlfriends in his past?

He bought her flowers. He always asked her about her day. He checked that she wasn't too tired or feeling sick. He was the perfect, solicitous partner. But if she asked him anything more personal, he'd make a vague comment and switch the conversation away from himself. And his stock response to everything was, 'I'm fine.' Even when she was damned sure he wasn't.

Still she tried to get through to him. 'How was your day?' she asked.

'Fine. I need to go back to Rome,' he said.

She froze. Did he mean for always, or just to sort out some business? He'd once told her that Rome was the only place he ever wanted to live. And she hadn't thought about whether he'd expect to move back to Rome once the baby was born, or even before that when he'd finished his business in London. 'Right,' she said carefully.

'I'll be away for three or four days.'

Not for always, then. Relief flooded through her. 'OK,' she said. Was he going to ask her to go with him?

'Will you be all right on your own while I'm away?' he asked.

That answered her question. He obviously didn't want her with him. She tried to shrug the hurt aside. 'Sure. I'm a big girl. I can look after myself,' she said brightly.

But she wondered. Would absence make Rico's heart grow fonder, or would it give him the space and time to realise that he was never going to be able to do this?

* * *

Home.

He was *home*.

Rico knew he was supposed to be feeling glad to be back in Rome, but instead he felt as if he were a stranger. He didn't really belong in the city any more. Plus that weird feeling of something being missing in his life, the one he hadn't been able to shake after Ella left but he hadn't felt since he'd been in London—that was back, big time.

And he knew why.

Because Ella wasn't here with him.

Which was ridiculous. He was going to be away on business for three or four days. Hardly any time at all. Why on earth was he missing her so badly? And so soon?

He tried dealing with it the way he always dealt with things—by blocking it out with work. Except it failed. Everywhere he looked, he saw families. Babies. Women carrying a newborn in a sling, men giving toddlers a ride on their shoulders. New parents sharing the joy of their children.

The thought slid insidiously through his head, tempting him. That was what life could be like with Ella and their baby. It didn't have to be the way his childhood had been. He just had to be brave enough to trust her with himself. To tell her that he loved her, and he was so scared that he was going to get it wrong and mess it up because he didn't have a clue how to love.

He wanted it. He wanted it so damned badly.

But he couldn't find the right words to tell her.

The first day he was away, Rico sent Ella flowers. Gorgeous summery flowers, sweet-smelling stocks and exuberant daisies and beautiful blush-pink roses. She didn't want to disturb him while he was in a meeting, so instead she took a photograph of the flowers on her phone and sent it to him with the message, *Thank you, they're gorgeous.*

His reply, a couple of hours later, was short and to the point. *Prego.*

You're welcome. That didn't bode well, she thought with a sigh. Or maybe she was reading too much into it. He was busy. At least he'd taken the time to acknowledge her text.

Though she noticed that he was too busy to call her even for two minutes.

OK. She could deal with this. As she'd said to him, she was an adult and she could look after herself.

The second day, he sent her chocolates. And a seriously nasty thought hit her. Was Rico choosing the gifts, or had he delegated the task to his secretary? Particularly as his only contact with her was a brief text message in reply to her thanks for the chocolates, saying he hoped she was OK.

On the third day, there was a delivery of a blu-ray disc of a film she'd mentioned casually that she'd like to see. She smiled wryly. She didn't actually have a blu-ray player, though she didn't quite have the heart to tell him that his gift had misfired. He'd listened enough to get the film right; it wasn't his fault that she hadn't upgraded the format. Although she really, really wanted to hear his voice, Rico had made it pretty clear that he was communicating by text only while he was away, so she tried not to mind and sent him a text to thank him.

'How did you know Sofia was the right one for you?' Rico asked his best friend, turning his wine glass round in his hands. He couldn't look Giuseppe in the eye. They never talked about this sort of thing, about emotions and love and family. But Rico really needed to know, and his best friend was about the only person he could ask. *How* did you know someone was the right one for you?

'Because life without her was unthinkable,' Giuseppe replied simply.

Yeah. That worked for him, too. Life without Ella... He'd been without her for three days and he was a total mess. He couldn't wait to get back to London. Back to *her*.

'Why are you asking? Is this the woman you borrowed the plane for?'

This time, Rico met his gaze head on. 'Yes.'

'It's serious, then.' Giuseppe raised an eyebrow. 'I never thought I'd see the day. Are you OK?'

'Yes.' But Giuseppe had known him for years. And he was the only person Rico had let close to him. The only one Rico trusted, or he would never have started this conversation in the first place. 'No.' He sighed. 'I hate this, Seppe. I don't feel in control any more.'

'Sounds about right,' Giuseppe said. 'If it helps, it does get better.'

'Does it?' Rico wasn't so sure. 'And what if I get it wrong?'

'Then you learn to apologise. Flowers and chocolates usually work.'

Rico smiled wryly. 'I've already sent them.'

'And the words?' Giuseppe asked. 'Because that's what Sofia expects more than anything. The words.'

'What words?' Sofia asked, coming in and leaning on her husband's shoulder.

Giuseppe stretched up to kiss her. *'Ti voglio molto bene.'*

She smiled. 'I love you very much too, Seppe.' She looked at Rico. 'I only caught the last few words, but does this mean you've finally stopped dating those awful women and you've found yourself someone nice?'

That wasn't the half of it. He decided to cut to the chase. 'How do you two feel about being godparents?'

Sofia's jaw dropped. 'You're kidding! You…baby… You…'

He'd never seen his best friend's wife lost for words before. Sofia could talk the hind leg off a donkey. Rico grinned. 'Yes. I'm going to be a dad.' It was the first time he'd said the words out loud. And something cracked inside him; his skin felt too tight. As if he were going to burst with love and pride.

Ella was having their baby. And the world, which had seemed so messed-up the last few weeks, tilted and righted itself. Except everything was different. Like walking from a monochrome into full, vibrant colour. Because the woman he loved was giving him the most precious gift in the world. And now he knew what to tell her.

'I was intending just to offer to get you two some more wine and leave you both to another boring conversation about cars,' Sofia said, 'but not now.' She took a glass from the cupboard and topped up their glasses as well as filling her own. 'I want to know *everything.*'

'Uh.' Panicked, Rico looked to Giuseppe to rescue him.

Giuseppe simply spread his hands. 'You heard the lady.' He smiled. 'I want to know, too. But I do know one thing. She has to be special.'

Rico frowned. 'Why?'

'To make you fall in love with her. Because you always keep people at a distance—even us, to some extent,' Giuseppe said gently.

'Yes, she's special. And yes, I love her.' Actually saying

the words made him feel a whole lot better. Rico smiled. 'OK. You want to know about my Ella *bellezza*. I'll tell you.'

Later that evening, when the horn beeping outside signalled the arrival of Rico's taxi, Sofia hugged him. 'Stay happy,' she said. 'And next time you come to Rome, bring Ella with you.'

'Or you could come to London to meet her. I know a nice little hotel where you could stay,' he said with a smile. 'And bring the children. I know some places they'll love.'

Giuseppe patted his shoulder. 'I never thought I'd hear something like *that* from you. But it's good. You've finally put the past where it belongs. And, for what it's worth, I think you're going to be a great dad.'

'Not perfect,' Rico said. He knew he was very far from perfect.

'Nobody's perfect,' Sofia said gently. 'Just do your best. That'll be good enough.'

Rico only hoped that she was right.

Back at the hotel, he glanced at his watch. Even allowing for the time difference, it was late. And pregnancy had made Ella sleepy. It wouldn't be fair to ring her and wake her up, just to tell her that he loved her. He didn't want to say it in a text, either. These were words he needed to tell her out loud. In the end, he just sent her a text. *Back tomorrow.*

And in the morning he'd make time to go shopping. For something he should've bought her weeks ago.

This was the fourth day without a single word. Rico hadn't even sent her a text today.

Ella had to face it. He wasn't ever going to be able to

love her. Sure, he'd sent her gifts—thoughtful gifts—but that wasn't what she wanted. She wanted his heart, and he'd never be able to give it to her.

Which meant their marriage was going to be loveless.

Promise me you won't make the same mistakes I did, Ella.

Falling for a man who couldn't love her back? A good man, but nevertheless that was exactly what she'd done. So very, very stupid.

No way could she marry him. And, even though she knew he was probably busy, in a meeting or something, she needed to tell him.

But when she called, his phone went straight through to voicemail.

She knew she should leave it until she spoke to him in person. Doing this by voicemail was utterly selfish. But she also knew she was weak, where he was concerned. If she left it until she saw him, she might not have the courage to tell him how she felt. And that wasn't fair on either of them. 'Rico, it's Ella. I'm sorry. I can't do this. Obviously you'll have access to the baby, if you want it— we'll sort that out so it's fair for all of us—but I'm sorry, I can't marry you.'

When she hung up, she drew her knees up to her chin and wrapped her arms round her legs. Though she couldn't cry. Sometimes pain went way too deep for tears.

Rico was glad he'd brought next to nothing back to London with him. Just one piece of hand luggage and his laptop case. He would've gone crazy if he'd had to wait at baggage reclaim.

Customs seemed to take for ever.

But finally he was through. He switched his phone on, intending to ring Ella and tell her he'd be home in less than an hour, when his phone beeped to let him know there was a voicemail.

Well, it could wait. Ella was more important.

But her mobile phone was switched off, and there was no answer from her landline. That meant she was either up to her eyes in the kitchen, or she was out on a delivery and had forgotten to switch her mobile on. She'd become incredibly scatty over the last couple of weeks and had to leave herself sticky notes all over the place.

Smiling at the thought, he listened to the voicemail. And his blood went cold.

I can't marry you.

What?

Why?

He tried her mobile again, and her landline, still with no result.

Oh, hell. He needed to see her, find out what was going on. Why couldn't she marry him? A seriously nasty thought struck him. Had she met someone else? No. Ella wasn't like that. Though she'd said that her ex had talked her round before. Had he talked her round again? Was Ella still in love with him?

He drove too fast on the way back to London, and only a near miss when someone pulled out in front of him made him slow down. It felt like for ever until his key was unlocking the front door, and he took the stairs up to the flat two at a time.

She wasn't there.

And her mobile phone was *still* switched off.

He paced the flat. Made himself coffee. Paced the flat. Tried her phone again. Paced the flat. And he was a hair's-breadth away from going insane when he heard the front door being unlocked.

Thank God. She was home. And they could sort this mess out.

She looked wary when she saw him. 'Rico. I didn't know when you were going to be back.'

'I should've told you. I'm sorry.'

She swallowed hard. 'Did you…did you get my message?'

'Yes.' And it hurt like hell. 'Why can't you marry me, Ella?'

'Because I've had time to think while you were away. You didn't call me—and I don't think you're ever going to be able to love me. I can't handle a loveless marriage.' Tears shimmered in her eyes. 'I'm sorry. I won't ever fight you, the way your mum fought your dad. I want you to be as much a part of the baby's life as you want to be. But I can't do this any more. I can't pretend everything's OK. And I'm not going to make the same mistake my mum made, falling for someone who's never going to love me back.'

Never going to love me back.

Those words gave him the courage that her voicemail had leached away. She loved him. Right now, she didn't believe in him, but that was his own fault for holding back. And he could do something about that.

'You're not making your mother's mistake,' he said. 'You *haven't* fallen for someone who doesn't love you back. You've fallen for someone who's totally rubbish at emotions and who isn't very good at telling you how he feels. But I'm going to try to change that, Ella. I'll need your help, but I swear to you I'm going to try my hardest.'

She stared at him as if he were speaking Martian.

He frowned. 'I'm speaking English, yes? Not rambling on in Italian?'

That made her smile. 'You never ramble, Rico.'

'Maybe I should learn.' He couldn't stand being apart from her any more. He closed the space between them and wrapped his arms round her. 'I'm going to need help with this. I've never told anyone I loved them before. Opening myself up like this—it feels weird. Scary. As if I'm standing on the edge of a precipice and someone's about to shove me over. But I love you, Ella. I really do.' He pulled away so he could look her in the eye. 'It scares me to death. I'm so scared of failing you. But I love you.'

'Really?' Her eyes were full of tears.

'I love you and I want to be with you. And our baby.' He rested his hand protectively on her abdomen. 'I don't exactly have good role models when it comes to parenting. Except Sofia and Seppe—and Sofia tells me that nobody's perfect and my best will be good enough.'

'Sofia?'

Was it his imagination, or did she sound just the tiniest bit jealous? 'My best friend's wife. And I have a confession to make.' He dragged in a breath. 'I, um, asked them to be godparents, just as I'm godfather to their children. Except they'll be better at it than I am. Do you mind?'

She blinked. 'You told them about me? And the baby?'

'Everything. They already know you're special.' He smiled. 'Seppe says for me to let anyone close, she has to be seriously special. And you are.'

She swallowed hard. 'You really love me?'

'I've been trying to tell myself I didn't. When I looked you up in London, it was to prove to myself that what we had was just sex.'

'Acquaintances with benefits.'

He grimaced. 'You're so much more than that to me. I was in denial even then. The very fact I had to prove to myself that you weren't special—well, it was because deep down I knew you *were*.' He blew out a breath. 'And

Rome—Rome isn't home to me any more. I hated being there without you.'

'Why didn't you ask me to go with you?'

'Because I didn't even want to admit to myself that I needed you. But I do need you, Ella.' He stroked her face. 'And I'm sorry. I should've told you that first day I was away. But I didn't know how to say it. And I didn't want to send you a text.'

'You sent me flowers.'

'The nearest I've ever got to love in the past is expensive presents. And I know that's not what love's about. I got it so badly wrong. Will you give me another chance, *bellezza?*'

A tear trickled down her cheek. 'You love me.'

'And our baby. I can't wait to be a dad. And I can't wait to marry you. I know you said you couldn't marry me, but that was when you thought I didn't love you. Now you know I do…will you change your mind?'

Ella could hardly believe what she was hearing. Was she dreaming? Imagining the words she'd so longed to hear from him?

'I went shopping this morning. For something important. I know you've been here before—but I'm not Michael. I'm not going to cheat on you. I'm not going to lie to you. And I might need reminding to open up to you, but I'm going to try my hardest to make you happy. To make you know how very, very much I love you.' He dropped down on one knee in front of her and drew a box from his pocket; he opened it to reveal a very simple band of diamonds in what looked to her like platinum.

She gasped. 'It's like the Sisi star you bought me, all sparkly—it's beautiful.'

'I'm glad you like it, because I need to ask you something. Last time, I got it wrong. I demanded. This time, I'm going to do it properly. I want to do it right.' He took her hand. 'Will you marry me, Ella? And I need you to know that I don't want to marry you just because of the baby. I want to marry you because of *you*. Because my life's a lot better with you in it. And you make me whole.'

She felt the tears gather in her eyes. 'Oh, Rico.'

'And I want to make sure that our baby knows from their very first breath that they're loved for who they are. Just as I love you for who you are, and you love me the same way—at least, I hope you do.' His breath caught. 'And I'm not good at this stuff, so I'm going to need your help in getting it right. I need you, Ella. I love you.'

She blinked the tears back. 'I love you, too. I love you for who you are. I don't give a damn about your money or your status or any of that rubbish. It's you I love. If you lost everything tomorrow, and my business went under, we'd still cope.' She stroked his face. 'Yes. I'll marry you, Rico. I'll be proud to marry you. And…' She took a deep breath. 'If you really need to go back to Rome, I'll go with you.'

'I can be based anywhere. If you want to stay in London, we'll stay here. Or we can live in Rome. Vienna. Even Timbuktu!' He kissed her. 'It doesn't matter where we live, as long as we're together. You were absolutely right. It doesn't matter whether we live in a broom cupboard in London or half the top floor of a posh hotel in Rome. It's being together that matters. You've taught me that and I'll never, ever forget it.'

He meant it. She knew he meant every single word.

And she also knew that she could trust him, and he'd never let her down. 'You've taught me a lot, too. You've made me see that not all men are liars. Well, I knew they weren't, but you know what I mean. You've taught me that it's safe to rely on you, because you'll never let me down.'

He slipped the ring onto the third finger of her left

hand. 'And there's a lot we've still got to learn. But we'll get there, because we'll be learning together.'

'Together,' she echoed with a smile.

And she knew that, as long as they had each other, everything was going to work out just fine.

* * * * *

THE MORETTI
SEDUCTION

KATHERINE GARBERA

USA TODAY bestselling author **Katherine Garbera** is a two-time Maggie winner who has written more than sixty books. A Florida native who grew up to travel the globe, Katherine now makes her home in the Midlands of the UK with her husband, two children and a very spoiled miniature dachshund. Visit her on the web at katherinegarbera.com, connect with her on Facebook and follow her on Twitter @katheringarbera.

One

The corporate offices of Moretti Motors were lush and exquisite, combining the best of Italian architecture with the cutting edge of modern design. No expense was spared in the five-story office building in Milan or in the state-of-the-art factory next door where the fastest and priciest production car in the world would soon start rolling off the line.

The only problem was a little sticking point with the name of the car. The Moretti Motors engineering team had reenvisioned the classic and most-talked-about model they had ever made—a 1969 sport roadster that had taken the sports car world by storm and made Lorenzo Moretti a billionaire. Now forty years later they were reintroducing the world to the Vallerio—the car named after the second Formula 1 driver to race for Moretti Motors.

The rights to the name were in question, something that Dominic, Antonio and Marco—the current generation of Morettis—hadn't realized until they had sent out a press release announcing their new car and gotten a cease-and-desist order from Vallerio Inc.

Pierre-Henri Vallerio had started the company after leaving Moretti Motors. Pierre-Henri had been a genius with engine design, and Vallerio Inc. was still at the forefront of that industry today. So it seemed to Antonio that they should be excited to have their name on the tongues of car aficionados everywhere.

The only problem was, as with everything that Antonio's grandfather Lorenzo touched, he'd somehow managed to piss off the Vallerio family.

"Do you ever wonder if *Nono* just had no mojo when it came to women?" Antonio asked his older brother, Dominic.

Dominic was the head of Moretti Motors operations. His title was CEO but he'd always been bossy even when they had been kids.

"The thought has crossed my mind a time or two.

Regardless of what his problem was, he left us a mess to inherit, didn't he?"

"You like the challenge of unraveling his messes," Antonio said. Dom was one of those men who lived for work. Bringing Moretti Motors back to the forefront of the auto world wasn't an easy thing to do. But a challenge like this latest wrinkle with the Vallerio family wouldn't ruffle his older brother. Nor him.

"We need the Vallerio family on board—yesterday."

"I know. It would have been much easier to handle it if we had realized that the rights to the name reverted to them. I mean, who would have signed a contract that said after twenty years of no production car we lost those rights?" Antonio asked.

"Papa," Dominic said.

Their father was a wonderful man and the best father in the world, but when it came to business, Giovanni Moretti just didn't care. Which was why he and his brothers had grown up the poorer relations of the Moretti family.

"Well, I have a meeting scheduled with the attorney." Antonio closed the file folder. The family's attorney was the older daughter, Nathalie Vallerio. From her corporate photo he'd sensed a keen intelligence, as well as an innate beauty that reflected her family's French heritage.

"Good," Dom said. "With Marco falling for Virginia, I'm afraid that our luck may be changing. I don't want to let anything compromise the new production car."

Antonio didn't know if his brother's falling in love with the granddaughter of the woman who'd originally cursed the family was going to change their luck or not. Antonio had never put much stock in luck.

The curse had been put on their grandfather by his onetime lover Cassia Festa. Lorenzo had spurned her love and Cassia, being a Strega—an Italian witch—had gone home and spent days getting angrier and angrier at Lorenzo. When Lorenzo decided to marry Pierre-Henri Vallerio's sister, Cassia had come back to Milan and put a curse on Lorenzo. The words of the curse had been written in her diary, and Virginia, Cassia's granddaughter, had figured out a way to break the curse. Antonio recalled the curse. No Moretti male would ever be lucky in business *and* lucky in love.

Antonio's father had no head for business—hence this mess with Vallerio Inc. But Gio had fallen in love with Philomena and those two had found a deep love and happiness in their life.

He and his brothers had grown up realizing they could be either wealthy or happy in love. Being practical boys, they had taken an oath long ago not to mess things up the way their grandfather had. That meant that they would be lucky in business and not risk falling in love and losing everything they worked to build.

Antonio had found that determination and drive covered what luck didn't. That and his refusal to accept defeat. His entire life he'd never lost at anything once he put his mind to it. And he certainly wasn't about to let Nathalie Vallerio win this battle.

"No problem. The Vallerio family will sign our agreement and I'll bring you back the contract."

Dom rubbed the back of his neck. "I don't need to tell you this, but I won't feel right unless I say it."

Dom rarely worried about the effect of his words, so Antonio raised one eyebrow at him in question. Whatever was on his brother's mind must be something outside the bounds of morality or business ethics. Though at times they'd considered doing things that were in that shadowy gray area, they never had.

Antonio believed that with his determination, Marco's racing talent and Dom's drive, the Moretti brothers didn't need to do anything shady.

"Are you still worried about the corporate espionage?" he asked his brother. They had first realized there was a leak of proprietary information last year at the start of the Grand Prix season. Somehow their main rivals, ESP Motors, had announced an engine intake that was exactly the same as the one that Moretti Motors had been working on for the previous six months.

"I think we can find our leak without doing anything illegal," Antonio said.

"Tony! I'm not going to ask you to do anything illegal. I have got a lead on our corporate spy."

"Then what were you going to ask me?"

Dom leaned over his desk, both arms resting on the dark walnut finish. "Use any means necessary, Tony. If you have to seduce her, then do it. Women like romance."

"Comments like that are the reason why you are single."

Dom made a rude hand gesture, but Tony just laughed. His brother was a great businessman and a natural leader, but when it came to women, Dom didn't trust them and he treated them like disposable commodities. Tony knew that was because of Liza, the woman whom Dom had loved and lost.

There was a knock on the door and Dom bade the person to enter. It was his secretary, Angelina de Luca.

"Sorry to interrupt, Signore Moretti, but the Vallerio family is here for Signore Antonio."

"*Grazie,* Angelina. Please direct them to the conference room and get them some refreshments."

Angelina nodded and left the room. Dom watched his secretary leave and Tony wondered to himself if his big brother wasn't as immune to women as he appeared to be.

"You know, with Marco's engagement to Virginia, it might not be a change in our business luck, only our love luck."

Dom shook his head. "For you maybe but not me. I think I have *Nono*'s bad woman mojo."

Tony laughed and stood, clapping his brother on the back.

"I don't have that mojo. And Ms. Nathalie Vallerio," Tony said, looking back down at her photo in the folder, "isn't going to know what hit her."

"Buon!"

Nathalie Vallerio had heard all about the Moretti family. Her earliest memories were of her grandfather and father plotting to bring down Lorenzo Moretti. The man was a legendary race car driver who was one of only four drivers to win the Grand Prix championship numerous times. The only person to win more championships was another Moretti. Marco.

And now she was sitting in the lion's den. Back in the one place her grandfather had vowed that no Vallerio would ever stand again. For being her personal hell, the boardroom was quite comfortable.

There was a trophy case at the end of the room with all the Formula 1 racing trophies won by the Moretti drivers, including the ones her grandfather had earned.

On another wall hung photos of the Moretti drivers and of their production cars. They were all good-looking men who had an air about them that seemed to say life was one big adventure. Her grandfather, Pierre-Henri, had always taken great pride that the bestselling production car had borne his name. And of course when Lorenzo broke Nathalie's great-aunt's heart and caused her to die early of heartbreak, Pierre-Henri had done everything in his power to see that Lorenzo no longer had use of the Vallerio name.

Lorenzo's son Giovanni had let the rights to the name lapse in the late '80s and since then Moretti Motors had floundered. But recently under the helm of Dominic, Antonio and Marco the company had resurged and was once again on the verge of taking the car world by storm.

Something that Nathalie was here to make certain they did without involving her family or their name.

She paced around the room, well aware that Antonio was keeping her waiting. Their appointment was supposed to have begun five minutes ago.

One of her pet peeves was tardiness. Disrespect

was the only reason Antonio was keeping her waiting and she would make sure he understood that she wasn't someone to toy with.

"*Ciao*, Signorina Vallerio. I am sorry to have kept you waiting."

She turned to see Antonio Moretti striding toward her. With dark curly hair and classic Roman features, he was quite striking. But that wasn't what held her attention. It was the intelligence and humor she saw in his obsidian eyes. This was a man who made her catch her breath—and that wasn't like her.

She lifted her hand to shake his and then realized that she'd been doing business with Americans for too long. She'd forgotten that Italians always greeted with a kiss on the cheek.

Antonio took her hand and pulled her close. The woodsy scent of his aftershave was intoxicating as he dropped a brief, warm kiss on her cheek. She stood transfixed feeling as if it were her first time in a boardroom.

All because of a handsome face, she thought, disgusted with herself and so very glad that her sister Genevieve wasn't here to see this.

In Antonio's eyes she saw a hint that he knew how he'd rattled her. She forced herself to kiss his cheek and totally ignored the fact that the five o'clock shadow on his jaw made her lips tingle.

She stepped back and retrieved her hand. "I only have twenty minutes to talk to you, Signore Moretti."

"Then I had better talk fast," he said with a grin.

She fought to keep her face stoic. She could see that he was charming. He wasn't trying hard; he just seemed unflappable.

She was too. She had spent her entire life being the reliable sister. The one that her father and grandfather could count on. She wasn't going to be a disappointment to them the way her great-aunt Anna had been when she'd lost Lorenzo's attention and the family name.

"I don't really see the point to this meeting. As you know, Moretti Motors has resigned all rights to the Vallerio name when you let that contract lapse. At this time we aren't inclined to license it to you again."

"You have not even heard what we are offering."

"I don't need to. You have nothing we want," Nathalie said. But she was interested in hearing what they were offering. Even her father thought that the Morettis must realize that they couldn't come to the bargaining table without offering substantial compensation. Her father wanted a half share in Moretti Motors. To be honest, Nathalie was confident they'd never go for that and she thought this entire exercise was one big time waster.

But she was here because her father had asked her to try to get this deal on the table. That was the problem with family feuds, she thought. There were never really any winners. No matter what deal she and Antonio negotiated.

"Are you sure about that? Everyone wants something they can't have," Antonio said.

"Well, if they can't have it, then they are just asking for frustration," Nathalie said.

"*Touché.* But I'm offering you whatever you want."

"Anything, Signore Moretti?"

"*Sì*, Nathalie. But you are going to have to do something before we can go any further with these negotiations."

Nathalie liked the way he said her name. The Americans she was used to dealing with didn't know the right emphasis to place on it the way Antonio did. "What is that?"

"You must stop calling me Signore Moretti. I am Antonio to my business associates and Tony to my intimates."

"Very well, Antonio."

He laughed and she found herself smiling. She liked this man and she hadn't expected to. From reputation she knew he usually won most of his corporate encounters, but then so did she and she'd expected him to be like other men.

She was pleasantly surprised to see that he wasn't. She had to remember that he was being charming for only one reason. He wanted something from her and he wasn't planning on taking no for an answer.

Antonio seldom met a woman he couldn't easily charm, but then he seldom met a woman who blinded him with only her smile. It didn't matter that there was something about Nathalie that said she saw through him. He tried to keep his eyes on business, but all he could think of was how soft her skin had felt when he'd shaken her hand and kissed her cheek.

He wanted to kiss her lips, to feel that full lush mouth under his. Every time she spoke he felt a little jab as she no doubt intended him to. He'd known from the moment he set up this meeting that negotiations between the Vallerio family and the Moretti family weren't going to be easy.

All of the research he'd done on Nathalie had helped him form the opinion that this was a woman who wasn't going to be easily swayed by charm.

Seduction, as Dom had suggested, wouldn't work either. She was too smart and she watched him carefully, adjusting her plan of action to fit his.

"Have a seat, Nathalie. And we will see if I can't find something the Vallerio family will take in exchange for letting us use the name that your grandfather made famous."

Nathalie brushed past him, her scent clean and re-freshing, and sat down at the head of the table. He bit the inside of his cheek to keep from smiling. It was obvious to him that she was used to being in charge.

He was the type of man who didn't like to let anyone take the lead. But he knew sitting at the head of the table didn't give one power. Power came from the person who wielded it.

Nathalie too knew that, he suspected. She'd learned it from her grandfather. Pierre-Henri Vallerio was a proud French F1 driver who loved racing, de-signing cars and, at the end of his life, anything that would upset Lorenzo Moretti—the man who had once been his best friend and his teammate on the F1 circuit for Team Moretti.

"Antonio, we do want something from Moretti Motors," she said.

"Of course you do," he said. "I'm here to make sure we both get what we want."

"*Bien.* Vallerio Incorporated wants half share in all of the profits from Moretti Motors and seventy percent of the profit from the Vallerio production model. We also want the right to change the styling of the Vallerio trademark."

Antonio shook his head. "I said we'd negotiate, not give away everything my brothers and I have worked to rebuild. What we are offering is a share in the profits from the Vallerio model and a seat on the board for the head of Vallerio Incorporated."

"Êtes-vous fou?"

"No, I'm not crazy. We think this offer is very generous."

She shook her head. "Of course you do. You are used to holding all the cards, but in this case, you must realize that you do not. Without the Vallerio name, you cannot release your new production car."

"Of course we can, Nathalie. We'd just have to rename it, which we are prepared to do if need be," Antonio said. He wasn't lying. It was a car that everyone talked about.

And they wanted to recapture the magic that *Nono* had first discovered with Moretti Motors.

"Then I suggest you start redesigning your car. As you know you can't use the name or any likeness to the original Vallerio Roadster."

She pushed to her feet and reached for her designer leather briefcase and he knew that this woman wasn't going to be an easy opponent. And damn if that didn't excite the hell out of him.

"Nathalie, we are just starting our talks. There is no need to get up from the table yet."

She shook her head, that beautiful red hair swinging gently around the shoulders of her conservative black Chanel suit that accented her curves. "Are you willing to meet our terms?"

"No, I am not. We can talk about a small share of profits for your company, but it won't be fifty percent."

"I'm afraid that our terms aren't really negotiable," Nathalie said.

"Then why are you here? You know that we won't agree to give you that kind of money."

"You asked for this meeting, Antonio. No one on the board at Vallerio Incorporated cares much for Moretti Motors. They would rather have Grandfather's name drop into obscurity than license its use to your family."

Antonio leaned back in the leather chair and thought about Nathalie. He couldn't keep just turning on the charm and hoping that would crack her composure.

She was smart and willing to stand her ground, so that meant he was going to have to reevaluate how he dealt with her.

"Why are you staring at me like that?" she asked. She rubbed her fingers over her lips and then tucked a strand of hair behind her ear.

"Am I staring?"

She tipped her head to the side. "You know you are."

"Indeed I am. I am looking for a chink in your

armor. Trying to figure out what makes you tick," he said, knowing that honesty was a very powerful tool in the boardroom because so many of his opponents often felt the virtue overrated.

She nibbled on her lower lip. "I don't have any chinks."

He threw his head back and laughed at her bravado. Damn, but he liked this woman. If she wasn't a Vallerio he'd even ask her out, but he knew that his family and hers had bad karma between them. And despite what he'd said to Dom earlier, he didn't want to take the chance that *Nono*'s bad woman mojo might touch him.

"I like the way you laugh," she said.

"Really? Why is that?"

"It makes you seem human."

He wanted to laugh again. "I am human, Nathalie. Do not ever doubt that."

"Well, your reputation would say otherwise."

"What does my reputation say about me?"

She leaned forward, bracing her arms on the table. The movement caused her blouse to hang away from her skin and he saw the briefest hint of the curve of her breast. He wondered if he should follow Dom's advice and seduce Nathalie—not to win the negotiation but because he wanted her.

"Well, the gossip about is that you are cold-blooded when it comes to business."

"I've heard the same thing about you," he said. And he had. She was known as the Ice Queen, and men that had dealt with Vallerio Incorporated spoke of her in unkind terms, often using words like *bitch*.

"That simply isn't true," she said.

"Then what is the truth about you?" he asked.

"I just believe that all is fair in love and war," she said.

"Me too."

"Well, then we are evenly matched and I'd say let the war begin."

Two

Nathalie knew exactly how she'd come to be sitting at Cracco Peck on Via Victor Hugo in the City Centre of Milan later that evening. She'd never met a man who was uniquely suited to her. But Antonio was.

He was smart, savvy and sexy as hell and she knew that no matter what the outcome, she was going to enjoy her negotiations with him. She liked being with him because unlike the previous lawyers she had dealt with, he didn't seem to resent that she was a strong woman.

He was several yards away talking to the chef-owner, Carlo Cracco, which allowed her to study him unabashedly. He had an easy way about him, and she realized the charm that she'd first noticed in the Moretti conference room was a part of him, not something he turned on strictly for women.

"Nathalie?"

She smiled as she stood up to greet an old family friend, Fredrico Marchessi.

"*Buona sera,* Fredrico," she said, kissing him warmly on the cheek. He had been at the university with her father. "Is Maria with you?"

"I'm afraid not. This is a business trip for me."

"For me as well," she said.

"With the Moretti family?"

"*Oui,* Fredrico."

"Your father is worried about this," Fredrico said.

Nathalie got annoyed at the way Fredrico talked to her as if she were still twelve. She'd been successfully handling the Vallerio family business for a number of years now.

"Papa knows he can trust me to do what is right by our family."

"*Bien,* Nathalie. We must have dinner when you are back in Paris."

"*Bien sur.* I will call your office."

Fredrico left and she felt a hand on her back as she started to sit back down. Antonio was back at their table.

"Nathalie, allow me to introduce you to Carlo Cracco."

They exchanged pleasantries and then the chef left and she was alone with Antonio at the intimate table for two.

"I am sorry for leaving you alone."

"It's okay," she said. "I'm not your date."

"And if you were?"

"Well, then I'd expect you to not leave me alone. A woman deserves to be the center of her man's attention."

"What does a man deserve?"

"The same thing."

"Are you a romantic?" he asked.

She shook her head. "No. I just don't believe in wasting my personal time with someone who's not worth it."

He gave her that crooked grin, revealing his straight white teeth. "Another point we agree on."

She shrugged one shoulder, trying not to acknowledge that Antonio was the kind of man she didn't believe existed. Someone who could be her equal in the boardroom and out of it. "What did your chef friend recommend for dinner?"

"I've never been disappointed with anything I've ordered here. My favorite dish is salt-crusted sole and dark chocolate crochettes with caviar."

She pretended to study the menu. This meeting was supposed to be about the Vallerio family. She had to concentrate and keep reminding herself that her family had been waiting for this moment for a long time. No matter how much she enjoyed the novelty of Antonio Moretti.

He was just that. A novelty. This was nothing more than a chance for her grandfather to even the score with Lorenzo Moretti, even though the latter was long gone from this world. Her grandfather wouldn't have a moment's peace until he knew that he'd been able to retrieve the honor that Lorenzo had swindled him out of.

"You look very serious, *mia cara.* Would it be so bad to let me recommend a dish for you?" He named two selections.

She looked up at him. "I see you are the type of man who will exploit any sign of weakness in your opponent."

"I thought we were beyond pointless shows of power."

Was that what he thought this was? She was always aware that she was a woman in a man's world and that she couldn't for a minute appear weak. She never cried, she didn't chat or laugh with the other women in the office and she certainly didn't let a man order for her at a business dinner. That was too feminine, too girly, and she knew a man's man like Antonio Moretti would see it as a sign of weakness.

"Thanks for the recommendations. I'll consider them."

He laughed. "You do that."

The wine steward arrived and Nathalie again felt the pressure of their roles. The steward automatically talked to Antonio about the wine selection, and even though he selected the exact vintage she would have chosen, she spoke up and picked something different.

Meals and drinks ordered, she sat back at the table and took control of this evening. "Tell me more about the Moretti Motors plans for the Vallerio model."

"I can only share so much information with you before we hammer out an arrangement. As I am sure you can understand, it's privileged."

"Of course. Tell me why we should even consider doing business with the Moretti family again. The last time we did my beloved great-aunt Anna was destroyed by her dealings with your grandfather and my own grandfather was swindled out of his share of the profits."

The feud between their families had at its heart the emotions of a young bride. Decades ago her *tante* Anna had married her brother's best friend—Lorenzo Moretti—and then found herself ignored and very unhappy. Lorenzo was a womanizer and Anna spent three miserable years married to him before she left him, something that Lorenzo didn't even realize for another six months. It was that treatment of Anna that had started the feud. When Anna divorced Lorenzo, something that left her ostracized from her devoutly Catholic community in Paris, Lorenzo had terminated production of the Vallerio Roadster, saying that he wouldn't share profits with a family that had betrayed him.

He felt Anna should have sucked up her hurt feelings and stayed with him.

"You make us sound like the Machiavellis. I assure you we aren't."

"Assurances are okay, Antonio, but I'd rather have some facts that I can take back to my board of directors."

"How about the fact that Vallerio Incorporated hasn't had a new innovation in the car world in over twenty years?"

"We know what our history is," she said. "We aren't in the automobile world anymore."

"Which is why you are here with me. The Vallerio-Moretti collaboration went all wrong last time. Our generation will be the ones to put both of our family names back into the limelight and give them the place in history they deserve."

* * *

Milan was vibrant and alive on this cool spring night and Antonio took a deep breath as he led Nathalie through the center of town to the Piazza del Duomo.

He knew the key to getting the Vallerio team to sign the deal was to break down the monster that his *nono* had become to them. And this square was the very place to do that.

"Why did you bring me here?" Nathalie asked. She seemed a little tired and a little leery.

He hoped to use that to his advantage. "I wanted you to understand why history is so important to us at Moretti Motors.

"I know that the Vallerio family harbors some bad feelings toward the Moretti family, but I believe that that stems simply from misunderstanding the man that my grandfather was."

Nathalie tipped her head to the side. Her red-gold hair swung against her shoulder and distracted him, made him want to touch the cool silky waves.

"Your grandfather may have had another side, but I doubt he showed it to anyone outside of the Moretti clan."

"Then let me tell you about him now."

Nathalie sighed. "Do you really believe this will make a difference?"

Antonio looked at her standing there in the moonlight and knew that even if it didn't he wanted to tell her about his family. He wanted to change the image she had in her head of the Morettis as the big bad guys. "When I was a boy I'd come to Milan to visit my *nono,* he'd bring me here to church every morning. He never missed a day."

"My *grandpere* was the same way. He said it was because God had blessed him on the racetrack," Nathalie said.

Antonio smiled to himself. *Nono* had told him how Pierre-Henri had been a devout man. It was one of the few positive things that *Nono* had ever mentioned about Pierre-Henri. Lorenzo Moretti had known from an early age that the Lord watched over him each time he got in his race car and attempted things no other man had ever done.

"See? We already have something in common."

She arched one eyebrow at him. "Really? That's the connection you are going to make?"

"In this battle, with the stakes being what they are, I'll start as small as I have to."

"Why do you want this so bad? As you said, Moretti Motors can rename the car."

"Because Moretti Motors' Vallerio Roadster is revered by car collectors all over the world. The demand for this model, the styling and racing lines that Lorenzo designed along with Pierre-Henri's engine design are legendary."

"So you do need us?" she asked.

"Maybe."

Antonio took Nathalie's hand and drew her closer to the cathedral. "Did you know that Duomo here has never really been completed?"

She shook her head. "I don't know that much about this church."

"I won't tell you the history, only that she is constantly being updated and added to. The church itself is never going to be finished because there is always some way to improve on its beauty, to improve on its function.

"It is the same for Moretti Motors. We are not content to sit around and think that we have accomplished one thing and that is enough. We must constantly change, constantly drive forward into the future. What we are offering you, Nathalie, and the entire Vallerio family and its investors is a chance to be a part of our drive to the future."

Nathalie drew her hand free of his. "You are a smooth talker, you know that, right?"

"*Sì,*" he said with a smile. "I think you like that about me."

"I like a lot about you, Antonio. But that doesn't

mean that I think doing business with your company would be in our best interests."

"Why not?" he asked.

She walked around the entrance to the cathedral. The statues that guarded it looked down upon them. This cathedral was one of the most famous in the world, the second largest to St. Peter's Basilica in Rome itself. Every Catholic in Milan was proud that this was their house of worship, and Antonio offered a quick prayer that God would make this moment a turning point for him and Moretti Motors.

"*Grandpere* used to say that Lorenzo was a smooth-tongued devil who had a way of seducing even the staunchest rival," she said. "And I can see now what he meant. I think you inherited Lorenzo's charm."

"You should meet my father."

"I guess all of the Moretti men have that gift. Do you know what we Vallerios have?"

"A gift for speed and a quest for knowledge," he said. The legacy of Pierre-Henri wasn't one that he took lightly. That was one of the main reasons why he, Marco and Dominic had decided to go this route. They could have taken an easier path with relaunching their production car, but the only car they wanted to relaunch was the Vallerio.

"We also have a way of seeing through the smoke and mirrors to the truth behind them," she said.

"Keep looking, Nathalie. There is nothing but truth and sincerity here. At Moretti Motors we want both of our companies to grow and prosper. We want both of our names to be remembered by history."

"You paint a pretty picture, Antonio, almost as pretty as this Gothic cathedral you've brought me to see, but I know that inside the walls of this place and behind the beauty of your offer lie more secrets."

"In the church perhaps, but I have laid all my cards on the boardroom table."

"Somehow I doubt that. It would leave you with nothing new to negotiate with."

He laughed at that. "Well, maybe I've kept one or two back."

"I have too. I'm not going to change my position tonight. To be honest I doubt we will ever be able to reach an agreement. There is too much bad blood between our families."

"But not between us. That was two stubborn old men who liked to argue. We are two young, vibrant people who know that there is more to life than fighting," Antonio said.

"Do we?"

"Yes, Nathalie, we do," he said, and drew her into his arms. "The night is young and so are we. Let's make the most of it."

* * *

At the end of the evening Antonio walked her back to her hotel. She was tired but pleasantly so. She had enjoyed the evening with him and she understood now what real charm was.

Her *grandpere* had been a brusque man by the time she'd gotten to know him, and a part of her was saddened by that. And she knew that the Moretti family—especially Lorenzo Moretti—was responsible for his bitterness.

But right now, as Antonio walked her to her room, that didn't seem to matter.

She knew starting an affair with Antonio Moretti was about the dumbest thing she could do. But she was so tempted.

They stood right outside her suite and though she had the feeling it would be unwise, she wanted to invite him in for a nightcap.

Antonio broke into her thoughts. "You are looking at me like I have something you want."

"You do."

"Name it and it is yours."

She tipped her head to the side. "Did you mean it when you said that all's fair in love and war?"

"Yes, I did."

"You aren't going to renege on that?"

"No, I'm not. Are you?"

"No. But I've found that men get mad when they don't win, regardless of what they've said before everything got going."

"I think you are trying to ask me if I'm going to act like a baby if I don't get my way. You should know that I am a man…not a boy."

She smiled at the way he said it. She knew Antonio was trying to seduce her. He wanted her to get to know the man behind the corporation and it was in her interest to do the same. Let him get to know the woman she was. Without that she'd never get the advantage over him.

"So, *bella mia*, are you going to tell me what you want?"

"Maybe."

"Maybe?"

"I think being mysterious has some benefits," she said.

"Indeed it does in a woman as beautiful as you."

She suspected that comment was at least seventy-five percent bullshit, but… "It's hard to resist such charm."

He laughed again, his deep, melodious tones wrapping around her in a dangerous way. She knew she needed to get rid of Antonio. She wasn't going to invite him in tonight, not after an evening of a full moon shining down over the city as she listened to him weave his tales of the past in that deeply erotic voice of his. Tonight she wasn't up to sparring with him.

Her plan was to let him think *he* seduced *her* and she wasn't sure yet if she could sleep with this man and keep her emotions at bay.

To be honest she'd never been able to do that.

"Good night, Antonio."

"I will see you first thing in the morning for a tour of the Moretti Motors facility."

"I'm not sure—"

"You already agreed to it," he said. "It will do you good to meet the people who have worked on the design of the Vallerio model. I think you should see the pride that our workers take in being part of that legendary car."

"I think you should stop referring to the car as the Vallerio."

"Of course. It's just that I feel that once you see this car you will change your mind."

His passion for the car and for the company was obvious and it made her realize she'd made the right choice in not inviting him into her room. She had to understand that with Antonio the company was always going to come first.

And Nathalie had a personal vow about men who were workaholics. She'd never get mixed up with one. Her father, uncles and grandfather all had been workaholics—and had been absent in the lives of their children and wives, something that Nathalie didn't want for her own life.

Not that she was thinking of having kids with Antonio. It was just that getting involved with a man when you knew you were destined to be second in his life was not a smart thing to do.

And she was a smart woman.

She met Antonio's gaze and nodded. "I like your confidence. Tomorrow we will see if you are simply bragging or if you have the goods."

He arched one eyebrow at her. "*Cara mia,* do I look like a man who doesn't have the goods?"

She shook her head. "I refuse to answer that on the grounds that no matter what answer I give you, you will take it as a positive."

Antonio shrugged his big shoulders. "I'm used to making everything into a positive. That is why Moretti Motors is where it is today."

"I'd heard that about you. That you never take no for an answer. Much like Lorenzo Moretti when he ran right over Anna Vallerio."

"That is very true about my not taking no for an answer. But I promise you, Nathalie, I'm not going to run over you or your family. This generation of Moretti Motors is committed to doing business differently."

He walked away on that note and she watched him leave. She wanted to believe his words, but at the end of the day Antonio was still a Moretti. And he was going to put those interests before her or her family.

Three

Antonio's mobile phone rang as soon as he pulled out of the parking lot of Nathalie's hotel. He glanced at the caller ID. Damn. His brother was very well connected in Milan—hell, they all were—but if Dom was seriously following his moves that closely, then there was more at stake than just the Vallerio car model.

"*Buona sera,* Dom."

"How'd the meeting with Ms. Vallerio go?"

Dom wasn't one of those guys who wasted time on small talk. There had been a leak in their office over the last year and though they had gotten closer to the snitch, they still hadn't found him. Something that Antonio knew annoyed Dom to no end.

"Fine."

"I'd say better than fine. Genaro said that you were upstairs with her for more than thirty minutes."

"Gee, Dom, I hope that you don't think I seduced her in thirty minutes."

"Well…it is a little quick, but I figured you might have your mind on other things."

"No wonder your relationships don't last longer than a tank of gas. Women want to be seduced by a man. They want a man who will linger and act interested in them."

"Which is neither here nor there. What did she say?" Dom asked.

Antonio activated the hands-free option that was built into his GPS.

"Can you hear me?"

"Yes," Dom said. "What happened?"

"We talked. The Vallerio family isn't going to be easy. Are you sure we need his name?"

"I'm going to pretend I didn't hear that," Dom said.

"I just wanted to make sure. The negotiations are going to be long and hard on this one, and right now we don't need that."

That was an understatement. Not only was the

production date breathing down their necks, but they still hadn't identified the leak in their office.

As if he read his mind, Dom said, "I am close to figuring out the leak. I have set some things in motion now that will take care of it."

"What things?" Antonio asked.

"More proprietary information given only to two people. I've almost narrowed it down. If I'm right about who it is, it's going to be someone close to us."

"Whom do you suspect?" Antonio asked, not even thinking about the Vallerio business for a minute. Corporate espionage was a big deal and the leaks they had lately were enough to seriously cripple Moretti Motors.

"I'd rather not say at this moment. I'll take care of the leak. You just do what you need to with Vallerio. So, if you didn't seduce the girl, what's your plan?"

Antonio had turned onto the street where he lived. He had a nice place with assigned parking on the street. There were times when he wished he had the space his parents did in their palatial house outside of the city limits, but he liked city living.

He switched his phone back to the handset and got out of the car. His street was quiet this late at night.

"My plan is the same as it always is. Find her weakness and then use it to our advantage," Antonio said. Though for the first time he was torn. He really did believe that all was fair in love and war, but this time he didn't know that he wanted to exploit the weaknesses he found in Nathalie. He would, he knew, but this time he might regret it.

"Her weakness or Vallerio's?" Dom asked.

"Aren't they the same?" Antonio asked.

"In most cases I'd say yes, but if you are going to seduce the girl, then I imagine your thinking could get muddled."

"I have to remember that. There is no gray area here."

"Don't let Nathalie get her hooks in you. I don't think *Nono's* legacy is going to withstand two of us falling in love."

"So you don't believe that Marco and Virginia have broken the curse?" Antonio asked. He had read the words of Cassia Festa's curse in the journal that Virginia had. He thought about the curse he'd read.

My love for you was all-encompassing and never ending and with its death I call upon the universe to bring about the death of your heart and the hearts of succeeding generations.

As long as a Moretti roams this earth, he shall have happiness in either business or love but never both. Do not disdain the power of my small body. Moretti, you may be strong, but that will no longer help you. I am strong in my will and I demand retribution for the pain you have caused me.

Virginia might have broken the curse for Marco by combining Festa and Moretti blood, but Antonio wasn't too sure.

Dom replied, "Maybe as far as Marco is concerned they have, but I have the feeling you and I aren't out of the woods yet."

"You better be careful, old man. I would never be so weak as to fall for any woman."

"That's what Marco thought."

"Our baby brother was distracted by the races. I am not about to be."

"Remember that, Tony. We are on the cusp of taking Moretti Motors to heights that it has never seen before," Dom said.

Antonio knew that better than anyone. He and his brothers had been born to a legacy of both pride and powerful determination but also to the curses that Lorenzo Moretti had left behind. This mess with the Vallerio family was only one of them. If Dom was right and Marco managed to appease the curse put on them by Cassia Festa, Lorenzo's spurned lover, then thank the stars. The fact that no generation of

Moretti men had ever been lucky in business and in love wasn't going to be easily forgotten by either himself or Dom.

"Do I have your permission to act without checking in?" Antonio asked.

"Why?"

"I might need to act quickly to get Nathalie to agree."

"Nathalie?"

"Ms. Vallerio."

"Yes, you can act without checking in with the board. I will back you. But make sure that you get the results we need, Tony."

"Have I failed you yet?"

"No. No, you haven't."

He rang off with his brother and entered his house. The town house was opulently decorated and quiet at this time of night. He had never noticed the silence of the place before, but tonight with Dom's words echoing in his head and after the evening he'd spent with Nathalie, he wondered if he, like *Nono,* was doomed to spend his life alone.

Nathalie had a restless night's sleep and woke early. She stood on the balcony of her hotel suite and looked out over the city of Milan. In the distance she saw Duomo and heard the bells of the cathedral still calling the faithful to worship. She touched the small gold cross at her neck and thought of her father.

He wanted her to succeed because it had been his aunt who had been so badly used by Lorenzo, and his father who had been duped by his onetime friend.

She took a sip of her cappuccino and leaned back in the cushioned wrought-iron chair. Her family wasn't used to failing. After their disastrous business deal with Lorenzo Moretti, the Vallerios had made it their mission to never walk away from any deal the loser.

And Nathalie followed a proud tradition of being the one to make sure that her family won.

There was a knock on her hotel door and she glanced at her watch to check the time. It was too early to be anyone from Moretti's office coming to check on her.

She walked across the room with a feeling of dread. The timing was exactly right for someone to arrive if they'd taken the early flight from Paris.

She checked the peephole and groaned out loud.

"Papa, what are you doing here?" she asked as she opened the door.

Emile Vallerio crossed the threshold and kissed her on both cheeks. "We wanted to make sure that everything was okay here in Milan."

"We?"

KATHERINE GARBERA   47

Like magic, her sister appeared in the doorway. "I decided to come with Papa to see if I could help out in any way," Genevieve said.

Nathalie's older sister was renowned for her beauty and charm. Nathalie had never really minded being the smart sister, but if her father had brought Genevieve he must think... "Why?"

"Let's discuss this over coffee. I see you aren't ready for your meeting."

"Papa, I've been handling these things for a long time. I don't need you and Genevieve here. I can handle it. Go back to Paris."

"We will. After we are sure you know what you are doing," Emile said.

"I love you both very much, but I don't need you to tell me how to do my job."

"I know," Genevieve said. "But the Morettis can be tricky."

"I'm not untried. I can handle Antonio," she said, wondering if the words were true. Could she handle him? Last night had tested her and she suspected each day they spent together in the boardroom was going to make resisting him more difficult.

"Antonio?" Genevieve questioned.

"How is he in person? I've heard that he's a shark," Emile said.

"He's a lot like me. I think we'll get some of the

things we want, but we're not going to be able to rake
them over the coals as you might have wanted."

"At the end of the day, I just want a fair deal for
our family. Lorenzo manipulated my aunt out of her
share of the Moretti fortune. We don't want that for
this generation. She was promised a share of Moretti
Motors and in order to get Lorenzo to sign the annul-
ment so she could marry again he made her give up
her rights to those shares."

"I agree, Papa. I've told Antonio that we aren't
going to take just any deal. There's nothing in this
for us unless they sweeten their offer."

She glanced down at her watch. "I have to start
getting ready."

"Go ahead," her father said. "We will wait here for
you."

She rolled her eyes. She knew how important this
was to her family. Her great-aunt had been in a bitter
marriage and had died young. They had almost no
contact with her son and his family. The split of the
Vallerio and Moretti families was complete.

"What are you going to wear today?" her sister
asked.

"I don't need fashion advice, Genie."

"I know. But this man is used to very sophisticated women."

Her sister had a point. She was used to winning

in the boardroom based on her smarts and her determination. But with Antonio, maybe she could use
clothing and feminine wiles to distract him.

She sighed. "What do you think I should wear?"

Genevieve laughed. "I took the liberty of bringing
a dress with me that I think will look super on you."

"Do you really think so?" Nathalie asked. In this
case she deferred to the pretty sister.

"Nat, you goof, of course it will. You probably
already have him dazzled. This is just going to take
away his ability to look anywhere but at your cleavage."

She shook her head. "I don't like to use my body
as a tool."

"Why not? Nature made us this way, Nat. We're
not stronger than men but we are smarter." Genevieve winked. "And sexier."

"You haven't met Antonio."

"Really?"

"Yes," she said. "He's very sexy."

"Good. Then he'll use his looks to his benefit. You
won't be taking advantage of him by bringing sex
into the boardroom."

Her sister had a point. And Antonio had agreed that
all was fair in love and war. And this most definitely
was war, she thought. Last night he'd pushed the
boundaries of the attraction between them. Normally
Nathalie wouldn't try to be some sort of femme fatale,

but in this instance and with Genevieve's help she had the feeling she couldn't lose.

The meeting went long into the afternoon. Everyone else looked tired and frustrated, but Nathalie looked more beautiful than when she'd first come to the Moretti Motors building this morning.

Her father and sister were also at the table, and Dom had joined them when he'd realized there were more Vallerios in here other than just Nathalie.

"Let's take a break," Antonio suggested. "We need to all stretch and get some air. I've asked my staff to set up some drinks in the garden."

"I don't think fresh air is going to resolve the issues on the table," Emile said.

Nathalie's father had the same sharp intelligence as his daughter but none of her charm. He was still angry with Lorenzo and because of that he was a liability at the negotiating table. He sensed Nathalie knew it, but how did one tell a family member to get lost? He knew it couldn't be done. When family and business were mixed, there was no way to win.

"I realize that, Emile. I thought a break will give us all a chance to regroup and then get back to work."

"Sounds good," Dom said. "My assistant, Angelina, will lead you to the garden."

"Where will you be?"

"In my office," Dom said. "Antonio and I need a moment and then we'll be right down."

Angelina led the Vallerio family out of the boardroom and he turned to Dom. "What did you need to discuss?"

"That Emile is an ass. I don't see the point to all of this. His only agenda seems to be to taunt us with the fact that we can't use his father's name."

"I know. Give me a few minutes to think this over."

"I already have. Screw them. We are going to use Marco's name instead. He's made a name for himself on Grand Prix. One that even Pierre-Henri didn't have."

"But he doesn't have the cachet that Pierre-Henri does, thanks to that roadster he helped design and gave his name to. No matter that Pierre-Henri drove for our team—Team Moretti. The Vallerios think they are owed more than the compensation they were given. And because of the way *Nono* treated Anna Vallerio, I guess Emile is right to feel that way."

Dom stood up and walked over to the floor-to-ceiling windows and looked down into the courtyard garden where the Vallerio family was assembled. "I'm not going to play Emile's game. Whatever *Nono* did to his aunt, we're not responsible for it. This is business, not revenge."

"I'm not ready to throw in the towel yet. I need

some time alone with Nathalie. We both are seasoned at negotiating so I'm sure we can get to something workable."

"Not if her father is in the room. And why is the sister here? She didn't add a single thing."

"I have no idea. Why don't you offer to take them on a tour of the factory and show them the mock-up of the new Vallerio? That will give me a chance to talk to Nathalie privately."

"I think I'll have Angelina take care of that."

"You can't. Emile will be offended if it's not you or I doing the tour. I think it's important that we give him his due here. What *Nono* did to the Vallerios…well, from their perspective wasn't right."

"We didn't exactly prosper from his actions either. But I understand what you're saying. I'll do my part. It's just Marco's luck that he's not here."

"He will be next week and then we can send him to deal with Emile and Genevieve."

"But not Nathalie?"

"No. I'm the one who can handle her."

"Are you sure? You seemed distracted a few times."

He had been distracted. Yesterday he'd been struck by Nathalie's brains and wit more than her looks. But today she'd pulled out all the stops and he couldn't help but remember how she'd felt in his arms the night before.

"It was nothing. I can handle Nathalie," Antonio said. "Any word on the leak?"

"No. Nothing. But the information I am using as bait is highly sensitive and I don't think we'll hear about it for a few days."

"Should we bring in an outside company?"

"I thought of that. I hired Stark Services to help."

"Good. I like Ian and he's not afraid to go for blood. He sees corporate spying as a real international crime."

"I agree. He's going to get stuff we can use in court."

"Good. Does he know about the bait?"

"Yes, it was his suggestion. He's on his way here from London. We should see him in the offices in the next day or so."

Ian Stark had been a college friend of Dom's and he'd gone into his family's business of protecting the rich and famous. Not as a bodyguard but as an intellectual properties security officer. He protected the secrets of the famous and he did a damn fine job of it.

"I'm glad Ian's working for us."

Dom shrugged. "I was hoping to handle it ourselves, but I'm not taking any chances on this."

Antonio knew that. He felt the same way. There was something about going from moving in wealthy circles to being beholden on their wealthier relatives that had cemented in all his brothers the belief that success was the most important thing in life. Money might not be able to buy happiness, but it did buy security and that was a very important commodity.

"We've come too far to fail now," Antonio said.

Dom looked him straight in the eye and smiled. "True enough."

"You seem relieved to hear me say that."

"Sometimes I feel like I forced my dreams on both you and Marco."

Antonio shook his head. As teenaged boys, Marco, Dominic and he had made a vow to never fall in love. They had promised and sealed it with blood that they would be the generation to be lucky in business. "We took that blood oath together, remember? We all want this."

"Yeah, until a pretty face comes along."

"I think that little Enzo won Marco over as much as Virginia did," Antonio said.

Dom shrugged. "If he broke that curse on our family I'll be happy, but I'm not convinced."

"Me either. I know that Virginia thinks the mingling of their blood broke it, but I remember that she said that they couldn't fall in love. That seems like a mighty big oops on their behalf," Antonio said. "Not that I've ever put much stock in the curse."

"That's because you've never been in love."

"Nor tempted to be," Antonio said. "Women are meant to be enjoyed and savored but never permanently."

Dom's mobile rang and he stepped into the hall to answer it. Antonio straightened his papers on the boardroom table and felt someone watching him. He glanced up to see Nathalie standing there.

"So women are like chocolates?" she asked.

"I never said that. Just that men and women seldom want things for the long haul."

"What about your parents?"

"They are the exception to the rule. And I'm not sure that they would have survived as a couple if my papa was interested in business."

"I'm not following," she said.

"I'm the kind of man who is all or nothing, so a woman could never compete with my business interests."

She nodded. "That's good to know."

Four

Nathalie had come back upstairs to see if she could have a minute of Antonio's time. His brother and her father were both so stubborn and not at all suited to the kind of discussions that needed to happen if they were going to come to any sort of arrangement.

Hearing him say so baldly that love and forever with a woman was the last thing on his mind didn't really surprise her. From her experience, men couldn't have both a family and a successful career. Her father was interested in her and Genevieve only because they were involved in the family business.

Before they had graduated from college he'd only

been a distant figure, leaving their upbringing to their mother. Which Genevieve hadn't minded. But Nathalie always had. She'd craved her father's attention and from her earliest memory knew that the only way to get it was through Vallerio Inc.

"Dom is going to take your father and sister on a tour of the car factory so that we can have some time to talk about what we both want. I think together we can find a solution that will work for both of our families."

"I agree."

Nathalie did agree. She wanted this over with. She needed to finish up the negotiations in Milan and make her way back to Paris where her real life was. She didn't need to stay here under Antonio's influence any longer than necessary.

"Would you like to continue working in here?"

"Yes, I think it would be for the best."

"Okay, then, please have a seat."

Nathalie took the same seat she'd had before, expecting Antonio to sit across from her. Instead he took the seat right next to her.

"At the end of the day what will please Vallerio Inc.?"

"Besides our original offer?"

"Yes. You know I won't agree to those terms."

"I'm not sure. I know we want to make sure that the new Vallerio production car represents Pierre-

Henri's legacy. Profits are something we can haggle on, but *Grandpere*'s legendary status as a racer…I'd like to see that brought forward."

Antonio leaned closer, the scent of his aftershave surrounding her. Last night after he left she'd noticed that she still could smell and feel him around her. And she realized she was going to be feeling that until this business meeting was over.

"How do you want to handle that?" Antonio asked.

"He's already in the hall of fame, but I think I'd like to see the marketing campaign focus on why the car is named for my *grandpere.* I'd like him to be the focus and not Lorenzo."

Antonio made some notes on the yellow pad in front of him. His handwriting was scrawling and masculine.

"We can't leave Lorenzo out completely, but I'll see what we can do. What else do you want?"

"We will take the seat on the board that you offered."

"Of course."

"And we want profit sharing for our investors."

Antonio shook his head. "I'll have to talk to our board. Are you offering a reciprocal arrangement for our shareholders?"

"No. Why would I?"

"I don't know that we are going to go for it. What else do you want?"

"I'm still thinking seventy percent of the profits from the Vallerio Roadster."

"Well, you go back and see if you can get a reciprocal arrangement for us and I'll see about giving you fifty percent of the profits. Dom wanted to offer you guys thirty."

Nathalie jotted down a few notes. She thought she could talk the board and more importantly her father into accepting a fifty percent profit margin from the Vallerio production model. But the reciprocal deal…that was going to be harder. No one wanted another company to be a part of Vallerio Inc. On the other hand, they wouldn't turn down the money to be made from the roadster. R & D was expensive and they could always use more money for that. Though they didn't build cars, they developed engines and Vallerio Inc. was on the cusp of launching a new biofuel engine.

That was why they weren't too concerned about coming to an agreement with Moretti Motors for the Vallerio. The company stood to make huge profits from its groundbreaking engineering patent.

"I will have to go back and discuss it with my board. Why don't we reconvene in a couple of weeks?"

"You haven't heard what else we want," Antonio said.

"What else do you want?"

"If you can get your board to go for reciprocal profit sharing, then we'd like a seat on your board. Just so we can keep track of our investments."

"Antonio, let me be straight with you. The chances of us doing a reciprocal deal are slim."

"Then your shareholders should know they'll get no stake in the Vallerio Roadster."

She knew he wasn't going to give away the shop. And he knew at the end of the day that he wasn't going to give up until he had everything he wanted.

But then she remembered his comment from yesterday. *All's fair…* Pivoting her chair to face him, she leaned forward so that she was almost touching him. He glanced away from the table and down her body.

Inside she smiled. Genevieve's dress was right on the money and the perfect tool to distract Antonio. "I think we're both too tired to discuss this anymore today. How about if I send you an e-mail with the things we want?"

She was careful to keep her shoulders back so that her breasts were thrust forward. Inside she knew her business school mentor, Professor Stanley Muchen, would have told her that this behavior was deplorable.

But as Antonio leaned forward and took her hand in his she realized that she didn't care. She wanted to flirt with Antonio, and using her "wiles" to distract him was exactly what she needed to get what she wanted.

Nathalie suspected that Antonio wasn't paying as close attention to the meeting as he normally would have. She had to wonder if it was because of her new clothes. But that seemed a bit silly to her. Antonio was a sophisicated man who was used to attractive women.

But this wasn't like her normal boardroom maneuvering, and frankly, as Antonio leaned closer to her, she knew she was out of her league. The dress was just a costume she wore. It hadn't changed who she was on the inside. To be honest he knew she had no idea how to use her body to manipulate the deal.

"What are you thinking?" he asked.

"That I've started something I can't finish."

He stood up and leaned against the table in front of her. She arched her neck back to maintain eye contact.

"What do you mean, *cara?* This?" He gestured to the two of them.

"Yes, this. My sister said… Oh, man, am I really saying this out loud?"

"What did your sister say? That you should seduce me and get me to agree to all of your terms?"

She tipped her head to the side and realized that either he had thought of the idea of seducing her or someone on his team had suggested the same thing. "Perhaps."

"We are both adults, Nathalie," he said. "We are

attracted to each other. It doesn't have anything to do with our families or the companies they own."

She wished it were that easy. That she could simply turn off the corporate lawyer part of her brain and pretend that an affair with Antonio would have no repercussions beyond the emotional ones she felt when affairs ended.

"I'm trying to decide if you really believe that or if you are just trying another tactic to get me to agree to your terms," she said.

Antonio reached down and took her hand in his. "I always believe what I say. I might not tell you all the reasoning behind it, though."

"I am not sure—"

"Don't think about this, Nathalie. We both have agreed to go back to our board of directors and to discuss the new terms. There is nothing more to be said or done this day. Why not enjoy each other's company?"

"Why not?" she asked, shaking her head. "I imagine Romeo must have said the same thing to Juliet."

He laughed. "I don't intend for either of us to die and I'm pretty sure that Dom and Emile won't draw blood while touring the car factory."

"I'm not trying to be melodramatic. It's just we aren't two people whose paths have crossed without consequences. As much as I might want to have an affair with you—"

"You want to have an affair with me?" he asked, leaning forward.

Any other man would have been crowding her, but with Antonio he couldn't get close enough. She stood up and put her hands on his shoulders.

"You're a smart man. You can figure that out."

He reached up and touched the side of her face with one long finger and she shivered under that touch.

"I already have," he said, leaning up to rub his lips over hers.

She tunneled her fingers into his thick hair and held his head still. She wasn't about to let Antonio take control of any part of their relationship, and she had realized over the last few minutes that they were going to have a relationship. There was too much spark between them for her to ignore it. That wasn't true, she thought. She would have been able to ignore it if Antonio wasn't attracted to her.

But he was.

His tongue sliding over her lips made her entire body tingle. She tipped her head to the side and opened her mouth as he deepened the kiss. She had never reacted this quickly to a man before.

He tasted so good, so right. And for once everything about a man felt as though he was made for her.

He slid his hands down her back, stroking the length of her spine and then drawing her closer to him. As he sat there, she was nestled between his legs and felt the warmth of his body heat wrapping around her.

She pushed his suit coat off his shoulders and he shrugged out of it. She put her hands on his chest, wanting to feel his pulse beating under her fingers. She sucked his lower lip into her mouth and felt his hands flex against her hips. He lifted her up and set her on the table, then nudged her legs apart to make room between them for his hips.

The skirt of the dress she wore flowed over her thighs and onto the conference room table. She looked down at their bodies knowing that the time for talking was long gone.

"Antonio…"

"Sì, la mia amore?"

She realized she didn't know what to say. She wasn't going to call a halt to their lovemaking, so instead she took his face in both of her hands and brought their mouths together again. She kissed him with all the pent-up passion she'd carried for a lifetime. She refused to think of anything but this moment. Refused to occupy anything but his arms right now.

He groaned into her mouth and she felt his hands sweep up her sides to cup her breasts. She found his hips with her hands and drew him closer to her. She

felt his erection nudging her center, but it only made
her hungrier for him. She wanted—

A sound in the hallway made them pull apart.
Antonio looked at her, something solid and steady
in his eyes. Something she'd never really seen on a
man's face before.

"I'm going to lock the door."

All she could do was nod because she knew she
didn't want this moment to end.

Antonio locked the door and turned back to
Nathalie. He knew the boardroom wasn't the place
for this kind of encounter, but he couldn't wait to
have Nathalie. Filled with the demands and pressures of their families as they were, he knew their
coming together like this was a complication. Yet he
couldn't walk away.

She looked so tempting with the sun streaming in
from the tinted windows onto her red-gold hair. Her
creamy pale skin was like a beacon, guiding him
back to her. Unable to resist, he loosened his tie and
hurried back to her side.

She was sitting just as he'd left her, her legs
parted, those impossibly high peep-toe shoes on her
tiny feet, the skirt of her dress draped over her thighs.
Her breasts rose up and fell with her breaths.

"Lean back on your elbows for me, *cara*," he said.

She did as he asked. She was temptation incarnate, everything a man could want, and she wasn't doing anything but sitting there, just as she had all morning. She'd cast a spell over him just as powerful as the curse that Cassia Festa had put on Lorenzo all those years ago. But this spell was enchanting and he wanted nothing more than to indulge himself in her.

And he could. He wasn't going to deny himself the pleasure of Nathalie and her body.

Her green-gold eyes were shy as he tossed his tie on the credenza and unbuttoned his shirt, but once he touched her, took a strand of that red-gold hair of hers in his hand, all that melted away.

She stayed where he'd asked her to as he leaned down to take her mouth in his. She was the first woman he'd kissed who tasted like home to him.

She smelled of spring flowers and her skin was softer than anything he'd ever touched. He ran his hands down her arms, linking their fingers together as his mouth moved over hers.

He slid his hand down her side, finding the zipper hidden in the seam, and lowered it slowly. "I want you naked, *cara mia.*"

"Me too, Antonio."

Blood rushed through his veins. Antonio knew the boardroom wasn't the sexiest place in the world, but with Nathalie that didn't matter. The fabric of her bodice gaped away from her chest and he wanted to see more.

"Arch your shoulders," he said.

"Like this?" Her shoulders moved and the loose bodice gaped further.

"What are you wearing under this?" he asked, tracing his finger along the seam where fabric met flesh.

"Why don't you find out?"

He growled deep in his throat. Leaning forward, he brushed soft kisses against her shoulder and collarbone, following the lines of her body down to where the loosened bodice was and then he took the soft fabric in his teeth and pulled it away from her skin. There was no strap from a bra there. Just the smooth skin of woman.

He pushed the fabric out of his way, letting it pool at her waist. She was exquisite, her breasts just the right size for her frame, her nipples a pretty pink accent to her creamy white skin. He hesitated to touch her, wanting to just look at her for a long moment.

"Take your shirt off," she said.

But he shook his head. "You do it."

She shifted on the table and reached between them, pushing his shirt off his shoulders. He took her wrists in his hands and drew them to his hips. He caressed the length of her arms and then slid his hands down her chest, caressing every bit of skin he touched.

"Come closer, Antonio."

"Like this?" He drew her into his arms, held her so her nipples brushed against the light dusting of hair on his chest.

"Yes."

He rotated his shoulders so that his chest rubbed against her breast. She squirmed delicately in his arms.

"I like that," she said.

Blood roared in his ears. He was so hard right now that he needed to be inside her body.

Impatient with the fabric of her dress, he shoved it up and out of his way. He caressed her creamy thighs. *Dio,* she was soft. She moaned as he neared her center and then sighed when he brushed his fingertips across the crotch of her panties.

The lace was warm and wet. He slipped one finger under the material and hesitated for a second, looking down into her eyes.

Her eyes were heavy lidded. She bit down on her lower lip and he felt the minute movements of her hips as she tried to move his touch where she needed it.

He was beyond teasing her or prolonging anything. He ripped her panties aside, plunged two fingers into her humid body. She squirmed against him.

He pulled her head down to his so he could taste

her mouth. Her mouth opened over his and he told himself to take it slow, but Nathalie was making him go naught to sixty in less than 3.5 seconds. She was pure fire. Like putting jet fuel in a car, she was sending him skyrocketing.

He nibbled on her and held her at his mercy. Her nails dug into his shoulders and she leaned up, brushing against his chest. Her nipples were hard points and he pulled away from her mouth, glancing down to see them pushing against his chest.

He caressed her back and spine, scraping his nail down the length of it. He followed the line of her back down the indentation above her backside.

She closed her eyes and held her breath as he fondled her, running his finger over her nipple. It was velvety compared to the satin smoothness of her breast. He brushed his finger back and forth until she bit her lower lip.

Her intelligence, wit and unwillingness to back down at the bargaining table had turned him on before, but seeing her today as a sexy, confident woman had been more than he could handle.

She moaned a sweet sound that he leaned up to capture in his mouth. She tipped her head to the side, allowing him access to her mouth. She held his shoulders and moved on him, rubbing her center over his erection.

He scraped his fingernail over her nipple and she shivered in his arms. He pushed her back a little bit so he could see her. Her breasts were bare, nipples distended and begging for his mouth. He lowered his head and suckled.

He held her still with a hand on the small of her back. He buried his other hand in her hair and arched her over his arm. Both of her breasts were thrust up at him. He had a lap full of woman and he knew that he wanted Nathalie more than he'd wanted any other woman in a long time.

Her eyes were closed, her hips moving subtly against him, and when he blew on her nipple he saw gooseflesh spread down her body.

He loved the way she reacted to his touch. He kept his attention on her breasts. Her nipples were so sensitive he was pretty sure he could bring her to an orgasm just from touching her there.

He suckled the inside of her left breast, needing to leave his mark on her so that later when she was away from him and surrounded by her family, she'd remember this.

He kept kissing and fondling her until her hands clenched in his hair and she rocked her hips harder against his length. He lifted his hips, thrusting up against her. As he bit down carefully on her tender, aroused nipple, she screamed his name and he hurriedly covered her mouth with his, wanting to feel every bit of her passion.

He rocked her until the storm passed and she quieted in his arms. He held her close. Her bare breasts brushed against his chest. He was so hard he thought he'd die if he didn't get inside her.

Then he remembered he had no protection with him.

Maybe this time it was better to leave things as they were, he told himself. He'd just realized that keeping his head and his heart separate were going to be harder than he'd thought.

Damn, did he say heart? He wasn't the kind of man to fall for a woman. Even one as sexy as Nathalie Vallerio.

Five

Nathalie heard the door rattle a second before Antonio moved off her. She didn't regret what had just happened. How could she when every nerve ending in her body was still pulsing? But now the thought of getting caught horrified her.

"Mon dieu," she said.

"Shh, *cara mia*," he said, helping her off the table. Her dress started to fall down her body, but Antonio caught it and drew it back up her body. "We will finish this later."

She nodded. There was no way she'd deny herself an affair with this man now. She put herself to rights and turned to see he'd done the same. His shirt was buttoned and he had his tie back on.

"Antonio—"

"Shh. Say nothing now. We will talk later," he said, shrugging into his suit jacket.

She sat down in her chair and drew her notes to her, staring down at the table as if it held some kind of answer, but all she saw was what she should be focused on. Her family and the board of directors at Vallerio Inc. were expecting her to beat Antonio Moretti at this game. They'd expected her to get him to agree to her terms.

Instead she'd just been writhing in his arms. Even now she could fall into a simpering puddle at his feet because that had been the best orgasm of her life.

"Nathalie?"

"Hmm?" she asked, looking up to see Angelina standing there.

"Your family insists we accompany them on the tour of the factory."

"Very well. We had finished our discussion any-way," Nathalie said. She gathered her folders and put them into her leather briefcase.

"I can hold that for you at my desk, Ms. Vallerio," Angelina said.

The other woman was shorter than Nathalie with an hourglass figure that she showcased in her form-fitting sweater and pencil skirt. Angelina had big brown eyes and thick curly hair and a hesitant smile as she took the case from Nathalie.

"Thank you."

"My pleasure. They are waiting for you in the lobby of the factory, Antonio."

"*Grazie,* Angelina."

They left the boardroom together and Nathalie tried to force her mind to accept that nothing had changed between the two of them, but it had. The awkward silence between them underscored that for her.

"Antonio?"

"*Sì,* Nathalie?"

"I don't want this to interfere with our negotiations."

"It won't. I'm still going to be hard on you."

She had no doubt about that. Had she meant her words more for herself? Did she really need a reminder that she had made a mistake?

Had she?

Antonio hadn't been uninvolved and unless he was more of a playboy than his reputation indicated, she had to assume he felt something for her.

Did she use that to her advantage?

He paused to put on a pair of sunglasses and she wished she'd brought hers, for the midday sun in Milan was bright on this spring morning. He put his hand at the small of her back as they walked across the courtyard and she realized he'd fallen back into the mode that she needed to.

"I will send you an offer when I get back to Paris. It will expire in a week, Antonio. After that time we will no longer need to be in contact for the sake of our companies."

"What if I accept the offer you send?"

"I'm assuming you will," she said, not thinking about defeat. She had nothing to lose. But those words didn't ring true for her anymore. She did have something very personal to lose.

"Good. Will you join me for dinner tonight?"

"Um…"

"Not to discuss anything about Vallerio Incorporated. As a date."

"I don't think it's a good idea for us to be dating."

"Too bad. I don't care what other people think and you didn't strike me as the kind of woman who'd let that stop her either."

"I'm not going to go out with you because you dared me to."

"You're not? What would it take?" he asked.

The sincerity in his voice made her stop walking and all she could was look up at him. "I guess if you promised we'd go somewhere private, then I'd say yes."

"Consider it done. I'll pick you up at the hotel—"

She shook her head. "That won't work. I know we aren't teenagers and sneaking around might not be what you want."

"I like it," he said. "Right now being seen in public isn't in our best interest, for either of us. Tell me what you had in mind."

"I'll meet you in front of Duomo and we can go wherever you have planned."

"Okay. Be there at nine," he said. "Dress casual."

"Fine," she said, taking a step away from him. But his hand on the back of her neck stopped her. It was a light touch, a casual caress, but she shivered from it.

"If our families weren't waiting behind that glass door," he said softly, "I'd take you in my arms and kiss you again."

"I might let you," she said, just to let him know she wasn't passive. She walked away, anticipating the coming night as she'd looked forward to nothing else in the last few years.

Antonio stood to the back of the group as Dom led the tour through the factory. He'd heard the stories before and seen the model of the car they were already producing a million times before. This car—the Vallerio Roadster—was the cornerstone of the Moretti plan to retake their place in the car-making world.

He was more interested in planning his total conquest of Nathalie. He knew he'd made a lot of headway this afternoon in breaking down barriers between them. Tonight he'd do the rest of what he needed to.

He felt a twinge of something that might be guilt as he thought about using her, but it was the only way he knew how to take control of his feelings for her. He had to make their relationship about the Moretti-Vallerio feud. Otherwise he'd never be able to keep himself on track.

And that was the one thing he had to do.

He wasn't about to let all of the work he, Marco and Dom had done go by the wayside because of a woman. No matter how pretty she was. Or how much he liked her smile or even sparring with her in the boardroom. He and his brothers were the Morettis that would set the world on fire.

That wasn't going to be easy to do if he was lusting after a Vallerio.

While the Vallerio family congregated around the model car and Genevieve got behind the wheel, Dom came over to him. "What were you two doing locked in the conference room?"

"Do you have a life outside of following me around?"

"No, I don't. Moretti Motors is my life."

Antonio clapped his brother on his shoulder. "It's mine too."

Dom looked him in the eye, his hard stare very reminiscent of their grandfather's. "Good. I'm not sure what the Vallerio family is up to, but Emile is sitting on something big. He sounded very smug when we talked earlier."

"Maybe it's just his French attitude."

"Or maybe he's a bastard."

"Dom. We have to work with them. *Nono* messed around with a woman in their family. How would you feel if the situation were reversed?"

"I'd be out for blood."

"Exactly my point. Having Nathalie do the negotiation was probably the best thing Emile could do. I know that we will come to some sort of arrangement that works for all of us."

"I wanted to give you more time alone, but—"

Antonio shook his head. "We will probably do the next phase of the negotiations via e-mail. I think you and I need to show them that they can't walk away from this deal. I've given in on a few things, but they want the moon."

"This car should make them want it."

"I know that and you know that, but now we need to show them why," Antonio said. Dom was a first-class salesman and if he could genuinely talk to the

Vallerio family, Antonio knew he could win them over. And that really was the first step, because until they wanted to be a part of the new roadster they weren't going to give in. They weren't going to be willing to let Nathalie truly bargain with him. Without that, the Vallerio was never going to be more than a pipe dream.

"Why is there only a V on the hood and not the signature lion's head emblem that Pierre-Henri used on his racing uniform?" Emile asked.

"We don't have rights to that," Dom said. "We wanted to use it and incorporate as much of the Vallerio legacy as we could, but we only own the rights to this new V we've created."

"Well, if we are even going to be serious about talking of using my father's name, you are going to have to use the lion's head."

"Perfect," Antonio said. "I've asked Nathalie to go back to your board and send us an e-mail of the things you want. She knows how far we are able to go on some issues."

Emile glanced at his daughter. *"Tres bien."* Then he turned back to Dom. "I'm interested in seeing the rest of the factory. No sense in not knowing everything we'd be getting involved in."

"We do have some proprietary areas that I'm afraid we can't show you," Dom said, moving to the front of the group. "But given our shared past in F1 racing, I think you'll want to see this next area."

Dom led the way into the showcase area for their F1 program. The open-wheel car that Marco had driven the last season in his final victory was on display there. On the wall were photos of his brother in Victory Circle, and Antonio felt a rush of pride as he looked at Marco. Their younger brother was really dynamite behind the wheel. When they had been younger and talking about who would do what in Moretti Motors when they grew up, they all knew that Marco would be the face of Moretti. He craved speed the way Antonio craved winning and the way that Dom craved power.

Everyone walked around the car, which was polished to perfection and looked showroom perfect. But Antonio smelled the oil and tire rubber that had been in the air in Sao Paulo, Brazil, when Marco had become the winningest driver in Grand Prix history.

"Will you be running the Vallerio Roadster in any rally races?" Emile asked.

"That is our hope. We'd like to use it at the 24 hours of Le Mans," Dom said.

Emile stepped forward and ran his hand along the edge of the racing car. Antonio wondered if the other man had ever wanted to be a driver like Pierre-Henri.

From his own perspective he knew that not everyone inherited the desire to drive at top speeds.

"This is a fine machine. Even my father could never find fault with your F1 program."

"That is at the root of our company and something vital to Moretti Motors. We will always preserve this first, which is the main reason we are reissuing the Vallerio Roadster. We want to pay tribute to those who helped build the Moretti name to the heights it once enjoyed and will enjoy again."

"We want the same thing for the Vallerio name. My father shouldn't drop into obscurity," Emile said.

"If you are reasonable," Antonio said, "I'm sure that we will be able to come to an acceptable arrangement."

Nathalie convinced her father and sister that she needed time alone that evening to think over the proposal that Antonio had outlined. In truth she'd already made notes and recommendations to the board of the directors and had an e-mail ready to send to them in the morning. Feeling very much like a teenager, she got dressed and snuck out of the hotel to meet Antonio.

She wore a pair of slim-fitting jeans and a button-down white blouse that made her feel very American. She draped one of her favorite scarves over her head and took the stairs instead of the lift to the first floor.

Instead of hailing a cab out front, she walked the short block to the Metro station and found the proper train to Duomo.

She couldn't wait to see Antonio again. To be with him away from the pressures of their families. She rubbed the spot on her breast where Antonio had left his mark.

She felt she was doing something illicit and daring. And it was out of character for the straitlaced business-focused woman she'd always been.

She walked through the Piazza del Duomo. The crowds of people were a nice buffer and helped her to feel anonymous as she walked to the cathedral. She stood on the steps where she and Antonio had been the night before. Looking up at the wedding-cake perfection of the old stone church, she had a sense of how small her slice of time was. That her lifetime, like her grandfather's, was going to be nothing more than a wrinkle in time. Legacies, especially one like this, were all that they'd have.

She realized she was going to do whatever she could to make sure that her father and the rest of the board came to an agreement with Moretti Motors. Sure, she wanted to win and it would be nice to get this deal sealed. But she also wanted her grandfather to be remembered for generations to come. She wanted the car named after him to be talked about the way the Shelby Cobra was to muscle-heads of the world.

"Are you ready?"

He'd come up behind her, startling her.

"*Oui.* I wasn't sure where to meet you. Am I dressed okay?"

Antonio took her hand in his and led the way through the crowded piazza to a stand where motor-cycles were parked. "You look perfect as always."

"Flattering me won't win you any points," she said.

"Why not?"

She studied him for a moment. He wore casual jeans and a cashmere sweater. His hair was perfectly styled and his Italian leather boots were shined. The bike he stood next to was slim and sleek. "Because I don't like lies, even the social kind, and I am very aware of what I look like in the mirror."

He opened up the seat and took out a helmet, handing it to her. "You will never convince me you don't know you are a beautiful woman."

She shook her head. "Beauty is in the eye of the beholder and I know that emotions can make a man see a woman in a different light, but you don't feel anything for me, Antonio."

"What makes you so sure?"

"Do you?" she asked, because she was fairly confi-dent he was still playing a game with her. A game he was desperate to win. After seeing the Moretti show-room and the hall of trophies, she understood why succeeding was important to him, but she still didn't know exactly how she personally figured into his plans.

He set his helmet on the seat of the bike and then took the one from her hands. "Yes, I feel something for you. Didn't this afternoon prove that?"

"Ah, lust."

He laughed. "Women always treat that emotion with disdain, but it's very important to the mating ritual."

Mating ritual. Was he thinking of his time with her as more than just an affair? Or was he simply trying to throw her off her guard?

"Stop thinking so much, *cara mia.* Let's enjoy the night and the time that we have together."

"Where are we going?"

"To Lake Como. I have my yacht waiting for us."

"Isn't that a bit far for dinner?"

"Not at all. I wanted the evening with you and I want privacy. We won't have that here in Milan."

Still, driving two hours to the deepest lake in Italy didn't sound practical. But Antonio wasn't trying for practical. This was romance, she realized, looking into his dark blue eyes. He was going to a lot of trouble to seduce her; the least she could do was enjoy it.

"Fine," she said. "I've never ridden on a motor-bike before."

"I promise you are in good hands."

She sensed that she was.

He put the helmet on her head and pulled her hair free of the back. There was a sincerity and a caring to all of Antonio's moves that made her realize that he was thinking about her. Not about the Moretti-Vallerio feud or the deal that each was fighting tooth and nail to win at the other's expense.

"Is this okay?" he asked. "We can go to my place and pick up my car. But I thought this mode of transportation was more autonomous."

"It's fine. I think. I mean I've never ridden on anything without doors before."

"You'll enjoy it, *cara mia.* Riding on the bike is a sensuous feast."

She believed him. And when he helped her onto the bike and then put his own helmet on and climbed on in front of her, she realized how intimate the ride was going to be.

"Put your arms around me," he said, but she heard it close to her ear in the helmet. His voice was strong and deep and sent a sensual shiver through her.

She scooted forward and wrapped her arms around his lean waist. He put his hand over hers for a moment and then the bike roared to life as he started it. The machine vibrated between her legs and Antonio pressed against her breasts.

This was going to be the most sensual night of her life. For once she was going to forget about being a Vallerio and just enjoy being a woman.

Six

His family had had a home on Lake Como for as long as Antonio could remember. Lake Como was a jewel-like oasis of tranquility, a magical combination of lush Mediterranean foliage and snowy alpine peaks. It was one of the most beautiful spots in Italy and Antonio always felt more at peace as soon as he came out here.

He also remembered the five long years when they had to rent it out instead of coming here in the summers because money had been tight. All of that had changed as soon as Dominic, Marco and he had taken over Moretti Motors and rebuilt the family

fortune in the last five years. It was that knowledge—
the fact that his family had been so close to losing all
of their legacy—that really drove him and his brothers.

He liked the way Nathalie felt pressed against his
back as they drove through the winding streets toward Lake Como. Feeling her against him immediately brought back his arousal from earlier that
afternoon.

He wanted her. No mistake about it. And he was
past debating whether that desire had anything to do
with Moretti Motors. He was going to be as fair as
he could be with the Vallerio family. Not because of
his interest in Nathalie but because he'd seen the
pain in Emile's eyes when he'd spoken of his own
father.

Antonio understood where Emile had been coming from. He knew too that pride was an important
commodity. At Lorenzo's knee he'd grown up learning that the Moretti name was the most important
thing that he, Antonio, had inherited.

"What did you tell your family you were doing
tonight?" he asked to distract himself from the feel
of her hands on his body.

"I told them I needed the night alone to prepare
your terms." She hesitated, then added, "I don't want
you to think that lying is a habit of mine."

"I don't," he said. He had a sense that Nathalie

was the type of woman who prided herself on doing what was necessary. He knew from his own experiences in life that sometimes meant white lies.

"You're a grown woman. I doubt your sister and your father are your keepers."

She laughed, the sounds soft and melodious in his ear. He liked riding like this. It had been a gamble to take her out of Milan where the deck was definitely stacked in his favor. But he had guessed that she needed to see more of the man he was than just the Moretti Motors company man.

He certainly wanted to see more of Nathalie. He wanted to see the part of her that wasn't tied to Vallerio Inc.

"My father still thinks of us as his little girls when we are in a situation like this. And he feels so tied to the Moretti Motors issue that he can't let me handle it."

"I can understand that."

"I bet you can't. Isn't it different for men? I mean your parents don't treat you like a boy, do they?"

He thought about that for a moment. His mother always did things for him that she'd done when he was little. Silly things like making sure his favorite soft drink was stocked in the house and sending him her lasagna for dinner once a week…

"I think it's different. My brothers and I are more interested in business than our father was, but I know

he worries when we travel a lot. And my mother…
well, she just mothers us."

Nathalie stroked her hand down his chest, resting
her hand on his thigh. "It is different. My dad thinks
I'm twelve."

Antonio laughed, taking her hand in his. "You
are definitely not twelve."

"Definitely."

He noticed she'd neatly turned the subject away
from business, which suited him. The last thing he
wanted to do was have Moretti Motors be between
them tonight. He wanted them to just be Antonio and
Nathalie.

Two lovers who were enjoying the romance of
this beautiful spring evening in the countryside.

"What are you thinking?" she asked.

He shrugged and turned off the motorway and
onto a small road that curved around the lake to
where his family's summer home was.

"That I'm glad you took a chance on me tonight."

"Is that what I'm doing?"

"Aren't you?" he asked, very aware that Nathalie
could be playing a game with him. Hell, she probably was. All's fair, he reminded himself.

Though he had set out to seduce her with the
romance of the evening and the beauty of his home
on Lake Como, he realized that he had to be careful

not to be seduced himself, because there was something about Nathalie tonight. Maybe it was the way her curves pressed against his back and the way her arms wrapped around his chest as he maneuvered the bike through the curves and turns of the road, or maybe it was something more.

"Are we close to your house? I read somewhere…"

"What?"

"Something very silly."

"If you read it I doubt it is all that silly."

"Well, this is. I was going to say I heard that celebrities lived in the area."

The comment was out of character for the woman he'd come to know in the boardroom. "My brother is considered a celebrity in some circles."

"Dominic?"

"Marco. You must know drivers too, right? Vallerio Incorporated is still very involved in the racing world."

"That is true," she said. "We still have patents for engines and stuff that my grandfather designed."

"Stuff?"

"Yes. Where is your home?"

"Right up here," he said, turning off the road and onto the long winding driveway that led to the stone cottage. He pulled to a stop next to the house and turned off the bike.

He removed his helmet and took Nathalie's from her when she did the same. He hung them both off the handlebars of the motorcycle and then got off the bike.

He held his hand out to her. She took it and slowly dismounted, losing her balance when she stepped off and falling right into his arms.

He only hoped she'd fall as easily into his arms later tonight.

Nathalie tried to pretend this was nothing new to her, that being on a private yacht in the middle of the very romantic Lake Como was like every other date she'd been on, but in her heart of hearts she knew it wasn't.

It had little to do with the yacht or the setting and everything to do with the man who was with her. Antonio hadn't brought up business since they'd set foot in his home. And clearly this was his home. He pointed out the home his parents owned and the ones that were his brothers'.

But he didn't focus too much on anything that wasn't personal. "Where did your family go on holiday?"

She tried to recall. She didn't dwell in the past and she'd attended a year-round boarding school with Genevieve. "We have a flat in London and my grandparents have a house in Monte Carlo. And we had holidays in London growing up. But otherwise we didn't really go anywhere. Except I had a pen pal in Cairo when I was a girl and I visited her one time."

"What about as an adult? Where is your favorite place to go on holiday?"

"I don't take them."

"How very American of you," Antonio said.

"It's not that…. You know how earlier I said my father still thinks I'm a girl?"

"Yes."

"I still feel like I'm proving myself to him and to the board."

Antonio handed her a pomegranate martini. They were anchored in the middle of the lake, music played through the speakers and a small table had been set on the deck of the yacht. There were lights draped from the mast.

"I can understand that. I think I've been trying to prove myself for most of my career."

"To whom?" she asked. "You said your father wasn't interested in business."

"Lorenzo. Dom, Marco and I made a promise to each other that we'd be the generation to get back the promise and the fortune that Lorenzo had made."

That made sense. It also explained why they'd come to Vallerio Inc. for permission to use the Vallerio name.

"Isn't it odd that no matter how old we get we are still trying to prove something to our elders?"

"Not necessarily odd," Antonio said. "I think we are both tied so much to our families that failure is simply not an option."

She smiled at him. "Maybe that is why we are both used to winning."

"Probably. But that doesn't matter tonight. I want this evening for us."

"You've said that a couple of times. I'm not thinking about work with the moon shining down on us."

He smiled over at her. "*Buon*. Are you hungry yet?"

She shook her head. She didn't want to eat right now. She could eat any time, but this moment with Antonio wasn't going to last forever.

"Dance with me?"

"Yes." She set her martini glass down. The music was slow and bluesy. A pure American sound that sounded familiar to her but she was unable to identify the artist. She soon stopped trying when Antonio drew her into his arms.

He put one arm around her waist, drawing her as close as he could, while the music slowed its pace. His hips moved in time with the drumbeat and hers soon did the same. She wrapped her arms around his shoulders as she'd wanted to do since they'd gotten off that motorcycle of his. She had been invigorated by the ride out here, and more than ever craved his solid body pressed to hers.

The passionate encounter they'd had in the board-room that afternoon had whet her appetite for him. And now she wanted more.

He kept his other arm in the middle of her back, stroking her spine as he danced her around the deck of the yacht. He sang softly under his breath and she thought she felt herself falling for him.

Maybe it was the magic of this night or the fact that she'd spent all day battling more with her own family than him, but at this moment she realized there was something likeable about Antonio.

His hands skirted along her sides and around to her front. "You have the sexiest body."

"Thank you," she said with a confidence that she was definitely starting to feel with this man.

"You don't give an inch, do you?"

"Do you?" she asked.

"Never."

They were perfectly suited, she thought. Perfectly suited for not only the negotiations they were bro-kering but also a love affair.

"Antonio?"

"*Sì?*"

"I want more than this dance with you," she said, taking the bull by the horns. Neither of them would be satisfied with anything less than this.

"Me too. I want this evening and many more, *cara mia.*"

"Am I really yours?"

He tipped his head to the side to look down at her. It was hard to see his expression in the dim light, but when he spoke she heard his confidence and the sincerity in his voice.

"You will be."

She stood on her tiptoes and met his mouth as it descended toward hers. Their lips met and she darted her tongue out to taste his, but he opened his lips and sucked her tongue deep inside his mouth. Both of his arms wrapped around her, making her feel she'd found in his arms the one place she'd always searched for.

They ate a light supper and then he drew Nathalie to the aft of the yacht where he'd had his staff arrange large soft pillows for them to lie on. The staff had followed his instructions exactly.

He left her standing by the bow to go and change the music on his iPod/Bose system.

Soon soft music filled the air. The breeze was cool but not cold, and to be honest Antonio couldn't remember the last time he'd enjoyed an evening with a woman so much. And they hadn't even had sex, he thought.

"*Merci,* Antonio."

"For what?" he asked. He loved the soft sound of her voice. But mostly he loved the feel of her in his arms. He pulled her back into his arms, dancing her around the deck.

"For this evening. I really enjoyed it."

"It's not over yet."

"Good," she said.

He caressed her back and she shifted in his arms. Blood rushed through his veins, pooling in his groin as she turned in his arms and smiled up at him. An expression of intent spread over her face.

He led her over to the pillows and drew her down to them. He lay back against them and drew her into his arms. She curled against his side, her head resting on his shoulder and her arm around his waist. He stroked her arm.

"Climb up here," he said, gesturing to his lap.

"Not yet."

He arched one eyebrow at her. "Do you have something else in mind?"

"Yes," she said. "Take off your shirt."

He arched one eyebrow at her but sat up and did as she asked. "Now you do the same."

She shook her head. "I'm going to be in charge."

He captured both of her hands and turned so that she was under him. "I don't think so."

He held both of her hands loosely in one of his and undid her white blouse with the other one. Once it was unbuttoned, he let go of her hands and drew the blouse off her body.

The bra she wore was creamy white lace and afforded only partial coverage. He could see the pink color of her nipples through the pattern on her bra.

"Now you can do as you wish," he said, trying to pretend he wasn't her slave at this moment. He might want to believe he was in charge, but he knew he wasn't.

He growled deep in his throat when she brushed kisses against his chest. Her lips were sweet and bold as she explored his torso, then nibbled their way down his body.

He watched her, loving the feel of her cool hair against his heated skin. His pants felt damned uncomfortable. When her tongue darted out and brushed against his nipple, he arched off the pillows and put his hand on the back of her head, urging her to stay where she was.

Still, she eased her way down his chest. She traced each of the muscles that ribbed his abdomen and then slowly made her way lower. He could feel his heartbeat in his erection and he knew he was going to lose it if he didn't take control.

But another part of him wanted to just sit back and let her have her way with him. When she reached the edge of his pants, she stopped and glanced up to his face.

Her hand brushed over his erection. "Did you like that?"

"Sì, cara mia," he said, pulling her to him. He lifted her slightly so that her lace-covered nipples brushed his chest.

"Let's see what you like," he said.

She suddenly diverted her gaze and nibbled her lips, and he realized she didn't want to let him see what made her vulnerable. Moments before, he had no problems with letting Nathalie know exactly how much her body and her touch turned him on.

He told her so, in softly whispered words. He buried his face against her neck and drew her body close to his until she was pressed to him, tucked tightly to him.

He skimmed his hands all over her body, up and down her back, unclasping her bra and pulling it down her arms and tossing it away.

"I like the feel of your chest against me," she said.

Blood roared in his ears. He was so hard right now that he needed to be inside her.

But he took his time making love to her. Slowly he unbuttoned her jeans and drew them down her legs. They were long and lean and so soft to his touch. He pushed the fabric aside and then sat on his heels near her feet and just looked at her.

She lay back against the multicolored pillows. Clad only in a pair of pink panties, she was exquisitely beautiful and he was glad that he was the man who would claim her tonight.

He caressed her creamy thighs. *Dio,* she was soft and so responsive. It was as if she were made to be his. They were equals in other areas of life, so he shouldn't have been surprised that they were here as well.

She moaned as he neared her center and then sighed when he brushed his fingertips across the crotch of her panties. When her long legs shifted and opened, he moved between them, keeping his eyes on her.

The cotton was warm and wet. He slipped one finger under the material and hesitated for a second, looking down into her eyes.

Her eyes were heavy lidded. She bit down on her lower lip and he felt the minute movements of her hips as she tried to move his touch where she needed it.

He wasn't done teasing her or himself with the building passion between them. He nudged her panties aside and teased her opening. Tracing with his fingers, feeling the humid warmth of her body spilling out, beckoning him to come deeper. He teased her with just the tip of his finger, and she moaned and reached down to grasp his shoulders.

"What are you feeling?" he asked in Italian, needing to know.

"I can't translate Italian now," she said breathlessly.

He laughed. She'd brought him down to the very base of the man he was. He'd forgotten to speak English, which they'd almost used exclusively in their conversations. "Pardon me. You go to my head."

"Good." She squirmed against him.

He kissed her, and her mouth opened under his, her tongue tangling with his. He was so hard right now he thought he'd come in his pants. She was pure feminine temptation and he had her in his arms.

He nibbled on her and held her at his mercy as his fingers continued to tease between her legs. Her nails dug into his shoulders and she arched into him.

He rolled over so that he was under her. He stroked her back and spine, scraping his nail down the length of it. He followed the line of her back down the indentation above her backside.

She closed her eyes and held her breath as he fondled her. A sweet sound escaped her lips before he captured them. She tipped her head to the side, allowing him access to her mouth. She held his shoulders and moved on him, rubbing her body over his erection.

He shifted her back a little bit so he could see her face and watch her expression. Her breasts were bare, nipples distended and begging for his mouth. He lowered his head and suckled.

He buried his hand in her hair and arched her over his arm. Both of her breasts were thrust up at him. He had a lap full of woman and he knew that he wanted Nathalie more than he'd wanted any woman in a long time.

He realized that he wanted to erase all other men from her memory. Whatever lovers she had in the past he wanted to ensure she never recalled again. That when she thought of sharing her body with a man, his was the only face she saw.

Her eyes were closed, her hips moving subtly against him, and when he blew on her nipple he saw gooseflesh spread down her body.

"Nathalie?"

"*Oui,* Antonio?" Her voice was husky and her words spaced out. And he loved it. Loved the way she reacted to him.

"You're mine," he said.

He kept his attention on her breasts. Her nipples were so sensitive he was pretty sure he could bring her to an orgasm just from touching her there.

The globes of her breasts were full and fleshy, more than a handful. He licked the valley between her breasts. She tasted sweet and a bit salty. And like nothing he'd tasted before.

He kept kissing and rubbing until her hands clenched in his hair and she rocked her hips harder against his length. He lifted his hips, thrusting up against her. He sucked hard on her tender, aroused nipple. "Come for me, *cara mia.*"

But she braced her hands on his shoulders and pulled her body away from his. "I don't want this to just be about me."

"It won't be. I want you to come for me, Nathalie, and then we can come together."

"Promise?"

"Yes."

She lowered her body to his again and he rebuilt her passion, aroused her with all the skill he'd learned since he'd had his first woman years ago. He was glad for the knowledge gained from his past lovers because he needed to do so much more than just please Nathalie.

When he felt her hips moving against him, he caressed her feminine mound and then slowly entered her with one finger and then two. She moaned his name as he teased her. He couldn't help but smile as he continued to draw the reaction he wanted from her. He kept touching her and whispering words of sex against her, telling her what he wanted and how to give it to him.

She gasped and he felt her body tighten around his fingers as her orgasm rolled over her until she collapsed in his arms, falling down on his chest.

A moment later he set about arousing her again. He held her close, enjoying the feel of her rapid breath against his neck. The creamy moisture at the apex of her thighs told him that he'd done a good job of bringing her pleasure.

He glanced down at her and saw she was watching him. The fire in her eyes made his entire body tight with anticipation.

"I want you inside me this time, Antonio," she said, no shadows in her eyes now. "I really want you. Come to me now."

Shifting off him, she settled next to him on the pillows. She opened her arms and her legs, inviting him into her body, and he went. He took his pants off, tossing them on the deck next to her shirt and jeans. Then he lowered himself over her and caressed every part of her.

She reached between his legs and fondled his sex, cupping him in her hands, and he shuddered. He needed to be inside her now. But he had to take care of a condom first. He fumbled in his pants pocket and pulled out the condom he'd optimistically put there earlier. He sheathed himself quickly, before coming back between her legs. He shifted and lifted her thighs, wrapping her legs around his waist. Her hands fluttered between them and their eyes met.

Mine, he thought.

He held her hips steady, entered her slowly, then thrust deeply until he was fully seated. Her eyes widened with each inch he gave her. She clutched at his hips as he started thrusting, holding him to her, her eyes half closed and her head tipped back.

He leaned down and caught one of her nipples in his teeth, scraping very gently. She started to tighten around him. Her hips moved faster, demanding more, but he kept the pace slow, steady. He wanted her to come again before he did.

He suckled her nipple and rotated his hips to catch her pleasure point with each thrust and he felt her hands clench in his hair as she threw her head back and a climax ripped through her.

He varied his thrusts, finding a rhythm that would draw out the tension at the base of his spine. Something that would make his time in her body, wrapped in her silky limbs, last forever.

Leaning back on his haunches, he tipped her hips up to give him deeper access to her body. Then she scraped her nails down his back, clutched his buttocks and drew him in. His blood roared in his ears as he felt everything in his world center to this one woman.

He held her in his arms afterward, neither of them saying anything, and he feared that was because both of them knew that this had changed the stakes in their friendly little game. The family feud that had started with her great-aunt and his grandfather couldn't be continued with their generation.

Seven

Back in Paris, life seemed too hectic. Her father and sister had gone back to their lives and now that she was home Nathalie thought that Antonio and the night they'd spent together would seem less intense, but it wasn't. She had been working day and night not just on the Moretti Motors negotiations but also on the other work that crossed her desk.

Her parents had invited her to dinner tonight and she'd tried to turn them down, but Nathalie never could disappoint her mother.

It was the same with Genevieve. Maybe it was because they'd grown up closer to their mother than their father. Whatever the reason, she admitted as she drove her Peugeot on the roundabout in front of the Arc de Triomphe, she didn't care. She wanted to get through dinner as quickly as she could and then get back to work.

It was the only way she'd found to keep her mind off of Antonio. When she was at home in her luxurious condo, all she did was imagine him there with her. When she slept he haunted her dreams, making love to her and speaking to her in that beautiful Italian voice of his. When she worked out at the gym, she sometimes thought she heard his footfalls on the treadmill next to hers.

He was haunting her. Damn him.

In the office he'd sent her a very official-sounding e-mail telling her that he looked forward to hearing from her on the Vallerio Roadster matter.

And then at home she'd received a vase of yellow daffodils, which were still on her front hall table. They were the first things she saw when she came home and the last things she noticed when she left. The note he'd sent was sweet and sexy. Everything she'd expect from Antonio.

And a part of her…okay, all of her hoped that this relationship was more than an affair. But she was afraid to believe it.

He had said that they should keep their dating

private and that it had nothing to do with the negotiations they were both embroiled in right now, but she worried that she wouldn't be able to.

Her mobile rang as she approached the restaurant and pulled into the valet lane. She glanced down at the caller ID and saw that it was an Italian number. Antonio?

She hurried out of her car and into Ladurée. The restaurant was over a century old and a famous institution on the Champs-Elysées.

"Bonjour, c'est Nathalie," she said, answering her phone.

"Ciao, cara mia. Did you get the flowers I sent?"

"Yes, I did. Thank you for them."

"You're welcome. What are you doing?"

"Having dinner with my family. I'm sorry I haven't sent you a thank-you note."

"That's nothing. Why haven't you returned my calls?" he asked.

She shrugged and then realized he couldn't see that response. "I'm not sure. I've been busy."

She realized she was making excuses and she knew better than that. "I guess I wanted a chance to get you out of my head."

"Did it work?" he asked.

"No. Not at all."

"Well, then you should have called me back. I've missed the sound of your voice."

"Have you?"

"Indeed. When will you be back in Milan?"

"Next week. I'm meeting with our board tomorrow and I should have a counteroffer for you."

"You know how far I'm willing to go," he said.

She wondered if she really did know. How far was Antonio willing to go to get the deal closed? Was he willing to seduce her?

She didn't know. She doubted seducing her would be of benefit for him.

"Why so silent?"

"I'm just thinking," she said. She was dreaming of this man who was her rival. This man who wanted something from her family that they had fought to hold on to. And she was going to try to find a way to make it work for him. Because she wanted to honor her grandfather's memory, but also because she wanted to get this deal off the table so she could see what lay between them.

"Nathalie?"

"Um…pardon me. I've got to go. My parents are waiting."

"Call me when you are done with dinner," he said.

"It will be late."

"That's okay, I'll be up."

She hesitated. But then she thought, why the hell not? She'd be thinking about him anyway.

"All right. I'll call. I only have your office number."

"I'll send you a text with all my numbers. I'll be at home after ten."

"Very well. *Bonne nuit,* Antonio."

"Until later."

He disconnected the call and she held on to her BlackBerry for another minute, standing in the crowded foyer of the restaurant trying to regain her equilibrium.

"Nathalie!"

She turned to see Genevieve waving at her. She made her way over to her sister and hugged her. "Are Mom and Dad here?"

"Not yet. I told them we'd meet them in the bar," Genevieve said, leading the way to the bar. They both ordered a glass of wine and found a seat at one of the high tables.

"What happened that last night in Milan?"

"What? Nothing. I told you I stayed in," she said.

"I followed you to Duomo and saw you leave with Antonio."

"Busted?"

"Big-time. So what's up?"

"I...I don't know. It really has nothing to do with the negotiations."

"How can you say that? He's a Moretti. Lorenzo already proved that the men in that family are all about business."

Nathalie took a sip of her drink. "I know. But Antonio is different."

"Is he really?"

"Yes, I think he is. I know that I might be making a mistake, but I think I can handle him in the board-room and out."

"I hope you are right," Genevieve said.

Nathalie did too. And she knew no matter what, she had to be very careful that she didn't forget that with Moretti men, business always came first.

Antonio strolled down the hall to Dominic's office. Angelina was sitting at her desk despite the fact that it was well past five.

"*Ciao,* Antonio," she said.

"*Ciao,* Angelina. Is my brother available?"

"*Sì.* Marco has just gone in."

"*Grazie.*"

He entered the office and closed the heavy oak door behind him. Marco looked relaxed and happy, despite the fact that it was the beginning of the F1 World Championship race calendar. "*Ciao,* Marco. Congratulations on your win in Behrain last weekend."

He smiled. "*Grazie*. Everyone is gunning for me this year."

"I would imagine so," Dom said.

"How is Virginia and little Enzo?"

"Very good. We'd love it if you'd join us for dinner tonight."

He nodded.

"If that's settled, can we get down to business?" Dom said.

Antonio sat in the other guest chair, listening with half an ear as Dom caught Marco up on everything that had been happening the last two weeks while he'd been out of town.

He studied his younger brother and realized, for the first time since Marco had fallen in love with Virginia, that he envied his brother. Which was ridiculous. He was a bachelor. He loved his single life, yet a part of him wanted someone to come home to. Wanted a partner that would always be there for him.

He rubbed the back of his neck, knowing that he wasn't going to find that with Nathalie. He couldn't. No matter how much he wanted her in his life, his priority had to always be Moretti Motors.

"Tony?"

"Hmm?"

"Did you hear what I said?" Dom asked. "The leak is in the corporate offices. I've asked Ian to meet us after the dinner hour tonight. He has some information that he didn't want to give to me at the office."

"I don't like the sound of that," Antonio said. "He must think that the problem is in one of our offices."

"I'm not going to guess at anything. Can you join us after dinner?"

He thought about the call he'd coerced Nathalie into making. He wanted to talk to her, but canceling an important meeting for her... Well, that would be giving her too much power in his personal life and he wasn't willing to do that just now. "*Sì*, I'm available."

"*Buon.* So, where do we stand on the Vallerio negotiations?"

"I offered them a share of the profits from the roadster, and a seat on the board for the CEO of Vallerio Incorporated. They want to do profit sharing companywide for all of their shareholders. I've told them we'll consider it if it's a reciprocal arrangement."

"Is that fiscally a good idea?" Dom asked.

"I am doing some research on their profit and loss statements for the last couple of years. They are expecting a huge profit in the third quarter this year, but I haven't been able to figure out why."

"Doesn't Nathalie know?" Dom asked.

"I'm sure she does but I haven't asked her yet. She

is busy with figuring out what her board will accept and preparing a counteroffer."

"I thought you were working on seducing her to get more information," Dom said.

"It's never that easy with women," Marco said. "You must know that, Dom."

"Indeed, but this time I think it's important that Tony pull out all the stops."

"Are you giving him romantic advice?" Marco asked. "What have you two been up to while I've been racing?"

Antonio knew this was going to continue going downhill. Marco would tease him endlessly because Dom had suggested he seduce Nathalie. Antonio realized that to anyone on the outside the ploy was going to seem cold and calculated.

Still, Antonio knew he hadn't seduced her for any reason other than that he wanted her. He was attracted to her body and soul, he thought.

"Tony?"

"Dom suggested I use sex as another means of weakening her defenses."

"Did you? That's ethically wrong," Marco said.

"Of course it is. Nathalie and I are both very aware of our family rivalry," Antonio said.

"That's good. Do you like her?" Marco asked.

He shrugged. No way was he going to talk about

Nathalie with his brothers. Dom would find it uncomfortable if he mentioned that he was attracted
to Nathalie in a way he'd never been attracted to
another woman. And he knew that he didn't want
to have to choose between his loyalty to his brothers
and to Nathalie.

Was he loyal to her? He didn't like to think that
she had any control over him, but he knew she did.

"Of course I like her. She's sexy and smart, a
lethal combination in any woman."

Marco laughed and Dom looked uncomfortable.

"Can you handle her?"

"She's only a woman," Antonio said. Now if he
could only convince his emotions of that fact.

Nathalie waved her mother and sister off as they
went to the bakery section of the restaurant to buy
something yummy for all of them. Her father was
going to ride back to her parents' house with her. He
wanted, as he'd said, to make sure she still realized that
the Vallerio family had been done a grave injustice.

The valet brought her car and she got in after
tipping the man. Her father sat quietly until she'd
navigated out of the traffic on the Champs-Elysées.

"Thank you for all your hard work with the Moretti
Motors people," Emile said, "but I don't think this
newest offer of theirs is going to be one we can accept."

"Why not? I think the terms are good and that we will make the profit that we wanted to from this agreement."

Nathalie made a left turn and then glanced over at her father. His mouth was pinched tight and he looked like a very old man for a minute. "Papa?"

"I'm fine. We don't need the Morettis to make a profit. I don't want to give away the farm just to have a piece of their pie."

She shook her head. "I know what I'm doing."

"Do you? I've always been impressed by your business savvy and the way you conduct yourself, but Antonio Moretti…he's slick and smooth and I'm not sure you can handle him."

If her father only knew. She'd faced men like Antonio on more than one occasion and always come back a winner. "Papa, don't you trust me?"

"*Oui, cherie,* I trust you."

"Then why are you asking me all these questions?"

"I guess it is simply that I don't trust the Moretti men not to do something underhanded. And you are my daughter, Nathalie. I don't want you hurt the way my aunt Anna was."

She understood that. "I'm not *Tante* Anna, Papa, and I'm not going to let Antonio use me the way that Lorenzo did her. I'm more than capable of handling myself around Antonio."

"*Bien.* That's all I wanted to say. Also we cannot accept less than seventy percent of the profits from the roadster. I talked to the rest of the board already and they are adamant as well."

Nathalie turned onto the street where her parents lived. "Papa, that's impossible. Antonio has already turned that offer down."

"Then tell him he'll have to try harder to come up with a better offer than he has so far."

"I will."

Nathalie parked on the street in front of her parents' house with a feeling that her father was never going to accept any relationship she had with Antonio. And that made her a little sad because she had started to see Antonio as a man. Not the Moretti monster that her family had always painted the Moretti heirs to be.

Holding his nephew reinforced to Antonio how important it was to focus on the legacy of Moretti Motors. Marco and Virginia were obviously in love and Antonio saw no latent signs of the Moretti curse in his brother's house, but as they left to go meet Ian Stark and Antonio handed his nephew back to Virginia, he realized that he didn't want to take any chances.

He didn't want Enzo to experience what he and his brothers had when their house had to be sold and they had to move to *Nono*'s house. That wasn't acceptable to him.

He knew that meant he had to cool it with Nathalie. He had to treat her the same way he would treat any other woman he'd started an affair with. Sending flowers was okay, but one-of-a-kind nightgowns probably wasn't the right tone if he wanted to keep this relationship like all of his other affairs.

But it was too late to cancel the sexy negligee he'd ordered to be delivered tomorrow morning. Earlier he'd thought he'd seduce her further over the phone and then send her that sexy nightgown for her to wear the next time she came to Milan. But now… Oh, hell, he wasn't sure.

He followed Dom to his home, which was only three streets from Marco's. They'd all purchased homes in the same area of Milan so that they were close to the Moretti Motors corporate offices and each other. They were only eighteen months apart and had always been very close.

There was a Porsche 911 in the driveway and Antonio shook his head as he got out. Only Ian would drive a rival car to Dom's house.

Luigi, Dom's butler, let him in and directed him to the den, where Ian and Dom waited for him.

"Dom, you've got a big piece of trash in front of your house," Antonio said as he entered.

"Most people don't consider a Porsche trash, Tony."

"I can't speak to others' ignorance," Antonio said.

Ian laughed and stood up to shake his hand. "Good to see you."

"You as well. So, did you find our leak?" Antonio said.

"I did. I think it's going to shock you both."

"Nothing would shock me," Dom said.

"Not even the fact that the leak is your secretary, Angelina de Luca?"

"What? Are you sure?" Dom asked. He crossed to the bar on one wall and poured two fingers of whiskey into a highball glass and swallowed it in one long draw.

"Positive. She's been feeding information to ESP Motors. I saw the last drop myself."

"What the hell?" Dom said.

Antonio was surprised and concerned. "She's had free rein of our corporate offices. She knows everything."

"I know that," Dom said.

"What should we do next?" Ian asked. "I have enough evidence to go to the police. We can have her arrested and press charges."

"Do you have enough to prove ESP was behind it?" Antonio asked. ESP was the company founded by Nigel Eastburn, Lorenzo Moretti's biggest rival on and off the racetrack. Both men had started their own car companies after retiring. The launch of the Vallerio model had pushed Lorenzo ahead of Nigel, but in the '80s when Moretti Motors had started to fail, ESP Motors, named after Nigel and his two partners Geoffrey Saxby and Emmitt Pearson, had moved ahead. And that was why Moretti Motors wanted the roadster to be a success—to take back the pride that they'd lost when ESP had become the name synonymous with roadsters.

"If you give me another week or so, I'll get the proof. I need to make sure their guy isn't working independently."

"Who is it?"

"I believe it's Barty Eastburn."

"Nigel's grandson? That is big. Well, I'd rather take him down than just Angelina."

"She can't get off with no punishment," Antonio said.

"She won't," Dom said. The fierceness of his tone made Antonio realize that Dom was furious at Angelina's betrayal.

Eight

Nathalie was no closer to figuring out anything about her relationship with Antonio when she arrived in Milan a week later. She hadn't called Antonio or spoken to him since their one conversation before her dinner.

She was trying very hard to convince herself that she was only happy to be in Milan to resolve the outstanding issues she had with Moretti Motors, but she was failing.

She wanted to see Antonio. She was a bit mad at herself that she hadn't called him back, but after her conversation with her father she'd felt it was important to keep her distance. Now as she waited in the Moretti Motors lobby she knew nothing was more important than seeing Antonio.

As soon as he stepped off the elevator and started walking toward her, she had the insane desire to run to him.

"Good afternoon, Nathalie. Welcome back to Milan," he said. He welcomed her with a kiss on each cheek.

She turned her head toward him at the last second and her lips brushed his cheek.

"It's good to be back."

"Why didn't you call me, *cara mia?*"

She held her briefcase in one hand and followed him through the hallway to the conference room. "I...I don't know. I mean I had good reasons at first, but now that I'm here they don't seem valid."

"We can discuss that later, over dinner and drinks."

"Antonio, do you think that's a good idea?"

"Yes, I do. Did you get the gift I sent?"

"I did. I'm sorry I haven't thanked you properly." She'd put the negligee on and slept in it every night since he'd sent it. It was exquisite and since she knew the store where he'd purchased it, she also knew it was one of a kind. She'd been touched that he'd sent her the nightgown, but afraid to call him. Afraid that if she talked to him she'd forget to remain strong on the negotiations.

"You can do so later."

"Can I?" she asked, refusing to let him get away with bossing her around.

"Yes, you may," he said, with an unrepentant grin. "I've invited Dominic to join us. He has a counter-offer since we are at an impasse."

Antonio's words made her realize she needed to put all of her personal thoughts on hold and focus on this meeting. How could she tell Antonio that the Vallerio board wasn't going to be satisfied with anything less than a deal that was on their terms? She decided to be straightforward.

"I'll be happy to listen to your proposal, but I'm afraid nothing less than what we've asked for will suffice."

"Is there nothing I can do that would make them change their minds?"

She shook her head. "If you want to back down on your stance, we could move forward."

"I don't see that happening."

"So it's back to the drawing board," she said.

"Hear Dom's presentation. I think it'll make a huge difference."

"You know this isn't just about business," she said. "Almost everyone on the board is related to my grandfather and he was so angry about what Lorenzo did to Anna."

"What did he do?" Antonio asked. "Because from what we heard, she left him. Went back to Paris and never returned."

"He kicked her out, Antonio. He told her she wasn't the wife he needed to build his dynasty with."

Antonio looked over at her. "Some men don't know how to handle themselves with a woman who offers too much temptation."

"Is that a problem for you?" she asked.

"It never has been, but to be honest you do stay on my mind more than I wish you would."

"Do I?" she asked. She didn't want to talk about them, because if she weren't careful she'd fall for him—harder than she already had. It already was a very real danger because she was ready to go back to her board of directors and do whatever it took to convince them to take this deal.

"*Sì*, you do. Why is that?" he asked. He glanced at the closed boardroom door to the table and she almost blushed when she remembered what had occurred the last time they were alone in this room.

She tipped her head to one side. "Perhaps because you've met your match."

"I think I have," he said, leaning back against the

table in the exact spot where she'd sat when he'd pleasured her. "But then you must have too."

"I don't know about that. I'm more than capable of taking whatever you have to dish out."

He reached for her, his hands on her waist as he drew her closer to him. He spread his legs and less than a second later she was in his arms. Nestled there where she'd secretly wanted to be.

"This is so inappropriate for the business we are conducting."

"That might be, but I've missed you, *amore.*"

She glanced at the closed door and then leaned up on her tiptoes and kissed him. For a week now she'd gone to sleep with only the remembered feel of his arms around her and his mouth pressed to hers. The reality was so much better than her memories.

She kissed him as if this was the last embrace they'd have. In a way it was. After her talk with her father she'd known that nothing lasting could come of her affair with Antonio. No matter how much she might want something more.

That evening when he picked Nathalie up, Antonio wasn't sure he was doing the right thing, but he knew that unless he got her to see his family as something more than monsters she was never going to be able to convince the Vallerio board to soften their position.

And truly the only way to do that was to let Nathalie meet his parents. His father was as different from Lorenzo as any man could be. Giovanni had filled his life with one passion and that was his wife, Philomena. Antonio knew that once Nathalie met them she'd see that the Moretti men weren't out to crush the Vallerio family once again.

He wanted to make her see that they were sincere in their offer to put Vallerio back on the lips of car connoisseurs the world over.

"Are you sure about this?" she asked once they were seated in his car.

"Positive. I had the opportunity to meet your father and sister and now I think it's time you had the same."

"Aren't they going to be angry that I haven't convinced my board to accept all of your terms?"

"No. I doubt they will say anything to you about business. My parents aren't concerned about that at all."

"What are they concerned about?"

Antonio thought about that for a moment. "Each other. And that my brothers and I are happy."

"I can't imagine that Lorenzo's son wouldn't be as passionate about car making as he was."

"Wait until you see my parents. They have a love that consumes them."

"I still don't understand," she said. "Many men are married and still manage a company."

"But those men weren't cursed to be lucky either in love or in business," Antonio said.

"And your family was?" she asked.

"Indeed. In fact your great-aunt may have fallen victim to the same curse."

"How do you figure?" she asked.

"Lorenzo broke the heart of a girl he'd left behind in his village to go and seek his fortune, and she cursed him when he didn't fulfill his promise to her."

"What promise?"

Antonio glanced away from the road and over at Nathalie. She seemed very interested in his story. And he wanted to share it. Wanted her to understand that there was more to Lorenzo than his callous behavior might have indicated. "The promise to marry her once he had won the Grand Prix championship and started his car company."

"Promises he didn't keep?"

"No. Lorenzo needed more time to make his fortune. His parents were poor farmers who never did more than eke out an existence and he wanted better for his children."

"So he asked her to wait for him, or did he send her home?" Nathalie asked.

"He told her he couldn't fulfill his promise until

he was certain he'd have the future they both wanted. He asked her to wait awhile longer. She returned home to her village and waited."

"How do you know all of this?"

"Marco's wife, Virginia, is the granddaughter of Cassia, Lorenzo's first love. She has Cassia's journal."

"She cursed your grandfather but your brother married her granddaughter?"

"That makes us sound crazy, I know, but the curse she put on Lorenzo was also put on succeeding generations. When you meet my parents you will see they have a love that is just as successful as Moretti Motors was under *Nono*'s leadership. As successful as it will be now that Marco, Dom and I are running things."

She gave him a very queer look, then turned away, glancing down at her hands, which were laced together in her lap. "Does that mean your brothers don't expect to find the love your parents have?"

Antonio tried not to think of love. It wasn't really something that he'd craved. He had his parents' love and he had never lacked for feminine company and he had his brothers. What more could a man need?

"I don't know," he said honestly. "Love... romantic love just isn't something I've ever really wanted to have."

"Why not?"

"Maybe because of how badly *Nono* screwed it up. Virginia's grandmother cursed him, hated him so much that she wanted to make sure he never felt love again. Your great-aunt hated him so much that she turned Pierre-Henri against him.

"With that kind of a legacy do you think I'd even entertain falling for a woman?"

"But your father isn't that type of man," she said.

Antonio had often thought the same thing. But he'd seen Dom crash and burn with a love affair when he was in university and Antonio had realized whether they wanted to believe in a curse or not he and his brothers had inherited *Nono*'s bad mojo when it came to love and women.

"He's also not the businessman Lorenzo was."

"I see. Since you are good at business, it follows you'll be a screwup with women."

Antonio turned on the long winding driveway that led to his parents' estate in San Giuliano Milanese. He stopped the car in the circular drive at the front of the house. "I have never been a screw-up with women. You asked about love and that's an emotion I've never really sought out."

And it had never found him, he thought. Until now. Seeing the disappointment in Nathalie's eyes, he wanted to be the man who could give her everything she wanted. Including love.

He wanted to be able to make a grand gesture as his father had when he'd walked away from Moretti Motors.

"I guess I understand what you are saying. You haven't looked for love and it hasn't found you."

"Have you?" he asked. The thought of Nathalie loving another man made a red rage fill him. He didn't want any other man to have any claim on Nathalie. And that very possessiveness bothered him as nothing else ever had.

She shook her head. "I've always been too focused on making a name for myself at Vallerio Incorporated."

Antonio's family was warm and welcoming to her. They had dinner in the garden under the stars and it didn't take her long to realize what Antonio had meant by the love his parents shared.

The men left the table to have a cigar in the lower part of the garden. Nathalie felt a moment's panic when she realized she was going to be alone with two women she had nothing in common with—Antonio's mother and his sister-in-law.

"I'm so glad you could join us tonight for dinner. The boys are so excited about their new car, and working with your family to get the Vallerio name is so important to them," Philomena said.

Antonio's mom was short, curvy and still had ebony-colored hair. She had held her own during dinner, but it had been obvious to Nathalie that she doted on the men in her life, and hearing her call Antonio and his brothers "the boys" was something that made her smile.

"Thank you for inviting me. I'm glad to see my grandfather's name being used in conjunction with a car again."

"Marco said your grandfather was pure magic when it came to open-wheel racing," Virginia said. She was a lively woman who had an aura of earthiness about her. She held her son cradled in her arms and often bent down to brush a kiss on Enzo's forehead.

Nathalie sadly had never seen her grandfather drive. She was more acquainted with the man he'd been after Lorenzo Moretti had married and divorced his sister. The man who had retreated into his workroom and focused more on what was happening under the hood. "I never got to see him drive until today."

Dom had put together a documentary that they were going to run in their suite at the F1 races for the rest of the year. The film showed Lorenzo and Pierre-Henri in their glory days. To be honest, the film had done a lot to make her look at all the Morettis in a different way. They had honored her grandfather in a way she hadn't believed they would.

She hoped even her father realized that. If he didn't, she was now determined to convince him.

Philomena's question intruded on her thoughts.

"How long will you and Marco stay in Milan?" she asked Virginia.

"Just another night. Then we are off to Barcelona for the Catalunya Grand Prix. Actually, I'm not sure if Marco mentioned this to you but we were hoping you'd babysit little Enzo here. It's our anniversary of sorts," Virginia said.

"We'd love to. You know I had a nursery prepared here as soon as we had the news of your pregnancy."

"Thank you," Virginia said.

"I've always wanted grandchildren, but I feared my boys were never going to settle down."

Nathalie understood why. "Moretti Motors is as important to them as family."

Virginia nodded. "I think sometimes that to them it *is* family and not a business at all. And of course the curse my grandmother had placed on the Morettis hung over the boys' heads."

Not a superstitious person herself, Nathalie found it hard to believe that so many of these people were. Virginia hardly seemed like a witch, but she'd told the story at dinner of how she'd used her limited knowledge of the old Strega ways to break the curse on Marco.

The curse that Cassia had placed on Lorenzo and every generation that followed.

Nathalie thought that Antonio and Dominic might believe they were still cursed. That by not finding love they hadn't found a way out of the blight that Cassia Festa had put on them. She couldn't help but sympathize with the close-knit Morettis.

"How often do you all get together?" she asked.

"Not often enough. Marco and Virginia travel most of the year for the Grand Prix. Antonio is here in Milan, but he is always busy, and Dominic goes between the offices here and the Grand Prix races."

"Do you attend the races?" Nathalie asked Philomena as they sipped coffee. Night had fallen and the sweet smell of flowers filled the air.

"Mostly the ones in Europe and always the first and last race of the season."

"You should come to the race in Barcelona next week," Virginia urged Nathalie. "There is so much excitement and energy at the races."

Nathalie doubted she would. Her father would have a fit if she attended a Grand Prix race before they had a deal with Moretti that satisfied him. "Thank you for the invitation. Is it always exciting to watch or are you ever afraid?"

Philomena blessed herself and uttered a small prayer under her breath. "I am afraid every time Marco gets in the race car. One of the Team Moretti drivers almost died last year."

Nathalie reached over and put her hand on Philomena's. "I'm sorry. I didn't mean to bring up bad memories."

"You didn't," Virginia said. "But it is a scary profession and even though I know that Marco is a very skilled driver I am reminded most weeks that this is a very dangerous profession."

Nathalie could see that. She was worried about falling in love with the son of her family's sworn enemy, but Virginia had to worry about the man she loved possibly dying. It put a lot of things in perspective for her.

She realized that she didn't want Antonio to be in danger. Then it hit her sitting her in this garden with his mother and his sister-in-law that she was in love with Antonio.

And once that realization opened her eyes, everything else fell into place. She hadn't returned to Milan to broker a deal. She'd returned to Milan to be with Antonio. In Paris it was easy to ignore the truth and to pretend that she didn't love Antonio, but tonight under the Milan moon there were no denials. Only the truth. And she was still dealing with that truth twenty minutes later when Antonio returned.

He looked at her and she could do nothing but smile at him. The man she loved.

Nine

Antonio drove to Nathalie's hotel in Milan in silence. Something was on her mind but he had no idea what. It had been a calculated move to bring her to his parents' house, and now he was wondering what the aftereffects would be. "Are you okay?"

"Yes. Dinner was very nice."

"I'm glad you enjoyed it."

"And I think I see what you meant about your parents' love. Your father is positively smitten with your mother."

"Yes, he is."

"Funny to think that a curse would have given him that much love in his life."

Antonio turned to her when he stopped for a traffic light. "I don't think he's cursed at all."

"Do you think the men in your family are? When we talked earlier I couldn't tell if you really believed you were doomed."

"Doomed to spend my life alone?" he asked. "Maybe I did. I guess that when you grow up with that kind of love in your home and then you visit with friends, you start to see that not everyone has that kind of love."

He didn't elaborate and she wanted to ask if he had wanted to find what his parents had. She knew that she and Antonio couldn't have that. She was never going to be like his mother and stay home and give up her own ambition.

She shook her head. Realizing she loved Antonio was one thing. Thinking about marriage was another. Had she lost it? Too much needed to be resolved between them businesswise before they could ever consider anything permanent. "What is it about your parents' love for each other that you really envy...I mean want?"

"I've never really thought about it," he said. He pulled into the parking area of her hotel, where the valet took the car.

She looked at him and asked, "Would you like to come up?"

"I was hoping you'd ask me. I've missed holding you."

That little confession eased the worries she had felt since she'd first realized that she loved him.

"Me too."

They walked next to each other through the lobby. In the lobby bar Antonio saw a few associates who waved him over, but he shook his head. "I don't want to talk business tonight."

"Is this going to be awkward tomorrow?" she asked when they entered the elevator alone. "This isn't the first time we've been seen together."

"I think my family knows how I feel about you. I didn't just invite you to dinner tonight as a representative of Vallerio Incorporated."

Or had he? He was a brilliant strategist and he had to know that seeing his family would make it harder for her to stand firm on what her board of directors wanted.

He had made the Morettis human to her. He had shown her the people behind the car company and that was softening her attitude toward them.

"It was nice to meet your family, but I have to wonder if you didn't plan it that way…use it as a way to soften me up," she said once they were in her suite.

"Why would I do that?" he asked. He shrugged out of his suit jacket and draped it over the back of the love seat.

"All's fair in love and in war," she said, crossing to the wet bar and taking out a bottle of mineral water. "Would you like something to drink?"

"I'll have a beer," he said.

She handed him a bottle, and he took her hand in his.

"Listen, Nathalie, I stopped trying to find an advantage to use to get you to give in a long time ago."

"Did you really?"

"Yes. I don't want you to surrender to me. I want to find a solution that will make us both happy."

"If I said that Moretti Motors should go ahead with their alternate plans you'd be fine with that?"

He took a swallow of his beer and then looked her straight in the eye. "No, I wouldn't. I think you know that. What would make me happy is coming to an arrangement that both of our boards will find pleasing."

She stepped back from him and walked to the window of her suite. "I'm…I'm confused, Antonio. For the first time in my life I can't just focus on work."

"Why is that?" he asked.

"You made me invest more of myself in this negotiation than I wanted to."

"I made you?"

She shook her head. "Not like you forced me into it…I guess I don't really mean that. I meant that I am different this time because of how I feel about you."

He put his beer on the coffee table and walked across the small room to her. He stopped when only an inch of space separated them.

He took her water from her hand and put it on the bar. "How do you feel about me, *cara mia?*"

"I…" *I love you,* she thought. But she couldn't say the words out loud. Though he'd claimed to have softened his stance on the negotiations, she couldn't hand him the powerful weapon of her love to use against her.

She shook her head. "I care about you, Antonio."

He drew her into his arms. He hugged her close to his chest and whispered soft words against her temple. She felt safer in her love with his arms around her.

Antonio claimed Nathalie's lips with his and didn't let her go until they'd reached the bed. He'd had enough talking. He was never going to be able to say the right thing to her. The thing that would make her forget that he was a Moretti and she was a Vallerio. That was always going to be between them.

Earlier tonight Dom had been very blunt that he wanted the Vallerio deal closed. He wanted Antonio to pull out all the stops. Antonio couldn't tell his brother that he wouldn't do it. That he was falling for the tall French redhead who was just as strong as he was in the boardroom and in the bedroom.

But now he was in control. And it was important to him that he make her understand this as well.

In three strides he was to the bed. He set Nathalie on her feet and peeled back the covers of the bed. He toed off his loafers and reached down to remove his socks. She still had her shoes on. He bent down and lifted her foot, carefully removing one high heel and then the other.

He stood back up. She looked exquisite in her sapphire wrap dress, like a male fantasy come to life. The neckline plunged deep between her breasts, revealing the creamy white tops of each one, while the hemline ended high on her thigh.

The only light in the room spilled from the city lights outside the window. Darkness enveloped them in a cocoon, as if no one else existed but the two of them. Antonio intended to make the most of their privacy.

He lowered his head and with his tongue, traced the edge where fabric met skin. She smelled of perfume and a natural womanly scent that he associated only with Nathalie. The scent of her skin had haunted him during the week they had been apart. Now he closed his eyes and buried his face between her breasts, inhaling deeply.

Shifting slightly to the right, he tasted her with languid strokes of his tongue. Her skin was sweeter and more addicting than anything he'd ever tasted. He followed the curve of her breast from top to bottom; the texture changed as he reached the edge of her nipple.

The velvety nub beckoned him and he pushed the fabric of her dress out of the way. He wanted to see her.

"Stand here."

He crossed the room and flipped on the light switch flooding the room in light. Nathalie stood where he left her, her red hair hanging around her shoulders in long curls. Her lips looked full and lush, wet and swollen from his kisses. Her breasts spilled from the fabric, full and white and topped with hard little berries that made his mouth water.

He crossed back to her side in less than two strides. "That's better."

"Is it?" she asked.

"I want to see you, Nathalie. The real you, not the dream that's been haunting me."

He didn't give her a chance to respond. He might be playing the fool, but right now he didn't care. He already knew he was compromised where she was concerned. She had a power over him that he could only hope she never realized she had. And he had a new goal—one that had absolutely nothing to do with Moretti Motors.

That goal was to get as deep inside her body as he could.

He lowered his head once more to the full globe of her breast, scraping the aroused nipple with his teeth. She shuddered in his arms. He used his hand to stimulate her other nipple, circling it with his finger and scraping his nail across the center very carefully while at the same time using his teeth on the first one.

She moaned his name, undulating against him. Her hands swept down his body and she unzipped his pants. His erection sprang into her waiting hands. He wanted her to grasp the length of him, but instead she only teased him by running her finger up and down the sides of his shaft.

He suckled her nipple deep in his mouth and slid his hand up under her skirt, where he encountered a sexy thong. He caressed her sticky curls through the lace, and her touch on him changed, became more fevered, more demanding.

He slipped his finger inside the crotch of her panties and into her humid opening. She moaned and lifted her leg to give him deeper access. The moan was nearly his undoing. He couldn't wait much longer to take her.

He turned and lay back on the bed, pulling Nathalie on top of him. She braced her hands on his chest and leaned up over him. Their groins pressed together. She bit her lower lip and rotated on him. It felt deliciously hot and he wanted nothing more than to let her rock against him until they both came. Later, he thought. Right now he needed to be inside her.

He pulled her down to him and rolled until she was underneath him again.

"Do you have to be on top?"

He smiled at her. "It's a male thing."

"Why?"

"Because you are too strong. I want you to know that you are ceding to my will," he said.

He didn't want to say any more, but for once he wanted to feel he was really in control. In control of their lovemaking and in control of this woman who gave away so little.

He tore his shirt off and tossed it across the room and then kicked his pants down. He reached for the bodice of Nathalie's dress and tugged until the fabric ripped, leaving her body bare.

He slid his hand down to her panties.

"Stop."

He did, glancing up at her. She reached underneath his body and pushed the panties down her legs. "I like these and don't want you to tear them."

He chuckled. "I wasn't going to rip them."

He bent his head and followed the path of her skimpy underwear with his mouth. Some of her wetness had rubbed against her thigh and he licked her clean. Then he rose over her.

He bent her legs back against her body, leaving her totally exposed to him. Leaning down, he tasted her pink flesh, caressing her carefully with his tongue until her hips were rising against him and her hands clenched in his hair. He slid up her body, holding her hips in his hands, tilting them upward to give him greater access.

He grabbed one of the pillows from the head of the bed and wedged it under her. Then draping her thighs over his arms, he brought their bodies together. Nathalie reached between them and grasped him, guiding him to her entrance.

"Take me," she said.

He did. He entered her deeply and completely, stopping only when he was fully seated within her. He felt her clench around him. He knew she was doing it intentionally and smiled down at her. He lowered his head and took her mouth, allowing his tongue to mimic the movements of his hips. Soon he felt close to the edge. It wasn't going to be much longer until he climaxed in her arms.

She rotated her hips against him with each thrust and soon she was gasping for breath and making those sweet sounds of preorgasm. He reared back, so he could go deeper, her feet on his shoulders.

He held her still for his thrusts and she tilted her head back, her eyes closing as her orgasm rushed over her. It was all he needed to send him over the edge. He felt the tingling at the base of his spine and then emptied himself into her.

Knowing she'd said too much earlier, Nathalie didn't wait for Antonio to say anything now that they were in bed. When he made love to her she felt like a woman. Not the Vallerio daughter or the Vallerio Inc. corporate shark, just a woman.

His woman.

"Do you want to see the negligee you sent me?"

"I'd love to see it," he said.

The light was still on and she went to the wardrobe where she'd hung her clothes earlier in the day. She drew out the gown.

It was a Carine Gilson gown. The exclusive lingerie couture was one of the most expensive in the world. "How did you know I like Gilson?"

"I noticed your bra the first time we made love," he said.

"Most men wouldn't have noticed."

"I'm not most men. Put on the gown. I had to rely on my imagination when I ordered it."

She did as he asked. The sheer gown fell to her knees and she stood in front of him boldly, allowing him to feast his eyes on her. The gold fabric made her skin look even creamy in the light, and the black designs on the side and at the hem added a hint of elegance.

"Come here," he beckoned from the bed. She couldn't help but notice his erection and inwardly she smiled, knowing she had the power to make him hard.

"Turn around."

She did as he said and felt his hand on her thighs, teasing up under the hem of the negligee, then caressing the crease in her buttocks. She shivered with awareness.

Reaching behind her, she found his erection and encircled it with her hand, tugging on it once and then letting go as she stepped away.

Suddenly he came up behind her, his arms coming around to grasp her breasts. He nipped at the shell of her ear. "Gotcha."

She shivered. He plucked at her aroused nipples with his fingers while his mouth continued to play at her neck. Sensation spread throughout her body.

His erection nestled between her buttocks through the fabric of her gown and she shifted a little, rubbing him between them.

One of his hands slipped down her body. He lingered at her belly button, and then slid lower, parting her nether lips. He didn't touch her, just held her open so that the fabric of her gown brushed against her clitoris. She moaned.

"Please," she gasped.

She felt like a prisoner to her desire and to this man. She tried to escape from Antonio's grip but couldn't.

He chuckled in her ear. "You're mine."

Deep in her soul, those words sounded right. She ignored that feeling and focused instead on the physical. She reached behind her to his erection, taking him in her grip. But he pulled his hips back, not allowing her to touch him.

"Antonio," she said.

"Sì, cara mia?" he asked.

"I…" She couldn't think, couldn't speak. She just wanted him inside her. Now.

"You can say it. You need me."

"I do."

"Say it please," he said. He rubbed the fleshy part of her labia with long strokes of his fingers. First one side and then the other. But she ached for more. She shifted again, trying to bring his hand where she wanted it, but he wouldn't be budged. She shoved her own hand down her body, but he caught her before she could bring relief to herself.

"Impatient?"

"You have no idea," she muttered.

He chuckled. Finally he touched her, just a light brush of his fingertip. She reached for him but again he canted his hips away from her touch. "Antonio, no more games."

"Agreed. Lie on the bed on your back."

She did. He pushed the fabric of her negligee high to her waist, parted her legs and moved between them. "Part yourself for me. Show me where you want my tongue."

She did as he said and felt his breath on her. She knew he was seeing her swollen with need and hungry for his mouth. He lowered his head and exhaled against her sensitive flesh.

Her thighs twitched and she wanted to clamp her legs around his head until he made her scream with passionate completion. She felt his tongue against her, lapping at her with increasing strength. Then she felt the edge of his teeth and she screamed with pleasure.

He thrust two fingers inside her, rocking up against her g-spot while his mouth worked its magic on her. He feathered light touches in between shockingly rougher ones that brought her quickly to the edge of orgasm. Still she fought it off, not wanting to end it too quickly.

He added a third finger inside her body and stretched them out when he pulled back and then thrust back into her body. Everything inside her tightened and her climax rushed through her.

Antonio put his hands on her thighs and pushed her legs back against her body before entering her so deeply she felt impaled on his length.

But he stopped there. She opened her eyes and met his gaze. "What are you waiting for?"

"You."

She shifted onto him. Holding his shoulders, she lifted herself off him and then slowly slid back down.

"Faster," he urged.

"Not yet," she said.

She tightened her muscles around him, milking him as she pushed herself up his length and letting him slip out of her body.

He grabbed her hips and pulled her down while he thrust upward. He worked them together until she felt every nerve ending tingling again and her second orgasm rushed over her just as Antonio screamed with his own release.

The sex was phenomenal, the best she'd ever experienced, but as he turned off the lights and took her in his arms and she relaxed against him she realized that the real power that Antonio held over her was this. The sense of rightness she felt in his arms as he held her gently and they both drifted toward sleep.

Ten

The next two weeks were the most intense of his life. Antonio felt more alive than he ever had before. He was exhausted from traveling between Milan and Paris but he thought the fatigue well worth it.

He had ensured that Nathalie and Vallerio Inc. would accept Moretti Motors latest offer. And tonight he was going to propose to Nathalie. From the conversations they'd had about love and that fairer emotion, he sensed that she was in love with him and he felt deeply pleased by that.

He couldn't admit to loving her. He was hedging his bets on the curse that had been a part of his life for so long that he couldn't just admit it. He wouldn't compromise all that he and Dom and Marco had worked for by admitting he'd fallen for Nathalie Vallerio, but he did need her in his life.

"Antonio, do you have a minute?"

He looked up from his computer screen. "Sure, Dom, come on in."

Dom came into his office and closed the door but not all the way. He stood there in the middle of the room, and for the first time Antonio saw that Dom wasn't confident. Not the way he'd always been.

"What's up?"

"Nothing really. Nothing important, I just wanted to let you know that Angelina will be continuing as my secretary."

"Are you sure that's a good idea?"

"Well, I have decided to use her to leak false information to Barty Eastburn. If he wants our company secrets, then he'll get them."

"She agreed to do that?"

"Yes."

Antonio signed off his computer and stood up, walking around to where his brother was. "Good. The Vallerio Roadster is almost ready for rollout. I think we've finally come up with terms that both sides can live with."

"What did you give them?"

"A partial share in the profits from the roadster and a seat on our board. We will be getting a seat on their board as well."

"Did you find out what their anticipated revenue will come from in the next quarter?"

He'd asked around and the Vallerio family was playing this one very close to the chest, but near as he could tell they had filed for new patents and would be releasing an updated carburetor design. A more energy efficient one. "It has something to with engines."

"That's good. See if we can get the exclusive rights to use it on our production cars for the first year."

"I will. I haven't broached the subject with Nathalie yet."

"Why not? You spend a lot of time with her."

"How do you know that?"

"Do you honestly think that I wouldn't pay attention to what you are doing? There is a woman involved and I don't want you to fall like Marco did."

Antonio shook his head. "Dom, it's time you stopped worrying about the curse. I think that Marco did break it. He's still winning and he seems happy."

Dom ran his hand through his hair and sighed. "I don't believe it. We haven't launched the new roadster and until it is successfully launched, we can't afford to take chances."

Antonio clapped his brother on the shoulder. As the oldest, Dom bore more responsibility than any of them. He was the one that *Nono* had groomed for the CEO position from the time they were old enough to talk.

"We will make this work. I can promise you that."

Dom nodded. "Some days just seem longer than others."

"I hear you," Antonio said. "I've been traveling too much. I'm ready to get everything taken care of so I can start loafing around again."

"You have never spent a day loafing in your life."

Antonio had to laugh at that. "Of course I haven't, but it does sound good."

"Indeed," Dom said.

Antonio looked at his older brother. They were workaholics, both of them, and he feared sometimes that if he didn't grab on to Nathalie with both hands, he was going to end up alone. Not that there was anything wrong with living a solitary life, but now that he'd a glimpse of what life could be, he wanted more.

"Do you ever wonder if we should have just followed Papa's path?" Antonio asked.

Dom turned and looked at him, studied him really, and Antonio regretted his words. Dom probably never doubted himself, and hinting that he, Antonio, doubted himself wasn't going over well.

"Never mind."

"No, I can't just dismiss this. If you are thinking along these lines, it can only mean one thing," Dom said.

Antonio shook his head. "It doesn't mean anything. Seeing Marco and Virginia together just made me curious."

Dom narrowed his eyes. "I was curious once, Tony, and I got burned. I didn't need a curse to harden my heart. I did it myself when I realized just how vulnerable a man can be to a woman. And most women can use that to their advantage."

Antonio knew that Dom's ex-lover had betrayed him in the worst way and that his brother would never risk his heart again. But he thought of Nathalie and the burgeoning feelings he had for her. They included trust, he thought.

He already trusted her and even if he never said the words out loud, he knew he loved her.

"I know I suggested romancing Nathalie Vallerio, but has that turned into something more?"

Antonio looked at his brother, straight in the eye, and told the biggest lie he ever had. "No, Dom. It's nothing more than an affair."

Nathalie backed away from Antonio's office almost running to get away from what she'd just heard. She refused to cry, but somehow her eyes didn't get the memo and tears burned the back of her eyes. She blinked rapidly trying to keep them from falling. She made it to the elevator and then had to stop.

She pressed the call button.

What was she going to do? She had taken back to her family the deal that she and Antonio had worked out. She'd compromised on things, believing that he was dealing with her fairly and that he was going to stand up and be the man she'd fallen in love with.

She should have remembered the lesson her great-aunt had learned the hard way...that Moretti men had only one true love and that was Moretti Motors.

She sniffed and blinked some more, but the tears were pooling in the corners of her eyes. She had no tissue to wipe them away. She never cried. She just wasn't the type of woman who would ever break down like this.

She heard the rumble of Antonio's voice and was horrified by the thought that he might catch her crying. She walked down the hall to the toilets on this floor.

She went inside and startled the woman already in there. She was clearly crying, her face red and splotchy. "Angelina?"

"*Ciao,* Nathalie. I'm sorry you've caught me this way."

It was funny but seeing the other woman's distress made her forget about her tears. At least for this moment. And that was all she needed. When she was alone she would deal with the heartache.

"Are you okay?"

"*Sì,*" Angelina said. "I wish I were one of those women who cried pretty."

Nathalie laughed. "Me too. Luckily I don't cry often."

"Unfortunately I do," Angelina said. There was an aura of sadness around her today.

"Do you want to talk?" Nathalie asked.

Angelina shook her head. "Not unless you know some way to keep from crying in front of others."

Nathalie thought about something her sister had read in a psychology journal a few years ago. To be honest she didn't believe it worked, but it always made her and Genevieve laugh when they mentioned it and laughter was a great mask for sadness.

"I did hear something, though I've never tried it," Nathalie said. "Don't laugh but if you tighten your buttocks, it's supposed to make you stop crying."

"And start laughing?"

"Well, it always has that affect on my sister and me."

Angelina laughed and then took a deep breath. "*Grazie,* Nathalie."

"You're welcome."

Angelina left the bathroom and Nathalie stood in

front of the mirror, trying to hold on to the laughter she'd shared with the other woman. She pushed her emotions down deep inside and tried to bury them, but it was hard for her to do.

She'd never been this vulnerable to a man before. And she didn't like that. She didn't like the fact that Antonio Moretti had done this to her.

She remembered what they had said in the beginning and realized she couldn't really get mad at him. She'd agreed that all was fair in love and war. It didn't matter that the circumstances of their relationship had changed for her. They'd laid down the ground rules at the beginning of their negotiations.

She was the one who had forgotten them. It was a mistake she couldn't afford to make again.

Breathing deeply, she left the ladies' room with a confident stride. Walking down the hall to Antonio's office, she practiced what she'd say, how she'd pretend that everything was normal until she got out of here.

She debated leaving now, not seeing him again. But he was expecting her and she had to use the new knowledge she had to her advantage. Something she wouldn't be able to accomplish if she left now.

Antonio's secretary, Carla, was at her desk this time when Nathalie came into the office.

"Is Antonio ready for me?" she asked after exchanging greetings.

"*Sì*, go on in."

The moment she pushed the door open and stepped into his office she knew this was a mistake. When Antonio turned to face her from the far side of his office and smiled at her, she wanted nothing but to confront him.

To demand he tell her to her face that she meant nothing more to him than a little affair to make the negotiations easier.

But she bit her tongue. She channeled her anger into a need for vengeance. Or at least that was what she told herself. Inside she realized that she'd trade vengeance for one more night in his arms.

Antonio was still distracted from his conversation with Dom. He wanted to get away from Moretti Motors and forget about his family for a little while. That was the past and Nathalie was his future. He didn't know how but he was going to convince Dom that there was no harm in falling in love.

He had spent a lot of time the last two weeks trying to make sense of everything, and having Nathalie here with him now made him realize that if he couldn't find a balance between Moretti Motors and Nathalie… Well, he'd have to choose between them, and Nathalie offered him something the car company couldn't.

She offered him a life beyond work.

He walked over to her to kiss her, but she turned her head so that his lips grazed her cheek.

"Are you okay?"

"Yes. Just had a long flight from Paris and I don't feel that your office is the best place for kissing."

"The boardroom is more to your liking?" he asked, teasing her.

She flushed and he saw an expression cross her face that he couldn't identify. "I guess so."

"Did your family agree to the terms we worked out?" he asked. They'd both spent long hours trying to make sure that the deal was fair for both sides.

"We can talk about that later. I'm here for a date with my main man."

"That's right. Pleasure first and then business," he said, but he could tell that something wasn't right with Nathalie. She never talked like this and he wondered if she wasn't having doubts.

Doubts about the deal or about them? Or was she simply tired? It was Friday evening and he'd asked her to come to Milan because he was going to propose to her. He wanted to do it at the house on Lake Como. He thought returning to the place where they'd first made love would be a nice touch.

In fact he'd planned for them to have cocktails and hors d'oeuvres in the boardroom first. "Will you come with me to the boardroom first?"

"Why?"

"I have planned a surprise for you, *cara mia*."

He escorted her out of his office, glancing over at Carla. She nodded to him, letting him know she'd set up everything as he'd asked her to.

When he opened the door of the boardroom he saw flowers on the sideboard, a champagne bucket at the end of the table with a tray of food. And most importantly a slim gift-wrapped box as well.

"After you," he said.

She entered the room and then stopped. He stepped in behind her and locked the door so they wouldn't be disturbed.

"What is this?"

"Just a little predate."

"Antonio," she said, "you didn't have to do all of this."

"Yes, I did," he said. "Have a seat while I pour the champagne."

He held out one of the chairs for her and she slowly came to sit down. He put his hands on her shoulders and leaned over her to kiss her. This time she didn't turn away, but he noticed she was blinking a lot. "Is this okay?"

"Yes," she said, her voice a bit husky.

"Open this while I pour the champagne."

He handed her the box. He hoped she liked the

strand of Mikimoto pearls he'd gotten her. The creamy color of the pearls would look exquisite against her skin.

She held the box in her hands and stared up at him. "Why all of this?"

"To celebrate. Now that we aren't adversaries in the boardroom anymore, we can concentrate on our relationship. I see this day as a new start between us, *cara mia.* Open your gift."

She opened it slowly and he heard her breath catch as she stared down at the ocean-inspired strand of pearls. The pearls were offset by blue sapphires.

"This is beautiful."

"It is nothing compared to your beauty," he said.

He reached around her and took the pearls from the box. "Lift you hair up."

She did as he said and he fastened the necklace around her neck, bending to drop a kiss underneath the white gold clasp. She put one hand at the base of her throat where the pearls rested. He turned the chair around so he could see her eyes.

A sheen of tears glistened there and he knew this was a moment he'd remember all of his life. Having Nathalie here with him made him feel he'd been given the keys to the kingdom. And it was a kingdom he'd never thought to belong in.

That was what he wanted from her love, he

thought, what he needed from it. This acceptance and the desire to be with this woman for the rest of his life.

He knew that their marriage and engagement would not be easy, but he had a strong feeling that they could make it work.

He tipped her head back and kissed her, trying to show her with his mouth all the emotions he felt, all the words he couldn't say.

She parted her lips for him, her tongue thrusting past the barrier of his teeth. Her hands wound around his neck, drawing him closer to her.

He leaned in, put his arms around her waist and lifted her out of the chair and spun around so that he could lean against the table and hold her in his arms.

She pulled back and he saw something in her eyes he'd never seen before. He wasn't sure what emotion it was, but he knew it wasn't love.

"What is it, Nathalie?"

"I'm just trying to figure out something."

"What?"

"Are you giving me this gift as a thank-you for what I did to help Moretti Motors with the Vallerio Roadster? Or…"

"Or?"

"As a sop for your conscience since you romanced me around to your way of thinking?"

Eleven

"I didn't give you this for either reason. These are engagement gifts."

"There are more?" she asked, so afraid to believe what this man was telling her.

"Yes. I want you to be my wife, Nathalie. It has nothing to do with Moretti Motors."

"Really?" she asked.

"*Sì*. Sit down here. Listen to me. Over the past six weeks while we have argued and talked and become lovers, I've come to realize how much you mean to me. How much I need you in my life."

"How much?" she asked again. It was odd. She

should feel like crying now, but instead she felt oddly detached. It was almost as if she were watching the events unfold instead of actually participating in them. "Enough to give up the Vallerio name on the new roadster?"

"Why are you asking me that? You know that our affair has nothing to do with business."

She stood up and paced away from him. "No, Antonio. I don't know that."

"What is going on here?" he asked.

"I heard you talking to Dom earlier. I heard you tell him that I was just a romance."

"*Merda.*"

"Cursing won't change the facts. And all of this is so lovely, but really it is over-the-top for the kind of affair you and I have…at least according to you."

"Nathalie—"

"Don't. Don't try to explain it to me, Antonio. I can't do this. I thought I could have it all. A man who cared for me…really cared about me and my family's respect, but I can see now I was wrong."

"What do you mean? The Vallerio and Moretti deal is done, just waiting for signatures," he said, walking over to her. He took her shoulders in his hands. "And our relationship is just starting. I couldn't tell Dom what I have only just figured out myself."

"What is that?"

"That you mean more to me than any woman ever has before."

He let his hands fall to his sides and she knew he was telling the truth. She did mean more to him than another woman, but for her that wasn't going to be enough. She wanted to be the love of his life. She wanted him to be enamored of her the way Gio was with Philomena. And that wasn't ever going to happen.

She could tell from the moment he mentioned marriage that he wasn't talking about a love affair and she knew that was what it would take for her not to grow bitter.

"That's not enough for me, Antonio," she said.

"Why not? We are both new to this relationship stuff. Give me time to get better at it."

She shook her head. "I can't."

"I don't understand, Nathalie. I have everything here that a woman could want. I will give you everything you need."

"Will you?"

"If it is within my power, it is yours," he said.

She wondered if she was being too hasty. Maybe she had misunderstood what he'd said to Dom. This boardroom certainly made it seem that way.

"What if I said all I really need is your love?" she asked quietly.

She felt the air go out of the room, as Antonio

stared at her. In that instant she had her answer and the tears started to roll down her face. She didn't try to stop them, knew that asking a man for his love and getting silence wasn't something that tricks could combat. She reached up behind her neck and took off the pearls and put them on the table.

"I think that answers my question," she said, walking to the door.

"No, dammit, it does not," he said.

"Yes, it does. Because without love, all of this is hollow. You'd think a man who grew up surrounded by the real thing would know the difference."

"You'd think a woman who spent her entire adult life in the business world would know a good deal when she sees it."

"I want more than a good deal from the man who asks me to marry him."

"I didn't mean that," he said.

"What did you mean, then?" she asked.

He raked a hand through his hair. "I don't know."

"What do you feel for me, Antonio? Is it only lust?"

He shook his head. "It is so much more than that."

"That's something at least. I think I made a mistake by starting an affair with you while we were adversaries."

"No, we didn't make a mistake. You and I we were drawn together from the very first."

"That doesn't mean we were meant to marry," she said. "We both wanted to win and I guess in the end I gave in because— Well, the why doesn't matter anymore…but I almost gave in on some important points for Vallerio Incorporated."

"Are you backing out of the deal we brokered because I can't say that I love you?"

He made her feel small and petty when he said it that way. "No. I'm backing out because we decided we don't need the money we'd make from the roadster."

"Fine. Walk away from the deal if that's what you feel you must do. But remind your board of directors that I treated you fairly and it's only your wounded pride that has you running back to Paris."

She had no rebuttal for him. She just unlocked the boardroom door and walked away as quickly as she could. She didn't want to think that she was using pride to protect her broken heart. To be fair, nothing could protect her broken heart. The pain there was already too intense for her to control.

Antonio glanced around the now empty boardroom. He had no idea how things had gone so wrong. Granted he had never proposed to a woman before, but he wasn't sure that he could screw it up that badly.

"What happened in here?" Dom asked from the doorway.

"Nothing. I…I had some— I asked Nathalie to marry me."

"What? I thought— Never mind that, are you okay?" He stepped into the boardroom.

"Yes, Dom. I know what you are thinking. I had it all under control this afternoon and now I'm afraid I may have messed everything up."

"The deal with Vallerio Incorporated on use of their name?"

"Yes. But more importantly my relationship with Nathalie."

"Which is more important to you?" Dom asked.

For once Antonio didn't stop to think about what answer his brother would want to hear. Instead he spoke the truth. "Nathalie is. And I let her go, Dom."

"You had to. You know that Moretti men don't make good husbands."

"How do we know that? Dad's happy and so is Marco."

"Yes, but they aren't cut from the same cloth as we are. We crave success the same way *Nono* did. What are you going to do? Would you choose Nathalie over Moretti Motors?"

Antonio thought about it. There was no way that he could pick between the two of them. And suddenly he realized he didn't have to. Without Nathalie in his life he didn't care if Moretti Motors was successful. "I can't choose."

"Then that's your answer," Dom said.

"What is?"

"You love her."

"I know I do. I was hoping that by not saying those words out loud I would be able to protect us from the curse. I'm sorry, Dom."

Dom shook his head. "I'm sorry, Tony, sorry that you feel like you have to apologize for falling in love. I was wrong to put you in that position."

"You might not feel like apologizing when I tell you that she's probably going to convince her board not to accept any deal with us."

Dom shrugged. "If that's what she has to do and if that's what you have to agree to in order to prove you love her, then we will find another way."

For the first time since everything went awry with Nathalie, he felt a ray of hope. "Yes, we will."

"I guess this means the curse is still in affect," Dom said.

"How do you figure?" Antonio asked.

"Well, if she's going to take the rights to the name…"

Antonio thought about it for a minute. "You know, I don't believe that's what the curse was about. I think the real curse is the fact that we would deny ourselves love to make the company successful."

"Really?"

Antonio shrugged. "I don't know for you, but for me I think that is the answer."

"What are you going to do?"

"Figure out a way to win Nathalie back."

Two weeks later Nathalie was back in Milan. Her sister and parents and the entire board of directors of Vallerio Inc. were in attendance as well. They'd taken the company jet and Nathalie was so ready to be alone by the time they got off the plane. She was tired.

Tired of sleepless nights and countless recriminations about the last time she spoke to Antonio. She'd tried to get out of this meeting, but Moretti Motors flatout refused to talk to anyone else from Vallerio. And so now they were all here for a big announcement from Moretti Motors. Something that demanded every one of them attend.

She'd tried to find out what was going on, but no one would share any details. Even Genevieve, who normally couldn't be shut up, just sat quietly next to her.

She had confessed to her sister that things had gone wrong with Antonio, but hadn't been able to tell her that she'd let him break her heart. She was a sadder but wiser woman when she entered the Moretti Motors building with her family.

Angelina greeted them all. "If you would all follow me to the garden. We have a special presentation before we go up to the boardroom."

"What presentation?" Nathalie asked.

"That's fine," Emile said, preempting her. "We will give you the time you need for the presentation."

"We will?"

"Oui, ma fille."

She shook her head and followed the rest of her family through the building and out into the courtyard. In the center of the courtyard was a canvas-draped car. She suspected it was the Vallerio Roadster coupe, though she doubted seeing the car would convince her board to go for the deal that Moretti had offered. But she'd have to wait and see.

There were several seats in the courtyard and Angelina directed them all to sit down. "Signore Moretti will be right with you."

"Merci," Emile said.

Nathalie found herself sitting between her father and her sister, tired and heartsick. Sitting here in this garden, she remembered the first time she'd been here and how it had been the start of her affair with Antonio.

She had hoped that her anger would be enough to

inure her to the love she'd felt for him, but it wasn't. And it saddened her to think that a man could use her and she'd still love him, but there it was—the truth of the matter.

"Thank you for joining us today," Dom said, stepping out of the factory and walking toward them. "I know that we have yet to reach an agreement for the use of Pierre-Henri's name on our legendary roadster and that very fact might be on your minds, but my brother has something very important he must do before we can go back to the boardroom."

She noticed that Philomena, Gio, Marco, Virginia and little Enzo were standing behind Dom. Why were they here?

Dom came over to her. "Will you come with me?"

She shook her head. "Why?"

"To make up for the trouble I caused," Dom said.

"What trouble?"

"Making my brother believe that he couldn't have the woman he loves and not disappoint me."

Woman he loved? Did that mean Antonio loved her? She stood up, putting her hand in Dom's. "Where to?"

"Right here," he said, leading her to the center of the courtyard right next to the canvas-covered car.

"Nathalie."

She turned to see Antonio striding toward her.

"Thank you, everyone, for coming today and for allowing me to do this in front of you," he said, speaking to their assembled families.

"As you are aware, our families have some misunderstandings between us. And because of that we haven't always communicated well with each other. I allowed that to ruin something precious to me."

Antonio turned to her. "I allowed the past to have more power over me than it should. I love you, Nathalie Vallerio. And I don't want to live without you."

"Antonio—"

"Shh. Let me finish, *cara mia.*"

He dropped down on one knee in front of her. "Please do me the honor of being my wife."

She stared down at him for a long moment and then drew him up to his feet. "Did you mean it when you said you loved me?"

"More than anything else in this world."

"What if my family won't agree to letting you use the Vallerio name?"

"That is why I'm asking you to marry me now. There is nothing that can change my desire to have you as my wife," he said, drawing her into his arms.

Nathalie looked at Antonio. She wanted to believe that he was sincere, but how could she be sure this wasn't the Moretti charm? The same charm that

Lorenzo had used on Anna. Was she simply being fooled because…because it was what she wanted to hear so badly? She realized she wanted Antonio's love. Not because it would end a family feud but because her life was so much better with Antonio in it.

She knew then if she was going to be happy for the rest of her days she needed Antonio and his love.

She hugged him tightly to her. "Yes. Yes, I will marry you."

Her family congratulated her and everyone agreed to go to the Moretti family home in San Giuliano Milanese after the meeting to celebrate.

They went into the boardroom and after a lot of haggling, Moretti Motors had the rights to use the Vallerio name on their roadster. They also got the rights to the new engine that her father had designed.

Everyone seemed happy with the way things worked out and when they went downstairs after the meeting, Emile and Gio both placed a temporary nameplate on the Vallerio Roadster. To see the sons of two men who fought and had grown to hate each other standing side by side felt right to Nathalie.

She hoped that with the bitterness of the feud in the past, both of their families would go on to much greater things.

"Are you happy?" Antonio asked, holding her

hand in his as they walked through the gardens at his parents' house.

"Happier than I ever thought I could be," she said. "What made you change your mind?"

"Nothing," he said.

She pulled away. "Nothing? Antonio, are you doing this on a whim?"

He pulled her back into his arms and kissed her. There was so much passion in that embrace that she knew without a doubt he loved her.

"I knew I loved you before you walked out. I had thought that confessing my love would doom it, but then I realized that by hiding it I was cursing us to a life without each other."

"Are you sure you love me?" she asked, unable to believe she was really going to get to spend the rest of her life with Antonio.

"Positive, *cara mia.* And I'm going to make sure you never doubt it or me again."

"How will you do that?" she asked, though she already felt his love surrounding her.

"By telling you of my love often, by paying attention to the little things that make you happy, by making you feel like the center of my world, because that is what you are."

"And what will I do for you?"

"You've already done it. You brought color to my life and made me realize that business wasn't the only thing I could live for." And he kissed her to seal the deal.

* * * * *

THE BOSELLI BRIDE

SUSANNE JAMES

Susanne James has enjoyed creative writing since childhood, completing her first—sadly unpublished—novel by the age of twelve. She has three grown-up children who were, and are, her pride and joy and who all live happily in Oxfordshire with their families. She was always happy to put the needs of her family before her ambition to write seriously, although along the way some published articles for magazines and newspapers helped to keep the dream alive!

Susanne's big regret is that her beloved husband is no longer here to share the pleasure of her recent success. She now shares her life with Toffee, her young cavalier King Charles spaniel, who decides when it's time to get up (early) and when a walk in the park is overdue!

CHAPTER ONE

'WHY don't you go back to the hotel, Coral, and have a lie down…? It *is* pretty stifling today.' Emily glanced sympathetically at her friend as they sauntered along the sun-hot streets of the capital.

'I think "pretty stifling" is a bit of an understatement—it must be all of forty degrees,' Coral said plaintively, taking off her hat for a second to wipe perspiration from her forehead. She sighed. 'Perhaps I will get a cab and go back… Do you have much more to do, Ellie?'

'Not really—but I'll look in on one more place before I call it a day,' Emily replied. She glanced at her watch. 'I'll be back before five o'clock, and then there'll be time for me to have a rest and a shower before we find somewhere for dinner.'

The two girls were staying at a small hotel in Rome on the outskirts of Trastevere. Emily was on one of her normal working assignments, where she had the task of vetting certain hotels and restaurants for the travel firm who employed her, and this was the first time she'd ever been accompanied abroad while on business. But Coral's long-term boyfriend, Steve, had recently dumped her and, in an attempt to cheer her friend up, Emily had suggested she come to

Rome, too. 'A complete change will do you good, Coral,' she'd said and, after a little persuasion, Coral had agreed.

Although her grasp of Italian was rather poor, Emily was determined to become sufficiently fluent to make herself well understood by the staff at all the places she'd been asked to investigate—while also expecting that their English could cope with the continuous influx of visitors from Britain.

Stopping for a moment to buy herself a cappuccino ice cream, she started to stroll up a side street which appeared almost completely shaded by the tall buildings on either side. She paused briefly to lick her tongue quickly around and around the smooth, creamy ice cream as it threatened to melt before she could eat it, then wandered on again somewhat listlessly. Perhaps she should have gone back to the hotel as well, she thought—but there was this one other restaurant she needed to visit before finishing for the day.

Soaking up the atmosphere of the ancient city, she wondered whether her parents had actually walked up this very street when they had done all their travelling. The thought of her mother, who had died so suddenly four years ago when she, Emily, was twenty-one, made the girl's eyes mist and she swallowed a painful lump in her throat. Even though her father, Hugh, had picked up the pieces of his life and carried on alone, she knew that he didn't find it easy... They'd been such a close couple, and wonderful parents to her and her brother, Paul. Paul was just a few years older than her, but he had a rather serious nature and outlook on life—which might be partly explained by his work as a lawyer. Emily wished that he was here now, so that she could give him a hug.

Lost in her own thoughts, her reverie was brought to a

sudden—and ignominious—halt as she almost fell over someone sitting on the pavement outside a small shop whose open-fronted entrance exhibited a colourful array of pottery and glass. Half-sitting, half-lying on a canvas chair with his long legs stretched out nonchalantly in front of him, his large-brimmed hat completely shading his face, he might have been fast asleep because he made no discernible movement as Emily paused to glance at the wares on offer. Slightly embarrassed at how close she'd come to nearly sitting on his lap, she cleared her throat and busied herself with picking up one or two items, even though she had no intention of buying anything. If she'd purchased something in every place she'd been sent to since working abroad, her small flat would be hopelessly overloaded. But then—there was always room for just one more jug, she thought.

Venturing just a little way inside the shop, she gingerly picked up a round, chunky marmalade jar—her father had started making his own marmalade, and she thought how he would love this.

'Unique.' The man's voice was cruelly seductive.

Turning quickly, Emily found herself looking way up into the blackest of black eyes—eyes which twinkled mischievously into her soft grey ones…. The inert figure outside had come to life! Standing now, he had removed his hat and his thick, dark and lustrous hair hung haphazardly over his forehead, while the deeply tanned skin of his outrageously handsome face shone slightly with perspiration.

'I'm sorry…?' Emily found herself fluttering inside like a silly schoolgirl! Come on, she thought, this isn't the first Italian male you've met! Get a grip!

'Unique,' he repeated, averting his gaze from hers just long enough to pick up one of the jars and to slowly turn it around in his long, sensuous fingers. 'Each one unique.'

Emily smiled inwardly. He was a man of few words, his somewhat sparse way of communicating clearly suggesting that his English was about as good as her Italian.

'They're…very…attractive,' she murmured, speaking slowly. 'How much…?'

Now he smiled down, his glistening, perfect teeth enlivening the density of his tan. Without taking his eyes from her, he pointed to the small price tag at the base of the jar, raising one eyebrow quizzically.

'Of course—I should have spotted that,' Emily said quickly, taking her purse from her bag.

'No problem.' He spoke carefully—and Emily thought, well, he'd obviously learned the necessary phrases to get by. So far he'd only uttered about six words, but he was doing all right. Quite well enough to run this small, unassuming shop. She smiled up at him, handing over her euros, conscious that his fingers seemed to linger on hers for several seconds longer than was necessary but admitting that she'd not objected to the feel of his hand on hers like that. He was not offensive in any way, just…just warm…warm and even affectionate. What she had seemed to need just then.

She watched as he carefully wrapped the jar in brown paper before putting it into a small bag. He handed it to her slowly.

'For you?' he asked.

Emily couldn't help smiling at him again. 'No. A gift,' she replied, her comments as economically spoken as his. 'For my father. He…he likes to make his own marmalade these days.' Now why had she bothered to tell the man that? He was only being polite. He didn't need to know her business.

'Ah, yes.' The dark eyes grew solemn for a moment. 'Your father… He is alone, yes?'

She hesitated. 'My mother died. Not so long ago,' she said quietly, and suddenly his brown hand caught hers again and squeezed it gently—not like before, but impulsively, sympathetically.

'I'm sorry,' he murmured, letting her go and moving away. Then his eyes twinkled again and the moment had gone.

Emily turned decisively. 'Thank you very much…for the jar,' she said.

He bowed his head slightly to one side. 'You are very welcome,' he replied formally.

Emily walked away and up the street, admitting that she felt strange inside. What on earth was the matter—had she got sunstroke? But that unlooked-for encounter with possibly the most overtly sensuous Italian male she'd ever spoken to had shaken her up. Had made her feel quite giddy. What on earth had they put in that ice cream?

With slightly narrowed eyes he watched her as she walked away. Of course he'd seen her coming up the street towards him a few minutes ago, his natural antennae homing in on her delectable appearance, on the cool, straight dress just above the knee, revealing gently tanned slim legs, her long fair hair falling casually onto her shoulders, her glitzy strappy sandals twinkling in the heat as she strolled. She was obviously in no hurry, he'd thought as he'd observed her enjoying her ice cream. She'd paused briefly a couple of times as she'd licked at the ice cream, then he'd watched as she'd nibbled at the last piece of the biscuit before taking a tissue from her bag to wipe her lips. He'd recognized at once that she was not of his own nationality—probably English, he'd thought, or German— or Swedish. A familiar shiver of desire had rippled right down his spine as he'd seen the slight figure come nearer, and he'd deliberately lowered his head even further on his chest while still maintaining his undisturbed scrutiny of her. And then she'd given him the perfect opportunity to come and stand close to her as she'd stopped to examine some of the merchandise on display. And to buy something. He had taken his time wrapping up what she had chosen, inhaling the light, tantalizing drift of her perfume.

Now, he sighed as he watched her disappear out of sight. She had been like a welcome apparition in the rather sickly afternoon heat, and now she had gone. He glanced at his watch, feeling somewhat irritable. He only had another hour here before someone came to relieve him, and then he could go and have a long, satisfying drink to cool himself down.

Emily had some difficulty finding the restaurant on her list that she wanted to visit—no one seemed to know where it was—but eventually she tracked it down and had a brief interview with the manager. It seemed a friendly, well patronized place, just the sort she herself might like to eat in, she thought and, taking away some menus and other literature, she hailed a taxi and went back to the hotel.

Coral was lying on her bed reading a magazine.

'Oh, good, you're back,' she said. 'Did you manage to finish what you had to do?' She stared at Emily for a second, thinking how pretty her friend looked. She had the same slim figure she'd had when she'd been in her teens. 'You look as cool as a cucumber, Ellie—and you're very lucky you don't burn in this sun,' she remarked. 'Not like me. With your fair skin you ought to look like a lobster.' She sighed. 'There's no justice.' Coral's red hair and freckled skin needed a lot of protection in these conditions.

'Well, I may not look burned up, but I feel it right

now—' Emily smiled '—so it's a cool shower for me.' She took a long cotton skirt and fresh top from the wardrobe and went into the bathroom. 'Shan't be long.'

Later, refreshed and looking forward to their evening, the two girls left the hotel and took a taxi to the centre of town.

'With your experience and expertise, you ought to know all the best places to eat,' Coral said as they strolled along the busy streets.

'I still have a lot to learn,' Emily said. 'I've only been sent here once before, but there'll certainly be plenty of choice.' They went on, passing one restaurant after another, the early evening atmosphere muted and relaxed, and presently they stopped for a moment outside a particularly well-lit place to examine the menu. 'This looks good,' she said. 'Shall we try it?'

They took their seats at a table outside under the sun awning and Coral sighed. 'Why does the thought of food always fill me with such delight?' she asked, glancing across at Emily. 'At this moment in time, I do not wish to be anywhere else, *with* anyone else,' she added meaningfully.

Emily smiled at the words, knowing that Coral had always loved food. But since the split with her boyfriend, Steve, a month ago, she had definitely started to look thinner—and it didn't suit her. Coral's normal appetite was legendary, and it went with her popularity and usually bright outlook on life.

'The only thing to complete this idyllic picture,' Coral said as she examined the menu, 'is for a drop-dead gorgeous Italian male to present himself at my feet and whisk me off to some exotic rendezvous. But not until I've had my meal,' she added.

Emily felt pleased that a change of scene seemed to be

having a positive effect on Coral's frame of mind. Her recent depression seemed to be less in evidence, anyway—at least for the moment. Coral and Steve had been an item for four years—with neither, apparently, wanting to commit themselves, when one day, out of the blue, he'd announced that enough was enough and he wanted to call it a day. To describe it as an emotional bombshell was an understatement and Emily had felt it too—the girls shared their lives in a flat together. It was horrible to see the normally happy-go-lucky Coral so downcast.

As she ran her finger along the huge menu, Emily frowned slightly. It was all very well thinking about other people's affairs and relationships...but what about her own love life? She had to admit that it didn't stand much scrutiny at the moment—and who could blame her for that? Her confidence in human relationships having a hope of surviving in the long-term had been shattered when Marcus, her last boyfriend, had been targeted by her best friend from university, who had made no secret of the fact that she'd always fancied Marcus. But it had never bothered Emily, who'd trusted him so naively...so, when he'd unbelievably succumbed to the determined charms of the other woman, Emily had suffered a bombshell all of her own. Then, it had been Coral's job to pick up the shattered pieces of her ego and her bruised heart. Emily sighed briefly as her thoughts ran on. The event was a whole year ago and, although she barely thought about him now, she'd been taught a hard lesson. Beware of those you thought you could trust. Especially handsome men, who were naturally attractive to the opposite sex.

Presently, they gave the young Italian waitress their order, and within a couple of minutes two large glasses of white wine arrived. Coral picked up hers straight away, beaming across at Emily.

'Cheers,' she said, taking a generous gulp, and Emily smiled back, picking up her own drink. It was good to have her friend's company on this trip, she thought. Even if she *was* beginning to get used to finding her own way around new places and fending for herself.

Coral leaned back in her chair and looked around. 'There seems so much talent everywhere,' she said, almost ruefully. 'I mean, just look at those two guys over there, Ellie— gorgeous or what?' She paused. 'Hey, they're looking at us… Do you think we might get lucky later on…?'

'Well, *you* might,' Emily said cheerfully, 'but count me out. I've got my busiest day tomorrow, and after we've eaten it'll be back to bed for me.'

'Spoilsport,' Coral said. 'Anyway, I was only joking.' But she continued staring across at the men, returning their rather suggestive smiles.

Emily said mildly, 'Don't encourage them, Coral. It'll really complicate matters if they think we're giving them the come-on.'

Soon their meal was put in front of them and for the next ten minutes Coral didn't say another word as she began rapidly consuming everything on her plate.

'This veal is so tender,' Emily said appreciatively, 'and I wish I knew what the dressing on the salad is. It's fantastic.'

'And I love, love, *love* these chips!' Coral said theatrically. 'I was so afraid we were only going to get pasta on this holiday.'

The portions were generous, so the girls decided that fruit and coffee would be all they'd need to complete the meal. But Coral insisted on ordering more wine, waving away Emily's protest.

'Don't be a party-pooper, Ellie,' she said beseechingly. 'We're on holiday, remember.'

'You are—I'm not,' Emily replied, but she drank the wine anyway. She certainly didn't want to be accused of being a drag. Anyway, Coral was having such a good time it was hard not to be affected by the girl's exuberance.

As they sat sipping their wine, the men whom Coral had been smiling at came over and, without asking, pulled out two chairs so that they could sit down.

'Is OK,' one of them said, 'to sit?' and, although Emily merely shrugged pleasantly, Coral was thrilled.

'Of course it's OK,' she said brightly, darting a quick glance at Emily.

Immediately, one of the men beckoned a waiter and insisted that the girls should have more wine. They were young—probably barely twenty years old, Emily thought—good-looking and well turned-out in their casual clothes, and it was obvious that they'd been encouraged by Coral's overtly friendly eye signals.

It didn't take long for the men to find out that the girls were English and on holiday and, in their halting attempts to make themselves understood, they became more and more animated, throwing their heads back and roaring with laughter at the mistakes they were making. But when one of them leaned across and took hold of Emily's hand, looking into her eyes and telling her how beautiful she was, the girl had had enough. While she was quite ready to go along with this—up to a point, for Coral's sake—it was becoming clear that this was going to lead to a situation she definitely did not want. She took her hand away, glancing at her watch.

'Well—great to have met you,' she said, 'but we have to go now.'

'Oh—no—no,' her admirer said. 'Is too early…'

Emily looked helplessly at Coral, hoping for some

support, but her friend refused to meet her gaze, clearly enjoying the situation, and for a few moments Emily felt at a loss. The men were only being friendly and she had no sense of being threatened. Yet this was the very thing she had wanted to avoid. How was she going to get out of it without appearing to snub these local lads?

And then her good fairy alighted on her shoulder, literally, as the warm hand of the handsome Italian she'd met earlier in the day rested on her bare arm for a second. He looked down into her rather startled gaze and smiled the smile that set her heart racing.

'We meet again,' he said calmly. 'I was sitting inside in the bar having a drink and saw you come in.' He paused. 'Is—is everything all right?' The words were uttered in perfect English, which had the effect of throwing Emily off balance for a moment. What she'd thought of earlier as his halting ability with the language was obviously a ploy he used in order to avoid having to make tiresome conversation with customers! But she admitted to feeling relieved that he'd turned up then—because now the situation was different—and the younger men saw it at once, standing up almost deferentially.

''Giorno, Giovanni,' the men said, almost in unison. He was obviously well known, Emily thought—and why not? He ran a local shop, and these were local youths. She smiled up at him.

'Oh, hello again,' she said. 'We…were just explaining to these…guys…that we are actually just leaving now…'

'Giovanni' spoke in rapid Italian to the men, who answered back in the same way, all three laughing loudly and clearly enjoying a joke—probably at her and Coral's expense, Emily thought—and then they were gone, smiling back as they went, leaving Giovanni standing there

alone. He looked down at the girls, treating Coral to one
of his disarming grins before introducing himself, holding
out his hand to each of them in turn.

'My name is Giovanni,' he said, 'but my friends call me
Joe…Gio.' He paused, his eyes flickering over Emily's
upturned face.

Quickly, she said, 'Oh—I'm Emily, and this is Coral.
We're only here for a few days—on a sort of holiday…'
she went on rather stumblingly, aware that her friend was
staring at her open-mouthed. Not just because it was
obvious that Giovanni was somehow known to Emily, but
also because he was looking so stunningly handsome she
knew that the girl's curiosity would be killing her. Emily
knew she had some explaining to do!

'Um…do sit down…Giovanni…' she said hesitantly,
and immediately he pulled out a chair. She looked across
at Coral. 'I bought a lovely present for my father at
Giovanni's shop this afternoon,' she began, 'and that's
when I met…Giovanni…Gio…'

Although Coral might have been disappointed at the
hasty exit the younger men had just made, she was so entranced at the most recent arrival she could hardly speak!
He was wearing well-cut jeans and a loose, immaculate
white cotton shirt open at the neck, exhibiting a teasing
expanse of muscular brown chest. His hair was stylishly
untidy, one or two dark fronds falling over his broad
forehead. And his bewitching eyes were fringed by long,
curling lashes. But when he leaned across and took Coral's
hand in his briefly, saying, 'I am so delighted to meet you,
Coral,' Emily thought her friend was going to faint!

'Oh…' Coral said at last. 'Pleased to meet you, Gio.'
She darted a quick glance at Emily, as if to say—*Well, you
might have said something*—before giving the man her

close attention. And his perfect English, with only the occasional mouth-watering Italian accent, made conversation easy—and wonderfully entertaining, as he turned on the full power of his Latin charm. He beckoned to the drinks waiter and turned to Emily.

'May we celebrate our acquaintance?' he asked. 'What would you like to drink—and you, Coral…? What may I order for you?'

'I'd like another coffee, please,' Emily said firmly. She'd already had several generous glasses of wine. Any more would be too many, she thought. But Coral had no such problem, and soon she was sipping at yet another large glass of the expensive bubbles as she regaled Giovanni with her life story, allowing Emily to add one or two comments about herself while he listened intently.

Presently, Emily decided that for her the evening was over. 'I want to go back to the hotel now, Coral,' she said. 'It's late.'

'Where are you staying?' Giovanni asked casually, and when they told him he said, 'I can take you, if you like. My car is just a few minutes away.'

'Oh, lovely!' Coral said at once, but Emily interrupted firmly.

'Thank you, but we can easily get a taxi. We wouldn't want to bother you.' She stood up and shot a warning glance at Coral, who stood up as well. Then she held out her hand. 'It's been very…pleasant…to meet you…Gio,' she said. 'And thanks for the coffee.'

He smiled at her, tilting his head briefly to one side. 'You're welcome,' he said. He hesitated. 'By the way, if you have trouble locating the places you need to visit tomorrow, I'll be at the shop, so you know where to find me. I can always point you in the right direction.'

'Oh…thank you, but I'm sure I'll manage,' Emily said.

'Why didn't you accept his offer of a lift?' Coral demanded as they were driven swiftly back to the hotel in a taxi.

'Because we don't know him, Coral!'

'He wasn't exactly a stranger…'

'As good as,' Emily replied.

But later, as Emily listened to Coral's gentle snoring from the other bed, she instinctively felt that there would have been no need to fear Giovanni's intentions. He was clearly a well known member of the local community and, if the younger men's reaction was anything to go by, highly respected.

Emily turned over, flinging her arm across her pillow. Behind her closed lids she could still see those ruinously seductive eyes gazing at her. Then she half sat up, pushing her hair away from her face. This would not do, she thought. She was here chiefly on business, not to indulge herself in sensitive thoughts about the first Italian who'd paid her any special attention. It was just a shame that she and Giovanni would probably never meet again…especially as there were only two days to go before they returned to England.

Back in his luxury flat in the heart of the city, Giovanni dragged his shirt over his head and unbuckled his jeans before going into the bathroom to shower. What a piece of good luck that he'd come across Emily again. She might have gone to any one of the countless restaurants on offer, or indeed might have already been on her way back home. And what luck that fate had given him the opportunity to approach her without causing any offence. He'd observed the young men attach themselves to the two girls, and had spotted at once that Emily had seemed uncomfortable about it. She'd certainly not appreciated the rather clumsy gesture she'd received from one of them. It was that which had made Giovanni intervene.

He stared at himself in the mirror for a second, a slight grin on his rugged face. He met many lovely women all the time, and this was hardly the first occasion that his masculine propensities had been briefly shaken and stirred. But, somehow, this felt different... He suddenly felt alive inside again, the persistent sense of guilt which he'd been suffering for the last eighteen months lessening slightly. He bit his lip. He was being introspective again, he thought. He must stop it. Wasn't it time to give himself an emotional break and start looking forward, instead of back? And he was not going to deny that Emily had lit a particular spark in him which was both exciting and unexpected. On so short an acquaintance he was, quite simply, enchanted by her. She was not only beautiful, she was...thoughtful...wistful, maybe...some other quality that he couldn't quite identify, but everything about her made him want to hold her and protect her. He had never, ever felt that instant, deep attraction to a woman before in his life—and the realization came as something of a shock.

Stepping into the shower, he let the water rush in cool, satisfying waves over the length of his taut, muscular body before beginning to soap himself vigorously. At least he knew where she'd be staying for the next few days, but he didn't have long and he wanted to know more about this Englishwoman before it was too late.

He finished showering, then knotted the huge white towel around his waist and padded barefoot into his bedroom, feeling elated. Feeling eighteen again. Emily Sinclair had definitely sprinkled some magic dust over him that day, he admitted—and who knew what may lie ahead? Didn't all his friends call him 'Lucky Gio'?

CHAPTER TWO

'OH, WHAT a night I've had!'

Coral sat on the edge of her bed with her head in her hands, then peered through her fingers at Emily, who was barely awake. 'But I'm glad that I don't appear to have disturbed *you*,' she added a trifle sarcastically.

Emily sat up and stared at her friend sleepily. 'No, I didn't hear a thing. In fact, I had the best sleep I've had in ages. But—what happened—or shouldn't I ask?'

'Oh, it's just that I've been in and out of the bathroom for the entire night,' Coral replied. 'I suppose it was something I ate for supper,' she added.

'Well, we had the same thing and it didn't affect me,' Emily said mildly, thinking that it was probably more to do with the amount Coral had had to drink. She'd almost single-handedly consumed the bottle of expensive wine which Giovanni had bought, and she'd had a lot before that. 'Do you think you can manage breakfast?' she asked doubtfully. The girl was still looking very white-faced.

'Don't! Don't mention food!' Coral said theatrically. 'It'll be nil by mouth for me today.' She got up slowly and went across to the window, clasping her stomach. 'It looks as if it's going to be another scorcher,' she said, 'but I shan't be coming with you, Ellie. I couldn't trust myself to be anywhere but here for the next few hours.' She turned to glance at Emily. 'Do you mind?'

'Of course I don't mind,' Emily said at once. 'But you're probably over the worst.' She climbed out of bed, yawning. 'I'll ring your mobile at lunchtime to see if you're able to come and meet me later.'

As soon as she'd had her breakfast, Emily took a few moments to read the instructions she'd been given. There were two hotels and two restaurants on her list for today and, although her map-reading skills weren't particularly impressive, she felt reasonably confident that she'd be able to get around. A couple of the places looked fairly close to each other, but the others seemed more spread out.

After feeling as if she'd walked fifty miles on the un-yielding pavements, Emily had tracked down the two more central establishments before deciding to stop at a small café for a few minutes to make some notes. And to order a long glass of freshly squeezed orange juice.

Sitting with her pad on her knee, she sipped her drink, staring pensively out at the fast-moving traffic. She was doing OK, she thought, feeling quite pleased with herself—even if she *had* gone round in circles when given conflicting directions by two passers-by. But she decided that she'd hail a taxi to take her to the next stop—a rather nice-looking hotel, if the description on her notes was anything to go by.

Standing uncertainly on the pavement, she held out her hand as one cab after another swept past her, obviously all occupied, and after several fruitless minutes she began to walk a little way up the street before trying her luck again. She saw another one approaching her rapidly and, stepping off the kerb in order to get the driver to stop, she stumbled and almost fell as he, too, roared past her. Emily bit her lip in frustration—why was it proving so difficult? she asked herself, beginning to feel hot and bothered all over again.

Suddenly, a sleek black car pulled up alongside her and, glancing in quickly at the driver, she felt a rush of pleasure—and relief—when she saw who it was.

'*Buon giorno, signorina,*' Giovanni said through the open window, a roguish smile on his lips, his black eyes unashamedly taking in her appearance.

'Oh…hello, Giovanni—I mean, Joe…' Emily replied, hardly believing her luck. He'd be sure to offer to help find the place she was looking for—and in this heat she wouldn't be turning him down.

Without switching off the engine, he got out of the car and came around to open the passenger door for her. Well, well, well—Lady Luck was on his side again, he thought. It was as if she had been planted neatly on that pavement for him to offer her a ride. He didn't usually drive his car around the city at this time of day.

He got in beside her, turning to look at her for a second, noting her flushed cheeks and aware that she seemed out of breath. 'You were obviously trying to get a taxi,' he said. Well, there couldn't have been any other reason for her to stand there alone with her arms in the air. 'It can be difficult sometimes,' he added.

'So I see,' Emily replied as they drew away smoothly. 'None of them seem to need my custom today.' She leaned her head back and sighed, grateful for the air-conditioning—and to be with someone who knew where he was going. 'I need to visit two hotels today… My work involves assessing places that might meet all the criteria for British visitors,' she explained, 'and I don't know how to get to either of these.'

'Well, what a good thing I'm not at the shop this afternoon,' Giovanni said, 'so I can take you wherever you want to go.' Effortlessly, he pulled the car to the side of the road for a moment and looked across at her. 'What names are you looking for?'

Emily handed him the sheet of paper with the instructions and a small map, and after a few seconds he nodded. 'They're a bit out of the way,' he conceded, 'but easy enough to find. That's if you…are happy…for me to take you,' he added.

Emily looked at him quickly, realizing that today it hadn't struck her that the man was still the stranger that he'd been last night when she'd refused his offer of a lift. So why did she feel so relaxed…so happy…to be sitting alongside him now? She turned to look in front of her. 'If you're sure it's not inconveniencing you, Gio, I'd be very grateful,' she said simply.

'Which travel company are you with?' Giovanni wanted to know as they drove away and, when Emily told him, he nodded. 'They're well known,' he said briefly. 'How long have you worked for them?'

'Almost a year,' Emily replied.

'And before that?'

'Oh, I had a couple of years with a small art gallery in London,' she said, glancing across at the handsome profile, the strong neck and firm chin. His white shirt exposed heart-throbbing muscular arms and shoulders which tensed and rippled as he moved. She swallowed, looking away. 'And what about you?' she asked, thinking that it was his turn to answer some questions. 'How long have you owned the shop?'

He grinned without looking at her. 'Oh, it's not mine,' he said. 'It belongs to a friend. I just mind the place for him from time to time.'

There was silence for a few moments after that and
Emily thought—well, that didn't say much. If it wasn't his
shop, what else did he do?

'So, when you're not selling beautiful marmalade
jars…?' she enquired.

'My friend also owns the restaurant you were dining in
last night,' he said, 'and I help out there, too, in the bar
sometimes—but mostly I manage his paperwork for him.'
He paused. 'By the way,' he went on, changing the subject,
'where is—Coral—today?'

'Oh, I'm afraid Coral might have had too much sun yesterday,' Emily said. She wasn't going to go into details. 'So
she decided to stay at the hotel and rest for a few
hours…which reminds me—I must ring her to see if she's
feeling any better.'

Taking her mobile from her bag, Emily dialled Coral's
number and was relieved that her friend answered almost
immediately and sounded her old self.

'Good,' Emily said into the mouthpiece, 'I'll be back
about six o'clock and we'll go out to supper later—if
you're still feeling OK… What? Oh—I'm phoning from…
from… I'm in a car on my way to one of those hotels, but
once I'm there it shouldn't take long,' she added as she
rang off.

Now why hadn't she told Coral that it was Giovanni's
car that she was sitting in? she asked herself as she
replaced her phone in her bag. And Giovanni must have
been thinking the same thing because he gave her a wicked
sidelong glance and said bluntly, 'Is my name a dirty word
then, Emily? You're not…ashamed…of me, I hope?'

Emily felt her cheeks beginning to burn. 'Of course
not!' she said. 'It…it was somehow difficult to try and
explain to Coral how you…I mean…how…I'll tell her

later, of course.' The fact was that Coral had fallen madly in love with Giovanni and when they'd got back last night hadn't stopped going on and on about him until the small hours. If Emily had said, *Guess what? Giovanni just happened to be passing by and now I'm sitting in his fantastic car and yes, he's just as gorgeous as he was last night!* Coral would have demanded to know how *that* had happened, and her shriek of amazed jealousy would have been deafening and very difficult to explain to the man in the driving seat!

It took about twenty minutes to reach the quite imposing hotel, and Giovanni glanced across at Emily. 'Do you have an appointment, or do you just turn up unannounced?' he asked.

'It varies,' Emily replied. 'It's quite good not to let them know when you're coming, for obvious reasons, but I usually do ring first. Let's hope the manager is available today. I'm hoping to see Signor Saracco, but in any case I can get a good feel of the place and see if it's the sort which our clients might approve of.'

They got out of the car and together they went into the large foyer. This would obviously have to feature in the brochure for one of their more expensive holidays, Emily thought, looking around her at the impressive glass cabinets containing luxurious clothing and jewellery. The girl standing behind the huge oak reception desk looked up as they entered, her eyes glancing briefly at Emily, but lingering for a lot longer on Giovanni, immediately captivated by his ruthlessly seductive appeal.

Emily stepped forward. *'Parla inglese?'* she asked, and the woman nodded hesitantly.

'A leetle,' she replied.

In the following few moments it was obvious that the

receptionist was having a struggle with the language, and Emily made a mental note of the fact. It would be important for British visitors to feel comfortable at this early point, she thought, and for any queries they might have to be dealt with efficiently. Then Giovanni spoke quietly to the girl and for what seemed like ten minutes to Emily they conversed rapidly in Italian, the receptionist clearly relieved to be speaking her own language, laughing excitedly now and then—and also obviously enjoying talking to the handsome visitor. Then he glanced down at Emily.

'This young lady is only standing in for the permanent receptionist,' he explained, 'owing to illness. She only started today and says it's been the longest morning of her life. Another girl is coming in tomorrow, apparently. She is only seventeen,' he added, and Emily was amazed. 'Carla'—for that was the name on the identity tag the girl was wearing—looked at least in her mid-twenties. She was immaculately dressed, her black outfit pristine and enlivened with gold jewellery, her dark hair swept back elegantly. 'I also asked if Signor Saracco was available, and she says that he is due back in one hour,' Giovanni went on. 'Do you want to hang on that long, or shall we find the other place first?' He paused. 'I don't know about you, but I didn't have any lunch. They do very good light meals, served all afternoon, so Carla tells me…'

Suddenly, the thought of sitting down to a gentle Italian repast sounded just what she needed and Emily smiled, realizing that her 'lunch' had been that glass of orange juice. 'I'd love something to eat,' she said, 'and we might as well wait for the manager now that we're here.'

'Good,' he said at once, cupping her elbow in his hand and leading her towards the other end of the entrance hall where late lunches were being served.

Without looking back, Emily knew that Carla would be watching them. The young girl had been instantly flattered by Giovanni's kindly attention to her, flashing her artificially long eyelashes at him as he'd looked across at her. And Emily could quite see how any female would be touched by his attitude. He'd been attentive, understanding…and deliciously sensuous, yet not creepy or overpowering. She'd give him full marks for the way in which he demonstrated his particular art—or was it craft?

He led her to a small round table in the corner, by a window which looked out across a beautifully green lawn. In a lazy circular movement, a hose was lightly playing water over the grass and Emily glanced up at Giovanni as he held out a chair for her to sit down.

'They must employ a lot of staff to keep this place up to standard,' she said. 'It does seem a very well run establishment.'

For a few moments they studied a copy of the menu, then both decided on something called the House Special, which was ravioli accompanied by freshly cooked spinach.

'I hope the service is good,' Giovanni remarked as he clicked his fingers to attract the attention of the drinks waiter, 'because I'm starving.'

Emily had to admit that she was beginning to feel the same way, and soon they were tucking into what turned out to be a really delicious version of the simple Italian dish. 'When I do ravioli at home,' she said, running her knife around her plate to scoop up the last of the sauce, 'it doesn't taste nearly as good as this.'

Giovanni smiled across at her, realizing how much he was enjoying the company of this Englishwoman whom he barely knew. His eyes narrowed briefly as he continued watching her. Although she was not cold towards him, he thought—no, not at all—he sensed a sort of protective film around her persona which seemed to exclude him. So why didn't he stick with his own kind? he asked himself. It wouldn't take long for that young receptionist to respond to his male ego!

Emily looked up at him now and he smiled, thinking that there was a little time to go before the manager turned up. Time to find things out.

'So,' he said smoothly, finishing the last of his beer, 'are there any more like you at home, Emily? Or are you an only child?'

'I have a brother,' Emily replied, folding her napkin and sitting back contentedly. 'He's a lawyer, and slightly older than me.' She paused. 'Although we both live and work in London, we don't see as much of each other as we'd like—there never seems enough time, somehow.'

'One must always make time for relationships,' Giovanni said, his expression darkening momentarily.

'Are your parents alive?' Emily wanted to know.

'I still have my mother with me,' he replied, 'but my father died ten years ago.'

So, Emily thought, they were both semi-orphans. 'Does your mother live in Rome with you?' she asked.

'No, we have a family home in the country, a few miles outside,' he said. 'She is happy there—though she sometimes comes into the city and stays at my flat when she feels like it.' He paused. 'And your father? You told me that he is alone now, but where does he live?'

'In the same house in Hampshire where my parents lived all their married life,' Emily replied, wishing that she hadn't had that small glass of white wine.

There was silence for a few moments, then he said

casually, 'And what about your love life, Emily—you have a partner longing for your return?'

Emily was a bit taken aback at the way he'd put the question—she didn't usually discuss her 'love life' with anyone! 'No, I do not have a partner—at the moment,' she said coolly, and he looked at her quizzically. There was a fleeting expression on her face which he couldn't interpret, didn't understand… Surely there must be a long queue of men lusting for her? he thought.

And Emily, looking out of the window thoughtfully, would not be telling him about Marcus—that was all in the past. And she was surviving life without specific male company too, she thought. Life was blissfully uncompli- cated now. Life was OK, wasn't it? She swallowed. It was time to talk of other things.

Just then a murmuring of voices coming from the re- ception area made them both glance up as three men, dressed formally, entered. Immediately, Giovanni stood up—he'd obviously seen someone he knew, Emily thought, and almost at once the taller one of the trio came over to them. He was about forty-five or so, Emily guessed, and extremely good-looking.

'Giovanni,' he began, his hand outstretched in greeting, and there followed a rapid exchange of Italian between the two of them. Then Giovanni looked down at Emily.

'Um…allow me to introduce you, Emily,' he said. 'This is…Aldo.' And to the man he added, 'The young lady is Emily. She is here on business.'

Aldo took Emily's hand in his and looked down at her, his searching Italian eyes seeming to unwrap every bit of her at a single glance. 'I am charmed to meet you, Emily,' he said smoothly, not letting her go, but turning his head to Giovanni. 'Another delightful creature to add to your

list, my friend?' he said, and the remark seemed almost
sinister to Emily. It held a definite touch of spite. She
looked uncertainly at Giovanni—whose expression was
non-committal, but there was suddenly a very cool atmosphere—and it seemed obvious that there was no love lost
between these two.

After some more rather stilted discussion between
them, Aldo made his gracious departure and joined his
friends at a table at the opposite end of the room. Giovanni
looked across at Emily as he sat down again.

'Well, I did not expect that,' he said, 'and I must apologize that we did not speak in English.'

Emily shrugged. 'Doesn't matter,' she said. 'Is he—is
Aldo—a friend? You've known him a long time?'

Giovanni grimaced briefly. 'Too long,' he said.

'You don't like him?' she asked.

He shrugged. 'I neither like nor dislike him,' he replied
casually. He paused. 'The more important point is that he
resents me… He does not like me.'

No, Emily thought—she'd seen that straight away.
'Well, sometimes certain…friends…just don't fit somehow, do they?' she said. 'It's impossible to get on with each
and every one of them.'

Giovanni nodded. 'Oh, I do OK with friends,' he said.
'They're no problem. Families are different.' He glanced
over at the three men, who were giving the waiter their
order for drinks. 'Aldo is family, unfortunately,' he said, a
note of resignation in his voice. 'He's my uncle. My
father's younger brother.'

'Oh,' Emily said, wondering why Giovanni hadn't mentioned that when they'd been introduced. Then she
shrugged inwardly. She knew that Italians were known to
be great family people, but even in the best of families

there'd be bound to be friction now and then. She glanced at her watch. It must surely be time for the manager to return, she thought.

'You speak wonderful English, Gio,' she said, changing the subject. 'You've obviously spent a lot of time in the UK.'

'Explained by the fact that I was educated mostly there,' he said briefly.

Now, why did it surprise her, Emily asked herself, that he'd gone to school in England? 'Where did you go?' she asked him.

'Boarding school in Surrey, then Marlborough College in Wiltshire, followed by London University. And, before you ask, I gained a Masters in Business Law.'

Emily was almost bowled over by all this information! Despite being born in Italy, and in appearance and attitude being a perfect example of typical Latin charm, he was nearly as English as she was herself! She almost laughed out loud at the thought.

'So,' she said, 'if you only help out at the shop, and at your friend's bar when you're in Rome, where else do you work?' she asked. 'Where has all that education led you?'

He waited a moment before reaching into his pocket and handing her a small business card. 'Oh, I help my mother with a…um…family concern in Rome,' he said. 'Which means I have to come to the UK every now and again,' he added briefly.

Emily looked down at the card he'd handed her. *Giovanni Boselli,* she read. *Financial Consultant,* followed by his qualifications and the telephone number and address of the London office he apparently used. An address which was just a few streets away from her own office in Mayfair!

CHAPTER THREE

'WELL, I think that's everything sorted—thanks to you, Gio,' Emily said, glancing across at him as they travelled back into the city later. 'It would have taken me a lot longer to find my own way around.'

'My pleasure,' he said easily. 'And—you were satisfied with both hotels?'

'Perfectly,' she replied. 'I shall be able to put ticks in all the right boxes.' She leaned her head back, feeling satisfied with the day's work. 'It was lucky for me that you happened to be free this afternoon—and also that you saw me trying to hail a taxi,' she added.

He looked across at her and grinned. 'Lucky for me, too,' he said. 'I've certainly enjoyed seeing you in action, Emily. You knew exactly how to handle those two managers, leaving them in no doubt what you expected—what your clients expected—of holiday accommodation.'

Emily was genuinely pleased at what he'd just said. Although she'd never been particularly shy or retiring, she'd had to get used to meeting complete strangers in foreign places, and assess their establishments without causing offence. And it could be difficult sometimes, when

she could see straight away that some were totally un-
suitable and would not get her recommendation.

It was six-thirty before Giovanni drew up outside the
hotel and, switching off the engine, he said casually, his
eyes glinting mischievously, 'As a small reward for having
given you my undivided attention this afternoon, may I
have the pleasure of taking you and Coral out for supper
later?' he asked.

'Oh, but…I've already taken up far too much of your
time, Giovanni,' Emily began, and he interrupted.

'Which I have very much enjoyed—as I've already
said. So—why not make a day of it?' He paused. 'You're
going home tomorrow, aren't you?'

'Yes,' Emily said, realizing that, for the very first time
since she'd been doing all this travelling, she felt regretful that the trip wasn't going to be extended for a few
more days. And she was honest enough to admit that
meeting Giovanni had something to do with that!

'Well, I must speak to Coral about it,' she said. 'But
thank you for the offer,' she added, knowing full well that
her friend would be ecstatic at the thought of spending the
evening with Giovanni.

He tilted his head to one side in acknowledgement of
her words. 'You've got my card,' he reminded her, 'and my
mobile number is on that. Give me a ring after you've
mulled things over, and if you decide to accept my invitation I could pick you up at, say, eight-thirty or nine and
take you to a place you'd probably never come across on
your own—but which I can guarantee you'd like. But—'
he touched her arm briefly '—don't worry if you decide
to have an early night instead.' He paused. 'There'll be
other occasions.' His lips parted in a brief knowing smile.

As soon as Emily got back to the room, she was almost

bowled over by Coral's excited welcome. 'Oh—hi, Ellie!' the girl exclaimed. 'Had a good day?' And, without waiting for a reply, she went on, 'You'll never guess what—I've pulled! We're going out tonight!'

Emily sat down on the edge of the bed for a second and looked up at Coral—who had obviously fully recovered, her eyes shining with girlish excitement. 'Go on—enlighten me. What have you been up to?' she asked, a faint note of resignation in her voice.

'Honestly, I haven't been up to anything!' Coral exclaimed. 'But this afternoon I was feeling so much better that I went down to Reception to order a tray of tea and that *gorgeous* guy—Nico—was on duty. You know, the one we've spoken to a couple of times?'

'Yes, of course I know who you mean,' Emily said. Yet another dashing and attentive Italian, she thought.

'Well, we sort of got chatting,' Coral went on, 'and I said I didn't know Rome very well and guess what—he wants to take us out to show us the sights. He's off duty at eight o'clock! What do you think of that?' She looked at Emily searchingly. 'It might be fun, Emily—and it *is* our last night.'

Emily got up and went over to put her laptop in the wardrobe, then turned to Coral. 'Strangely enough, I've had an invitation for us as well,' she said lightly, before going on to explain how Giovanni had arrived and had escorted her to the hotels on her list. 'And he's asked if we'd like to have dinner with him tonight,' she added.

Coral was speechless—but only for a second. 'How weird—that he should have turned up at just the right moment,' she said. 'But—now we've got *two* invites! Choices, choices!' She paused, thinking it over for a moment. 'But—it'll work perfectly, Ellie. I mean, I wouldn't want to turn Nico down—not after he was so sweet to me this afternoon—and you can't possibly disappoint Giovanni. That wouldn't be fair, since he's obviously been so wonderful to you today. So there you are—we'll go our separate ways tonight…and compare notes later!' she added darkly.

Emily smiled, shaking her head briefly at Coral's excitement. Her friend was obviously going to make the most of this final bit of her holiday—and what better way to end it than to be escorted around town by the handsome Nico?

Presently, as she washed away the day's dust under a cool shower, Emily couldn't help feeling pleased for Coral. Having an unexpected date was just the sort of thing to add a little sparkle to a holiday, she thought, and her friend was quite old enough—and sensible enough—to treat it as the light-hearted, inconsequential thing it was. And Emily had to admit that the thought of spending her last evening with Giovanni—just the two of them—held a little sparkle of its own! And why not? The occasional fleeting evening spent with an attractive man was the sort of thing which pleased her these days… No expectations, nothing heavy, which might threaten to cloud the long-term plan for her life. Go with the flow, but keep things cool—that was the best way.

Later, dressed in her white slim-leg cotton trousers and ocean-green low-necked top, Emily tripped lightly down the steps of the hotel to find Giovanni standing at the bottom waiting for her. Looking up, he grinned slowly, taking in every detail of her appearance and making no secret of his admiration.

'You are a very beautiful woman, Emily,' he murmured, and although Emily knew very well that easy compliments flew from the lips of amorous Italians like flocks of migrating birds, coming from Giovanni it seemed different. It seemed genuine, and she accepted it graciously.

'Thank you…Giovanni…' she said, lingering over his name for a second. He was so obviously a 'Giovanni' rather than a 'Joe', she thought briefly. That rather blunt derivative of his name could only be thanks to one of his English friends and somehow, to her, it didn't suit him. And tonight she could have added that he, too, was worth more than one glance. His black, well-fitting designer trousers were teamed with an ivory cotton shirt, casually open, showing off his golden chest. He obviously liked dressing well, Emily thought.

She glanced across at him as he drove them into town. 'Coral asked me to thank you again, for including her in tonight,' she said. 'As I explained on the phone, she'd already accepted an invitation which she didn't feel able to change.'

He looked back at her, his dark eyes glinting in the reflection from the brightly lit dials of the dashboard. 'No worries,' he said easily, thinking that, with another woman, he might have said that he was very happy to have her all to himself, so that he could treat her to the undivided attention that was his norm with alluring females. But he decided not to say that, happy to relax in the comfortable silence that seemed to exist between them. He frowned briefly. He had known so many women in his life—had always regarded the female sex as treasures to be valued. But would he ever meet a woman who didn't have an ulterior motive in wanting to belong to his family? That was what haunted him.

Feeling annoyed at his thoughts, he leaned forward to adjust something in front of him. The evening ahead was one to enjoy, for heaven's sake! And he was determined to do just that—and to make sure that Emily had a good time, too. When he'd first seen her yesterday—was it only yesterday? he asked himself—she'd had the usual instant effect on him, arousing an animal instinct of wanting to get close, even to possess. But there was this elusiveness about her which continued to intrigue him. And he had to penetrate it somehow, if only to convince himself that he could find out what it was, what lay behind the rather enigmatic expression he'd noted on her fine, perfect features.

Realizing that they'd not exchanged a word for the last few minutes, Emily said, without looking across at him, 'I hope today hasn't been too boring for you, Giovanni. I'm sure there were far more interesting things for you to do than transporting me around and hanging about…'

He interrupted her at once. 'I'm seldom bored, Emily. And I certainly wasn't today. I'm only too pleased that I was able to be of some use to you.'

'That's what you seem to do quite a lot of—being of use to people,' Emily said. 'Your friend who owns the shop and the restaurant seems to make good use of you when you're in Rome.' Now she did look across at him, chiding herself for the sensuous pleasure she was experiencing at being close to him, of seeing the strong brown hands on the steering wheel, his taut, muscular thighs visible beneath the fine fabric of his trousers. She swallowed, trying to think of Coral, and where Nico might be taking *her* tonight.

'Oh, well, my friends are good to me too, when I need them,' he said. Then, 'Are you hungry, Emily—would you like dinner straight away, or shall we go for a walk first?'

'I'd like to eat now—then maybe walk off my meal later!' Emily replied. 'Lunch does seem quite a long time ago.'

'Good. That suits me, too.' He smiled at her with that certain, gentle smile which had the effect of making Emily's pulse quicken. It *was* true, she thought—that Italian men had that certain something which could melt a woman's heart. She'd never really believed it, but now she was experiencing it first-hand… Giovanni exuded that courteous roguishness which personified the Italian male.

After he'd parked the car, they strolled along side by side, through streets which—although less busy—still seemed to ooze with the warm friendliness of the timeless city. They passed one or two families with small children in tow, couples sightseeing hand in hand, and now and then a cheerful group of young Italian men, maybe hopeful of a romantic assignation later, all adding to the laid-back atmosphere of the evening.

Walking along beside Giovanni, Emily felt a surge of unexpected happiness ripple through her. Being in the sole company of the most handsome man she'd ever laid eyes on was something she had not anticipated when she and Coral had left Heathrow the other day. She was not meant to be here enjoying herself—she was employed purely on a business basis. And she realized that it was the first time since starting the job that anyone had invited her out, or treated her as Giovanni was doing. She met plenty of pleasant—and not so pleasant—people during the course of an assignment, but no one had ever asked her out to dinner or treated her other than formally. But maybe that was down to her, she acknowledged. Although there were certain guidelines laid down by the company which she should conform to—mostly in her own interests—she was also aware that she seemed to have developed a natural antipathy to showing undue familiarity with people— notably with men. She hoped she wasn't thought of as stand-offish. Then she shrugged inwardly. So what? It was far safer, emotionally and in every other way, to keep slightly detached, to keep her distance. To try and enjoy life on the margins.

But, despite these thoughts, Emily was acutely aware that, although he was walking very closely by her side, Giovanni had not attempted to take her hand in his—and for a ridiculous moment she wished that he would! She could still recall the touch of his fingers on hers as he'd passed over the gift she'd bought at the shop yesterday—strong, protective fingers, sensitive and warm. Then she bit her lip. These thoughts must be thanks to the relaxed evening atmosphere, or to the occasional sight of two young lovers, their bodies entwined, as they passed, she thought.

He glanced down at her. 'Although I don't know your particular likes and dislikes, Emily,' he said, 'I'm pretty sure you'll approve of my choice of venue for tonight. There are so many places to choose from, of course, but we have to start somewhere.'

Emily smiled up quickly. 'It'll be great to have someone…to have *you,*' she amended, 'to make the decision for me. I'm only just getting used to being totally independent in strange places, to try and find my own way around. And, although it's getting easier, sometimes it can be…uncomfortable.' She didn't add that she frequently felt very homesick and wished that she was back in the comparative solitude and safety of the art gallery. But she'd made the decision to spread her wings, to search life out instead of waiting for it to find her—and you didn't do that by hiding away in the cool, protective atmosphere of an art gallery.

When they arrived at the restaurant, Emily knew straight away that she was going to love it. It was on the top floor of the Hotel Hassler Roma and, as they were shown to a table by the window, soft piano music started to play quietly. Giovanni held out a chair for Emily to sit down and she glanced up at him appreciatively.

'This is…lovely, Giovanni,' she said, her eyes moist and shining with unaffected pleasure.

He returned her glance, his seductive lips parted in a brief smile. 'I had a feeling it would be right for you, Emily,' he murmured, pausing for a moment with his hand resting lightly on her bare shoulder, and she shivered instinctively.

'You're not cold?' he enquired, moving away to sit down opposite her. 'You haven't brought a wrap with you?'

'No—no, I'm not cold! It's…I'm just excited to be here,' she said quickly.

He looked across at her thoughtfully. The gentle light from the single candle on the table seemed to enhance the delicate curve of her cheek, accentuating the length of her dark eyelashes. He picked up his copy of the menu which the waiter had just given them, trying to concentrate on the selection of dishes on offer.

'You've obviously been here before, Giovanni,' Emily said with her eyes on her own menu. 'What do you recommend amongst all this?'

'I can recommend just about everything,' he said at once, 'but it depends on what you feel like.'

After a few moments, Emily put down her menu. 'I've made my decision,' she said lightly. 'I've decided that you can order for both of us.' She paused. 'And I shall trust your choice unequivocally.'

He shrugged, grinning across at her. 'Well, if you're going to live dangerously, here goes,' he said. 'And anyway, in all matters, large or small, I like to think that any woman is perfectly safe in my hands.'

Just then, the waiter came to their table and, as Giovanni

gave their order for wine, Emily gazed out of the window, swaying her shoulders lightly to the rhythm of the popular medley the pianist was playing. The hotel was situated at a spot overlooking the Spanish Steps, affording a bird's eye view of the mellow roofs of old Rome, and Emily felt grateful, again, for having met Giovanni—because he was right. She would probably have never come across this charming restaurant, and at this moment, with stars beginning to pin-prick the darkening night sky outside, and the soft lighting and friendly atmosphere in the candlelit room, Emily felt as if she had been transported to an enchanted island. And she didn't want to be rescued from it—not just yet!

Giovanni broke into her reverie. 'I've ordered white wine, Emily,' he said, 'and for the meal, I thought grilled tuna with tomatoes and taggia olives, followed by suckling pig in sweet milk sounded about right. Plus a mixed salad.' He paused. 'I hope you approve.'

'Heartily.' Emily smiled.

'And we'll consider dessert later,' Giovanni went on as the waiter departed. 'Their chocolate mousse with hot chocolate sauce is a known favourite,' he added.

'Well, if I've room, that will certainly be the one for me,' Emily said lightly, and he grinned.

'I thought so,' he said. 'That's why I mentioned it.'

Emily kept her eyes lowered for a moment. If he thought he knew her so well, she'd better watch what she said in future. This man seemed able to infiltrate her persona without even trying. He was getting close— dangerously close—she thought. But…she'd relax and enjoy it—just for tonight. There was no harm in accepting the fact that she was liking the feelings which Giovanni was arousing in her—the sense that she was not only liked, but that she was desired. And, in any case, these trifling few days would soon pass into history and would simply come in the category of harmless holiday meetings which never came to anything—and which never meant anything. Which was exactly how she wanted it. This time tomorrow she'd be back in the flat—alone—because Coral was going to spend the weekend with her parents, with just the unpacking and the laundry to fill her thoughts.

Their wine arrived and Giovanni raised his glass. 'Let's drink to…let's drink to this evening,' he murmured.

Emily picked up her own glass and gently clinked it against his. 'To this evening,' she replied slowly, letting the sparkling bubbles tease her lips and tongue. 'This is wonderful,' she added.

When the food arrived, Emily looked down at her plate. 'This is rather…generous…' she said. 'I hope I can manage it all.'

'Do your best,' Giovanni said as he unfolded his napkin. 'You look to me as if you need just a little building up, Emily.'

But he didn't mean that, and shouldn't have said it, he thought as he watched her for a second. It was true that she had a slender figure—unlike many of his compatriots, who were more generously endowed, but she possessed the most exquisite curves and, in his experienced opinion, they were all in the right places!

Presently, he said, 'So, where are they sending you next, Emily?'

Emily picked up her glass to take a sip of wine. 'I'm not sure,' she replied. 'I shall know when I go back to work on Monday. But I normally spend the following week in the office after I've been away—to report back.' She picked up her knife and fork again. 'What about you,

Giovanni? When do you expect to leave Rome?' As soon as she'd said that, Emily wished that she hadn't because it looked as if she was trying to find out when he'd be in London.

'Oh, well, that's largely up to me,' he said casually. 'But I'll probably be there in the next week or so.' He leaned across to top up her glass. 'I have a flat in London, so I can come and go as I please.'

Hmm, Emily thought. A flat in London, and he'd said he'd a flat here in Rome too—all the education he spoke of had obviously provided him with a very sound income! She would find it difficult to be able to afford a flat of her own—sharing the rent and expenses with Coral was the only way it could work for *her*.

At that moment her mobile rang and, frowning, Emily reached into her bag to answer it. She hoped it wasn't Coral to say she'd landed herself in some sort of fix!

It wasn't Coral—it was Paul. And Emily smiled involuntarily at the sound of her brother's voice.

'Hi, Emmy,' Paul said. 'Just checking up—you're due home tomorrow, aren't you?'

'Paul! How good to hear you,' Emily said, smiling across at Giovanni briefly.

'Has it all gone well?' Paul wanted to know. 'Found your way around OK? Where are you now?'

'Everything's gone like…like a dream,' Emily said, 'and I'm sitting in a lovely restaurant having the most fabulous meal…'

'Is Coral there? Let me have a word,' Paul said. He and Coral had always got on well.

'Oh…well…Coral's not with me,' Emily said casually. 'We've sort of…parted company, just for this evening…'

'Oh? You're on your own?'

'No—not exactly…I'm having dinner with…with a friend.'

There was silence for a second. 'Someone you know?'

'Well, I do now.' Emily smiled, looking across at Giovanni again. She wished Paul wouldn't worry about her like this. 'I've met Giovanni…Giovanni Boselli,' she said hurriedly, 'and Giovanni has been a great help in finding me a couple of places I couldn't locate, and now we're enjoying a fantastic meal, Paul… I must bring you here one day.'

She could just imagine the expression on Paul's face. Where his sister was concerned, he saw predatory males on every corner.

'Oh…well, then,' Paul said. 'Have a good time, and safe travelling tomorrow, Emmy. I'll ring you later on…' He paused, lowering his voice. 'Take care, won't you…be *careful,* Emmy.' Then, 'Dad sends his love, by the way.'

They ended the call and Emily replaced the phone in her bag, not looking at Giovanni, but she knew he hadn't taken his eyes off her. She decided not to tell him that Paul was her brother. Let him think what he liked. And, for a ridiculous moment, Giovanni felt a surge of jealousy run through him at the way Emily's eyes had lit up as she'd spoken to the man at the other end. It had to mean that it was someone special…even though she'd said she wasn't in a relationship at the moment.

By the time they'd finished the meal—with neither of them having the chocolate mousse—it was almost midnight, and reluctantly they left the restaurant and began strolling back to where Giovanni had parked his car. Emily sighed, taking a deep breath as she looked up at the sky.

'This evening has been the perfect way to end my tour,' she said. 'Thank you, Giovanni.'

'I consider it to have been a…privilege to have your company, Emily,' he replied, and there was no teasing note in his voice as he said it.

What happened in the next couple of seconds would always remain a blur in Emily's memory—but, without any warning at all, her ankle suddenly twisted horribly and with surprising force—so that she found herself sprawling to the ground, her arms flailing helplessly at something, anything, to help her. And, although Giovanni had been walking very close beside her, he was not able to do a thing to stop her falling. Then, with an incoherent curse, he sprang forward and grabbed hold of her and pulled her to her feet.

With a gasp of unbelievable pain, Emily tried to put her foot to the ground, but could only lean against him as he held her in a tight, protective embrace. *'Oh,'* she said, gritting her teeth to stop from shrieking aloud, 'what on *earth* did I trip over?'

Still holding her, he glanced down at the pavement. 'Well, these slabs are very uneven—look at that one—that's what you must have caught your foot on.' He looked down at her, resting his chin on her head for a second. 'How…how bad do you think it is, Emily? Can you put any weight on it?'

Now her ankle was throbbing with hammer blows and, for a terrible moment, Emily felt her head swimming. She hoped she wasn't going to disgrace herself and faint in public! 'This has happened to me before,' she admitted. 'Perhaps I've weakened this ankle, so I'll have to be more careful in future.' With her full weight against him for support, she looked up into his eyes and, even in the dim mellowness of the street lighting, he could see that her face was ashen.

'Come on,' he said. 'We're very close to my flat. You need to sit down for a few minutes and recover.' With his arm firmly around her waist, he almost carried Emily the length of the street and around the corner. Half hopping, half walking, Emily was in no position to suggest any alternative, and in a couple of minutes they reached an ancient stone archway through which she could see a discreet block of shuttered dwellings.

'Mine's on the ground floor,' Giovanni said, 'so there are no steps to negotiate.'

Although the building was unprepossessing from the outside, inside it was a different matter. Giovanni gently guided Emily across the large tile-floored sitting room to lie her down on an elegant chaise longue.

'There, keep your feet up for a few minutes and let's see what you've done to yourself,' he said.

As he switched on the numerous table lamps, the room was immediately swathed in a gentle, soothing glow and, in spite of feeling extremely shaky, Emily couldn't help admiring her surroundings. It was a cool, comfortable room and clearly very expensively furnished.

He came over and knelt down beside her, not removing her sandal but taking her ankle very carefully in his warm hands. 'Can you move it about, Emily?' he asked. 'Try to turn it—very gently—from side to side.' He peered at it more closely. 'It does look rather swollen,' he added.

Emily did as she was told. 'Well, I'm sure it's not broken,' she said, 'and, as I said, this has happened before. I think I've probably just sprained it again, that's all.' She looked at him ruefully. 'Sorry to be such a pain, Giovanni…'

'Wasn't your fault,' he said. 'That could happen to anybody.' He massaged her foot gently for a few moments, smoothing it rhythmically with the palms of both hands.

'It does feel hot,' he said. He stood up and looked down into her upturned face, relieved to see that some colour had returned to her cheeks. 'I'll get an ice pack from the fridge to put on it…and would you like a glass of water—or anything else?' he asked.

She smiled up. 'Yes—some water, please,' she said, thankful that her heart rate had lessened and that the feeling of dizziness had passed.

Left by herself for a few moments, Emily had a good look around her. It was quite obviously a man's abode, she thought, having very few frills or ornaments—apart from several framed photographs displayed on a large mahogany cabinet. There was one of two little girls in swimsuits on a beach somewhere, and someone else crouching and hugging a dog around its neck, but in the front was one of a beautiful dark-eyed girl with a generous smile. She was obviously someone rather special, Emily thought—no doubt one of Giovanni's many girlfriends… Then her gaze flickered to a smaller one of Giovanni with his arm held protectively around the shoulders of the same girl, who was looking up at him adoringly.

Just then Giovanni returned and Emily sipped gratefully from the glass of water he handed her, leaning forward slightly to watch him as he placed the ice pack, which he'd wrapped in a small towel, around her foot.

'This will help,' he said, supporting it in place with two cushions. 'And presently I'll go and fetch the car and take you back to the hotel.' He paused. 'Do you have an early start tomorrow? What time's your flight?'

'Two p.m., if I remember rightly,' Emily replied, feeling suddenly as if she were in a dream. The whole day had turned out so unexpectedly, she thought…and being with Giovanni for so much of it was the most unexpected thing of all. But she knew that she'd enjoyed every minute of it, had enjoyed being with this—all right, say it, she told herself—being with this heart-throb of masculinity. And even now, being here with him in his flat, was rather unbelievable. It was certainly nothing which she could have anticipated.

He was still kneeling on the floor beside her, pressing the ice pack more firmly against her foot now and then, and looking up at her occasionally with that special sensuous smile which Emily was getting used to, and which had the effect of sending delicious shivers down her spine. She looked over his shoulder, nodding at the photographs on display. 'Are you fond of photography?' she asked casually, hoping he'd tell her who all the people were in the pictures. Tell her who that girl was.

'Oh—off and on,' he replied non-committally. 'I'm not someone who likes to snap away at everything in sight and clutter up my home with hundreds of albums, that's for sure.' He leaned back slightly. 'But it's my mother who's snap-happy. She keeps giving me fresh ones to put on show.'

Emily glanced up at him quickly as he spoke. Something in his tone, something in the unusually dark expression flickering across his features made her wish she hadn't shown any interest in his belongings. He'd already intimated that there was some friction somewhere in the family...

And Giovanni, acutely aware of Emily's vulnerable presence so near to him, couldn't help thinking how ironic the situation was. She was a beautiful woman, he enjoyed her company, enjoyed everything about her, had already imagined what it would be like to make love to her—and here she was, lying on his sofa with a sprained ankle!

How different it might have been if he could have invited her here for an intimate meal, if they could have talked long into the night, and then, later, much later, from the comfort of his king-size bed, could have watched the dawn break together. Some hopes!

After a while, Emily slid off the chaise longue and gingerly tried putting her foot to the floor—and, thankfully, Giovanni's treatment had worked like a miracle.

'It's fine now—really,' she said, looking up at him. 'Thank you, Dr Giovanni. I'll be OK now.'

He had got to his feet, still holding her protectively around the waist, then stood back. 'That's good—you stay right here and I'll fetch the car,' he said.

While he was gone, Emily limped over to the cabinet and peered closely at the girl in the picture. Her facial expression was so lively that Emily felt she could discern what the girl was thinking when that shot was taken. Whoever she was, Emily thought, she was a living part of this room. A presence. No wonder she had pride of place, right there in front of all the others.

Emily turned away, shrugging slightly. So what? What did it matter to her, anyway?

CHAPTER FOUR

'WELL, *you've* certainly made a night of it!' Coral exclaimed. 'Do you realize what the time is—I was beginning to get worried,' she teased.

Coral was sitting up in bed, half dozing, half reading, but now that Emily had returned she soon became fully awake and ready for a long chat. 'Come on,' she said. 'Where did you go...and was the sumptuous Giovanni good company—or shouldn't I ask?'

At this point Emily wished with all her heart that she had her own room, rather than sharing. She definitely did not feel like giving Coral a blow-by-blow account of the last few hours. But she knew she wasn't going to be let off easily.

'Oh—we had dinner in a lovely restaurant,' she said casually, 'and there was a pianist playing all my favourite numbers.' She went across to the bathroom. 'But how about you? Did Nico come up to expectations?'

Coral couldn't wait to pour out all the details. 'Ellie, he is just *gorgeous!* We strolled all around the city—to places you and I haven't been to—and we stopped by the Trevi Fountain and I threw a coin in and made a wish! Then we sat outside at a small restaurant and had a nice meal— nothing too extravagant, of course, because I don't think he's rich or anything, but Emmy he was so…so…special. So attentive. Made me feel like a princess,' she added somewhat wistfully. 'I mean, Steve never treated me like that, ever—but Nico, *he* did, and he was so charming… wanted to know all about me, what I did, where I lived.' She paused for breath. 'And, guess what—he's going to come to England—maybe next month, especially to see me! What do you think of that?' She flopped back on her pillow. 'I never dreamed for a second that I'd meet some-one—anyone—who could make me feel so…so…roman-tic.' She looked up at Emily. 'I think I'm in love. Do you think I'm mad?'

'Yes,' Emily replied, going into the bathroom and shutting the door firmly.

She switched on the shower and stood under the rush of warm water for several moments before beginning to soap herself gently. Coral was so—so—*suggestible,* she thought, so ready to read something into nothing. Of course, Nico seemed a nice enough man, but he was young—significantly younger than Coral—and he was obviously cutting his emotional teeth on this impres-sionable Englishwoman—and she would not have been the first, either. And now Coral was letting herself believe that she was about to have the grand love affair! Honestly!

Emily stepped out of the shower and started towelling herself briskly, feeling distinctly rattled. Suddenly, she didn't want to be here. Then she paused, glancing at herself in the mirror as she rubbed gently at her soaking wet hair. She knew very well why she was feeling suddenly mis-erable and deflated. And it was nothing to do with Coral's enthusiastic and immature reactions, either. It was every-thing to do with Signor Giovanni Boselli—how could she have allowed him to get to her so easily, to engender feelings in her that she thought she had got well under control? Emily realized how easily she had fallen under his spell—the dangerous spell of a handsome Italian who was obviously well practised at flattering the opposite sex. He'd certainly made her feel special—as no doubt he'd done with that girl in the photograph. And plenty of others like her.

She took her gown from the hook on the door and went back into the bedroom. Coral was still awake and Emily knew that there'd have to be more lively chat before sleep was allowed. Reaching for the hairdryer, she tried to smile brightly.

'So—has Nico been to the UK before?' she asked. 'Does he know anyone over there?'

'Not a soul,' Coral said, 'so I said he could stay with us—it would only be for a week or so, Ellie.'

Emily made a face. 'Coral—you shouldn't be quite so free with your invites,' she said. 'We only have the extra sofa bed in the sitting room, remember.'

'I told him that, and he said that would be great.' Coral sighed. 'He's going to teach me Italian,' she said. 'That's what we were doing over dinner. I've learned a few phrases already.' She sat up, drawing her knees to her chin. 'Now, tell me more about Giovanni… I can't believe that my evening was more exciting than yours.'

Emily filled in a few details, describing the moment that she'd fallen down, but when she went on to say that she'd been to Giovanni's flat, that was something else!

'You went to his place? Ellie! No wonder you were a bit slow telling me that! What was it like—and what was *he* like?'

'I have no idea what you're implying,' Emily said loftily, 'but his flat is in a luxury block—and it was quite sparsely furnished, but all obviously very well planned and very expensive.' She paused. 'And the only human contact we had while I was there was when he continued pressing a huge ice pack on my foot. *Very* romantic,' she said sarcastically.

'That was bad luck—you twisting that ankle again, Ellie,' Coral said seriously. 'It's about the third time you've done that lately, isn't it...and *next* time the gorgeous Giovanni may not be there to rescue you!'

They had plenty of time to spare the next morning, so after a leisurely breakfast Emily and Coral packed their belongings and went down to the hall to await the taxi which would take them to the airport.

'It's Nico's day off today,' Coral said, glancing across at the reception desk, which was being manned by yet another good-looking Italian. 'Where do they *get* all these men?' she added, lowering her voice. 'Just look at *him*!'

Emily sighed. 'I think it's high time we got back to London and reality,' she said. But she was relieved to find that this morning she herself felt more grounded, more normal. She realized that being away from home, with sunshine and good food and wine, could all be a heady combination and, although it would be a long time before she'd forget Giovanni's mesmerizing gaze, today she was totally in control once more. Today she wasn't experiencing those ridiculous schoolgirl feelings that she'd felt last night... The only physical hurt that remained was a slight twinge in her ankle now and then. Just enough to make her careful where she walked.

They arrived at the airport in good time and after they'd checked in Coral announced that she was going to use the Ladies' room.

This was not nearly so crowded a place as Heathrow, Emily thought as she stared around her—and the gathering queues seemed to be mostly holidaymakers. Glancing up at the monitors, she saw that their flight number had not yet been announced—but there was plenty of time, she thought idly.

Suddenly, to her total astonishment, she saw Giovanni. He was standing at the far end of the hall looking around him, and for a few seconds Emily didn't get up from her seat, aware that her heart was fluttering madly again... Well, he had to be the most fantastically attractive man in the building—in the universe, she could have added—so why wouldn't any woman's heart beat just that little bit faster? And how did he always manage to look so elegant—even in casual clothes?

She got up then and walked across to him slowly. He spotted her almost immediately and his face broke into a wide grin as he quickened his pace to come and stand by her side. He was holding an elegant spray of red roses. Emily was the first to speak.

'Giovanni...' she began, trying not to sound breathless. 'What...what are *you* doing here?' she said, though the answer was pretty obvious. The way he was looking down at her spoke volumes.

'I just had to see how you were today, Emilee-a,' he replied easily. He wasn't going to say that he'd lain awake most of the night, thinking about her. Wanting her. He put his hand lightly on her shoulder. 'Your ankle... I was worried that this morning it would not be good—that you might have difficulty walking.' He paused, then handed her the flowers. 'For you,' he said simply. 'To say sorry.'

Emily took the flowers from him, then bent her head to smell them. They were fragrant and perfectly shaped.

She looked up at Giovanni. 'To say sorry? What for, Giovanni?' she asked.

'I felt responsible, Emily,' he said. 'You trusted yourself to my care last night, and I should have spotted that loose stone…I should have prevented you from falling.'

Emily smiled up at him. 'Of course you shouldn't, Giovanni, it was my own silly fault,' she said quickly. 'I told you, it's happened before. You'd think I'd be more careful!' She looked down at the roses again. 'But I can't say I'm sorry that you've brought me these beautiful roses! Thank you—thank you so much, Giovanni. They're lovely.' She paused. 'But you really must not feel guilty. I should have looked where I was going.'

Although she hadn't imagined for a moment that she would be seeing him today, Emily couldn't help feeling flattered—and excited—that he'd turned up, despite the talking-to she'd given herself earlier about the perils of being in the company of gorgeous Italians. But it was really good of him to be so considerate, she thought. And, anyway, he was only being kind.

Just then Coral appeared, and when she saw the pair standing together, her reaction was fairly predictable. 'Goodness me…Gio…' she began, her eyes wide, and Emily cut in quickly.

'Giovanni was worried that I might be crippled this morning,' she said, 'so he just looked in to make sure I was…everything was…OK. Wasn't that thoughtful of him?'

'*Very* thoughtful,' Coral said, her interested gaze going from one to the other with unashamed interest. 'Don't worry, Gio,' she said, 'I'll make sure that Ellie gets home safe and sound.'

Giovanni looked down at Coral with his usual disarming smile.

Presently, it was time for them to go through to the departure lounge, and for Giovanni to take his leave.

'Safe travelling,' he murmured, his gaze lingering on Emily's upturned face. 'I'll...be in touch, Emilee-a,' he added softly.

'Goodbye, Giovanni,' she said, 'and thank you so much...again.'

Then he turned and walked rapidly away without a backward glance, and Coral stared at his retreating back. 'What a yummy Italian,' she said sadly. 'You've made a hit there, Ellie. He couldn't take his eyes off you.'

'Rubbish,' Emily said. 'He's just that sort... He was really concerned about me falling down last night, felt it was all his fault. That's the only reason he bothered to find me today. Just to make sure.'

When they got back home, Coral left for her parents' house and Emily took Giovanni's card from her bag and dialled his mobile phone number. Well, it was only polite... They'd barely had chance to say goodbye properly. He answered almost immediately and when he heard who was calling he said, 'Ah...Emilee-e-a,' with just that lingering intonation at the end of her name which had the familiar effect of making her knees feel slightly shaky.

'Giovanni,' she said quickly. 'I thought...I thought you'd like to know that we got home safely but really I want to thank you again for the roses... They are absolutely lovely. You shouldn't have spoiled me like that. But thank you so much... What have I done to deserve them?'

There was a moment's hesitation before he answered. 'All beautiful women deserve to be spoiled,' he said easily, and Emily shook her head briefly. She wondered how many times he'd used that one before.

He cleared his throat. 'I'm glad you called, Emily, because I've just heard that I need to be in the UK next week—just for a few days. It would be good to see you,' he added.

Emily bit her lip. This felt all wrong—it *was* wrong—and she knew it. During the flight home, she'd made up her mind that she wasn't letting this—association—with Giovanni go any further. It wasn't that she didn't trust him as a person—it was more to do with not trusting herself, and relationships in general. The problem was, he'd said he sometimes came to the UK so it was obvious that they'd meet up—something told her he'd make sure of that! And each time they did would make it more difficult…difficult to refuse to see him, and even more difficult to deny herself the pleasure! And, in any case, with the choice of women he so obviously would have, she'd soon slip down his list of priorities. No, thanks, she wasn't going down that road again, she thought firmly.

She waited before answering, trying to find the right words. She'd so enjoyed herself yesterday evening—the meal, the atmosphere in the restaurant, the slow stroll afterwards—even if it had ended rather dramatically. And she remembered all too clearly the feel of his arms around her, holding her so protectively after she'd fallen, remembered the feel of his hands, warm and consoling as he'd massaged her ankle in that firm but gentle caress. She cleared her throat.

'It's been really great to have met you, to have known you, Giovanni,' she said, adding softly, 'I've…enjoyed it. But I'm going to be very busy at work next week, so I don't think we'll be able to meet up. Sorry.'

Giovanni grinned to himself. He knew a rebuttal when he met it.

'No worries,' he said easily. 'I understand.' And, after chatting for a few more minutes, they finished the call and he rang off. And Emily sat where she was for several moments, staring at the phone. Well, that was easy enough, she thought. He had accepted her very firm refusal to see him again with no attempt to make her change her mind. He hadn't even bothered to prolong their conversation, keeping it short and sweet. She shrugged. Oh, well, it had been an experience, being with him for that brief interlude.

Standing by the window in his flat, a slow smile spread over Giovanni's dark features. The challenge ahead excited him. So, Signorina Emily was going to give him a run for his money, was she? Give him a hard time. But he was up for it, and he knew he'd win in the end. She liked him—he was sure of that—even fancied him, just a little. So he'd have to work hard at heightening any feelings she already had for him, until they burned with the same passion that he admitted, quite unashamedly, he had felt for her from the very first moment they'd met at the shop. She had seemed to light up the space around her with a kind of magic…and he'd wanted to be close enough to her to share in it. And he still felt exactly the same now—nothing had changed. But maybe *he* was changing, he thought, thanks to almost six months of complete rest from all the pressures, all the hurt that had weighed him down so relentlessly.

He bit his lip thoughtfully. He would be in England next week, he knew where Emily worked, and now he had her phone number. And, however busy she said she was, she'd make time for him. In his mind, there was no doubt about that!

He went across to the cabinet and poured himself a drink. 'To us, Emilee-a,' he murmured, raising his glass. 'To you and me. And Lady Luck.'

CHAPTER FIVE

'YOU *can't* turn me down tonight, Emily,' Justin said softly. 'Not on my birthday!'

Emily looked up quickly, trying not to look as irritated as she felt. Justin simply would not take no for an answer—and it was beginning to get on her nerves. What made it worse was that they were always seated next to each other, so he was a constant presence in the busy upstairs office. Not to mention the fact that he happened to be the boss's son—which made it doubly awkward for her to keep turning him down. But, the fact was, she didn't fancy him, not one bit, and didn't relish the thought of them being alone together off duty.

'But how much more celebrating do you need to do, Justin?' she said, giving him a rather watery smile. The entire staff had already been to a wine bar at lunchtime to honour the occasion, and someone had bought cream cakes to go with the afternoon cup of tea.

Justin gazed down at her thoughtfully. He couldn't understand her reticence. He'd tried so many times to get her to accept his offer of a night out somewhere, and he'd certainly never been turned down by anyone before. But Emily was different from all the others…and, as far as he knew, she hadn't been out with anyone else from work, either. He frowned slightly as he looked down at her. She always looked so fantastic in the regulation black suit and white shirt, her sheer black tights and high-heeled shoes doing full justice to her slim legs and dainty feet.

'Well, it's just that we might round off the day in spectacular fashion,' he said, a slightly teasing note in his voice. 'Make it one to really remember.'

Emily turned her attention back to her computer. She had made up her mind that she was not going with him anywhere tonight, but neither did she want to offend. He was a nice enough bloke, but his persistence was becoming over-familiar and she'd had enough of it.

'I'm sure you've a whole list of suitable partners to make your dreams come true tonight, Justin,' she said, 'but I'm already spoken for, I'm afraid.' She shifted some papers on her desk. 'I'm entertaining someone to dinner at home tonight—a long-standing arrangement which I can't possibly alter.'

He waited a moment before replying. Then, 'I don't believe you,' he said teasingly—but meaning it.

Emily felt really angry at that. How dared the man doubt her honesty? But it was too late—she'd told a lie and now she'd have to brave it out. 'Believe what you like,' she said flatly, her colour rising. 'The fact remains that I'm not free to accept your kind offer and, before I even begin to think about tonight, I've got all these lists to complete, so if you don't mind…'

As it happened, it had been an exceptionally busy day for everyone, and it was gone seven o'clock before all the staff finally left the office, spilling out onto the pavement and making their 'goodnights' to each other.

'What have you got lined up for this evening, Justin?' one of the other men asked. 'Something special?'

'It was going to be special,' Justin said breezily, glancing at Emily, 'but I've been turned down. Still, I shan't be spending it alone, I promise you.'

Everyone then went their separate ways and, to Emily's annoyance, Justin fell into step beside her as she began to walk away.

Then, from a doorway close in front of them, a dark voice suddenly uttered her name and Emily could have shrieked in amazement—and delight!

'Giovanni!' she cried and, without a moment's hesitation, she almost threw herself at him, clutching him around the neck and offering him her mouth to be kissed. And Giovanni, momentarily transfixed by her reception, wasted no time in closing his lips over hers—putting his arms around her waist and lifting her right off her feet.

'Emilee-a,' he began, putting her down gently but before he could say anything more, she cut in.

'Giovanni, this is Justin—who happens to work with me,' and, turning now to Justin, she said triumphantly, 'and this, Justin, is Giovanni Boselli.'

To give him his due, Justin managed not to look too taken aback at what he'd just witnessed—he'd never realized that Emily could express herself so...so freely, like that—and he cleared his throat.

'Good to meet you...Giovanni...' he muttered. 'So, you're the lady's choice, then, are you...? Well, I do hope that you have a pleasant evening with Emily.' He paused. 'I've heard that she's a fair cook, so I'm sure she won't disappoint you tonight.'

It hadn't taken long for Giovanni to size up the situation, and he made good use of it, his arms still wound around Emily's waist. He'd wondered what sort of greeting he'd get from her, because she'd had no idea that he was going to turn up—he'd decided to surprise her rather than give her time to think up an excuse. And it seemed to have worked better than he could have dreamed!

'Emily has never disappointed me in anything,' he murmured, smiling down into her upturned face, his eyes twinkling mischievously.

'Well, have a great evening,' Justin said. 'See you on Monday, Emily.'

As soon as he'd gone, Emily disentangled herself from Giovanni, who made no effort to stop her, merely grinning down at her.

'I had no idea that you'd missed me so much, Emily,' he said smoothly. Then, more seriously, 'I take it that I was a useful, shall we say, decoy just now?'

Emily glanced up at him rather shamefacedly as they began to walk towards the tube station, thinking how suave he was looking in his dark business suit and grey shirt, though the loosened tie around his neck hung down casually 'Yes, sorry if I embarrassed you, Giovanni,' she said. 'But I refused to go out with Justin this evening, even though it is his birthday, saying that I was entertaining someone at home tonight. And he didn't believe me—quite rightly, I'm afraid. But, when I saw you there, I was able to…well…play the part, shall we say. It was as if fate had stepped in to make things easy for me!'

'I'm always very…happy…to be of service,' he said softly, putting his arm through hers protectively and his touch—now that they were alone—made Emily's breasts tingle. She quickened her step.

'How did you know that I'd be around, anyway?' she

asked, not looking up at him. 'I didn't tell you where I worked...'

'I knew the firm, but not the branch office,' he said, 'so I took a chance and looked in earlier this afternoon and asked if Emily Sinclair was in today—and the girl on the desk told me what I needed to know. My own office is only a ten minute walk away, where I've had to be for the last few days, so it was no big deal. And, if you hadn't worked there, I'd have tried the other branches until I found you,' he added.

After a moment, Emily said, 'You could have rung me first.'

'What—to have you turn me down?' he said, that teasing note in his voice again. 'No chance!' He took her elbow more firmly, to steer her across the road. 'And now that I am here, you have no choice but to be my date for the evening. I've several suggestions where we might go.'

Emily's emotions were totally mixed up now. She freely admitted that she'd felt absolutely blown away to see Giovanni standing there—it couldn't have worked better for her to convince Justin that she was spoken for that evening—but it wasn't only that. She knew that the very sight of Giovanni had set her heart pounding. In the intervening days since they'd been together she'd hardly stopped thinking about him, and to see him again in the all-too-seductive flesh had set her senses spinning. Which was why she hadn't wanted to meet him again—if she could help it. He was threatening to thwart her plans to remain emotionally uninvolved with anyone at all—at least for the foreseeable future. *Remember Marcus,* she kept telling herself, *remember how you felt when he decided he didn't want you any more, that he loved someone else. Can you bear the thought of that happening all over again?* But Emily knew with a sinking heart that every time she was near to Giovanni it would be increasingly difficult to resist him, and it wasn't her fault that he'd turned up tonight. So she'd have to deal with it as best she could.

Pulling herself away from all these thoughts, she glanced up at him as they joined the teeming home-going masses on the Underground. 'Well, I think I owe you one, Giovanni,' she said. 'A meal, I mean,' she added hurriedly. 'If you think you can trust my cooking, I'd be happy do the honours this evening.' She paused. 'I am rather tired, as a matter of fact—it's been a long week, and going out anywhere doesn't really appeal.'

'Sounds perfect to me,' he murmured. 'I hope Coral won't mind my intruding on her space.'

'Oh, Coral won't be there,' Emily said. 'She's staying at her parents' home in North Wales. She'll be back on Sunday night.' She didn't look at Giovanni as she spoke. She was going to make it very clear at the outset that she was merely being polite and returning his generosity by providing him with supper. It wouldn't be quite up to the standard of the meal they'd had in Rome, but her reputation in the culinary stakes was fairly high. She was the one who usually cooked when she and Coral were together at home.

The flat which the two girls shared was in a quiet residential street in a suburb of the city and, as she opened the front door, Emily glanced up at Giovanni.

'I'm afraid our place isn't quite as grand as yours,' she said lightly. 'Not so big, anyway,' she added.

He followed her up to the first floor, and as they entered the flat he looked around him appreciatively. 'It's very nice, Emily,' he murmured. 'Perfect for two working girls, I should have thought.'

As Emily had said, it was not large, only boasting a

sitting room, two small bedrooms, a minute galley of a kitchen and a bathroom with only enough space to accommodate the usual facilities and a shower cubicle.

'I shall own my own place one day,' Emily said, 'but this will do for the moment—and sharing the rent and all the expenses with Coral means that I can save up.' She smiled at Giovanni, who stood with his hands in his pockets, glancing around him.

'It's a very…pretty…home,' he said. He looked down at her. 'Just the sort of place I'd imagine you to be living in, Emily.'

His speculative eye had noted the expensive curtains at the windows, the luxurious cushions scattered around and the framed pictures on the wall, three of which were graced with soft over-lighting. He went closer to inspect them, his eyes narrowing. They were all watercolours, mostly of charming pastoral scenes, with one seascape and a couple of still life.

'I don't recognize any of these paintings,' he said, turning to look down at her.

'No,' she said, 'because they're originals.' She paused. 'They're my own feeble efforts, I'm afraid.'

Giovanni was genuinely amazed—and impressed. He knew a good painting when he saw one, and these were, to his mind, professionally done. But then he remembered that she'd said she'd worked in an art gallery, so it was obviously a subject dear to her heart. 'They are not feeble—they are fantastic, Emilee-a,' he said slowly. 'You have a real gift.' He looked back at the pictures for a moment. 'But you must know that, without me pointing it out, surely? What on earth are you doing in a travel agency?'

'I did do an Arts degree at university,' she said, 'and I'm never happier than when I've got a paintbrush in my hand.

But I'd have to be exceptionally good—and very lucky—
to earn my living at it, so I work where someone will pay
me.' She turned away. 'Maybe one day I'll be able to
afford to just sit at my easel and paint…but goodness only
knows whether that'll ever happen. I'd need a fairy god-
mother—or a big win on the Lottery, which I don't do, in
any case.'

'Your family—your father—must think you're brilliant,' Giovanni said, still staring at the pictures.

Emily smiled. 'Yes, I suppose he does,' she said. 'But
he would, because I'm his daughter. All parents think their
kids are brilliant, don't they? And that's not a good enough
recommendation. He insisted on rigging up those lights,
and he's done the same for a few of the ones I've given
him at home,' she added.

'Well, I'd recommend your expertise any day,' Giovanni
said firmly—and meant it. 'Haven't you tried selling any?'

'I'd be too embarrassed to try!' Emily said at once. 'I'd
only have to be rejected once, and that would be it! So I
restrict myself to giving them away as presents to friends.'

'I hope that I come into that category,' Giovanni said,
'because I'd love one of your paintings, Emily—for my
flat.' He turned to glance at her. 'And I'd be happy to pay
your price—whatever it was.' He paused, looking straight
into her eyes. 'Feasting one's eyes on beautiful things
cheers you up,' he added. 'It's good for the soul.'

Emily suddenly felt almost overcome by all this flattery
and she said quickly, 'Look, I must just change out of my
work clothes, then I'll start getting our dinner. Make
yourself at home, Giovanni.' She switched on the television, handing him the remote control. 'And help yourself
to something from our rather modest drinks table,' she
said as she went into her bedroom.

Doing as he was told, Giovanni poured himself a small whisky, then wandered over to the window thoughtfully. He was quietly amazed at how things had turned out today—amazed that he'd been able to track Emily down so easily, and gobsmacked when she'd thrown her arms around his neck in the street like that—although the reason for that had been made very clear straight away. He smiled to himself. Thanks, Justin, he thought. If it wasn't for you, I mightn't be here at all, now. He took a drink from his glass. Just another piece of luck which had come his way so unexpectedly.

Sitting down on the sofa, he switched on the TV, flicking through the channels for a few moments, and presently Emily emerged, wearing tight jeans and a white T-shirt, her hair brushed out loosely around her shoulders. She seemed to have removed her make-up, he noticed, as he admired the natural, fresh glow of her skin, and he stood up immediately, deciding not to compliment her on her appearance, even though it was the first thing he would normally do with any female he happened to be with. And most of them responded to it very happily. But he knew he had to tread carefully where this woman was concerned... She seemed to have her feet very firmly on the ground, and wouldn't necessarily appreciate too much sweet-talk.

'It won't take me too long to get our food,' she said lightly, 'so do freshen up while I do it, Giovanni—if you want to.' She smiled, indicating the bathroom. 'You don't need a map to find your way around our flat.' She turned to go into the kitchen, saying over her shoulder, 'My brother was supposed to be spending the evening with me—but he hasn't been very well for the past few days so was going to go straight home to bed. And I always plan

something a bit special when he eats here with me, so I
hope you'll approve of tonight's menu.'

Giovanni grinned. 'There won't be any trouble on that
score, Emily,' he said. 'Especially as I only had a very
quick bite with the others at lunchtime.'

Emily took the two generously sized veal cutlets from
the fridge. She'd prepared them before leaving for work
that morning, wrapping them in cheese and a fine slice of
ham before coating them in breadcrumbs. They'd only
take a few minutes to cook, she thought. She'd also par-
boiled and sliced the potatoes, which were now ready to
be layered with onion, butter and cream and baked quickly
for a short time in the oven. And there'd be green vegetables or salad—Giovanni could make that choice, she
thought.

She smiled as she busied herself. She did love entertaining—not that she did very much of it now. There never
seemed much time, and she was often away from home in
any case. But this was what she liked best—just cooking
for two. Sometimes it would be for Paul or her father,
very occasionally, but more often it would be just her and
Coral.

She finished preparing the potatoes, popping them into
the oven just as Giovanni came to stand in the doorway.
Leaning casually against the wall, he said, 'This was something I did not expect, Emily—to watch you beavering
away on my behalf. I'd hoped to be able to buy you dinner
somewhere tonight.'

She looked up at him quickly. 'But you did that when
we were in Rome,' she said. 'Now it's your turn to be
treated.' She paused for a moment. 'Now, would you prefer
salad or green vegetables? Your choice.'

He stared down at her for a long moment, thinking that

his 'choice' wouldn't have anything to do with food. He'd glanced in at her open bedroom door as he'd gone into the bathroom—her bed looked extremely comfortable and very inviting! But he knew very well that his carnal instincts were not going to be satisfied—not here, not with Emily Sinclair. But he was an experienced lover of women, each of whom had to be treated as an individual, he knew that. No rushing in where angels fear to tread, he thought.

He cleared his throat, trying to keep his mind on food. 'Any green vegetable will be great, Emily,' he said in answer to her question.

'Good. I was hoping you'd say that,' she said lightly.

As she was fairly sure it would, the meal turned out well and Giovanni was unstinting in his praise. 'Not only does the lady paint like an angel, she also cooks like one,' he murmured, glancing across at her as they sat together at the diminutive table in the window. By now, it was getting quite dark outside. Emily had switched on the discreet lamps in the room and the effect was cosy, soothing and intimate. Giovanni, feeling relaxed and totally at ease, put down his knife and fork and looked around him. 'I imagine that the décor here is all down to you, Emily?' he asked casually.

'Mostly,' Emily replied, 'and it's a good thing that Coral is so easy-going. She never argues about anything, so she was quite happy for me to choose the material and make the curtains and the cushion covers.' She took his empty plate and began to clear the dishes. She paused for a moment, the dishes in her hand. 'There is one big matter on which we're disagreeing at the moment though,' she said. 'It's Nico... Do you remember that it was Nico who she spent the last evening with in Rome? Well, he not only turned up at the airport to see her off, but apparently he's phoned her every single day since we returned to England, stating his undying love for her, and Coral, being Coral, is falling for it!' Emily sighed. 'She keeps phoning me to give me all the details and she's so excited. I don't like to pour cold water on her enthusiasm…but honestly—can anybody be *that* gullible?'

'You obviously don't believe in love at first sight, then, Emily?' Giovanni asked mildly.

'No,' Emily replied flatly. 'Do you?'

'Yes,' he said slowly, 'I certainly do—for some people.'

Emily shrugged. 'Well, I don't think that Nico is right for Coral. Good heavens—they've only spent a few hours together! And he's much younger than her.' She turned to go into the kitchen.

After a few moments, Emily came back from the kitchen carrying a glass dish of perfect strawberries and a fondue full of melted dark chocolate. Striking a match, she lit a flame beneath it and looked across at Giovanni.

'I hope you like this pudding,' she said. 'It's my brother's favourite.'

'I don't often indulge in puddings,' Giovanni said, 'but I'm not going to turn this one down.'

There was silence for a few moments as they each dipped the succulent fruit into the piping-hot chocolate, transferring it to their mouths carefully and looking across at each other, Giovanni's eyes twinkling. There was some-thing intrinsically sensuous about hot chocolate—hot dark chocolate—he thought as he watched Emily savouring the thickly coated strawberry she'd just put into her mouth. As she raised her eyes to look back at him, he noticed the tiniest shred of chocolate staining her cheek and, without thinking, he automatically leaned forward slowly and gently, very gently, wiped it away with his napkin, pausing with his fingers caressing her warm skin before cupping her chin in his hands. For a second they both stayed quite still, looking into each other's eyes without speaking, and Giovanni was painfully aware of his heightened pulse-rate, while Emily felt almost transfixed in her chair. The nerves in her neck were jangling, tingling, and she felt an unbelievable sensation invading the whole of her body, right down to her toes. A sensation she had never, ever experienced before, and it left her shaky and bewildered.

He sat back then, still gazing at her, and Emily looked away quickly. It was time to make some strong coffee!

'Thank you,' she said, hoping that her voice didn't sound as odd to him as it did to her. 'Dribbling chocolate all over yourself may only be done at home,' she added, trying to erase the memory of the last few moments. 'Would you like some cheese?' she enquired.

He followed her into the kitchen, wishing that his body would leave him alone. 'No, I don't want anything to take away the taste of that delicious dessert,' he said.

'Then we'll just have coffee,' Emily said.

Presently, after they'd cleared up the dishes, they went into the sitting room with the coffee things and Emily leaned forward to pour the steaming liquid into two mugs. She already knew from the other times they'd been together that Giovanni liked his black with no sugar and, as she handed him his mug, he held her gaze for a second.

'That was *the* most fantastic meal, Emily,' he said quietly. 'In fact, it has been a remarkable evening,' he added huskily, and Emily stirred cream into her mug quickly to avoid having to interpret his remark. He was sitting next to her on the sofa, but there was no bodily contact between them—for which Emily was profoundly grateful. Why was she still feeling so churned up inside? she asked herself. Giovanni Boselli had struck a nerve in her which she hadn't known existed and, although it was the most delicious sensation she'd ever experienced, it had put her on the alert, making her almost dizzy with a mixture of exhilaration and anxious desperation. It could be described as the same feeling she always had on extreme fairground rides, she thought...when she was going upwards, upwards towards a terrifying apex, then to hover tremblingly for a few seconds before being catapulted forward into a mind-blowing, breathtaking vortex—yet not really knowing how it was all going to end. She took another sip from her mug. She must not let Giovanni get to her any further, she told herself. It was all very well giving Coral good advice—she needed some herself, right now!

Later, after they'd finished their coffee, he glanced at his watch. 'I ought to be going,' he said. 'Do you realize that it's eleven-thirty?' He smiled across at her, feeling that somehow he'd crossed a certain line with her that night. And it would do. It was enough. For now.

He got to his feet and looked down at her, and Emily said lazily, 'Are you staying at your flat tonight, Giovanni?'

'No, I decided to book into a hotel this time—as I was only going to be here a couple of days.'

She got to her feet at last, not wanting him to go—and not wanting him to stay! She'd fully expected that Giovanni would suggest they spend the rest of the night together—in her bed—and she'd rehearsed in her mind the gracious way in which she would turn him down. But that obviously wasn't necessary, which was just as well, she thought. Much as she liked him—really liked him—she still thought he was probably an opportunist, someone who took his chances with no questions asked, then walked away, unscathed. Yet she had to admit that he had not behaved in any way that she'd found unattractive or unacceptable—quite the reverse! She turned resolutely to show him out, just as the phone rang stridently by her side.

It was late for a call and, raising her eyes briefly at Giovanni, she reached over to pick up the receiver. It was Coral and, after listening to several moments of excited chatter, Emily said, 'Oh, great…all right—it'll be good to have you back… What? Oh…OK, then—no, no, there's no need, we've got most things, but I'm going food shopping in the morning in any case and I'll re-stock where necessary.' Then, 'Have you enjoyed your break with the parents?' Emily shrugged, glancing over at Giovanni briefly. 'OK—see you tomorrow, Coral,' she said.

She put the phone down slowly and looked up at Giovanni, who had been watching her—watching the changing expressions on her face. 'Coral is coming home earlier than expected,' she said. 'She wasn't due back until Sunday night.' She raised her hands in mild resignation. 'But first she's going to Heathrow to pick up Nico. Apparently, he's going to be staying here with us for a week!'

CHAPTER SIX

EARLY one morning of the following week Emily let herself quietly out of the flat so as not to disturb Nico, who was still fast asleep in Coral's room.

As she made her way swiftly towards the Underground, Emily's mobile rang. It was Giovanni, and she smiled instinctively. He'd already contacted her several times since Friday evening, not only to thank her again, but, it seemed to Emily, to just chat... About anything. About nothing. And she was honest enough to admit that, in spite of everything, she was beginning to look forward to his calls.

'*Buon giorno, signorina.*' His dark, melting tones filled Emily with the usual warm shiver of pleasure.

'Giovanni—hello...' She couldn't keep the smile from her voice. 'This is a very early call—couldn't you sleep?'

'Well, I knew the day would have started for you. And I just wanted to say hi.'

'Hi,' she said lightly.

'So—how's it going with Nico? Is he behaving himself?'

'Well, when *I'm* around he does,' Emily said. 'But, as I spent the rest of the weekend at my father's house, I haven't seen that much of him.' She shrugged. 'Anyway, I thought it was tactful to leave the two of them together.'

'That was thoughtful of you.'

'Hmm,' Emily murmured enigmatically. The fact was, she didn't want to be in Nico's company at all. As soon as Coral had arrived with him on Saturday afternoon, she was struck by the man's synthetic charm.

'I suppose Coral has to go to work this week?' Giovanni said.

'Yes, she's employed by one of the big estate agencies in town and they're very busy at the moment, so there's no prospect of her having any more time off to spend with Nico,' Emily replied. 'So, apparently he finds his way around by himself all day, meets Coral for lunch and again in the evenings. And I don't see them until quite late.' She paused. 'They seem to be enjoying themselves,' she added.

'He's lucky to have such a lovely place to stay while he's in London,' Giovanni said, 'and lucky that you were prepared to put him up.'

Emily made a face to herself. Actually, she felt quite annoyed with Coral about the whole thing. Their flat was not big enough to entertain someone who was, after all, more or less a complete stranger. But it was her friend's home as much as it was Emily's, so she kept quiet.

By this time Emily had reached the Underground. 'Well, thanks for your call, Giovanni,' she said lightly. 'I'll have to go—my train's due in.'

'Of course, Emily.' He paused. 'The weather is so wonderful today… I wish you were here so that I could drive you out into the countryside. We could have a long, long lunch at a favourite spot of mine…the food, the wine…'

'Stop!' Emily said. 'You're making my mouth water— and I haven't even had any breakfast yet! Anyway,' she added, 'aren't you expected to do any work today, like the rest of us?'

'Oh, yes—of course. I've promised to mind the shop later for Stefano, and apparently there's a sort of family meeting I have to attend this evening.' He paused. 'These are a necessary evil which take place from time to time, I'm afraid, and unfortunately Aldo will be there as well,' he added.

'Oh, yes—Aldo,' Emily said, remembering the handsome man she'd been introduced to in Rome, and wondering what it was that Giovanni didn't like about him.

Finally, they ended the call and Giovanni went into the kitchen of his flat to make his morning coffee. Glancing around at the spacious area, he couldn't help comparing it with the tiny room—not much more than a short galley—in which Emily had prepared their meal the other evening. Yet she'd handled everything with such deft efficiency, producing that fabulous meal with no apparent effort, he thought. He stopped what he was doing for a moment, remembering how he'd touched her cheek, had taken his time in removing that small trace of chocolate. He had felt such an unutterable longing to take her in his arms and cover her lips with his, to feel her feminine curves moulding to his body…and, for the briefest of seconds, he'd felt that she had wanted it, too. How had he let the opportunity pass? he asked himself—it wasn't his way to hold back. But he couldn't rid himself of the conviction that if he wanted Emily he would have to work hard to earn her respect, her love, to get her to the point where she would submit readily to his increasing physical need of her. There was a price on this woman's head, he thought, and it was nothing to do with money.

He sighed briefly as he poured boiling water onto the coffee grounds. He'd never before had to bide his time to get anywhere with a woman, was only too aware that they seemed naturally attracted to him from the start. But he couldn't be sure about Emily, feeling that he still had to get past the thin veneer that seemed to protect her from anyone—from any man—getting too close.

The damnable thing was, they were now hundreds of miles apart and prolonged absence did nothing for any re-lationship—Giovanni knew that well enough. A flame without oxygen would soon peter out—and there was no way that he was going to watch this particular flame die! He knew that it wouldn't be a good idea to go back to the UK straight away…Emily would definitely not appreciate being hassled or pressurized, the feeling that she was being cornered. Yet he knew he mustn't let too much time pass before seeing her again, and she could be sent anywhere abroad at any time—her firm was planning to send her to Estonia, so she'd said, but she wasn't sure when that would be. At this rate, he thought morosely, it was going to be like capturing a dainty butterfly without much of a net to do it with. He bit his lip thoughtfully, remembering seeing Emily with that man she worked with—Justin. He was a good-looking guy, a decent sort of bloke and obviously smitten with Emily—anyone could see that. Yet she clearly did not return his feelings. But why? Giovanni wondered. What, and where, was the golden key that would unlock Emily's heart?

On Thursday evening Emily arrived home earlier than usual, the boss having decided that, as everyone had been working flat out for days, he would make it a short after-noon, just keeping a skeleton staff on duty until six o'clock.

This was quite a treat, Emily thought as she unlocked her front door and ran swiftly up the stairs. She'd have a long cool shower, then maybe finish the book she was reading before thinking about her evening meal. One good thing about Nico's visit was that he and Coral always ate out, so there was no chance of her being disturbed—not for several hours.

How wrong could she be? As she went into the sitting room, Nico got up from the sofa, treating her to one of his disarming smiles.

'Oh—Nico… I didn't realize you'd be here,' Emily began awkwardly, and he interrupted.

'I hope…is OK…' he said. 'Coral is to work late tonight.' He paused. 'She suggest I come here for rest… then we go next door to Trattoria later…'

'Oh, yes…we eat at Marco's sometimes,' Emily replied, trying not to feel too disappointed that her own plans were going to be thwarted. 'The food is good—you'll enjoy it.' She paused. 'Did—did Coral say when she'd be home?'

Nico shrugged. 'She not sure…about eight o'clock— hopefully.'

Emily groaned inwardly. It was only five-thirty—how could she stand being here with Nico for nearly three hours? Why couldn't he have found something to do in town? Then she felt guilty—he was probably feeling worn out by now, having apparently trudged the streets each day to enjoy the sights, and having to suffer being jostled and pushed around by the crowds. And she had to admit that he'd not been as much of an intrusion as she'd feared, because she only really saw him later on each evening and, as soon as he and Coral came back from wherever they'd been, Emily had gone to bed almost straight away, staying up just long enough to show an interest.

'I'll make some tea—or some coffee for us in a minute,

Nico,' she said, smiling briefly at him as she went into her bedroom, shutting the door firmly.

'OK—*grazie*—' he murmured, his gaze following her as she went.

Standing for a moment with her back to the door, Emily frowned. So much for a long relaxing shower and wandering about the flat in next to nothing! she thought. Instead, she'd just have to change out of her office things, have a quick wash, then try to be an amenable hostess to their visitor. She sighed, feeling irritable all over again. To have a lovely long evening ahead, with no one but herself to please, had been such a wonderful thought... Now she was going to have to make small-talk with Coral's beau until her friend got back.

Slipping out of her clothes, she went into the bathroom next door, glancing at herself in the mirror as she soaped her face and hands. And thinking of a certain other Italian who she'd be quite happy to have lounging on her sofa. She had gone over and over the evening they'd spent together here, the way he'd gazed at her across the table with that special look in his eyes which always made her senses swim. Then she shook her head, cross at allowing herself these silly thoughts—like Nico, Giovanni was a mind-numbingly handsome Italian—a Latin charmer of women. But what about loyalty and devotion, that quality which her parents had demonstrated for the whole of their married life, and which Emily didn't dare to hope was likely to feature in her own experience. Everyone seemed different today, she thought, wanting so much more from life, and that meant new partners when the novelty wore off and boredom set in.

And what about honesty? Where a beautiful female was concerned, Emily could only believe that, for most men, the woman of the moment was all that mattered.

Presently, with her hair brushed and wearing a fitted white shirt and jeans, Emily left her bedroom and Nico, lounging on the sofa, turned lazily to look at her as she went into the kitchen.

Glancing back at him casually, she said, 'Would you like tea or coffee, Nico? Or maybe something stronger?' She smiled apologetically. 'I'm afraid that at this time of day chamomile tea is the only thing that works for me, but we've got the ordinary kind—as you know by now!'

He got to his feet and followed her into the kitchen. 'I'll have…whatever you have, Emily,' he murmured.

Emily was aware, suddenly, that she was beginning to feel uncomfortable in Nico's presence… He had come over to deliberately stand very close to her, and she had to gesture to him to move aside so that she could reach up to the shelf for the box of tea bags. Then, just as she reached upwards, she felt his arms slide around her waist, both hands resting provocatively against the flatness of her stomach, and she immediately thrust herself right away and looked up at him sharply. But he only gazed down at her, at the heightened colour of her cheeks and, narrowing his eyes briefly, he said softly, in his halting English, 'English girls are…so…enchanting…so cool…'

Then he moved back towards her again and, bending his head, he closed his lips firmly over Emily's mouth—at which unbelievable point she staggered backwards in protest.

'Nico!' she almost shouted. 'What on *earth* are you doing?'

But Nico was not going to be put off that easily and he moved towards her again, enfolding her in his arms. 'Emilee,' he said breathily, 'be nice…you are so beautiful…I cannot resist…'

Pushing him off her, she said angrily, 'Go *away*!' He raised his hands as if to say, *What's the problem? It was only a kiss*…but Emily was having none of it.

'You are totally out of order, Nico!' she said crossly. 'Do you understand what that means? It means your behaviour is not welcome! It's inappropriate! Learn those words *now,* because you're going to need them if you think you can take advantage of any woman who takes your fancy!' She swallowed, not really believing what had just happened. 'Now—go away!' she said.

He shrugged, but turned to do as she'd asked and, to her own annoyance, Emily found herself shaking inside. Nico was a tall, fit, strong young man…and practically a stranger, even if he had spent the last five nights staying in their flat. But he was Coral's guest, not hers! How dared he take that kind of liberty—because his whole attitude just now had been overwhelmingly purposeful, and she was sure that if she'd shown him the slightest encouragement things could have gone much further.

Fuming as she waited for the kettle to boil, Emily thought of her friend… Poor Coral.

As she made the tea, Emily wondered how she was going to convince Coral to let this man go out of her life before real damage was done. She could describe what had just gone on in their kitchen—but she knew she couldn't do that. It would be too hurtful. No, but somehow Coral must come around to Emily's way of thinking. Obviously, there would be many exceptions, she thought, but holiday flings spelt bad news, whatever nationality you were talking about. Here today, gone tomorrow…but what about the broken hearts left in their wake? No, Emily thought, definitely, *definitely,* not worth the risk!

* * *

At the end of the following week Emily found herself once more on the plane to Rome. Her recent assignment in Italy had been so successful that the boss had decided that she should return. 'It will all become so familiar to you, Emily, you'll be like one of the locals soon,' he'd joked. 'And there's plenty of work still to do over there!'

She had received the news with a mixture of feelings... In one way it would be good to go back because she had definitely begun to feel more at home in the place, more relaxed about everything—although how much that was down to knowing Giovanni, Emily didn't like to think. But, in another, she half wished she was being sent somewhere else—anywhere else—to help her forget how much she'd begun to like Giovanni Boselli. Really like him.

His telephone calls continued with determined regularity and, although Emily's heart leapt with pleasure each time she heard his voice, she knew this was not the way she wanted it. So she decided not to tell him that she was coming to Rome for a further four days—and, in any case, he was apparently not going to be there, so there was no point.

'I'm spending a week at home in the country,' he'd said during one of his calls. 'It's very hot in town at the moment and, anyway, there's stuff to do for my mother. But soon I'll be back in England.' He'd paused. 'I want to stroll down Oxford Street with you when it's cold and frosty and when the Christmas lights are on,' he'd said, 'and we'll eat hot chestnuts together.' Why did he make it sound so good? 'I'll peel yours for you,' he'd added darkly.

Now, gazing out of the window as the plane came in to land, Emily couldn't help comparing Giovanni with Nico... Well, there was no comparison, she thought. Nico was a silly young man trying his luck with life, while

Giovanni was much more mature, more understanding… more manly, more totally acceptable. And not once had he behaved in the absurd way that Nico had, not once taken that step too far.

She'd never mentioned anything to Coral about Nico making a pass at her, keeping out of their way until it was time for him to go home, and it had been a great relief to Emily when he'd finally departed.

Now, the plane landed safely and everyone made moves to leave the aircraft. Well, Emily thought, this time it was going to be up to her. She'd have to find her own way around, eat all her meals alone… No Coral—and no Giovanni, either. So—that was good. Wasn't it?

CHAPTER SEVEN

FOR obvious reasons, Emily chose to book herself a room at a different hotel than the one she and Coral had stayed at—she didn't want to have to make small talk with Nico, who'd be on duty again now, and who was probably already well into seduction mode again, she thought.

For the next couple of days, Emily surprised herself by finding everything so much easier. She'd learned how the public transport system worked and where to purchase tickets, and how to find short cuts through the countless winding streets until she found the places she was looking for. And, so far, there had only been one hotel which she was not going to recommend to the firm, though she hoped it wasn't only because the man on Reception reminded her of Nico!

By the fourth day of her visit, Emily had covered almost everything she had to do—which had been her deliberate plan so that she could have a few hours to herself to revisit St Peter's and the Sistine Chapel and the Raphael Rooms. To drink in all the works of art of the leading painters, though realizing that there was so much to see it would take a lifetime to absorb it all. But to be able to feast her eyes on all the glorious pictures was an amazing bonus to her job, helping to make up for her occasional minor bouts of homesickness.

It was another very hot day and, dressed in her ice-blue sundress, her sun hat pulled well down on her head and with her large dark glasses obscuring most of her face, Emily strolled along the streets towards the Basilica. There were, naturally, hundreds of people of every nationality milling around the ancient monuments—in fact, it seemed that the entire world was there—but suddenly, unbelievably and almost making her gasp out loud, she saw Giovanni's unmistakable figure. But he was supposed to be out in the country somewhere! Not here at all! He was standing outside a coffee house talking to a dark-haired, beautifully dressed woman, who was standing with her back to Emily, talking and gesticulating animatedly.

Emily stood still for a moment, not knowing what to do… Should she go up to Giovanni and announce her presence? But he'd want to know why she hadn't told him she was going to be in Rome—and she didn't have a valid answer! She could hardly tell him the truth—which was that she wanted to avoid being near him, avoid the possibility of falling in love with an Italian, it would almost certainly prove to be an unwise bet.

Quickly, Emily moved into the shelter of a nearby doorway, just as Giovanni's vivacious friend took her leave of him, walking rapidly away in the opposite direction. That had to have been the girl in the picture, Emily thought, swallowing over a dry tongue—but as the woman had turned her head her dark glasses had made it impossible to tell whether she resembled the girl in the photograph or not. But…there had been something special… intimate…about the body language between the two of them as they'd chatted. If that wasn't the girl, then it was another glamorous female in Giovanni Boselli's life. But—so what? Emily thought reasonably. He was a free individual, and how many women he had at the same time was no business of hers…just so long as *she* wasn't among their number! So what on earth was bugging her?

Emily waited until he had walked away and was out of sight before emerging from her shadowy hiding place and resuming her journey, admitting to feeling downbeat. She had not expected to see Giovanni—it was the last thing she'd thought of—and, whatever happened, she didn't want to bump into him and have to explain why she hadn't let him know she'd be in Rome again. They had had so many lengthy chats on the phone—the last one only a few hours before she'd caught her flight—it wouldn't look good that she'd omitted to mention it. And what explanation could she give?

Biting her lip until it nearly bled, Emily hurried her step a little. No, she thought, there was nothing she could say to him which wouldn't sound empty and pathetic—or insulting. So she'd better make sure that he never knew she'd been here this week.

Feeling quite overcome—and not only by the heat—she found a convenient café and lined up to buy herself a large ice cream, realizing that her problems were far from over. Soon, probably, Giovanni would be back in London. So, what then? Well, she'd meet that when the time came, she thought as, walking along, she took a generous mouthful of the minty confection. And before that, for now, she'd rest her poor senses by gazing at all those paintings.

And then, suddenly, an ear-splitting screech of brakes, quickly followed by a cacophony of screams and shouts, made Emily stop in her tracks. Just in front of her a speeding cab had half mounted the pavement, its horn still blaring, and, to her horror, she saw someone partly lying awkwardly beneath it. For a few seconds Emily stayed frozen to the spot, the shock of witnessing an accident at close hand robbing her of her power to move, and everyone around seemed to be in the same position because no one had gone forward to help. But then her lengthy course in first aid made Emily swing into action—doing nothing was not an option in these circumstances—and, yelling loudly, 'Someone—help—call an ambulance—quickly!' she dropped her ice cream and broke into a run, pushing her way past the groups of horrified spectators and dropping down onto her knees beside the prostrate victim. It was a young woman who—to Emily's relief—was sobbing and crying hysterically, which meant that her airways weren't blocked and that she could breathe unaided. She was trying desperately to raise herself up but, as she was trapped beneath the cab—fortunately clear of the wheels—there wasn't the space to do so. And by now an evil-looking gash was visible along her forehead and there was a lot of blood coursing down her arm, staining the road beneath her as her terrified eyes looked up beseechingly at Emily.

'Aiuto! Aiuto! Per favore!' she cried.

Emily forced herself to smile reassuringly as she grasped both the woman's hands in hers. 'It's OK…you're OK…stay still…you're going to be fine,' she said firmly, cursing the fact that she spoke so little Italian. But words of comfort in any language were easy enough to understand, she thought. 'What is your name… Name? Name?' she repeated. 'What is your name?'

'Anna,' the woman answered at once, trying to raise her head, and Emily's smile of relief broadened.

'Hello, Anna—I'm Emily,' she said, pointing to herself.

'Em—i—lee… Someone will come soon to help us.' She squeezed the trembling hands tighter. 'Try and keep still,' she said gently, 'in case you've hurt your back or your neck.' Her controlled tones seemed to quieten the sobbing, which was becoming quieter as they stayed locked together on the dusty road. Seeing that most of the blood seemed to be coming from a large wound on the girl's upper arm, Emily frantically unzipped her bag and took out the handful of tissues she'd brought with her, folding them quickly into a firm pad, which she pressed against the damaged area.

'Here—press this tightly, Anna…press…press…' Anna understood, doing as she was told.

Anna had not taken her eyes from Emily's consoling features and, with an instinctive movement, Emily put out her hand to move a stray lock of hair, sticky with blood, from the woman's forehead. 'You're doing so well, Anna,' she said. 'How old are you? How old are you…how old?'

After a moment, the girl got the message and she whimpered, 'Twenty years.'

'You are very pretty, Anna,' Emily said, smiling. 'Don't worry—they will soon get you cleaned up and back home…'

And then at last someone else did arrive, and stooped down beside them. And, with an overwhelming gush of thankfulness, Emily saw that Giovanni was right there, close to her. She looked up at him quickly, all other thoughts now far from her mind at that moment. 'This is Anna,' she said briefly, 'and it's only just happened. I don't know how badly she's hurt, but she's breathing OK, and talking…'

Hardly glancing at Emily, Giovanni took control immediately and, with both hands on the girl's shoulders, he spoke to her, asking questions in rapid Italian, his voice gentle but authoritative. Anna answered him equally quickly, responding to his persuasive sympathy, by this time her sole attention on the handsome face of the man crouching down beside her.

A few moments after that, with sirens blaring, the ambulance and *polizia* arrived on the scene and at last Emily stood back to allow the professionals to do their work. Giovanni was speaking to them, explaining as much as he knew about the accident, before coming over to Emily and taking her arm firmly, his face expressionless. At his touch she felt like bursting into tears. It's no good, she thought, nobody told you how frightened you'd feel if you had to help at a real accident, or a real heart attack…because now she was trembling all over, and even her teeth were starting to chatter.

Looking down at her seriously, Giovanni started leading her away from the scene and, feeling the comforting strength of his body, Emily found that she was able to walk calmly along beside him.

Neither spoke for a few minutes as Giovanni allowed her to recover from the recent ordeal, but as each second passed Emily knew that she had some explaining to do.

'Well, that was the last thing I expected to come across,' she said shakily, looking up at him.

'And you were the last person I expected to see,' he replied, not looking back at her, but with a pleasant enough smile on his lips.

Emily swallowed. 'Yes, I'm sorry I didn't let you know I was coming to Italy this week… It was…difficult…' she stuttered. How utterly vapid did *that* sound?

'Never mind,' he said. 'First things first. We'd better get you cleaned up.'

Cleaned up? Suddenly realization set in as Emily stared

down and with a quick intake of breath she saw the damage she'd sustained. She hadn't given herself a thought! Her pale outfit was covered in blood and gravel—probably beyond repair. What a total mess she looked!

Now he did look down at her, properly, before guiding her around the corner and into a quiet bar. 'I think you need a brandy,' he said briefly. 'Then we'll go to my flat and see what can be done. For both of us,' he added, because his own cream trousers were stained and dirty, Emily saw now.

At this time of the early afternoon there were few people in the cool and darkened bar and, removing her sunglasses, Emily sank gratefully onto the chair which Giovanni held out for her, noting impassively that in the panic she'd managed to lose her sun hat.

After ordering their drinks from the waiter, he sat along-side her, leaning back in the chair and gazing at her quiz-zically. But he didn't ask any questions, only thinking how ravishingly lovely Emily looked, even in her present state. The fact that her clothes were crumpled and stained did not seem to detract from her in any way. In fact, vul-nerability could be a seductive state, he thought. Her hair was tousled, there was dried blood on her hands and arms and dirt on her flushed cheeks, and every now and again he saw her shiver, as if the effect of the traumatic event she had just been part of refused to leave her alone. At that moment he wanted to crush her in his arms, to hold her close to him, to make her feel safe. But he knew that would not be a wise move—especially as it was obvious that she'd not wanted him to know she'd be in Rome. He frowned briefly, looking away and trying to harden his heart against her. What had he done to make her so...elusive? To him, she seemed a complete mystery.

Their two double brandies arrived and, picking hers up, Emily sipped at the warming liquid, looking at Giovanni over the rim of her glass. 'This is good,' she murmured, drinking again more freely, and he cautioned her.

'Take it easy, Emily. Don't rush it. You've had a shock and it'll take a little time for you to recover.' He smiled at her disarmingly, now. 'If you drink it down in one, I'll be obliged to carry you back home!'

He knew what he was talking about, and Emily put her glass down, relieved to note that by now her hands had actually stopped shaking. Smiling back at him, she felt the alcohol taking effect and almost at once she began to relax.

'So—how's the job going this time?' he enquired casually. 'Finding your way around OK…? No problems?'

Emily took a deep breath. He was purposely being kind, she thought, not quizzing her about her unexpected presence in the city and assuming that for her it was business as usual. So she would treat it in the same way.

'I've done brilliantly, thanks,' she said, picking up her glass again. 'And I've finished it all in record time, so there's a chance for me to do some touristy stuff before I go back home tomorrow…I want to see some more paintings.'

'Of course you do,' he said blandly, not taking his eyes from her face and noting that her colour was deepening by the second.

Emily could stand it no longer—she *had* to say something! 'Look, I'm sorry I didn't let you know I'd be here,' she said, trying to keep her voice normal. 'But…I…I was afraid of being a nuisance to you…I thought you'd feel obliged to…you know…offer your help, waste your valuable time on me…' *How* had she managed to think that one up? 'And, also, I felt I should really attempt to get things right by myself, she went on. 'I have a tendency to rely on other people sometimes…to let them do some of the work for me.' That was a lie, too. 'And you said that you had important work to do for your mother this week… I just didn't want to get in the way, that's all.'

Emily hoped that this explanation sounded more truthful to him than it did to her—but she was grateful for the little lies which had conveniently formed on her tongue.

Giovanni smiled at her slowly, as if considering what she had just said. 'You could never get in my way, Emily,' he murmured. 'You should know that by now. But thank you for your consideration,' he added.

That made Emily feel even worse. 'Besides, you said you wouldn't be in Rome, in any case…that you'd be in the country,' she said quickly.

'That is true,' he said coolly, 'but something came up and I had to drop back here briefly. But I'll be returning to the country later on this afternoon.'

Emily decided that she wanted to change the subject as quickly as possible. 'That accident,' she said, picking up her glass, 'it all happened in a split second. I was standing about fifty metres away, I suppose, and the first thing I saw was the cab mounting the pavement. But the noise! It was incredible! And people were screaming but no one seemed to be doing anything and when I got there that poor girl was frantic, and she couldn't get up and I was afraid to try and move her in case she'd really hurt her back, and then all that blood! It was horrible!' Emily shivered again. 'I think I remembered everything I'd been taught, but when the moment arrives and something is actually happening it's much, much worse than you ever thought it could be!' She paused for a moment to take another drink. 'I was so…so pleased when you turned up, Giovanni,' she said truthfully. 'At that moment, you seemed like a ministering angel!'

'I think the ministering angel was already there,' he said gently.

Giovanni had let her relive the experience, knowing that she had to get it out of her system, and he shrugged at her words. 'I heard all the commotion,' he said. 'That's what alerted me that something was going on. And, when I got there, all I saw was someone—who turned out to be you—kneeling on the pavement and talking to someone underneath the cab… It didn't take me too long to put two and two together,' he added drily. He paused. 'But I'm gratified to think that you were…pleased…to see me, Emily.'

Emily looked away quickly. From the way he'd just said that, he'd made it clear that he was feeling slightly hurt about her secretive behaviour—and also that he probably didn't believe her explanation about it. She sighed, wishing now that she had told him she'd be here again… Things would have been a whole lot easier for her!

For a while they sat in silence while Emily sipped and sipped at the brandy. Giovanni had got it exactly right, knowing it was what she'd need to calm her. She couldn't care less about her appearance, which seemed totally irrelevant now, the curious looks from one or two other drinkers passing her by unnoticed. She felt comfortable, relaxed—and sublimely at ease.

But not for long.

'Why didn't you tell me you'd be here, Emily?' he asked softly. 'What was the real reason? Tell me the truth.'

She waited a moment before answering. Then, 'I…I don't want to find myself in a position I might…regret…' she began, and he frowned.

'How so?' he asked.

'I'm afraid to get involved in something—or with someone—that might turn out badly,' she said, wishing that the words would come more easily.

'Why—don't you trust me?' he asked, and his tone was sombre.

'I don't think I trust myself—or fate—' she said slowly. 'And I'm unsure of...of...'

'Of Italians?' He finished the sentence for her. 'Have you known many, Emily?'

'Not many,' she admitted, 'and certainly not in a close, personal sense. But there *is* a cultural difference between us. Well, I think so anyway.' She paused. 'Your young men can be...impulsive sometimes and...and...' She wanted to say *audacious* but that would be going too far. Giovanni had never been audacious with her. It was the wretched Nico who was in the forefront of her mind as she spoke.

His expression had darkened as she'd been speaking, and he caught and held her gaze. 'I think you should explain that,' he said coolly.

'OK, I will,' Emily said, equally coolly. 'You remember me telling you about Nico—Coral's friend—the guy who stayed at our flat recently?'

'Of course.'

'Well, one evening I got home early from work—Coral wouldn't be back until later—and Nico was there, resting for a couple of hours.' She paused, feeling angry again at the way the man had behaved. 'So I offered to make him some tea, and when I was in the kitchen he came in and...and...'

'Go on,' Giovanni said, frowning.

'Well, let's just say that he took advantage of me,' Emily said. 'And I told him that he was out of order. That his at-

tentions were unwelcome.' She grimaced. 'He seems to
think that he's God's gift to womankind and, worse, it
didn't occur to him that he was betraying Coral—who,
after all, was putting herself out to see that he had a good
time in London.'

'What did he actually do?' Giovanni persisted.

'He put his arms around me and kissed me, full on the
mouth. And invited me to "be nice"—which, to my mind,
meant only one thing,' Emily said flatly.

'But it didn't get any worse than that?' Giovanni asked.

'How much worse should it have got?' Emily said,
suddenly irritated at his reaction—which shouldn't have
surprised her, she thought. It confirmed her opinion that
Italian men were passionate, intense—and ready to seize
the moment.

'But…there was no attempt to take it further?' Giovanni
went on. He paused. 'I think I can safely say that, as a
general rule, we are lovers of beautiful women.'

'Oh, really? Well, that's a comforting thought!' Emily
said crossly. He wasn't taking any of this seriously, she
thought, clearly giving the subject little significance. But
it was significant to her.

'I do believe that you are "lovers of women",' she said
after a moment. 'But what I don't believe is that one
woman—speaking generally, of course—would ever be
enough…that you're not really into long-term relationships—the sort which require loyalty, fidelity…and total
commitment,' she added, her eyes filling suddenly.

'Oh, and you think that fecklessness is confined to our
race?' Giovanni asked scornfully. 'Have a good look at your
own social statistics, Emily. British marriages, relationships, have a very bad track record. If you're making odious
comparisons, you'd better be careful in your assumptions.'

Emily realized that she *was* making assumptions—and her sense of justice made her hesitate. 'Yes, well, I'm sorry if I'm jumping to conclusions,' she said slowly, not wanting to admit that this was her own problem more than anything else. The dark-eyed, amorous Italians whom she had met did seem to have that special way with them which, at times, could be almost irresistible, their passionate instincts often equally matched by a caring, cherishing attitude which could melt the heart. They had the ability to make a woman feel she was a desired female who they wanted to love, admire and protect... Yet all the time she felt a nagging doubt that they could sustain that initial glow, that it was instinctive for the hot-blooded Italian to search out as many females as he needed to satisfy his carnal ambitions. And she was determined not to allow herself to become trapped by their powerful allure—a characteristic exhibited so captivatingly by the man at her side.

No more was said for a while as they finished their drinks and presently, aware that Emily had regained total self-control, Giovanni stood up. 'Come on. Let's get you to the flat and a wash in some warm water.' He glanced down at her. 'It's rather far to walk from here so we'll get a cab.'

'Maybe I should go straight back to the hotel,' Emily suggested, and he shrugged.

'Whatever you like,' he said, 'but I think it would be preferable for you to clean up and relax at my place first.'

Emily stood up then, too, surprised at how strange her legs felt. 'Yes, OK, we'll do that,' she agreed, thinking that, at the moment, if he suggested a trip to outer space she'd agree.

He took her arm as they left the bar. 'Besides,' he said, 'there's someone there I'd like you to meet.'

'Oh?' Emily looked up at him, surprised. Then realization struck. The woman he'd been talking to had to be the woman in the picture! Emily hadn't been close enough to have a good look, but it was obvious now, she thought. She was going to be introduced to that beautiful face—and Giovanni Boselli seemed to have no difficulty in bringing another woman into the equation.

Well, there was nothing for it, she'd have to fall in with his plans now, she thought, as they sat together in the cab, which sped at breakneck speed through the teeming streets. When they eventually arrived at the flat it seemed even more auspicious than it had before, as they entered the coolness of the large hallway.

'Ah, good, she's back already,' Giovanni said casually, seeing that his front door was wide open. 'She said she wouldn't be long,' he added, 'because we're leaving the city in an hour.'

As they went inside, a woman, hearing them come in, called from the kitchen, 'Coffee!'

Giovanni grinned down at Emily. 'Good, just what you need,' he said.

Just then the woman entered the sitting room carrying a tray and, with a jolt of surprise, Emily looked across at the attractive dark-eyed face...but it was not the face in the photograph, she realized as a thousand thoughts formed in her mind at the same time.

Giovanni gazed down at Emily. 'I'd like you to meet my mother, Emilee-a,' he said softly, pronouncing her name in that special way of his, making Emily's tongue go dry with desire. And to the woman he said, 'And this is Emily, Mamma—you remember me telling you about her?'

CHAPTER EIGHT

EMILY hoped that the look of total surprise wasn't written all over her face. This was certainly the same woman she'd seen talking to Giovanni earlier—but it was his mother, not his girlfriend! She was good-looking, short and about sixty years old, Emily guessed, and she had obviously looked after herself, her overall appearance still extremely attractive. She was dressed in a sheer cream skirt and smart summer shoes, her loose lemon top setting off her black hair and dark complexion. And her large, bright gold hoop earrings glistened in the afternoon sunlight, adding to the glamorous picture she presented to the world. She had Giovanni's searching eyes—which were raised questioningly now, as she stared at Emily, then at her son, then back at Emily.

'What on *earth* has got you both into this state?' she demanded, her English heavily accented. She turned to her son. 'Giovanni?'

Giovanni took a few moments to explain briefly what had happened earlier, and his mother put down the tray she'd been holding and came over to Emily, her hand outstretched.

'*Mamma Mia!*... How terrible! How terrible!' she exclaimed, then she broke into a smile. 'I am Maria,' she said, her voice warm, 'and I am pleased to meet you...to meet another of my son's many friends.'

Emily smiled back in response, taking Maria's hand lightly. 'Thank you, Maria.' She looked down at herself, then back at the woman. 'I am sorry to be in such a mess,' she said. 'Maybe I can do something about it in a minute, before I go back to my hotel?'

Giovanni picked up the tray with the two mugs on it. 'Sit down and have a coffee first, Emily,' he said. 'I'll go and make another one for myself,' he added, as he handed his mother hers.

Emily did as she was told, sitting down carefully on the pale chaise longue by the window—where she'd lain down once before, she remembered wryly. The room seemed vast in the daylight, she thought, glancing around her briefly, its tiled floor cool beneath her feet. And still there in the centre of the cabinet in front of her was that picture. Still smiling, those bewitching eyes sending out their message to any onlooker. *This is my place; this is where I belong,* it seemed to say.

Maria sat down then, a little way from Emily, but looking at her with a rather inscrutable expression on her face. Neither spoke for a moment as they sipped their coffee.

Then, 'I can't tell you how thankful I was when Giovanni suddenly showed up,' Emily said earnestly. 'I was the only person who seemed to be offering any assistance—and goodness knows, I could do very little. The way the poor girl was trapped made it impossible for me to find out if she was seriously injured, or even to put her into the recovery position.'

'You have medical experience?' Maria asked.

'No, but after my mother died I attended several first aid courses,' she said. 'I wanted to have at least some understanding of what to do in an emergency.' She didn't add that it had been her father who was uppermost in her mind. What if he suffered something dramatic, as her mother had done, and she, Emily, was there and not able to help? She shuddered. 'I'll be having nightmares about that accident for a few weeks, I expect. I felt so utterly helpless,' she added.

'But, from what Giovanni said, you were not helpless. You did the only thing which was possible at the time,' Maria said firmly. 'You were the one who gave her courage and reassurance.'

Emily took another sip of coffee. 'Well, I felt a whole lot better when Giovanni took over,' she said, 'and it's a good thing he was here in Rome.' Not bothering to add that she'd thought he was miles away in the country somewhere.

'Yes, well, if this had all happened tomorrow, instead of today, he would not have been in the city,' Maria said. 'He is taking me back home later... I travelled in to do some shopping today,' she added, smiling.

Just then, Giovanni returned with his coffee and sat down opposite them, and after a few moments Maria said, 'Giovanni tells me you are in the travel business, Emily.'

'Yes. That's right.'

'Do you enjoy that?'

Emily hesitated. 'Sometimes I do,' she said. 'But in every job there are highs and lows. I am not always thrilled to be away from home quite so much,' she admitted.

'So—what would you like to be doing—ideally?' Maria asked, and Emily began to feel that she was being interviewed!

Giovanni spoke for her. 'What she would really like to be doing is painting her pictures, full time, Mamma,' he said. 'Emily is an amazing painter—in my opinion, professional.'

Maria's eyes had narrowed slightly during this conversation, and she was staring at Emily closely—and the girl was very conscious of the fact. Well, everyone knew what Italian mothers were like where their precious sons were concerned, Emily thought. No woman was ever good enough for them, and Maria probably feared that Emily had designs on Giovanni. She finished her drink and put her mug down on the little table beside her. Maria need have no worries on *that* score, she thought.

Presently, Maria stood up, taking control. 'Go into the bathroom, Emily, and have a warm wash,' she instructed firmly. 'Then we will see about your clothes.' She put her head on one side. 'I think we can sponge the dirt off—but all that blood will need a cold water soak, I'm afraid,' she added.

Emily turned obediently to do as she was told and Giovanni stood as well, barring her way slightly. 'No, I think my en suite will be more suitable, Mamma.' He pointed to a door along the hallway. 'There's the bedroom— with facilities,' he said. 'Make yourself at home, Emily.'

Feeling as if she were in a strange kind of dream, Emily did as she was told. What was going on? She was supposed to be somewhere else, relaxing and admiring all those fabulous ancient paintings this afternoon, not here in Giovanni's flat—with his mother in attendance. And not with her clothes in this state, either. She'd only worn this designer dress once before; she made a face to herself. Was it any good, ever, to make plans? she thought. Life had a will of its own—well, hers certainly seemed to have at the moment and you just had to go with the flow. Go where it took you.

Giovanni's bedroom was spacious and cool, the king-size bed neatly made, its white covers smooth and inviting—and for a heady moment, Emily felt like stretching out on it for a short nap! Instead, she pushed open the other door in the room, revealing the en suite bathroom, and gazed at it in admiration. There was a massive corner bath with shower, the glistening porcelain and gold taps almost blinding her as she looked around, and there were fluffy white towels in abundance everywhere. The place was to die for, and if all this belonged to her, Emily thought, this was where she'd be spending a lot of her time! She paused for a moment…Giovanni undoubtedly had good taste— not to mention very expensive taste.

As she went inside, closing the door behind her, she suddenly noticed a long pink gossamer-like negligee hanging on a hook, and she caught her breath. That certainly did not belong to Giovanni! It was exquisite, and she let the fine folds slip between her fingers as she touched it gently. It was a young woman's—obviously *that* young woman's, who must have been staying here with Giovanni… So, *that* was what had brought him back… 'briefly'…he'd said!

Going over to the basin, she glanced up at the shelf above, her eye immediately caught by the sight of an exotic flask of the most fashionable scent from one of France's renowned perfumeries. And it was not for the Giovannis of this world!

Emily sat on the edge of the bath for a moment. Why did all this matter to her? None of it was any of her business! And Giovanni Boselli was nothing to her— nothing at all! Who he chose to entertain at his flat was of no interest to her whatsoever! Then another thought struck her… Of course! This had to be Maria's! That was it! Giovanni had mentioned once that his mother sometimes stayed at the flat.

Presently, she rejoined the others and Maria looked appraisingly at Emily's appearance. Somehow the girl had managed to make herself quite presentable again, had been able to sponge off most of the dirt from her dress.

'That's better,' Maria said gently, 'though there is still some work to be done on those blood stains.'

Emily smiled. 'My dry-cleaners have worked miracles in the past,' she said. 'I'll be leaving this up to them.'

'I'll take you back to your hotel now, Emily—if that's what you would like,' Giovanni said, looking down at her, and she smiled quickly.

'Thank you, yes, I don't think I'll be doing any sight-seeing today after all,' she said, thinking that an early night suddenly seemed very attractive. As Giovanni left the room for a moment, she turned to Maria, holding out her hand. 'It's been great to have met you, Maria,' she said. She paused. 'And I hope you don't mind me mentioning it, but…the negligee hanging behind the door just now…is absolutely beautiful. I don't think I've ever seen anything quite so lovely.'

Maria frowned, then shrugged slightly. 'Lingerie? Oh, no, I have not left any lingerie here,' she said. 'In fact, I haven't stayed here for months.' She shook her head. 'No, no—Rome is far too hot for me at this time of year.'

As Giovanni drove them out of the city later, Maria glanced briefly across at her son, her heart swelling with pride, as usual. He was so like his father, she thought for the hundredth time…not only handsome, but kind, thoughtful and diligent. He had accepted his responsibilities so young, and with not a single grumble, had been *too* hardworking, of course, handling that dreadful company matter—which Maria did not want to think about—with such adroitness, such natural skill. Her mouth tightened slightly. It had been good to see him with the Englishwoman today... Maria had begun to despair of him ever showing that kind of interest in a female again. And she had to admit that there was something about Emily that was particularly endearing—even to her. She gazed out of the window for a moment and cleared her throat.

'I think I can understand why you like this...Emily...' she began tentatively, trying to find the right words. Well, he would be expecting her to pass *some* opinion, but the past had taught Maria to be cautious. She would never make the same mistake again.

'It would be hard for anyone not to like Emily,' he replied casually, not taking his eyes from the road. His lip curled slightly. 'The sad fact is that it's harder to get her to like me. That's the problem.'

Maria was aghast! 'Why? What are you saying... What is it?' she demanded.

'I wish I knew,' Giovanni replied soberly. Then, after a second, he added, 'She is...warm, yes, but...not close. It is so strange.' He hesitated. 'I have no experience with that kind of woman.'

Maria would have none of it. 'She *does* like you, Giovanni, there is no doubt about that! I could tell straight away! I assure you that...'

'Yes, I think she does, Mamma,' he interrupted, 'but not in the way that I would...wish.'

Then neither of them spoke for a few moments after that, Giovanni admitting to still feeling shattered that Emily hadn't told him she was going to be in Rome, while Maria was quietly seething inside. How any woman could hold her son at arm's length was beyond belief—and she knew what he was getting at all right! She was Italian too,

was she not, with the same passionate blood in her veins…
had been loved by her husband in the way that only Italians
could love! Still, she decided to say no more. She had said
too much before—and look what had happened.

Presently, she said, 'Will you be seeing her again soon,
carissimo?'

Giovanni shrugged. 'I don't know… Of course, I can
find excuses to visit the London office, and I will try to
see her then, but my duties recommence here again soon
and I must say that I'm looking forward to it, Mamma. The
idea of six months off was pleasant, but…'

'Was necessary,' Maria said firmly.

'OK. But I want to get back in harness now, as soon as
possible. You've been holding the fort for too long.'

Maria smiled. 'With help from others, of course,' she
said. 'And our profits are holding up well, *carissimo*. Have
no fear about that.'

Emily had booked an early flight for the following morning,
and it was with some relief that she boarded the aircraft.
Yesterday had been a day to remember, she thought—and
not for particularly good reasons. Coming across that
accident had sobered her more than she cared to admit, and
meeting Maria Boselli in Giovanni's flat had been a totally
unexpected incident. Maria had been kind enough—in a sort
of way, Emily thought—but there was something going on
behind those shrewd, dark eyes that had made the girl feel
slightly uncomfortable. She shrugged inwardly. Maria was
the archetypal possessive Italian mother. Emily had heard the
two of them speaking in low tones while she'd been tidying
herself up—and she couldn't help feeling that she was being
discussed… She'd heard Giovanni's voice raised slightly
now and again, as if they were arguing about something.

Now, staring out of the window as the aeroplane left the ground, Emily remembered the last thing which had been said, as they'd made their goodbyes yesterday, and she smiled faintly to herself.

'Next time you're in Italy, you must visit us, Emily,' Maria had said in a tone which implied a directive rather than an invitation. 'La Campagna is the place to be at this time of the year…Giovanni will bring you.'

And Emily had accepted the suggestion graciously, while thinking there was more chance of being flown to the moon than of her visiting the Boselli family home. She was not going to get involved any more with Giovanni… Deep down, all her instincts told her to get out now, while there was still time.

Emily decided to prepare a special supper for herself and Coral on Friday evening. They'd not seen much of each other recently—with Nico being there, and then with Emily having to go away again so soon. It would be good to have a catch-up, she thought now.

Coral arrived home earlier than usual and, when she heard their front door close, Emily called from the kitchen, 'Hi, Coral…dinner's in forty minutes—you've time for a shower.'

Coral came and stood by the door, leaning against it for a moment as she watched Emily prepare the sea bass. Emily looked across, smiling.

'It's good to be home,' she commented, reaching for the black pepper. 'I hope they don't send me anywhere for a week or two—anyway, I've had enough of Rome for the moment,' she added.

'I'm sure you have, and you must tell me all about it,' Coral said, and there was something in her voice that made Emily look up quickly. 'I will have that shower,' Coral went on, 'but first, I could do with a drink.' She yawned. 'Do you want one? I'll open one of the bottles of red we brought back with us from Italy.'

'OK, fine,' Emily said as she started slicing some tomatoes for the salad. 'You sound tired, Coral—hectic at work?'

'No, actually, it's dead quiet at the moment and we're all bored out of our minds.' She paused. 'A flat day can seem twice as long as usual—but you wouldn't know anything about that.'

Presently, after they'd finished their supper—which Coral was very complimentary about—the two girls sat, elbows on the table in the window, drinking their coffee. Emily glanced at Coral briefly. She didn't really want to mention Nico's name at all, but it seemed odd not to say *something* about him—after all, he had occupied their flat for a week.

'Has Nico been in touch?' she asked casually. 'I hope he enjoyed himself as much as he thought he would—you certainly showed him all the sights while he was here.'

'Oh, yes, he's phoned a couple of times,' Coral said casually.

'And…um…have you made plans for him to come back at some point?' Emily went on, thinking that Coral wasn't being particularly talkative—she'd have expected her sometimes excitable friend to reveal all the details without this sort of prompting.

'No…well, we'll have to see,' Coral said. She drank some coffee. 'It was just one of those things…you know, with Nico…he's a nice enough bloke but…Italians are different, aren't they…I mean, they seem so…I would never be sure…' Her voice trailed off. So, Emily thought, it had taken a week of being full-on with Nico to make Coral have second thoughts. Poor Coral—any hopes she might have had for a whirlwind affair—and possibly even something more—with a seductive Italian had somehow turned out to be disappointingly not the case. And it was clearly the reason for the girl's rather melancholy spirit this evening. Involuntarily, Emily reached over and squeezed Coral's hand for a second.

'I totally agree with you about the Latin male,' she said. 'They're a race apart in the emotional stakes and I, personally, would think more than twice about getting involved with one of them.'

Coral raised her eyes briefly. 'What—not even with the gorgeous Giovanni?' she said. 'He certainly only had eyes for you when we were in Rome, and you've said he's been on the phone since…'

Emily bit her lip, looking away quickly. 'No, not even with him, Coral,' she said.

'Did you see him this week while you were over there?'

Emily hesitated. She'd intended not to say a word about any of it, but so much had happened that she couldn't be that evasive—not with Coral. They usually confided in each other.

'Well, now you mention it, I did see him,' she said. 'He didn't even know I was going to be in Italy because I decided not to tell him, but then, out of the blue…suddenly there he was.' She went on to describe everything about the accident and going back to Giovanni's flat and meeting his mother.

'And I think my summer dress is probably ruined,' she added. 'Even if I manage to remove all the stains, I'll never feel the same about it again.'

She paused for a second, deciding not to mention the woman in the photograph, or the negligee she'd seen in Giovanni's en suite bathroom. There was no need to go into all that because it didn't matter now. It was irrelevant.

Coral blew through her teeth, suitably impressed at what Emily had just told her. That's unbelievable, Ellie,' she said. 'It's as if you're a magnet to the man. He seems to know exactly where to find you.'

'Well, somehow I've got to persuade him that I don't appreciate his company,' Emily said flatly. 'It's not as if he's ever likely to be short of female company. I won't exactly be depriving him, will I?'

'Hardly,' Coral said. 'He has to be the most mind-numbingly handsome man on the planet.' She shot a brief glance at Emily. 'He even beats Nico in that department.'

'Oh, they're all the same,' Emily said a trifle scathingly. 'So good-looking it's abnormal. And they think all women are ready to fall at their feet.'

'Well, then, here are two who are definitely *not!*' Coral said, her cheeks flushed from too much wine. She raised her glass. 'Here's to us, Ellie—and the blessed joys of a single life!'

Emily got up to make some more coffee just as her mobile rang. She glanced back at Coral. 'Phone's there behind you on the windowsill, Coral,' she said. 'Answer it, will you?'

Coral did as she was asked and in a second she stood up, following Emily into the kitchen, her eyes bright. 'It's *him—Giovanni,*' she whispered. 'Shall I say you're not here?'

Reluctantly, Emily shook her head briefly, taking the phone from Coral. 'Hi…Gio…' she began, then her expression changed as she listened for a few moments.

'OK—yes, of course…no, I'll be here all weekend… Of course I will, Giovanni.'

She snapped the phone shut and looked across at Coral, who was staring at her open-mouthed. 'You're *going* to see him—after all we've just been *saying,*' Coral accused.

'The man has got you in his clutches, Ellie, and there's nothing you can do about it.'

'You wait and see,' Emily said shortly. 'But, for the moment, what I can do is offer him some support.'

'Why—what's going on?' Coral demanded.

'He's going to be in London mid-morning tomorrow—his best friend was taken dangerously ill yesterday, and is in hospital on a life-support machine.' She paused. 'Giovanni's asked me to meet him…to go with him to the hospital, and I couldn't refuse, could I? He sounded terrible!' She shrugged helplessly. Giovanni had seemed so upset, so unlike his normal confident self, it had almost unnerved her. It was obvious that he needed her—needed her badly—and she'd be there for him, of course she would. She'd do the same for anyone.

CHAPTER NINE

LATE the following afternoon they left the hospital, and Giovanni held Emily's hand tightly as they waited to cross the busy road. Glancing up at him briefly, she could see how shocked he still was.

'How long did you say you've known Rupert?' she asked matter-of-factly, thinking that Giovanni wouldn't want to talk about anything else at the moment. 'You said you met up at university…?'

'Before that,' he said shortly. 'We were at boarding school together—aged thirteen. So we go back more than twenty years.' He shook his head briefly. 'It was terrible to see him lying there like that, Emily… His parents are absolutely distraught. They haven't left his side, of course.' He looked down at her. 'I felt very touched—honoured, in a way—that I'm the only one, apparently, apart from his parents, who's allowed to see him. For now, of course,' he added hurriedly. 'As soon as he's better, he'll obviously be allowed lots of visitors.'

Emily didn't look at Giovanni as he spoke. They both knew that he was being deliberately optimistic that his friend might recover—from the little she knew, it was probably less than a fifty-fifty chance. And she had been more than happy to keep out of the way downstairs in the restaurant while Giovanni had been at Rupert's bedside.

'Well, you are obviously someone very special,' she began lightly.

He cut in, 'I think I've probably known him the longest, out of our crowd,' he said. 'Wherever we've been over the years, we've always kept in touch...I've stayed with him and his family in England many times, and he pops over to our place in Italy whenever he feels like it. My mother is very fond of him,' he added.

'Have the doctors been forthcoming about Rupert's condition...? Have they offered any prognosis?' Emily asked as they walked slowly along in the late afternoon sunshine, and he shook his head briefly.

'For a man of his age to collapse so suddenly like that—so dramatically—is not, apparently, unknown,' Giovanni said. 'One good thing—his heart is still strong—so it's to do with his brain, I believe...' Giovanni stopped for a moment, unable to go on. Then, 'He hasn't regained consciousness yet.' He paused, moving to one side of the pavement to let a woman and two young children go past them, before taking Emily's hand again. 'They're not sure how deep the coma is yet.' He bit his lip. 'It must be hell for his parents—Rupert's their only child. I tried to say the right things, you know, to offer a crumb of comfort—but what do *I* know?'

Emily squeezed his hand tightly, looking up at him. 'Whatever you said, Giovanni, I'm sure it was just the right thing,' she murmured.

'Well, it was little enough, goodness only knows,' he said. 'But they did seem pleased to see me—his mother hugged me so hard I didn't think she was ever going to let me go.'

'Then that says it all,' Emily said quickly. 'Just being there with them was enough.' She hesitated. 'What happens now? Must you go straight back to Italy?'

'No—the stuff I was going to do at home can wait. I told Rupert's parents I'll be staying in England until his condition stabilizes, and the situation is clearer.'

Giovanni looked down at her suddenly, loving the feel of her fingers entwined in his, gaining strength from her closeness. Why had Emily been the first—the only—one he'd thought to ring with the bad news? He could have got in touch with any of his and Rupert's friends, but it hadn't occurred to him to do that. There was something about Emily that seemed to warm him right through... He'd felt it from the moment he'd sold her that marmalade jar in Stefano's shop, had seen how she'd reacted to the accident in Rome. Of course, she was an intensely desirable woman by anyone's standards, but it went beyond that. He tried to pin down his thoughts about her, but couldn't, and he breathed in deeply. At this moment he felt like sweeping her off her feet and carrying her into the park they were approaching and making love to her under the trees in broad daylight. Glancing down at her, he was deeply ashamed of his lustful thoughts—especially today of all days—but he was aware that times of shock, or fear, or sudden turbulence could unhinge the male psyche... The last twenty-four hours certainly seemed to have unhinged *him,* he thought.

It was typical of Emily not to prattle on with unnecessary conversation, or to recite platitudes about Rupert's present condition... She seemed perfectly content to stroll along without saying anything, or expecting him to fill the silence. He wished he had the courage to put his arm around her and draw her into him...but something told him not to do that. He frowned briefly. When she'd been in Rome and they'd been unexpectedly thrown together again during that accident, he'd felt a distinct change in their relationship which might have given him some hope for the future. For a short time she had clung to him emotionally—and he'd revelled in her obvious need for him. But then, back at the flat a distinct change seemed to have taken place in her attitude. He shrugged inwardly. He didn't understand this woman—and he doubted that he'd ever be given the time or opportunity to find out what made her tick.

Bringing him abruptly out of his introspection, Emily suddenly said, 'Where will you be staying while you're here?'

'Oh, I've booked in at my usual hotel,' he said non-committally.

Feeling slightly awkward that he might feel he had to take her out somewhere this evening, Emily said, 'I don't imagine you've made any plans for tonight, Giovanni, but you're welcome to come back home to our place for a meal. Only if you want to,' she added hurriedly. 'Coral will be delighted to see you again.'

Giovanni hesitated. 'Well, if you're absolutely sure I won't be in the way, Emily,' he said, 'it would be good to relax somewhere more like home this evening.'

'Great,' Emily said. 'It's Coral's turn to do the food tonight, and she's a good cook. I think lamb cutlets are on the menu.' She glanced up at him quickly—the expression on his handsome features was unusually hard, the normally seductive eyes seemed to have become distant and solemn—not surprisingly, she thought. He'd been undeniably bowled over by the sight of his friend in that hospital bed—which was the only reason she'd invited him to come back with her to the flat, she told herself. It was nothing at all to do with wanting him to be there... Not after the discovery she'd made in that elegant bathroom of his!

Neither of them seemed in a hurry to go back just yet, and presently they entered a small park and sat down on one of the unoccupied benches. As the day was beginning to draw to a close, most of the children had gone home but there were still one or two floating their boats on the pond, their parents casually reading the daily papers nearby. Giovanni stared at them pensively, his legs outstretched, his hands thrust into his pockets. He turned to glance at Emily.

'It always strikes me as strange that when something bad is happening in your own life, the lives of others go on uninterrupted,' he said quietly. 'Those people, those kids—they don't know about Rupert...what his parents are going through...'

Emily smiled and moved slightly closer to him. 'I do know what you mean, Giovanni,' she said softly. 'Ideally, we'd like everyone in the world to suffer at the same time as us, wouldn't we? It doesn't seem fair that they're not sharing the burden.'

He stared at her for a long moment. 'Exactly that,' he said. 'That's exactly what I was getting at.' He paused. 'Thanks for understanding,' he said. 'Thanks for not thinking me a complete idiot.'

Emily opened her bag to take out her mobile. 'I'll ring Coral,' she said, trying to inject a lighter note in her voice. 'To let her know there'll be three of us for dinner tonight.'

It was gone seven o'clock by the time they got home and Coral met them at the top of the stairs, her face flushed—either from cooking or from one or two pre-dinner drinks, Emily thought instinctively. Giovanni greeted her in his normal attentive way, but Emily was struck by his reticence, the unusual lack of unnecessary compliments.

'Giovanni,' Coral said, without waiting for anyone to say any more, 'I'm so sorry about your friend… How did you find him? Is he going to be OK?'

They all went inside and Giovanni explained the situation. 'So—apparently things may become clearer in forty-eight hours,' he said. 'It's a waiting game at the moment, I'm afraid.'

'Well, there's nothing more you can do now,' Coral said practically, 'and I always say, look on the bright side.' Goodness only knew she'd been trying to do that for the last month! 'And I'm already halfway through a good bottle of wine—so come on, help me finish it, Giovanni. It'll do you good. Then we'll have something to eat— there's nothing like a good meal to sustain you and, even if you don't feel like eating it, food always comforts the body and cheers the soul! Well, that's *my* theory.' She glanced up at him and Emily spotted the telltale signs on her friend's eager face—she was fascinated by him, as usual, by his overtly masculine persona.

Giovanni seemed more than ready to comply with her suggestion and in a few minutes he'd seated himself comfortably on the sofa, a drink in his hand, while Emily laid the small dining table with cutlery and glasses.

As she went into the kitchen, Coral caught her eye and raised hers extravagantly. 'He's *such* a dish,' she whispered, and Emily nudged her, a warning look on her face.

'All this looks good, Coral,' she said, loud enough for Giovanni to hear. 'Anything I can do—though it looks as if you've done it all anyway?'

'You can't, and I have,' Coral replied, shooing her away. 'Just open another bottle, Ellie.'

Later, with every scrap of food—including a mouth-watering crème brulée for pudding—having been consumed, they were sitting together in a semi-doze, sipping the last of the wine, when their front doorbell rang, bringing them out of their torpor for a second.

'I'll go,' Coral said without much enthusiasm, but Emily stood up at once.

'No, I'll get it,' and she left the room, going out into the tiny hallway. As she opened the door, she was surprised to see the owner of the flats standing there.

'Oh—Andy…' she began, and the man cut in apologetically.

'I'm really sorry to encroach on your Saturday evening, Emily,' he said, 'but I need to tell you about some new regulations regarding the properties—and I'll need your signature. Can you spare me a few minutes?' He paused. 'It's so difficult to find people in during the week—or indeed at any time,' he said, 'and I'm sorry to intrude.'

Emily smiled at him quickly. Andy Baker, a short middle-aged man with grey hair and a permanently worried expression on his face, was a very good landlord, always willing to sort out any complaint they might have.

'Of course I can spare you a few minutes, Andy,' she said, 'but we've got someone with us at the moment…' She paused. 'Look, I could pop upstairs to your place instead, if that's all right? It would probably be more convenient for you anyway, wouldn't it?'

'Oh, thanks, Emily…yes, of course.' He turned to go. 'It should only take us ten minutes to go through the stuff—more safety regulations, I'm afraid,' he added.

Back inside, Emily explained what it was all about.

'Sorry about this, Giovanni,' she said, 'but I shouldn't be long… Coral, make some coffee, will you, while I'm gone?' she added, thinking that it was time her friend diluted some of the alcohol she'd been drinking so freely.

Andy occupied the top flat of the four-floor dwelling, and Emily followed him up the stairs thinking how lucky she and Coral were to rent in the building, and to have Andy as their landlord. He never bothered them and was always businesslike in his dealings—and tonight was no exception as he showed Emily the several sheets of paper which she needed to study.

'And your signature here, Emily, please,' he said, 'and take this form with you so that Coral can add her signature as well. Any time will do. Just post it through my door at your convenience,' he added.

Well, that was painless enough, Emily thought as she went back downstairs.

As she'd followed Andy, she hadn't bothered to close their door properly behind her and, almost silently now, she went back into the flat to join the others, when, to her utter amazement, she saw that Coral had left her armchair to sit next to Giovanni on the sofa and was locked in what looked like a passionate kiss. And the worst of it was— Giovanni seemed to be thoroughly enjoying it!

'Am I interrupting something?' Emily asked coldly, trying to subdue the unreasonable feelings of resentment which had overtaken her with the force of an unexpected tidal wave. What Giovanni Boselli did—with Coral or anyone else he happened to be near—was nothing to her! It was surely what she might have expected, after all. Staring down at him, she could see that he was totally relaxed from enjoying their good food and wine, and now the bodily nearness of an all-too-available female was just what was needed to complete his pleasure. And he obviously was not going to pass up the opportunity. Did she need any further confirmation of her opinion of the man—and his compatriots? Easy come, easy go. Here today, gone tomorrow. She tried to swallow a painful lump in her throat—and failed miserably.

With a muffled screech, Coral pulled herself away and rose hurriedly to her feet, rushing past Emily and going into her bedroom, slamming the door behind her. Her sobbing was clearly audible and Emily stared down at Giovanni, who returned her gaze, his expression unfathomable.

'Well?' Emily demanded.

'Well, what?' Giovanni replied, apparently confused for a moment.

'Well, thanks for taking the first opportunity to…spread your favours around,' she began, and he raised his eyebrows in surprise.

'Does it matter to you, Emily?' he asked seriously.

'It matters that you took advantage of my friend while my back was turned!' she said hotly, suddenly realizing how that must sound. That she might be jealous!

He shrugged. 'I can only apologize,' he said casually. 'Especially after you've been good enough to show me such kindness and hospitality this evening…and spending some time with me today.' He paused for a long drawn-out moment. 'You must have a very low opinion of me, Emily,' he said quietly.

She looked back at him squarely, her eyes suspiciously moist. He was dead right, she thought—she did have a low opinion of him. And, at this moment, it couldn't possibly go much lower! Then she regained control of her feelings.

'It's of no consequence,' she said evenly. 'After all, it's a free world.'

After a few moments of uncomfortable silence, Giovanni moved across to stand close to her. He paused, hating the situation he was in and not being able to do anything about it. He looked down into her upturned, flushed features, longing to close his mouth over hers. Then, 'Can I ring you—as soon as I know more about Rupert…what his chances are?' he asked hesitantly, and Emily replied at once.

'Of course… I would *like* to know how he is,' she said, 'just as soon as you hear anything.' She paused. 'I'm spending tomorrow with my family, so I shan't be here, but you've got my mobile number.'

He nodded gravely, then left without another word and after he'd gone Emily stood alone in the room, trying to stop herself from bursting into tears. How could Coral have allowed him to do such a thing? To kiss her like that? After all…Giovanni was *her* friend, not Coral's!

CHAPTER TEN

'DAD—your cooking is getting better all the time,' Emily said as she helped her father to load the dishwasher. 'I think you've been going to lessons and not telling us!'

Hugh Sinclair, a tall, handsome, rather spare-framed man with iron-grey hair and eyes to match, looked down at his daughter and smiled. 'Ah, well, I don't tell you everything, you know,' he said. 'But I'm glad you enjoyed it, Emily—and it's good to have a family to practice on.'

Together they took their coffee cups into the sitting room, where Paul was lounging on the sofa, idly turning the Sunday newspaper. Paul was a younger version of his father and, glancing at him fondly, Emily couldn't help wondering why he hadn't succumbed to the attentions of the women he came in contact with every day. She knew he'd had several girlfriends, and at least one serious relationship, but so far nothing had come of any of them.

'It says here,' Paul said, jabbing his finger at a page in front of him, 'that apparently we're all going to be living for ever. Medical science and high standards of living are going to ensure that it'll be the norm for everyone to reach one hundred and fifty, or even more. What do you think of that?'

Emily glanced at her father quickly. She knew that for a long while after the death of his wife he had not wanted to go on living at all…had told Emily, privately, that he didn't see the point now. And she'd tried to convince him that there was every point, that he was still loved and needed by his two children. She wondered what was going through his mind as he handed Paul his coffee. And his response to what Paul had said surprised her.

'Well, just so long as we can stay fit, mobile and in our right minds, I don't suppose that being one hundred and fifty will seem any different,' Hugh said. 'Just more of the same, though boredom may be the main adversary,' he added. 'I mean, how many more rounds of golf will it take to eventually cheese you off? Or how many more spring and summer plantings in the garden will finally get too much? Someone will have to invent other diversions.'

Emily looked at him as he stirred his coffee. His remarks were much more positive than she'd imagined they'd be… She might have expected him to say that he'd be happy to call it a day any time. In his darker moments, hadn't he told her that? But, after all, it was four years since the death of his wife. Perhaps time was doing its healing, after all, she thought.

Presently, sitting opposite his children, he looked at each of them in turn and cleared his throat. 'I'm glad you were both able to be here with me today,' he began, and immediately Emily put down her cup. Something in her father's voice alerted her sensitive intuition that there was something important coming…and she held her breath. Dad wasn't ill, surely? she thought, searching his face for telltale signs that something was wrong.

In his usual direct way, Hugh came straight to the point. 'You said you thought I'd been having cookery lessons,

Emily,' he said, 'and in a way I have been.' He paused. 'I've met someone called Alice who's been showing me a few tricks of the trade, so to speak… We met at the garden centre some time ago and got talking and, well, you know…she's in much the same position as me, and we've been kind of helping each other out with things now and again. I dug over a patch of garden for her earlier on, and helped her with some tax return stuff she didn't understand.'

For a moment there was complete silence as the others quickly put two and two together. Then Emily said slowly, 'You mean you have a…lady friend, Dad? Someone… special?' Even as she spoke the words, Emily could hardly believe it. Her father had always maintained that no one woman would ever—could ever—take the place of his adored wife…that he would never want another woman in his life. Yet he was several years off retirement age and still an attractive man…

Emily smiled a rather shaky smile. This was news indeed! 'Go on, Dad,' she said. 'Give us all the details.'

'Well, we've been seeing each other for about ten months,' Hugh replied slowly. 'Once or twice a week at first, then it became more frequent because Alice introduced me to her bridge-playing friends and we have regular card evenings…' He paused. 'I'm beginning to get the hang of it, but it's a fiendish game—mostly to do with being able to remember things—but it's very good for the brain-box, so they keep telling me.' He put down his cup. 'They're a great crowd, and I've been invited to one or two drinks evenings at their houses.' He glanced across at each of his children in turn. 'It's been very…pleasant…to be out and about with folk of my own age again, and to…have someone by my side. If you see what I mean,' he added quietly.

After her initial astonishment at this revelation, Emily felt a rush of warmth towards her father and, putting down her cup, she got up and went over to hug him.

'Dad, that's lovely—wonderful,' she said, smiling quickly. 'But…why haven't you told us before this? Why have you kept it to yourself all this time?' They had never been a secretive sort of family.

'Because for a long while I didn't think there was anything to tell,' Hugh said slowly. 'I didn't think our… friendship…was important, in that way.' He sighed. 'In today's language, I suppose you could say I was in denial. But I should have recognized my feelings sooner, admitted them.' He looked away for a moment. 'If I'd waited much longer I might have lost her.'

For the next few moments, the three of them stood with their arms wrapped around each other in mutual delight and understanding, with Hugh hugging his children so close they could hardly breathe. 'I was…worried that you might not approve…' he murmured and Emily held him away from her for a second.

'Dad,' she said softly, 'we only want what's best for you but…it all sounds rather serious—when are we going to be allowed to meet Alice?'

Hugh grinned, clearly relieved at the reception his news had received. 'Sooner than you might have thought,' he said mildly. 'She's coming over to have tea with us this afternoon.'

Much later, Paul walked Emily to the station to catch her train home. 'Well,' he said, looking down at his sister, 'I never expected to hear an announcement like that—did you? Good job I was sitting down at the time!'

Emily smiled happily. 'I'm delighted—for them both,'

she said. 'Wasn't Alice lovely? I know Mum would be happy for someone like her to keep Dad company.'

Paul was quiet for a moment, then, 'It's probably my own fault, but I have felt as if I've been in a kind of no-man's-land since Mum died,' he confessed. 'As if my own life has been on hold. But Dad's news frees me up to pursue some special plans of my own now…'

Emily stopped in her tracks. 'What? What's *this* all about?' she demanded. 'No more shocks today—please!'

'Oh, well, it's just that I've been given the chance to have a sabbatical for a year—to do some real travelling. Australia and New Zealand, for starters. You know it's been my ambition for some time, but I never felt I could leave Dad. He's not getting any younger.'

'Paul—that's brilliant!' Emily exclaimed, looking up at him eagerly. 'Will you go alone?'

'Not sure yet. Maybe, maybe not,' Paul answered, looking away.

'Hmm,' Emily murmured, deciding not to probe any further.

'Well, just let me point out that *you're* not getting any younger, either,' she said, 'so don't waste any more time—go ahead and spread your wings before they start to wither!'

'Thanks for the reminder,' Paul said drily, 'though I suppose I'll have to be prepared to fly home for the family wedding!'

Presently, as she sat in the train, Emily went over and over her father's news, admitting to feeling really surprised about it. Even though she was delighted for him, she'd never expected him to even consider the thought of another woman in his life—that that part of his existence was over. But…he'd obviously changed his mind, Emily thought pensively. A long-term single state was not for him, after all. She bit her lip. If her father could trust his life with someone again, perhaps there was hope that she, Emily, could do the same one day…

During the following week there was no message from Giovanni about Rupert, which didn't seem very optimistic and, although she was kept busy enough at work, Emily felt restless and on edge. The worst thing was, she and Coral had had a real showdown and she couldn't get it out of her mind. After hardly speaking to each other for a couple of days, everything had come out in a rush.

After a late-night shower, Coral had come into the sitting room where Emily was watching something on TV. 'I think we need to talk,' Coral had said, and Emily had immediately turned off the TV, looking up.

'I couldn't agree more,' she replied. 'Go on—enlighten me,' Emily said.

'I think you have a pretty good idea what I'm getting at,' Coral went on, and Emily frowned.

'I assure you, I have no idea at all.'

'Let's talk about our Italian friends, shall we…? Giovanni…and Nico? Remember Nico?'

Emily stood up, totally mystified. 'Who could ever forget Nico?' she said flatly.

'I surely don't need to spell it out!' Coral cried. 'He told me all about it, Ellie, how you were here together that evening and how you came on to him…almost begged him to make love to you! I mean, how do you think that made me feel? I would have trusted you with my life—never mind my boyfriend—and to say I was shattered is an understatement!'

Emily was transfixed by everything she was hearing. 'He…said…*what?*' she said unbelievingly.

'That you told him you'd always fancied him, and that you wanted him to…you know…'

Emily flopped her hands to her sides in complete resignation. 'Coral,' she said slowly, 'how could you believe such…such…total nonsense, such make-believe…such *lies*?' She shook her head slowly, while Coral looked across, her face flushed with emotion. 'Do you honestly think that I'd be capable of such a thing?' Emily paused. 'But I think you should know the truth. Nico was the guilty party in this case.' She hesitated, looking away for a second. 'I was in the kitchen, making us some tea, and he came in and almost trapped me against the sink—and I had to be really off with him, Coral. I didn't exactly tell him to get lost but it amounted to the same thing.' She paused, knowing that her heart rate had quickened at the memory of it all. 'I was never going to say a thing about it because it didn't matter. I was able to swat him like an irritating fly, and he got the message all right. But,' she added, 'I agonized over whether to tell you, to warn you, really, just what he's like.' She paused, reaching to put her hands on Coral's shoulders. 'I think you know that yourself. And I think you also know that I'd never betray you like that— we're mates, Coral. We do trust each other…don't we? Or I thought we did.'

In reply, Coral threw her arms around Emily's neck and held her tightly.

'Oh, Ellie,' she whispered, 'I'm sorry…really, I am.' She looked away for a moment. 'I'm really sorry I doubted you, even for a second, Ellie…and also that I…jumped on Giovanni on Saturday like that. I was only making a point, and I felt terrible afterwards. Disgusted with myself.'

The light suddenly began to dawn, and Emily whispered, 'You mean…Giovanni didn't…'

'He didn't do *anything,*' Coral sniffed. 'Of course, I'd had far too much to drink and I was grateful that he didn't try and push me off... Well, he's far too gallant for that, isn't he?' She blew her nose again. 'I was getting my own back on you, Emmy, that's all. Will you...forgive me?' she added.

Emily put her arms around Coral and held her tightly, suddenly feeling light-hearted—and light-headed. 'Of course I will, Coral,' she said, relieved, and embarrassed, by Coral's confession. Her own reaction at the time, and her attitude towards Giovanni, had spelt out its message all right. She did care about him! And she *was* jealous! She might just as well have shouted it from the rooftops!

Every time her mobile rang, Emily hoped that it would be some news about Rupert. Several times she'd been tempted to ring Giovanni herself, then decided against it. He had said he would get in touch if there was any change, and obviously there wasn't so it was better for her not to interfere. It wasn't as if she'd ever met Rupert, but Giovanni's haunted expression after he'd seen his friend would stay in her memory for a long time. The normal suave, somewhat devil-may-care confident manner had temporarily vanished, and it was obvious he'd been shattered by the appearance of his friend.

It wasn't until Thursday afternoon that Giovanni got in touch and at the sound of his voice Emily's heart leapt.

'Giovanni—I've been waiting for your call... How is...how is Rupert...?' She hardly dared to hear his answer, fearing the worst, but he cut in quickly.

'Rupert is going to be OK,' he said quietly. 'He regained full consciousness last night.' There was a long pause. 'They think he's going to pull through.'

Emily realized that her heart was pounding in her chest—this time with relief at the news—but why? she asked herself. Why did it matter so much to her, anyway? But of course she knew why. It was because she cared deeply about it for Giovanni's sake—and for Rupert's parents, of course—but mostly for Giovanni, whose obvious distress had upset her more than she wanted to admit, and whose happiness seemed to be more important to her than she'd imagined. Her voice was shaky as she answered.

'That's wonderful, Giovanni!' she exclaimed. 'Tell me everything. What caused his collapse? Was it…is it…?' She didn't want to frame the dreaded word.

There was silence for a moment. Then, 'Look, I can't tell you it all over the phone,' he said. 'I'm still at the hospital…but I'd love to see you, Emily. Can you meet me somewhere this evening?' As he spoke, Giovanni crossed his fingers. He'd expected a frosty reception to his call, and was massively relieved that Emily seemed her normal self.

'Of course I can!' Emily said at once. 'Oh, Giovanni, I'm so happy for you—for Rupert and his parents… They must be ecstatic. I was so…so afraid when there was no news…'

'So were we all,' he replied grimly.

Emily thought quickly. She didn't want to suggest that Giovanni came to the flat again.

'Giovanni, let's meet by the river,' she said, 'down by the London Eye. About seven-thirty? We could have a drink or a coffee somewhere.'

'OK, fine,' he agreed.

By the time Emily had finished everything she had to do at the office it was gone six-thirty and she knew she'd have to hurry if she wasn't to keep Giovanni hanging around waiting for her. Downstairs in the cloakroom, she changed into a pretty pink dress. Then, after a wash and touching up her make-up, she brushed her hair and tied it back in a long ponytail. Glancing at herself in the long mirror so thoughtfully provided by the management, she wondered why her appearance mattered...but she knew the answer to that. It mattered because she was going to be with Giovanni Boselli. She wanted him to like what he saw, and she stared at her reflection for a moment. She'd never intended for this to happen, had never intended that the unlooked-for relationship should deepen at all—but somehow it had started to and she seemed powerless to stop it. Then she shook her head, cross with herself. What she did, or didn't do, was entirely up to her and she could find plenty of good reasons not to see him ever again—if that was what she wanted.

She turned away resolutely and left the building. The only reason she was seeing Giovanni now was to let him tell her all about his friend—who, thankfully, was going to recover. So that particular panic was over.

She was almost twenty minutes late before she got to the Eye, and she spotted him at once—at the same time that he saw her tripping down the steps towards him. Walking swiftly to meet her, his smile broadened and he caught her hand in his, looking down at her approvingly.

'It's so good to see you, Emilee-a,' he murmured. 'I've booked us a short trip on the water... It's such a lovely evening. I hope that's OK?'

'Perfectly OK,' Emily replied. She loved a boat trip, and it would be a wonderfully relaxing way to sit and talk for an hour, she thought.

Still holding her hand tightly, he led her over to the moorings and helped her onto the boat, which was waiting.

There were only a handful of people already aboard and, pushing her gently in front of him, Giovanni indicated one of the seats at the back. Then he sat next to her and looked down, resting his arm across her shoulders. And Emily looked up into those mesmerizing eyes, feeling her whole body flood with an indescribable heat, making her almost breathless. Swallowing quickly, she turned away, watching the boat being untied, watching as the water began to move alongside them, watching the gulls soar hopefully. Eventually, Giovanni broke the silence between them.

'Thanks for postponing whatever else you had planned for tonight, Emily,' he said softly, and she interrupted.

'I wasn't doing anything,' she said. She paused. 'And I do want to hear about Rupert.' She hesitated, thinking that now was not the moment to mention Saturday night, if she could ever bring herself to do it. 'I thought you were never going to ring. As each day passed I thought the worst must have happened,' she said.

He tightened his hold on her. 'Yes—sorry I didn't get in touch, but there was nothing to say… All the waiting, watching, hoping, despairing…was awful, Emily. Like a nightmare.'

'Were you there all the time?' Emily asked.

'Yes, almost,' he replied. 'I felt I couldn't leave Rupert's parents to shoulder it alone… They seemed to gain strength from me being there.' He paused, swallowing, and, looking up quickly, Emily could see that he still seemed moved by the experience.

Then, little by little, all the details came out—how the three at the bedside had talked quietly about old times, funny things they remembered, new plans, new hopes, anything and everything to help pass the hours. How, once or twice, Rupert had seemed to come round, then would sink back to the oblivion which enveloped him. And, as Giovanni spoke, Emily leaned into him—as if she wanted to share the crisis—and the feel of her soft body melting so deliciously into his provoked such an intense desire in Giovanni that he had difficulty in restraining himself, in not telling her how much he desired her, longed for her, wanted her for ever.

Pulling himself together, he stared down at the water beneath them for a few seconds. 'Have you noticed how distant all the traffic seems, even though we're still in the middle of town?' he murmured.

'Yes,' Emily said. 'Any expanse of water has the effect of isolating you, doesn't it?' She paused. 'But—go on—about Rupert…'

Giovanni took a deep breath. 'Well, the breakthrough came last night,' he said. The nurses had made their final rounds and I was preparing to go back to my hotel. Rupert's mother was going to have a couple of hours' sleep in the side room while his father was going to stay up and keep watch.' Giovanni swallowed, and something—she didn't know what—made Emily rest her head on his shoulder, turning her face into his neck, his dark masculine scent making her body churn.

'Go on,' she said quietly.

Headily conscious, now, of Emily's action, Giovanni waited a few seconds, not wanting to interrupt the moment. Then, 'I was bending slightly over Rupert, squeezing his hand…and…you know…saying, "G'night, mate—see you tomorrow"…and suddenly his eyes opened, almost lazily, you'd say, and he said…he said…'

'Go on,' Emily murmured, looking up into Giovanni's eyes, which were wet with tears. 'What else?'

'Rupert looked straight at me and said, "Joe—Lucky Joe—what are *you* doing here?"'

Recalling the event, Giovanni couldn't go on for a second, and Emily squeezed his hand, swallowing a lump in her own throat. What a moment that must have been! For Rupert, for his parents—and for Giovanni! That he should be the first whom Rupert had responded to!

Releasing her hand briefly, Emily took a tissue from her bag and touched Giovanni's wet cheeks, and he didn't stop her. Seeing him emotionally upset did not detract in any way from Giovanni's masculinity, she thought. And it was nothing less than she would have expected from a passionate Italian male. It was part of his strength.

'So,' she said, 'what now?'

'Well, there is still a long way to go,' Giovanni said, 'but our worst fears are over, and Rupert's basically a strong man… They're sure he'll pull through, though it's bound to take time. But, as his mother said—when she'd stopped dancing around the place—we've got all the time in the world. And anything precious is worth waiting for.'

Sitting there together on the gently chugging boat, with occasional lights beginning to come on along the riverbank, there didn't seem any need to say much more at that moment…Giovanni revelling, not only in his good news, but in being clasped in Emily's soft arms. Because she had responded to him in the way he was used to with women…in the last half an hour he felt that a massive emotional barrier between them had been breached, and if his luck held he may still be in with a chance.

And Emily, with her head tucked into his neck, could only wonder at this man she was nestling into. At what a valued, loyal friend he must be to those he loved—and how disarmingly vulnerable he himself could be. Not to mention those other things—drop-dead good looks, a physique to make the mouth water and a sensuous tenderness to warm the coldest heart. So then—what of her good intentions? She mustn't let him get to her like this… Wasn't Giovanni Boselli the enticing chocolate that could have poison at its centre?

And then, unbelievably and almost in slow motion and as if it was the most natural thing in the world, Giovanni took her into his arms properly, turning her so that they embraced as two lovers, his arms encasing her soft body and his dark head bent to reach her mouth. And, without stopping to think, Emily responded eagerly, loving the feel of him, the feel of his body harden against hers, the intoxicating sensuousness of their moist parted lips melding as one. Her whole body throbbed with desire, every warning instinct flying away with the breeze as he slipped his hand inside her dress and held her breast in his palm. Her flesh yielded to the magical press of his fingertips and she had difficulty in controlling her breathing.

How long they remained there like that, neither would ever know. What they did know was that they both wished it could go on for ever, where nothing could interrupt this time of gentle lovemaking or break the delight of unexpected passion.

Presently, Emily regained something of her self-control and sat back, pushing a wisp of hair away from her face. And, easing himself away, Giovanni looked down at her, his eyes black with continuing desire for this beguiling woman. He cleared his throat.

'I could do with a drink,' he said huskily, 'and isn't it time for some food?' Though food was the last thing on his mind! 'We're almost back where we started from,' he added, 'so we'll be getting off in a few minutes.'

'I know somewhere nearby where they do good snacks,' Emily said, 'then I must go home, Giovanni…'

'Of course,' he replied, 'and it was good of you to meet me tonight, Emily. I appreciate it.' She'd never know *how* much!

By now it was getting dark and the lights of the city had come on, casting gentle shafts of gold into the night sky. Not daring to glance at herself in her handbag mirror, Emily wondered whether all the erotic feelings which had engulfed her were written all over her features! But she did not regret the experience, not for a single second… Giovanni was the very first Italian she'd ever known in a close sense—and all she could think was *Wow!* She couldn't begin to imagine what might have followed in a more private situation…!

They disembarked and found the place to eat and presently, as they sat with their coffee, he said casually, 'By the way, I have a very special invitation for you, Emilee-a,' and she looked up at him quickly. 'My dear Mamma is going to be sixty in October,' he went on, 'and there is to be a big party.' He paused, looking across at her, melting her heart with his gaze. 'Please say you will come, Emily. I will take you. We will go together.'

Emily couldn't help smiling. She'd not expected *that* kind of invitation. Not so soon after meeting Giovanni's mother. 'When is it to be?' she asked.

'On the twenty-eighth—I hope you are free,' he said earnestly.

'Well, I'll have to look at my diary,' she said, knowing very well that she was not booked up that month. 'But thank you for inviting me,' she added politely.

She smiled up at him. She'd have to think of something, a really good excuse not to accept, she thought, after what had happened to her on the boat earlier. Her common sense was trying to tell her something! He was alluring, she admitted that, and, heaven help her, she could begin to adore him! But her deep anxiety of not being able to trust would just not leave her... No, she would not be going to Italy with Giovanni Boselli for his mother's party, or for any other reason. Definitely, definitely not!

CHAPTER ELEVEN

AFTER what could only be described as an incident-packed week, Emily decided that, so far as relationships were concerned, she was going to have a complete rest and not think about anyone at all for a bit. Rupert's predicament, her father's announcement, Coral's confession and, most of all, her heated moments with Giovanni on the boat, must all be pushed into the background of her thoughts.

But the rest she'd promised herself was short-lived when one morning she received a call on her mobile and, hearing Coral's voice, she frowned briefly. The two girls rarely contacted each other during office hours.

'Coral, hi—what is it?'

'You'll never guess, Ellie. Steve's just called me, and he sounded awful! Said he had to see me.' There was a pause. 'Something's wrong, I know it is…I think he may be ill!'

Emily smiled briefly. Coral was such a softie, she thought—even after the casual, heartless way Steve had dropped her, she still cared about him. 'Well, what else did he say?' Emily asked.

'Not much—just that he had a big problem and needed to see me about it. Do…do you think I should see him, Ellie, talk to him?'

'I suppose there can be no harm in doing that, Coral,' Emily said guardedly. 'But, you know, keep things casual.' The memory of how hurt and upset her friend had been was still uppermost in Emily's mind.

They rang off and Emily sat staring into space for a few moments. The way that Steve had behaved had been so out of character it had completely shattered Coral—and mystified Emily. He was a decent, kind man—or so she'd always thought. How could he have changed overnight and been so cruel? Then her mouth tightened. Hadn't she been dealt the same kind of blow herself? Why should anyone be surprised by anything, or anyone? People did change, she thought bitterly, even the ones you least expected to. No wonder you had to be wary of the opposite sex—of people in general.

Although her curiosity about Steve's phone call was killing her, Emily decided not to contact Coral later in the day. Anyway, they were hectic again at work, which more than occupied her mind. It was seven-thirty before she got home and, unusually, Coral was there first.

'Well?' Emily said at once. 'How did it go—what's the matter with Steve?'

'He's asked me to forgive him, wants to know whether we can get back on track.'

This was news indeed! As far as Emily knew, there'd not even been a phone call since the split. 'I don't…believe… it,' she said slowly. 'What did you say to him?'

'Well, my first instinct was to say that I'd have to give it a great deal of thought,' Coral said, 'but I couldn't do that, Ellie. Because all I wanted was to put my arms around his neck and hug him, tell him it would be all right—that we could make it all OK.' She shook her head slowly. 'You know, I've never stopped loving him, not really. I tried to hate him, and for a while I think I did, but when all is said and done we go back too far. And he said he was sorry so many times, over and over again, that I had to tell him to stop.'

'He *was* the one at fault,' Emily reminded her gently.

'In the sense that he was the one who did the dumping,' Coral admitted. 'But there's more to it than that, Ellie.' She hesitated. 'I was more than half to blame—I did sometimes take Steve for granted, began to treat him like a convenient sort of...well...friend. Knew he'd always be there, be the same, so our whole relationship became rather mundane.' She got up and went over to the window. 'Last year he wanted us to be more committed to each other—to get engaged—and I put him off.'

'Why—why did you do that?' Emily asked. 'Were you having doubts?'

'No—no, of course not,' Coral replied. 'It was because... because it was just at the time that Marcus—you and Marcus—finished.' She turned to glance at Emily. 'How would you have felt with me flashing an engagement ring in your face? So I told Steve there was no hurry, and we could wait a bit. And then, somehow, we just went on as before.'

Emily was horrified to think that her problems had upset things. 'You shouldn't have turned Steve down, Coral,' she said slowly. 'Not for my sake. It could have been the worst mistake you'd made in your life.'

Coral's face broke into a wide grin. 'Well, I don't think so,' she said. 'We sat in that bar today, holding hands and looking at each other like a pair of love-struck teenagers.... He's my sort...that's all there is to it. And I was happy to tell him that.'

Emily breathed a long sigh of relief—and happiness for Coral. In her opinion, she and Steve had been like a pigeon-

pair from the word go—that was why it had been so stagger-
ing when they'd parted. She went over to Coral and hugged
her. 'So—you've obviously forgiven him,' she said teasingly.

'We've forgiven each other,' Coral said simply. 'But
we're not rushing things.'

'Very wise,' Emily said.

'No—we're going to take it easy—for at least the
next week!'

Two weeks later, Giovanni arrived back in London, his
longing to see Emily again almost overwhelming. It was
Monday morning and he knew she'd be in the office...
unless they'd sent her somewhere abroad. He kept his
fingers crossed against that possibility as he waited for her
to answer her mobile, and the sound of her voice sent his
spirits soaring. She was in England—and only a ten
minute walk away!

'Emilee-a,' he said breathily and, despite having given
herself a good talking-to all the time they'd been apart,
Emily felt a surge of excitement as she heard him.

'Oh...Giovanni...' she began. 'You're back.' Well, he'd
told her what his plans were on the phone a couple of days
ago. He'd been ringing her frequently while he was back
in Italy, keeping her up to date with Rupert's progress and
other less important things, and each time Emily had
managed to keep their conversations brief—either saying
she was busy or just going out or just getting into the
shower—any excuse not to let that seductive voice knock
her off balance. And Giovanni was well aware what was
going on... They were playing a discreet cat and mouse
game, this woman and him—and the only effect her
attitude had was to make him double his efforts, increase
his determination to capture this provocative female,

because he knew he wanted her more than anything else he'd ever wanted in his life. He had this instinctive feeling that they could be sublimely happy together… He knew he would love her for ever and could make her happy. All he had to do was convince her of the fact. And to make her love him.

'I certainly am back,' he said, 'to find plenty of work here waiting for me.'

'Your time is going to be precious, then,' she began, and he cut in.

'There will always be time to speak to a beautiful woman,' he said.

'And I'm sure there are plenty of those near you right now,' she said lightly.

'Hmm. Not so you'd notice,' he replied, thinking that there wasn't a woman within a mile who could compete with Emily. He hesitated, but only for a second. 'Can I see you tonight?'

Emily bit her lip. She'd tried to cool her feelings for Giovanni during the time he'd been back in Italy, had made a determined effort to keep busy with other things, other thoughts. She and Coral had managed to give the flat a good clean—something which didn't often happen, she admitted, because they never seemed to be there together long enough with the time to do it. Emily had also started on another painting—although that didn't always stop her thinking. In fact, it was often the perfect opportunity for introspection and, as she'd worked her brush delicately over the canvas, her mind had been constantly tormented by the recollection of those few moments on the river. Giovanni's magnetic animal energy as his lips had locked onto hers, the demonstration of his physical need for her, had shaken her equilibrium. And the short-lived incident

had left her vulnerable and open, hinting as it did of un-
dreamed-of passion. She knew that, despite all her reservations, she was longing for something else, something
even more beautiful with Giovanni. She had been kissed
many, many times before, but not like that. It was the air
of breathless intensity enveloping them which had excited
her beyond all imagining. *How* was this all going to end?
she asked herself hopelessly. How could she end it?

'Um…sorry, I'm busy tonight,' she murmured in answer
to his request. 'I've promised to help Coral with something.'

There was a pause. 'Oh, well, never mind,' Giovanni
said, clearly disappointed to be turned down. 'But are you
going to be busy every evening? Can I see you tomorrow
or Wednesday?' He'd wait for ever, if necessary, he
thought grimly.

'Well, OK—Wednesday, then,' Emily said, trying not
to sound hard-to-get, even though that was her intention.
She could not be ungracious or unkind. He didn't deserve
that. But how could she make him get the message that she
was afraid to trust him? Or that she wouldn't be prepared
to share him with any passing female who crossed his
path? Her eyes hardened as she remembered that seductive negligee hanging up in his bathroom. 'Shall we meet
outside my office at six-thirty?' she said briskly. 'Will you
have finished work by then?'

'Wednesday at six-thirty,' he agreed at once. 'I can tell
you all the plans for my mother's surprise party,' he added.

Emily shut her mobile and stared out of the window for
a moment. Of course, that party. Now he was going to
involve her properly, make her part of this family occasion,
draw her in like a fish on a hook. Sighing deeply, she picked
up her lists and started to type. She was not going to Italy,

she thought, to a party or to anything else. Not with Giovanni Boselli. No, no, no. It would just prolong the agony.

On the Saturday evening three weeks later, Giovanni drove slowly along the winding drive which led to the imposing building set into the gently sloping hillside. Emily caught her breath as she gazed in awe. She'd had no idea of exactly what Giovanni's family home might look like, and what she was seeing took her completely by surprise. The setting was spectacular enough, but the dwelling itself was magnificent to look at, its creamy high stone walls glinting in the rapidly setting sunlight and surrounded by acres of private olive groves. Emily looked across at Giovanni as he brought the car to a standstill outside the huge pillared entrance.

'Is this…is this really your "place in the country"?' she asked. 'Or are we just passing through?'

He looked back at her, his dark eyes unusually thoughtful, and his voice as he answered held a trace of caution. 'Well, yes, this is the family bolt-hole,' he said briefly. 'The one I've always looked upon as my home.'

The 'family bolt-hole!' Emily thought. It was a palace—by anyone's standards! She took a deep breath. 'It's fantastic, Giovanni,' she said softly. 'Why would you want to live anywhere else in the whole world?'

He smiled quizzically at that. 'Come on,' he said. 'You're probably tired and looking forward to dinner. I told them when to expect us.'

They got out of the car and went up the stone steps into the massive tile-floored entrance hall. The tall shuttered windows all around led Emily's stupefied gaze to the vaulted ceiling above and she had difficulty in keeping her jaw from dropping as she took it all in. This was the home of *very* wealthy owners, she thought. Giovanni had never even hinted at such prosperity.

Just then a pretty Italian woman approached them and Giovanni said, 'Ah, Rosa—this is Emily. Would you show her where she's going to be sleeping, please?'

'Of course, Giovanni,' the woman said, gazing up into his eyes in the sort of way that spaniels did to their owners. She smiled at Emily, taking her small case from her and ushering her towards the wide curved stone staircase. So there was staff in attendance, too, Emily thought—but anywhere this size would certainly need it!

Alone, Emily stared around the large room she'd been allocated, then went slowly across to the window, whose shutters were wide open, allowing her a breathtaking view of the scene in front of her. In the distance was the uninterrupted countryside, and surrounding the house were serried ranks of olive trees and grapevines. Almost directly below her window was the swimming pool. It was flanked by a series of bay trees and tubs of flowers and generously supplied with sun loungers, wooden tables and chairs and umbrellas—though these were closed now and the October air felt distinctly chilly as Emily turned away thoughtfully.

Someone had already switched on the lamps by the side of the double bed and, as Emily slowly unpacked the few things she'd brought with her for the weekend, she felt somehow uneasy—and distinctly irritated. In falling in—reluctantly, and after much persuasion—with Giovanni's insistence that she should come to this event, she felt she'd been caught on the wrong foot. Why hadn't she been given some idea of the sort of place she'd be coming to? Who else would be coming to the party, had she brought the right dress to wear—would she fit in with the obviously moneyed gathering? Emily cringed as she thought of her humble little flat, how Giovanni had sat at the minute dining table. His place in Rome had been fantastic enough—goodness only knew—but this was something else! And had he deliberately not told her about it to impress her? To sweep her off her feet? Because it certainly seemed like that to Emily. He'd never given her any idea of the opulence of his family home. Were they aristocracy, the Boselli family? Was there an illustrious Count somewhere amongst their forebears?

She finished unpacking her case and laid out her clothes anxiously. This evening was no problem—because she'd been told that it was to be just her and Giovanni here—so her cream trousers and purple shirt would do, she thought, though she knew she'd be glad of her favourite go-anywhere wrap later. It had been a birthday present from her father a couple of years ago, and Emily knew it had cost him a great deal of money because stitched in one corner was the tiny revealing logo of the famous fashion house that had designed it. The fabric was of sheer fine wool, with a pearl background and narrow, pale, multi-shaded stripes. And, delicately hinting at every colour in the rainbow, it always teamed happily with everything Emily wore.

But as for tomorrow night's big party—the one which Maria, apparently, wasn't aware of—Emily hoped that the dress she'd brought would be suitable for the occasion. It certainly wasn't new because she'd only agreed to come here two days ago, and there'd been no time to go shopping for something else. It was a raw silk number in a luminous jewel-green, low-necked and with a three-quarter length hemline. Its exquisite, simple cut and shape was perfect to display Emily's dainty waist and hips and, as she hung it carefully on a hanger, she couldn't help smiling to herself. It was the only designer dress she'd ever bought—or was ever likely to buy, she thought—and the only person who knew the charity shop it had come from was Coral, who'd promised not to tell. Admiring it again, Emily wondered who else had owned it—and why they'd not kept it for ever… Maybe the wearer had put on some weight! Well, *she'd* never get rid of it, she thought as she went into the bathroom. Anything of that quality should be cherished.

Presently, there was a discreet knock on the door. Giovanni stood outside. 'Everything OK, Emily?' he asked, glancing down at her, his eyes softening. She always looked so good, he thought instinctively. 'Have you everything you need?' he enquired.

Together, they went down the staircase and Giovanni said, 'We'll have dinner on the patio—they've put the heaters outside…' He cupped his hand under her elbow as they negotiated the last few steps, and Emily looked up at him.

'Where is Maria tonight?' she asked curiously. So far, she'd only met Rosa.

'She's being entertained to dinner by some friends,' he said briefly.

As they sat at a table on the patio a stout Italian woman appeared with wine in an ice bucket. She smiled cheerfully at Emily as she put it down in front of Giovanni, who immediately started to uncork the bottle. He introduced them casually.

'This is Emily,' he said, glancing up, 'and this is our irreplaceable Margherita, Emily, who's been keeping us all too well fed for as long as I can remember.'

Margherita raised her eyes extravagantly at Emily, murmuring *'Allora,'* before departing to bring in their dinner.

Presently, after they'd eaten the delicious meal, Giovanni poured their coffee and glanced briefly across at Emily, who he'd been aware was unusually quiet this evening.

'Is anything wrong, Emilee-a?' he asked. 'Are you feeling OK?'

Emily looked back at him steadily. 'I'm feeling perfectly well, thanks,' she said, 'but slightly confused, that's all.' She paused, trying to find the right words. 'I had no idea of the sort of place I'd been invited to and…it's taken me by surprise.'

Giovanni sighed and leaned back in his chair. 'Yes, I know…I apologize, Emily,' he said slowly. 'But it's very difficult to explain to people. Well, let's say I always find it difficult,' he added. Emily raised her eyebrows as he went on slowly, 'Do you know…have you heard of the Antonio chain?'

Interrupting him, Emily answered at once. 'You mean *the* Antonio…the famous couturiers?' she said. 'But of course I have.' Every woman knew the company whose modern but untrendy designs were coveted by thousands of devoted clients.

'Well—that's us. That's the family. The business—and the burden.' He waited a moment before going on. 'It all began a long time ago with my great-grandfather, Antonio, who was not only a talented artist but also a shrewd businessman, and he had the good sense to fall in love with, and marry, an accomplished seamstress.' He paused. 'Like many successful companies, it started in a very small way, with just the two of them to begin with, but it grew steadily over the years, becoming what it is today.' Giovanni drank from his cup, not looking at Emily, who was in a state of mild shock as she took in what he'd said. Antonio was best known for the quality of fabrics they worked with, together with their unique simplicity of style—and prices which were not totally out of the question for those with a steady income.

'Strangely enough,' Giovanni went on, putting down his cup, 'we have not been very successful on the family front. Antonio had two sons—one of whom died young, which eventually left my grandfather and his wife to carry the baton. Then they produced my father and his brother, Aldo—but, as you know, my father, too, died far too young, leaving me virtually holding the reins—with my dear Mamma very much in the front seat, of course.' He smiled.

'What's happened between you and Aldo?' Emily asked bluntly, feeling that she was entitled to ask whatever questions she liked.

Giovanni pursed his lips. 'A few years ago, Aldo acted shamefully...very dishonourably...over a certain matter with a competitor. There was great deal of harm done at the time,' he added. 'Our small team of directors wanted to vote him off, and out, but...I...persuaded them that Aldo was still part of the bloodline and that he should stay and be paid a small salary, and the firm pays his children's school fees. He only plays a nominal part in the business now, and has little say in important decisions. Anyway—' Giovanni shrugged '—I suppose it's inevitable that Aldo should resent me because my father left all his possessions to me, making me the majority shareholder. So what I say goes.'

'Where does everything all happen?' Emily asked curiously. 'Where is the factory, the workshops...?'

'Oh, well, in the very early days it actually functioned from here, from this place,' Giovanni said, 'but for many years we've rented design and factory space in the industrial estate outside Rome. There's plenty of room for everyone there.'

Emily sat with her hands in her lap and looked across at Giovanni. 'But…why all the secrecy?' she asked. 'Why wait until now before letting me know what company I've been keeping lately?' She shook her head briefly. 'Shall I drop a deep curtsy—or provide a roll of drums?' she added sarcastically.

Giovanni almost shouted in response. 'No! That is just the point, Emily! Oh… It is so much worse having to admit to a rich dynasty than to admit to having nothing! What should I say to anyone? *Hi, I'm Giovanni Boselli and I'm part of the Antonio fashion chain and I've inherited its fortune—plus the responsibility of carrying it on for the rest of my life.*'

Giovanni's handsome features were flushed under his dark skin as he spoke. 'It is very difficult for me, as a man meeting new friends who might…' and Emily interrupted before he could go on.

'Oh, I get it!' she said hotly. 'Beware of gold-digging females, is that it, Giovanni? Well! I'm surprised that it's taken you all this time to realize that I couldn't care *less* what you own, or who you are, or what your background is!' Emily felt her anger rising with every second that passed, and now Giovanni half stood up, leaning across the table to put his face closer to hers.

'It took me no time at all to know what sort of woman you are, Emily,' he said harshly, 'but I have been wrong… hurt…disenchanted…before. And I have hurt other people, too. It is so…difficult.' He sat down again heavily, and went on more quietly. 'I have been so sure of you, so *re*assured, from almost the first moment I met you, and yes, while I'm on the subject, I *do* believe in love at first sight, because I love you, Emily, more deeply than I can express…and don't look at me like that, because I mean every word of what I'm saying! But I wanted to make *you* love *me*—if that were possible—for *myself*. And for no other reason. I wanted you to love me, like me, want to be with me as much as I want to be with you. And for nothing—*nothing*—to get in our way, in the way of our happiness.' He paused for a moment, gazing at Emily with such uninhibited ardour that it made her senses reel. He was sweeping her off her feet—making her feel dizzy. And, in spite of all her reservations, she knew that she could be in imminent danger of admitting her love for him, too! She'd been trying to deny her feelings for weeks, trying to talk herself out of wanting to be near him, and it had been getting more difficult with each day that passed.

Shakily, she picked up her coffee and sipped for a moment, knowing that he was waiting for some response from her, but, despite the obvious sincerity of his words, Emily felt ruffled and hurt. He had been testing her, judging her all this time, sizing her up—presumably as a possible wife! That made her feel small and silly. She stared across at him, her mind so churned up with a myriad emotions she thought she was going to be sick. Why had she agreed to come here this weekend? All her instincts had warned her against it—but Giovanni Boselli was used to getting what he wanted. She took a deep breath, trying to calm down. She was here now—nothing could alter that— and she wouldn't embarrass everyone—embarrass herself— by sulking or being difficult. She wouldn't spoil Maria's party. But she still wasn't sure how to handle this, how to handle Giovanni and what he'd just told her. It was all too much—much too much.

'I think I must go to bed now, Giovanni,' she said slowly. 'Do you mind if we continue our...discussion... some other time?'

Much later the following evening, after an amazing display of fireworks had concluded the festivities and the last guest had departed, Emily stood alone in her room, her head bursting. She'd never before been to a party like it!

Earlier in the day Giovanni had taken his mother and Emily out for a long drive, taking them miles into the countryside, ostensibly for a relaxing time in remote villages to browse, and to have coffee and lunch. And when they'd arrived back home just before seven o'clock, what a sight had met their eyes! The place had been transformed into a film set! Coloured lights had swayed from every tree, huge displays of fresh flowers graced every corner of the huge patio, and already masses of people— all beautifully dressed for the occasion—had gathered around, waiting to greet Maria. Emily had wondered whether Maria would be overwhelmed by this totally unexpected celebration, but from the expression in her eyes as she'd hugged her son excitedly and then went on to embrace all her friends, no one need have worried. Maria had been in her element.

Presently, Emily and Maria had gone upstairs to their rooms to change before soon rejoining the gathering outside. A small band had already taken up position on an elevated corner of the area and soon medleys of current popular songs had added to the noisy gaiety, while uniformed caterers moved among the crowd with trays of mouth-watering canapés. There were so many guests, more arriving every few minutes, that Emily had difficulty keeping up with it all, and it was hard for Giovanni

to be everywhere at once, though he had introduced her to
as many people as he could. Left by herself for a moment,
Emily had searched around the milling crowds, hoping to
see that beautiful face in the photograph somewhere, that
special someone, but she couldn't spot her anywhere.
But—she *had* to be one of the guests, surely, the girl had
thought… It stood to reason.

Now, before she got ready for bed, Emily took from her
case the daintily wrapped present she'd brought for
Maria—who'd received so many presents at the party
tonight she must have lost count, the girl thought—but
Emily had decided she'd wait until tomorrow, Monday, the
actual birthday, before giving it to her. She bit her lip
thoughtfully, hoping it would be deemed good enough for
Maria. The woman's other gifts would have been fabulously expensive, judging by the obviously wealthy guests.
The present Emily was holding in her hand was one of her
own small framed water-colours, and it pictured a goose
leading a line of tiny goslings along a wooded path towards
a pond in the background. She smiled now, as she remembered the occasion when she and Coral had come across
the little feathered family. It had been on a warm afternoon
out that they'd enjoyed together a year ago, and Emily had
committed the scene to memory before getting around to
painting it. And, unusually for her, she had been pleased
with the result.

   Slowly, she undressed and got into bed, thinking what
a strange day it had been. Surreal, almost. She had spent
the entire time with Giovanni, yet neither of them had
referred to their conversation of last night. Well, Maria had
been there too, which of course would have made it difficult but, even so, it was almost as if their discussion hadn't

taken place. Every now and then she caught Giovanni
looking at her, but she deliberately didn't want to catch his
eye… She still felt totally bewildered at being here with
this family—this renowned family—with its fabulously
rich heir apparently wanting to make her part of it…and
she still couldn't get her head around it all. He had said,
with such conviction, that he *loved* her… But Marcus had
been good at that kind of thing, too, she remembered. She
turned over impatiently. She shouldn't have agreed to
come. She should have listened to her inner self.

Later, much later, Emily drew herself up to a sitting
position in quiet desperation. At this rate, she was *never*
going to get to sleep, she thought, as she rested her head
on her bent knees for a moment. She seemed to have been
tossing and turning for ever. Everything that had gone on
during the party, the loud conversation all around, the insistent beat of the music, the shrieks of uninhibited
laughter and the general carnival atmosphere which
Italians seemed so good at enjoying, had left Emily wide
awake. Not to mention everything Giovanni had said to her
when they'd been alone. But the eerie silence now, after
all the noise, was making it worse… Was everyone else in
the whole world fast asleep? If so, why wasn't she?

She switched on the lamp beside her and glanced at her
watch. Three o'clock! Still a long time to go before
morning. Getting out of bed, she went across to the
bathroom and poured herself a glass of water. Well, that
might go some way towards eradicating the effect of all
the champagne she'd had.

She took a long drink, then, after a moment, went over
to the window and quietly drew back the shutters, gazing
out at the now familiar scene. It was simply perfect here,
she thought, the now subdued lighting casting strange

shadows all around, the water in the pool moving gently as the breeze ruffled its surface. Emily took in all the details in her usual observant way… One day, she might like to paint all that she was seeing.

Suddenly, her attention was caught by the sight of two figures strolling onto the patio, their arms entwined, their faces close together, and Emily hurriedly drew back… It was Giovanni and that woman! The woman in the picture! It just had to be—even though in the dim light it was hard to be certain… But, yes, it *was* her…and she was looking up at Giovanni, who was murmuring softly into her ear, his lips caressing her face in the sort of intimate, unhurried manner of an attentive lover.

Emily's mouth had gone completely dry as she stood unashamedly watching them, and she realized that her legs were trembling slightly. But why? Wasn't this to be expected? These two were well-known to each other— very well-known! And what difference did it make to her, anyway? It just proved what she'd known all along— Giovanni Boselli liked women, full stop! And in the plural! Emily suddenly felt a wave of anger engulf her as she continued watching… Now the two were sitting, half concealed by a large shrub, but what they were doing was clear enough! The woman's head was resting on Giovanni's shoulder and he was holding her tenderly…whispering so tenderly…and, with a start of genuine surprise, Emily knew that she was feeling upset and jealous! *Jealous* of a two-timing character she wouldn't trust as far as she could throw! The man who only a few hours ago had professed his love for *her,* Emily Sinclair! Had given her all that drivel about wanting to make her love him as much as he loved *her!* Well, he must think she was born yesterday!

She stood back and closed the shutters softly, only just

stopping herself from bursting into tears. What the hell was the matter with her? *She* didn't want Giovanni, no thank *you!* So why was she feeling so…so…completely bewildered—and so devastated?

CHAPTER TWELVE

WHEN she woke the following morning, Emily felt tired and dispirited. If only she were home now, she thought, in their unprepossessing little flat that had no marble staircases or swimming pools or olive groves—and no Giovanni Boselli, either.

But she still had almost a day to get through before their flight, a day in which she must appear normal and friendly and happy to be here. How could she be happy, when all she could think of was seeing those two cuddling up, right there in front of her in the early hours?

It was nine o'clock when she went downstairs and, going towards the long room where the formal dinner had been served, she could hear Giovanni and his mother talking. They both looked up as she entered, Giovanni immediately coming over to greet her.

'*Buon giorno, signorina,*' he murmured, looking down at her in his special way, and Emily felt like punching him.

'Oh, hello…Giovanni,' she said coolly, deliberately stepping away from him. 'Good morning, and a very happy birthday, Maria,' she added as Maria beckoned Emily to come and sit beside her at the table, which was laid for breakfast.

'Good morning, Emily,' Maria said. 'And thank you. Wasn't it a wonderful party? And I had no idea! Giovanni is too good to his mother!' She paused. 'You are looking very pretty this morning, Emily—and what an exquisite dress you were wearing last night! It looked as if it had been made just for you! You must know exactly where to shop.'

'Thank you,' Emily replied, thinking—if only you knew!

'You have very good taste,' Maria went on, 'and, by the way—did you ever manage to rescue that summer dress— the one with all the blood and dirt on it? I'm afraid I had my doubts.'

Emily smiled briefly as she took her place. 'No, I'm afraid I have to keep it for lounging around at home, or in the garden,' she said. 'You can still see the stains, though they're a bit fainter.'

'The main thing is,' Giovanni said mildly, 'that the young lady in question was not as badly hurt as it looked at the time.' He paused. 'I checked up at the hospital a couple of days later, and she's going to be fine.'

Rather shyly, Emily reached into her handbag and took out Maria's present.

'This is just a small gift, Maria,' she said. 'I'm afraid it's not likely to compete with all the amazing presents you were opening last night, but…I do wish you many happy returns of the day.' She placed it beside Maria, who immediately started untying the dainty ribbon. She looked at Emily shrewdly.

'You should never apologize when presenting someone with a gift,' Maria said. 'There was no need for you to bring me anything, but thank you…I know I shall like it very much.'

Slowly, she undid the flimsy wrapping paper and took

out the picture…and the expression on her face needed no explanation, her small gasp of pleasure as she studied the painting telling its own story. 'This is…so…beautiful…' she said quietly, obviously touched, and Giovanni broke in.

'Is that one of yours, Emily?' he asked eagerly, bending over to gaze at it.

'Yes—it was a little scene which Coral and I came across when we were out walking one day—this lovely mother goose taking all her babies down to the water for a swim.' She smiled. 'A painting is never as good as the real thing, of course, but I thought this was getting close.'

'It's really good—isn't it, Mamma? I told you about Emily's paintings… It is professional—don't you agree?'

For a few moments Maria said nothing, but continued studying the picture. When she looked up at Emily, her eyes were moist.

'This…gift…outshines anything else I may have received,' she said, 'because it is not only a delight to look at, but also it must have taken many hours to achieve this standard.' She shook her head briefly. 'Thank you very much, *carissima*. It shall be a most treasured possession.'

Somehow, the last few minutes had helped Emily restore something of her good spirits—not just because it was obvious that Maria was genuinely thrilled with the painting, but it reminded the girl that there was so much more to life than finding a partner, finding love, daring to trust. Happiness existed in so many other ways, too. When she got home, she would make much more time for her painting, she decided.

They finished their breakfast, with Emily purposely not looking at Giovanni or catching his eye, but merely contributing to the desultory conversation, and Giovanni was only too aware of her coolness. Still, it didn't bother him too much. He knew what women could be like at times... Wasn't that part of their allure?

Presently, Maria stood up and touched Emily's arm. 'Let me show you around the place,' she said pleasantly. 'I know there has not been time for you to investigate... and a walk in the cloisters will do *me* good, anyway—I'm afraid I drank a little too much wine last night!'

Giovanni stood as well. 'That's a good idea, Mamma,' he said easily, willing Emily to look at him—which she didn't, 'and I can sort out that paperwork you showed me yesterday. It shouldn't take me too long,' he added, 'but Emily and I will need an early lunch—I want to leave here about three o'clock, if that's OK.'

Maria nodded. 'Margherita knows about lunch,' she said briefly.

Presently, Maria led Emily through the courtyard towards the entrance to the cloisters. It was a lovely morning, though the season was no longer very warm, and Maria glanced approvingly at Emily's wrap, which she'd tied loosely around her shoulders. Maria smiled, touching it with her fingers.

'I said you had very good taste,' she said. 'Do you like this? It is one of ours, of course.'

Emily smiled back. 'It is my favourite wrap,' she said simply. 'All my friends are envious of it, and I...just love it. My father gave it to me,' she added.

'We have sold many like it,' Maria said. 'It is always good when a garment meets such general approval,' she added. 'And you wear it so well, Emily...casually, lovingly, just as it should be worn.'

They reached the cloisters, and now quite a cold draught greeted them as they began their stroll. Maria tucked her arm into Emily's.

'Do you have plans for your future, Emily?' she asked bluntly, and Emily was almost caught off guard, remembering Maria's rather straight way of talking.

'Oh, well…yes…sort of,' she replied guardedly. 'I hope to do more travelling—for the firm—because it is helping to boost my confidence. And…I'd like to have more time for my painting, of course—but that's a pipe dream, I'm afraid. And I enjoy making things. I make curtains for my father when he needs them—though I shan't be doing that again,' she added.

'Oh? Why is that?'

'Well, very surprisingly, he recently informed my brother and me that he is to marry again soon, so his new wife will be doing his sewing.' She paused. 'We never imagined that such a thing might happen—he and my mother were always so close and, after she died four years ago, my father vowed that no woman would ever take her place. That he would never marry again. But…life can be unpredictable. And people can change. See life differently.' She bit her lip thoughtfully. Her father, whose opinion on things, on life in general, Emily had always respected, had decided to take a gamble with his life…perhaps trusting, just a little, to fate. To venture where his heart was leading him.

'Do you mind—that he is to marry again?' Maria asked.

'Oh, no, of course not!' Emily replied at once. 'It was wonderful to see him so…relaxed. And Alice seems a very nice woman indeed. I'm sure they can be happy together. And that'll make me happy.'

'So—what about you, yourself, I mean?' Maria persisted. 'Will you marry, too, one day?'

'Sometimes I think I will, and at other times I think the opposite,' Emily replied, surprised at how comfortable she felt talking to Maria. And that made her bold enough to ask a question of her own. 'What about Giovanni?' she said lightly. 'He, too, is still single.' She looked away for a second, then, 'Who is the girl in that photograph—the one in his flat, Maria? She is very beautiful...and obviously someone very special to Giovanni.'

Maria pursed her lips for a second. 'Ah, yes—that is a picture of Paulina,' she said quietly. 'My son's wife...'

If she'd been struck by lightning, Emily couldn't have felt more shocked. The woman was his *wife?* A wife who he still loved, obviously... Their behaviour in the semi-darkness last night had said it all. 'Oh...' she said faintly. 'I had no idea that Giovanni was married.' Was she going mad...what was going on? Had she dreamed all those things he'd said to her the other night?

'Well, sadly he is not any more.' Maria's expression was grim. 'Paulina died last year—after a very short illness.' She shrugged. 'But I'm glad to say that Giovanni himself is so much better now. He was instructed by his doctors to have some time off to recover from his ordeal...and I insisted that he should have a complete rest from all his responsibilities here in Italy.' She shook her head. 'But these sad things take their own time,' she added. 'And I have hated to see him so unhappy...so down. Not like him at all, to be that way.'

Emily was totally mystified—and baffled—at why Giovanni had never thought to mention such a dramatic event in his life, or that he'd been married. How could anyone be so secretive? And if the woman in the garden hadn't been his wife—which, clearly, she couldn't have been—who was she? Obviously another enchanting female who took his fancy! But, now that Emily had started, she couldn't stop. She cleared her throat. 'Giovanni's loss must have been terrible,' she said, thinking how strange her own voice sounded. 'I'm sure they were very much in love...'

Maria's lips tightened again, in the way that Emily was beginning to recognize. 'We had known Paulina—and her family—for many years,' she said, 'and I thought she was perfect for Giovanni... In fact, I told him so on many occasions and perhaps I should not have done.' She paused before going on. 'They had been married for only two years before Paulina was taken ill...but I'm afraid things had not been going well with them for some time before that.' She clicked her tongue. 'Life is a melting pot of good things and bad things, Emily...but that is what it is. Life. And one must always hope.' She tucked her arm more firmly into Emily's, not surprised that Giovanni wanted her so badly. The girl was different from any of the others her son had known... For one thing, she was obviously a 'family' person, clearly caring and loyal, but there was also an indefinable quality about her that was very seductive—to both sexes. Maria had sensed it at once. Not to mention the fact that Emily was beautiful... But, of course, Giovanni *deserved* a beautiful woman! Of that his mother was in no doubt! It was his right! But the thing troubling Maria so deeply was that Giovanni had said he'd known from the very first that Emily was the one woman he was sure could give him back some happiness, and that if he couldn't have her, then he'd settle for no one else. That never again would he look for another woman, trust another woman to share his life. What a state of affairs! No second marriage, no second chance, no babies! Aldo was no longer in the equation, and there were no other men in the family to see that the firm continued to develop and prosper as it had done for generations! Her son's flatly stated announcement during their long chats this weekend had been Maria's worst possible birthday present! And it left her in no doubt that he meant it. Once he made up his mind—about anything—nothing would change it. But it seemed that the one thing he had to do was to change *Emily's* mind—for hadn't he said that she did not return his feelings? How could she not? How could she not see what a wonderful man Giovanni was…? Surely everything any woman could desire!

Later, as Emily, Giovanni and Maria sat outside in a sheltered corner of the patio enjoying their mid-morning coffee, Giovanni glanced across at Emily. She looked pale this morning, he thought, almost waif-like…though he loved the red dress she was wearing. It hugged her slender neck and arms and emphasized her neat waistline. But appearances were not everything, he acknowledged, and it was impossible not to be aware of her mood. She seemed more distant than ever this morning, and it had to be all about the wretched dynasty, of course—and not being told about it before. He cursed inwardly. Why hadn't he plucked up the courage to tell her about his background earlier? Whatever had made him think that bringing her here and then telling her was a good idea? Well, her feisty reaction to the news had put him right on that point! She felt she'd been put at a disadvantage—and she hadn't liked it.

Giovanni sighed briefly as he finished his coffee. He'd always prided himself that he understood women, but he was beginning to feel that he didn't know them as well as he thought he did. And he also knew that, somehow, he was going to have to bring her round, make her forgive him for keeping her in the dark.

Giovanni had been looking forward to bringing Emily here to his home—the home he'd hoped would be hers one day—but, as he saw her staring implacably in front of her with that non-committal expression he'd often seen before, his doubts were growing by the minute. Yet, in spite of everything, he knew that she liked him—a lot—and also that—did he dare to even think it—she fancied him. His whole body tensed as he recalled the erotic feel of her body almost wrapped in his when they had been on the river, the soft roundness of her breast in his hand, her undoubted willingness to have travelled further. It all gave him a blood-rush as he lived it again.

But that was then, this was now. If he was going to win this woman over, he'd have to think of something—fast.

It was in a rather subdued mood that they made the journey back to the UK, with Emily staring rather listlessly out of the aircraft window while Giovanni tried, unsuccessfully, to concentrate on the first page of his newspaper.

He cleared his throat. 'I'm really sorry that I didn't tell you, you know, about all the stuff regarding my family,' he began, and Emily interrupted quickly.

'There's no need to apologize,' she said flatly. 'It doesn't matter—not one bit. I was very happy to meet Maria again,' she added, 'and it was a pleasant and very…informative… time for me.' Emily looked across at Giovanni, holding his gaze, but now her tone was soft. 'I was sorry to hear of your wife's untimely death, Giovanni,' she said, thinking that he must still find it hard to talk about—to anyone.

Emily turned back to look out of the window again, and Giovanni felt his blood rising in anger. Why had his mother complicated things by talking about that to Emily? he thought. She should have left it to him, to deal with in his own way at the right time. He touched her arm. 'The past is the past,' he said, 'and nothing can change that now. It's over. Gone. The only important thing remaining is the future, and what we make of it.'

'But the past *is* important,' Emily began, and he interrupted her.

'Only if we learn from it,' he said soberly. 'And try not to make the same mistakes again.'

It was quite late as they hailed a cab outside the airport, and Giovanni looked down at Emily. 'Thank you again, for coming with me this weekend, Emily,' he said quietly. 'I know my mother appreciated everything…and especially the painting you gave her. She hasn't stopped going on about it.'

Emily smiled briefly. 'I'm glad she liked it.'

They got into the taxi and gave the driver instructions. Then, 'I must see you tomorrow, Emily—I want to talk to you,' he added, almost desperately. He was not going to let Emily slip through his fingers, and he knew, he just *knew,* he could win her…that she would understand everything…understand him, eventually.

Emily looked up at him. 'Sorry, Giovanni, I can't possibly see you tomorrow,' she said. 'The firm are sending me to Estonia in the morning—didn't I say? I shall be away until next week.' Her voice faltered at this deliberate lie, but she was not going to see Giovanni again—this weekend had been just too much to take in. And her excuse was as good as any. She had to have some space to get her thoughts in order. She wasn't going to risk her life in this man's hands, and the first step in the procedure was to distance herself from him, forget how much she'd started to love being with him, being close to him, breathing in that subtle, evasive masculine scent that sent all her nerves twitching. Giovanni Boselli was dangerous. She wanted out!

CHAPTER THIRTEEN

IT WAS four whole days since they'd returned to the UK and Giovanni's current commitment at the branch office was complete—there was simply no excuse for him to remain in London and he was needed in Rome, now and for the foreseeable future. So it was time to go home. But not before he'd had a chance to see Emily again and try to restore something of the position he'd thought they'd been in before. He knew she was upset with him— perhaps understandably, he accepted—but he'd never dreamed that his background, his rather exceptional status, would be such a big deal for her...that he was who he was.

Now, he looked at his watch. It was nearly lunchtime— time to decide on some action! Because they'd not exchanged a word since Monday night and he knew he couldn't bear this silence a day longer. Emily's mobile obviously had a fault, he reasoned, or else she was not answering—which he thought was unlikely, because wouldn't her firm need to contact her while she was away? He bit his lip. He didn't really want to embarrass her by ringing her office, but there was nothing else for it. He'd think of some plausible excuse...

He dialled the number, and almost at once a voice answered.

'Justin Taylor. Can I help?'

Giovanni cleared his throat. 'Oh, hi. Sorry to trouble you...Justin... It's Giovanni Boselli here. I think we met some time ago. I was wondering if you could tell me how I can get in touch with Emily. Her mobile seems constantly on the blink.' He paused. 'Could you give me the name of the hotel she's staying at? I believe she's in Tallinn at the moment.'

'No, she isn't,' Justin replied at once. 'She's not due in Estonia for another ten days.'

This unexpected piece of news nearly floored Giovanni.

'She...she isn't?' he said incredulously. 'But she told me she was going—on Tuesday—for a week.' Giovanni quickly recovered his composure. 'Oh, well, anyway...is she there?' he asked. 'Can I have a word?'

'No, you can't, I'm afraid. She's not in the office, hasn't been all week,' Justin said. 'She phoned in sick on Tuesday morning.'

Giovanni put down the phone and stared into space for a few moments, his throat constricting at the thought that Emily might be really ill. Then he shook his head briefly. But...she'd *lied* to him, about going to Estonia! But why? It was a horrible thought. She didn't need to do that. But clearly she didn't want to see him, or even speak to him, which was why she wasn't answering his calls.

He went over to the drinks cooler and poured himself a generous cup of water. He was utterly confused emotionally, and hurt beyond belief that he'd been lied to, humiliated that he'd been taken in, had believed her. But, much, much worse, Giovanni couldn't bear to think that she may be really ill. He finished the drink and poured himself some more. At least she had Coral there to look after her for part of each day…unless Coral, too, had succumbed! Giovanni cursed to think that he didn't have Coral's number, to check.

Presently, his normal clear-headed thinking took over. When he left work he'd go straight over to their flat, he decided. Whatever explanation Emily had for her deviousness, he thought, he must hear it from her. He couldn't stand unresolved, unsettled matters. In his book, it was always best to get things sorted—then move on. Even if the outcome was not always the happy one you'd hoped for.

He left the office and took a cab straight to the familiar address. He glanced up at the first floor—he knew which was Emily's bedroom—and, through a tiny chink in the closed curtains, he could see a dim light. He paused outside the front door for a few moments before trying, yet again, to get Emily to answer her mobile, but with the same result.

It was almost dark by now, and Giovanni was conscious of one or two strange looks from passers-by as he stood hesitantly on the front doorstep. Looking up and down the street, he was praying that he'd suddenly see Coral coming home, but there was no sign of her and, eventually, reluctantly, he pressed lightly on the doorbell. Emily would not want to be disturbed, he appreciated that, but how else could he be sure that she was OK, or whether she needed anything? And if she was annoyed at the intrusion on her privacy, he couldn't help it. He *had* to know.

There was no response to his ring… If only she'd open her window and just talk to him, he thought desperately, just for a moment, tell him she was all right. That would be enough. But, apart from that small bedroom light, the place might have been deserted.

Standing there, Giovanni really didn't know what to do next... If theirs had been a ground-floor flat, he thought, he might even have tried breaking in! And then, quietly emerging out of the gathering gloom, someone came up the path towards him.

'Can I help you—are you looking for someone?' the man said, in a none-too-friendly voice.

Giovanni spoke quickly. 'Oh...yes.' He stood well back so as not to appear intimidating to the rather slight middle-aged man. 'My name is Giovanni Boselli, and I'm a friend of Emily's...Emily Sinclair?'

The man smiled now, inserting his key into the door. 'Ah, yes, Emily. I think they're both away,' he said. 'I haven't seen either of the girls for a few days, but then, I'm often not here myself.' He turned to look at Giovanni, who had come up behind him. 'I'm Andy Baker—I own this property.'

'Of course—I remember you called once, while I was having dinner with Emily,' Giovanni said, almost wanting to throw his arms around the man's neck in relief. He paused. 'The thing is...I believe Emily is ill in bed...I haven't been able to contact her all week, and I'm worried about her.' He hesitated. 'Do you have a spare key so that I can let myself in to check everything's OK?'

Andy couldn't help feeling sorry for him, but felt bound to express some doubt about doing what Giovanni had asked. 'Well, I don't know really...I'm only legally allowed to gain access in an emergency...' he began, and Giovanni interrupted.

'But I have a real feeling that this *is* an emergency,' he said. 'Look, if we could just open her door and call out—ask her if she's OK—there can't be any harm in that, surely?'

'Well, I suppose not,' Andy said rather reluctantly, and together the two of them went up the stairs. When they got to Emily's door, they paused for a second and Giovanni tapped lightly.

'Emily…it's Giovanni. Is everything all right?' he called.

There was no reply but, as Giovanni looked down at Andy, they both heard a low moan, followed by a crash and the unmistakable tinkle of breaking glass.

'Look, we must go in,' Giovanni said, trying not to sound as desperate as he felt. 'Please—open her door.'

As if making a world-shattering decision, Andy stepped forward and selected a key from the bunch in his hand, opening the door.

They went inside and, with Andy hovering anxiously behind him, Giovanni went straight into Emily's bedroom.

She was lying on her side on the bed, the covers thrown off and with one arm dangling towards the floor, and she half-opened her eyes as she became aware that she was not alone. Then she tried to struggle up into a sitting position and Giovanni moved forward to support her, stepping over the glass from the broken tumbler on the floor. Her appearance sent shock waves through him. She was deathly pale, with her hair tousled around her face, and her eyes looked huge and almost opaque as she stared up at him.

'*Emilee-a….*' he breathed, gathering her up into his arms, and she automatically leaned into him, flopping her head against his shoulder.

'What time is it?' she whispered through dry lips. 'I must get up…'

Andy cleared his throat as he stood awkwardly by the door. 'Well…I'll be going on upstairs,' he said, turning to leave. 'Let me know if there's anything I can do… You know where I am…' he added. He paused. 'Just as well we came in, wasn't it? Poor Emily. Doesn't look too good, does she…?'

When he'd gone, Giovanni laid Emily back down and drew the covers over her gently. She looked up at him, and now she was beginning to focus more clearly.

'What are you doing here?' she croaked, her voice hoarse. Then, 'I can't remember coming to bed... What's going on?'

Giovanni sat beside her, taking her hand in his. 'How long have you been lying here by yourself?' he asked. 'Do you know what day it is?'

'It's Tuesday—isn't it?' Emily replied. 'Yes, it's Tuesday...'

'No, it's Friday, Emily. And you've obviously gone down with something.' He paused. 'Where's Coral—shouldn't she be home soon?'

Emily was wide awake and aware now, and she struggled to sit up again. 'Coral's away on a course,' she said weakly.

'So you've been here all alone for four days,' Giovanni said. 'I was getting frantic with worry because I hadn't heard from you, Emily, so I rang the office...' He didn't go on because now was not the time for explanations. What *was* needed was to make Emily more comfortable. Seeing her so helpless and vulnerable made him want to hold her close. He suddenly had no feelings of resentment about her lying to him, he realized. What did that matter now? All he felt was intense compassion and an overwhelming longing to bring her back to normal, to make her feel good again.

For the next ten minutes, Giovanni busied himself with practical matters. He cleared the small bedside table of several empty tumblers and crumpled tissues, and screwed the top back onto the half-empty bottle of tablets Emily had obviously been taking. Then he went into the kitchen and found a dustpan and brush to clear up the broken glass, before putting the kettle on to make Emily a hot drink.

When he came back, she was sitting weakly on the edge of the bed, struggling into her dressing gown, and Giovanni went across to help her.

'Oh, dear,' she said faintly. 'I'm beginning to remember everything now.' She paused. 'I woke early on Tuesday morning—and knew straight away that I couldn't go to work… I felt terrible. But I thought if I had a day in bed, I'd soon recover.' She swallowed. 'And that's really the last thing I remember. Except…I do remember going into the bathroom and getting myself water to drink…and I think I took some tablets…but that's all, really.' She looked away, not wanting to gaze into the dark eyes that she knew were staring down at her.

Giovanni put his hand on her forehead gently. 'Well, you're cool enough now, so obviously your temperature's back to normal,' he said. 'But you must be ready for something to eat. What do you fancy? What can I get you?'

By now, Emily was right back on track and she knew she had to explain about not being in Estonia. But…she'd put it off for as long as possible, she thought, so she replied quickly, 'I feel like a slice of toast with some marmalade on it. The jar is in the cupboard above the sink.' She sighed weakly. 'And I think there's bread in the fridge.'

Giovanni grinned down at her, relieved to see that Emily was obviously coming back to the real world. 'Toast and marmalade coming up,' he said, going into the kitchen.

Getting up, and feeling as if she were floating a foot off the floor, Emily tottered into the bathroom and stared at herself in the mirror. Whatever did she look like? But by now she was past caring. She filled the basin with warm water and began to wash her hands and face, drawing the sponge up around her neck and arms before smoothing some of her moisturizer onto her skin. Then she reached for her toothbrush, squeezing some paste onto it, the strong peppermint making her tongue tingle pleasantly. That made her feel a lot better. Then she took her brush and eased some of the tangles from her hair, making a face at herself in the mirror... She still looked a mess, she thought, but it would have to do for now.

It was so good to have Giovanni here, Emily thought suddenly, pausing for a second. In spite of the doubts she had about him, he could be so utterly kind and thoughtful...everything any woman could want in a man, especially in her hour of need. And at every other time too! But—and it was a big but—could they last a lifetime together, as he apparently thought they could...and would *she* ever be enough for Giovanni Boselli? There was so much he hadn't told her. So much she needed to know.

Presently, she went to sit down on the sofa, just as he came in with the toast and two mugs of tea on a tray and, as Emily started to nibble at the first food she'd had for some time, he sat on a chair opposite and watched her. Some colour had come back into her cheeks, he noticed, and her beautiful eyes, as she glanced across at him, looked clearer now and as discerning as ever.

Then she said, 'I expect you were surprised to find that I wasn't in Estonia this week.'

Giovanni shrugged, as if he'd hardly thought about it. 'Obviously some last-minute change of plan?' he suggested, trying to make it easy for her.

She stared at him for a long moment before answering him truthfully. 'No, it wasn't that,' she said slowly. 'I wanted you to think I'd be away because...because—' she swallowed '—I didn't want to see you, Giovanni.' She sipped from her mug. 'I thought it best if…you see…I'm afraid, Giovanni,' she whispered.

'Afraid—of *me*, Emilee-a?' he said quietly.

'A bit,' she admitted, not looking at him.

Giovanni's face was expressionless. Then, 'You won't mind if I ask for an explanation?' he asked mildly. 'Are you still mad at me for not admitting sooner who my family was—is? And what my future is likely to entail?' He paused. 'Or, indeed, that I'd been married once?' he added as an afterthought.

Emily nodded slowly. 'I do still find it hard to think how anyone could avoid mentioning all that before,' she conceded, 'but it's not just that, Giovanni.'

Now he was really puzzled. 'So—what is it?' he asked.

There was a long pause before Emily spoke again. Then, 'I don't want to love you…I don't want to fall in love with someone who I'm afraid would find it hard to be faithful,' she said earnestly. 'Loyalty is the essential element which is needed to bind a relationship, to make it last for a lifetime.'

'I agree with that,' Giovanni responded at once. 'So—what are you trying to say?'

'Must I spell it out?' Emily said.

'I'm afraid you'll have to,' he said quietly.

'Well—what about that girl at the party…the one I saw you with from my window, much later on that night?' Emily said, suddenly feeling energized. 'I saw you two together, how you were holding her, kissing her…she must be someone very special to you, Giovanni.'

The slight frown which had started to form on Giovanni's features cleared briefly and he leaned forward and let out a deep sigh. 'Oh—what must you have thought, Emilee-a?' he said slowly. He shook his head. 'That very special woman is my sister, Francesca,' he said. He took a deep breath, realizing that there was even more for Emily to find out about his family. 'We see Francesca very infrequently, thanks to her working life,' he said. 'She did a politics degree at university and now has a high-octane job with the government...all top secret stuff which we never ask her about—and she wouldn't tell us, in any case. But of course she is constantly flying all over the world, and actually only got back from the States very late on Sunday night—you had already gone to bed—just in time to wish my mother a happy birthday. But she was collected again almost before dawn to accompany the Prime Minister's entourage to Japan.' Giovanni looked deadly serious for a moment. 'Did you really think that she and I...?'

'Well, you did look very close...' Emily began hesitantly, wondering how many more surprising revelations she was to learn. 'You seemed so deep in conversation.'

'That is certainly true,' he agreed, 'because I was telling her all about you, Emily...about this wonderful English girl that I'm in love with. But I also had to tell her that I didn't think you cared too much for me...not in the way I am yearning for.' He paused, finding it hard to go on for a second. 'My sister has always given me good advice,' he said, 'and her words were—*Never give up on your heart's desire. If something feels right, go for it. Never give up.*'

He looked so appealing, so earnest, that Emily wanted him to hold her close...wanted to feel his arms around her and not let her go. 'So...Francesca...has no part in the family business?' she asked, trying to keep her voice steady.

'No, she has never had any interest at all in fashion, or how the business works,' he said. 'And my parents respected that, respected her wishes to go it alone.' He smiled briefly. 'My mother is intensely proud of what Francesca has achieved in her own profession. After all, it isn't everyone who can say that they occasionally take tea with the Prime Minister, or who has met the President of the United States.'

There was a long silence while Emily ate the last of her toast slowly, admitting that her head was feeling almost as light as it had when she'd been suffering that temperature. But she was on an unstoppable train now, she thought. There was more she must know.

'And Paulina?' she asked steadily. 'Your wife? Tell me about her, Giovanni. I want to know everything—everything about *you*.'

His expression clouded, but only for a moment. 'That is one subject that I do not like to think about...do not like to talk about,' he said seriously, 'but I understand why I must tell you, Emilee-a. It is only right that I should.'

He had hardly touched his tea, and now he put down his mug, standing up and going across to the window, drawing aside the curtain and staring out into the night sky.

'Paulina—and Francesca—and I had been friends for many years, when we were all very young,' he said slowly. 'She was very beautiful... In fact, she looked so like Francesca they were sometimes taken for sisters.'

'Yes, I know. I've seen that photograph in your flat, Giovanni,' Emily said.

'I'd never really imagined that our relationship would develop into something deeper,' he went on, 'but sometimes life takes on a rhythm which is difficult to stop. She was...very much in love with me, that was the trouble... She was like a loyal dog, looking at me with those big eyes...and I found it hard to tell her that I did not feel quite the same way about her. I did try,' he said, 'and she even threatened to kill herself on one occasion.' He paused. 'Everyone else in the family—' Giovanni did not mention his mother '—told me so many times that we would be the perfect match, and I tried to believe that because I hated having to reject Paulina. To be rejected is the most hurtful thing.' Emily glanced up briefly. Yes, she thought, she would wholeheartedly agree with that.

'So—we got married,' Giovanni said, 'and life was pretty good…it was OK. But Paulina changed…she developed into a woman who was never satisfied with what she had, what she was given. She was constantly shopping, buying clothes, shoes, handbags, things she didn't really need or want…the perfect example of someone who was trying to fill her life with something she was lacking.' Giovanni paused for so long that Emily looked up curiously. This was hurting him, she thought, hurting him to speak about. But presently he continued, and his voice was sombre.

'I realized, too late, that it was all my fault,' he said. 'Because I neglected her—shamefully. I was working all hours—the business was going through a difficult patch—something that only I could really deal with. There was no one else, and my mother is no longer young. I could not expect too much of her.' He sighed, then, 'I always gave Paulina whatever she wanted—paid all her bills without question, but it started to become serious and I had no idea how to handle it. Money is not everything, and it can become a monster—and that is what it became for us. The more Paulina had, the more she wanted. I tried to talk to her about it, but then she accused me of being mean.' He gave a short, harsh laugh. 'The only thing I was mean about was not giving my wife the attention she deserved…

giving her time so that we could be together properly, to enjoy our lives as other married couples do.' He shook his head. 'At the time, I was totally stressed, my nerves hanging by a thread, or so it seemed. Then the unimaginable thing happened—Paulina developed a serious medical problem which no one suspected, and she died within a few months. Died before I could put things right between us, before I could make up for my lack of—thoughtfulness—of attentiveness—which is every woman's right, surely? I had put the family business—our wonderful, sometimes cursed dynasty—before more important issues like the feelings, the comfort of my wife. And I am left with a deep sense of shame. I can never forgive myself,' he replied.

There was such a long pause after that that Emily looked up at him, frowning.

'But the very worst thing, Emily, was something I have never told anyone before—anyone at all,' he emphasized. He swallowed. 'During one of her many outbursts, which were becoming more and more frequent, Paulina told me that she'd never been in love with me at all, anyway. What she was in love with was what I owned—and what she wanted access to. She said that from a young age she'd been determined that one day I would marry her.' He turned slowly and looked down at Emily. 'But, in spite of all that, I am left with a deep sense of shame...a sense of failure. And I can never forgive myself,' he repeated.

He came back to sit down beside Emily, whose throat had formed such a hard lump of sympathy she couldn't speak. But she took his hand gently as he went on.

'So—I was forced to take a long leave of absence from work recently and, apart from a couple of visits I made to the UK office, I've spent much of the time in Rome with

friends, doing simple things like minding shops belong-
ing to other people and generally chilling out. Which is
when I met you, Emilee-a, *carissimo.*' He squeezed her
hand tightly. 'And, even at that early point, I felt a surge
of something…a quite irrational hope that some miracle
might happen for me.' He hesitated. 'But perhaps, now,
you can understand my reluctance to say too much about
the past,' he said slowly, 'though it was never meant to be
a secret…something to be held back. But I like to think
that I've learned from it. I will never make the same
mistake again. Any woman who entrusts her life with me
will never be short-changed,' he added, thinking that he
was only going to give himself one more chance to prove
that—and it had everything to do with Emily.

She turned her head and looked right up into his eyes.

'I hope you *will* forgive yourself, one day, Giovanni,'
she said. 'Carrying guilt around with you for too long
isn't healthy. It doesn't achieve anything in the long run.'

'I know you are right,' he said, 'but I need someone to
help me with that, Emily…it isn't something I can do by
myself.' He looked down at her, his whole body tensing
with desire at her closeness, at the soft feel of her body, at
the sweet, warm smell of her skin. And, sensing that she
wouldn't stop him, he tucked her in tighter, reaching for
her lips and kissing her gently, cautiously.

And Emily felt her heart breaking into tiny little pieces
inside her…little pieces of unbelievable, undeniable surrender. Resting against him pensively, she wondered
whether she dared to ask one final question…

She turned her face to look up at him. 'Whose negligee
was that, hanging in the bathroom of your flat, Giovanni?'
she asked, trying not to make the question sound in any
way accusing, and he smiled down at her.

'That's my sister's,' he said. 'Francesca leaves it there permanently for when she uses the flat as a flying stop-over.' He answered the question as casually as Emily had asked it, and for a few moments there was a comfortable silence as they both relaxed there in the gentle comfort of the modest room.

Suddenly, neither of them could bear it any longer, and now his lips came down on to Emily's and he kissed her, properly, urgently, with such heightened ardour that it left her senses reeling. And Emily responded without hesitation… No man had ever filled her with such a passionate longing, such yearning…such unbelievable excitement.

In a moment, he whispered, 'Tell me you love me, Emilee-a, tell me I'm not hoping for something which will never be mine. Tell me that you will be my wife, my life…my everything—for ever…'

And, at last, in a breathless, timeless moment, Emily murmured, 'I have been trying *not* to love you, Giovanni, but I can't keep it up any longer.' She paused. 'Of course I love you,' she said, adding softly, 'How could I help it?' and his dark eyes, those mesmerizing windows of his soul, glistened with unshed tears of pleasure and happiness at the words he'd been longing, hoping, praying to hear.

But would his family ever accept her? Emily thought, as Giovanni's lips claimed hers again. She instinctively felt that Maria was a formidable woman… She could be a formidable enemy… What if she, Emily, wasn't deemed good enough for the illustrious Bosellis? She drew away and looked up at him. 'Do you…do you think I would fit in, Giovanni?' she asked. 'Come up to standard, shall we say…?'

'What on earth do you mean, Emily?' he asked.

'I'm talking about Maria…your mother. I know she

has strong views on important matters. Would I ever be good enough for her remarkable son?'

Giovanni gave a short laugh. 'My mother is as much in love with you as I am, Emily! Truly, I mean it. I have had long chats with her, and she has told me that if I can persuade you to be my wife, it will be her happiest day!' He paused. 'She liked being with you, talking to you. And she could not believe that the picture you gave her was not a copy…but that you had painted it yourself, using your own memory and imagination. And my mother is a very perceptive woman,' he went on, 'she knows a gifted artist when she meets one.' Giovanni's face broke into a broad grin. 'I think she would love to have you on board, on our design team…you'd be someone with fresh, modern ideas, and every company needs new blood from time to time.' He paused. 'Just think,' he said, 'it would be like turning full circle—you and me, the two of us, Emilee-a, taking on what my great-grandparents began all those years ago! Isn't that an amazing thought? Besides,' he added mischievously, 'Antonio needs some heirs—and I think you and I, together, can sort that one out. Only if that's what you want, too, of course,' he said quickly. 'Your feelings will always come first.' Giovanni's eyes glistened and, looking up at him, Emily thought, not for the first time, that she would never again know such an achingly desirable man. And someone who, at last, she *was* going to trust. Because she knew that she could. She remembered the words her father had used that day…that, if he'd waited much longer, he may have lost Alice for ever… Well, Emily wasn't going to hesitate any longer.

What was she waiting for? She knelt up on the sofa and put her arms around his neck, almost collapsing into him as she offered him her parted lips to be kissed again…to be tasted…and immediately his hands reached under her flimsy nightwear and roamed over her body, making every one of her nerves tingle as he caressed her back and her bare shoulders, sliding his fingers over the creamy softness of her breasts…gently at first, then with increasing passion, until Emily was forced to draw back reluctantly. Now was not the time, she thought breathlessly, even though their desire for each other was painful. Their love-making—which she knew would be beautiful and amazing beyond her wildest dreams—must wait for just a little while longer.

'Will…will this time next year do—for the first baby?' she asked teasingly. 'Is the firm prepared to wait that long— if we're lucky enough to produce any, that is?' she added.

Giovanni reached for her again. 'Don't worry about that,' he said darkly. 'Don't you know what my friends call me? I'm known throughout the entire world as "Lucky Gio". And, at this precise moment, Emilee-a, I *know* that my luck will never get better than this!'